JUDI FENNELL

my
fair
genie

My Fair Genie, Copyright 2012 Judi Fennell
Previously published as *Magic Gone Wild*

Cover and Interior layout by www.formatting4U.com

Published by Mergenie Books

All rights reserved. No part of this book may be reproduced in any form or by any electronic or mechanical means, including information storage and retrieval systems—except in the case of brief quotations embodied in critical articles or reviews—without permission in writing from the author. Please contact the author at JudiFennell@JudiFennell.com. This book is a work of fiction. The characters, events, and places portrayed in this book are products of the author's imagination and are either fictitious or are used fictitiously. Any similarity to real persons, living or dead, is purely coincidental and not intended by the author.

For more information on the author and her works, please see www.JudiFennell.com

First Edition 2012
Second Edition 2019

Books By Judi Fennell

Royally Sunk
In Over Her Head
Wild Blue Under
Catch of a Lifetime
~Making Waves ~ outtakes

Bottled Magic
I Dream of Genies
Genie Knows Best
My Fair Genie
~Your Wish Is His Command ~ outtake

Once Upon A Time Romance
Beauty and The Best
If The Shoe Fits
Through The Leaded Glass ~ prequel
Fairest of Them All (coming soon)

BeefCake, Inc.
Beefcake & Cupcakes
Beefcake & Mistakes
Beefcake & Retakes
Beefcake & Snowflakes

Manley Maids
What a Woman Wants
What a Woman Needs
What a Woman Gets
What a Woman
What A Man Wants (coming soon)

Every Time She Uses Magic Something Goes Terribly Wrong...

Vana wishes she hadn't dropped out of genie training. Now she's determined to get a grip on both her genie magic and her life. But the harder she tries to fix things for her intriguing new master, the more she drives him crazy...

Except There's Nothing Ever Wrong About Him...

Pro–football player Zane Harrison finally has control of the family estate and is determined to put to rest his grandfather's eccentric reputation. Until he discovers that behind all the rumors is a real, live genie who stirs feelings in him he's never known before. The more Zane tries to help Vana harness her powers, the more her madcap magic entangles his heart...

***

"Fennell brings us a lighthearted romp... Cleverly written, uproariously funny, with quirky, interesting characters. 4 Stars"   ~ RT Book Reviews

"Cute, fun and fluffy."   ~ Fangs, Wands and Fairy Dust

"Lighthearted and delightful..."   ~ Romancing the Book

"What a fun read, chock full of surprises and with humor at every turn... A magical tale, with a beautiful twist of romance."   ~ BookLoons.com

"A wild, funny, and delicious ride... Fennell has a voice that's unique and refreshing."   ~ Storm Goddess Reviews

"Creative and fresh and so incredibly fun... luscious and sizzling."   ~ Joan Swan's Blogr

Careful what you wish for...

Northeast Pennsylvania
41,646 days ago
But who's counting?

Vana cringed as the stairs vanished beneath Peter's feet.
Again.
Luckily, this time, he was holding on to the railing.

Which also started to disintegrate.

Holy smokes! Would her magic *ever* turn out the way she wanted it to?

At least she could manage Invisibility, and did so, standing at the top of the staircase and gripping the railing so it wouldn't fall apart. Luckily for everyone attending Peter's weekly gathering, the structure seemed sound—despite the stair-mangling efforts of the bear she'd accidentally conjured.

Vana winced. A *bear*.

Thankfully, Mr. Hornberger had chased it out before it could do any more damage, but she shouldn't have tried to repair the steps, let alone *varnish* them. Especially with the way her magic worked. Or rather, *didn't* work.

Judi Fennell

"I know you're here, Vana," Peter called loud enough for everyone at the luncheon to hear. Not the best idea. Peter still hadn't grasped the concept of secrecy when it came to having a genie—anymore than she'd grasped the concept of being one.

"And don't try fixing it again. I'll take care of it mysel—*agghh!*" Peter threw his hands in the air as the remaining spindle disintegrated and another stair tread caved in.

"Oh, dear, Peter's tippled too much again, hasn't he?" Mrs. Otto waddled out from the dining room with Mrs. Ertel following her, dressed in her Sunday best and tsk-tsking behind her gloved hands. "I'm sure it's understandable, Bertha. After all, a bear! Can you imagine? Quite the spectacle."

Just one in a long line of them. Vana had the feeling that the townspeople's appearances at Peter's gatherings had more to do with her and her magic than the food he served. Not that anyone ever saw her; no one had but Peter. Which was half the problem. Peter was what the locals liked to call eccentric. He'd made money in shipping and imports before she'd entered his life (obviously, or she would have lost it all for him), and he'd invested it heavily in the town, but not necessarily in things people wanted him to invest in.

But that was Peter. He'd erected a big statue to his grandmother, the sternest-looking woman to walk the earth, and considering Vana had lived for more than a few centuries, she ought to know.

He'd paved the path to the home for unwed mothers with cobblestones, saying it'd prevent falls when the path iced over in the winter. The church ladies disagreed and periodically took up a collection to have the stones removed. But each time, Peter would have them put back in place. After all, he did own the property; he could do what he wanted with the path. It became an unending cycle until the women eventually gave up.

2

No, Peter Harrison had been an oddity long before Vana had come along, but her special brand of ineptitude helped put the icing on Peter's cake of eccentricity.

Peter never seemed to mind, and that, more than the fact that he possessed her bottle, made Vana happy to be his genie.

"Jonas, why don't you send Mrs. Hamm to get your father?" one of the church ladies asked Peter's son kindly. "I think he might want to take a nap."

Sleep it off, she meant. Everyone thought Peter liked his whiskey, but the truth was, Peter couldn't stand the stuff. He did, however, like a special blend of chilled tea that Vana could manage to magick up correctly.

She would pour the tea into empty whiskey bottles to encourage the locals' belief that Peter liked his drink. That it had all started after the death of his wife (which, also not-so-coincidentally, coincided with the round-the-world trip during which he'd come across a certain bottle) lent credence to the story.

Everyone knew how distraught Peter had been, so what else could Vana do? Let them think he was full-blown crazy with his talk of genies and magic? He might own the town, but he'd also built that nice hospital at the far end, and there was a wing there with his name on it. She was half worried they'd send poor Peter there, and then where would she be? Where would the children and Eirik and all the rest be?

The children. Vana shook her head. The children had been dancing in the study earlier, which normally wouldn't be a problem. But when children were enchanted to be everyday dishware, and those dishes were twirling and swirling and leaping and do-si-doing all over the place, well, that was definitely an issue.

Especially if anyone had seen them.

"Out of the way! Out of the way!"

Vana winced once more when Mrs. Hamm, the

housekeeper, strode into the foyer, bellowing as usual. "The master needs his nap!"

The master would never get his nap with that old foghorn blustering like she was.

Vana smiled. She'd been able to manage a fairly good sleeping draught that Mrs. Hamm had really taken to. Alas, it was the middle of the afternoon and Mrs. Hamm would never be persuaded into napping during a Sunday gathering.

Peter stumped up the steps. "I'm not taking a nap, Mrs. Hamm. I'm not in my dotage!" Still, he allowed the housekeeper to herd him up what remained of the curved staircase.

"Don't fret, Vana," Peter said as he passed her, his hand unerringly finding her shoulder as it always did.

No, no doubt about it. Although Peter might come across as being dotty, he was as sharp as a needle.

But she *would* fret. After all, this was her fault. Honestly, *varnish*? How hard could that be?

With her screwy magic, pretty hard, apparently.

Vana sighed, kissed the air, her Way of doing magic, and *poofed!* herself inside the armoire in Peter's bedchamber. Travel magic wasn't as difficult as conjuring things, and once she'd practiced it, there'd been no mishaps similar to today's incident—Well, other than the time that Mr. Peale and Mrs. Hargetty had been too engrossed in what they *shouldn't* have been doing to each other to notice her sudden appearance in the drawing room, that is.

The door opened and Peter strode in, followed by Mrs. Hamm, who immediately set about flustering around Peter, arranging pillows and fluffing the comforter in an effort to get her master settled.

"Stop fussing, Mrs. Hamm." Peter tossed the silk pillow he'd bargained off old Mustafa in the *souk* onto the divan he'd won in a card game in Kiev. "It's the middle of July. I am not cold, nor am I tired. I told you. It's *her* again."

4

Mrs. Hamm and the rest of the staff thought Peter's "her" meant his wife, and Vana was fine with them thinking that. After all, Peter talking to his dead wife was more believable than him talking to a live genie, and since his supposed downward spiral into madness had begun in earnest after Millie died, it garnered him a certain amount of pity. Which was why Mrs. Hamm went about picking up the pillows and refluffing the comforter with merely a chorus of "Yes, sir"s and "Of course, sir"s tossed about with a fair number of "hmmm"s.

Vana sighed, torn between wanting Mrs. Hamm to believe Peter—for once—and feeling bad that she'd contributed to Peter's "madness" yet again. Really, she was just trying to do her job in the best way she knew. Was it her fault that her training had been cut short by a ruthless antiquities dealer who'd snatched up her bottle before she'd been given clearance to become a full-fledged member of The Service, that noble rank of Servitude every djinni aspired to?

Okay, so maybe she shouldn't have been in that bottle, since, according to The Djinn Code, a genie shouldn't be inside a bottle until she was assigned one. (Or someone accidentally locked her inside one, as had happened with that antiquities dealer.)

A couple dozen masters over the centuries, a few boat rides, one horribly memorable trek lashed to a mule, and here she was in the New World with Peter and the vanishing staircase.

Mrs. Hamm let the cord fall that held back the window curtains on one side of Peter's bed, then rushed around to do the same to the other side, bathing the room in shadow and stifling heat. It would soon be sweltering.

"There, there, Mr. Peter, you'll feel better after you wake up." Mrs. Hamm pulled the comforter up to Peter's chin.

No wonder Peter was getting sleepy. He was probably

suffering from heat stroke. The minute Mrs. Hamm left, Vana would get rid of the covers and cool things down. She could manage that most of the time, which came in handy for making Peter's favorite drink or lowering the temperature in the house on a hot day. She'd never tried to do so on a grand scale, however. Too much potential for trouble. She could only imagine how a snowstorm in July would go over. For today, though, she'd magick a few little cool spots all around Peter. They ought to do the trick.

Vana puckered her lips and kissed the air as the door closed behind Mrs. Hamm and she—

No! Not *actual* spots! Holy smokes, she'd given Peter cold sores!

Trying to keep her panic at bay, Vana puckered up again.

"Don't do it, Nirvana." Peter's voice was deeper and sadder than she'd ever heard. And he'd used her full name. He never used her full name.

"Whatever it is you think you're going to do, don't. I can't take any more right now, Nirvana. I just can't." Peter sat up on the bed, the horrid spots looking like some tropical disease.

"First the bear, then the stairs, and now this. This has to stop. We need your magic in good order if we're going to turn those dishes back into children." He lifted her bottle out of a drawer in the bedside table where he kept it, and pulled the stopper. "You've been trying so hard recently, Vana. I think you need a rest. Don't you?"

A *rest*? Vana bit her trembling bottom lip and rolled her shoulders back. She couldn't rest. The children and everyone else would be stuck in their enchanted forms unless she could figure out how to undo them. She needed to keep practicing.

"Vana?"

She sighed again. At least he'd asked. Most masters would have ordered her.

Most masters probably would have sent her into the Light by now.

She opened the armoire door and walked across the beautiful Persian rug he'd bought in the same *souk* where he'd found her bottle.

She stood next to his side of the bed, her head bowed, her hands linked in front of her. "I am sorry, Peter." He'd never insisted she call him "master," a kindness for which she'd forever be indebted to him. He'd never made her feel like his servant.

Until now.

"Vana, it's just for a little while. To give you time to calm down. To give everyone time to calm down. That's all. Just a little while."

Vana nodded. Peter was trying to be kind. She knew that.

That she felt like a failure was all her own doing.

One last breath of the stifling July air, and Vana dematerialized from the room and entered her bottle in a plume of pink smoke.

As her body regained its corporeal form, the stopper filled the hole above her head, sealing her inside where, theoretically at least, she could do no harm.

Later that evening, Vana braced herself against the cushions on her divan as Peter climbed the steps to the attic (ones she'd never attempted to varnish), placed her bottle stopper-side up in a trunk, cushioned it with a handmade shawl, and closed the lid—his way of protecting her from someone taking her from him, another kindness for which she was forever grateful.

***

Two days later, Peter was killed in a wild horse-and-buggy accident that Vana had had nothing to do with.

And no one knew about the bottle in the attic or the genie locked inside.

Chapter 1

Northeast Pennsylvania
41,646 days later
Vana *had been counting*

Zane Harrison stared at the woman on the other end of the scimitar and tried to remember exactly how he'd come to have a sword pointed at his chest.

"Holy smokes!" The woman sucked in a breath, clamped a hand over her mouth, and dropped the sword.

Right on top of him.

The pommel conked him on the head and the blade spun around, almost taking off his nose.

Zane leapt to his feet and grabbed the sword in one movement, the hours spent in football training drills thankfully having real-world application, although he'd never imagined that would be to defend his life during a trip back to his ancestral home in the middle of nowhere.

Then he got a good look at the woman. A more unlikely assassin he'd never seen. Hand-to-hand combat was not the ideal way to handle this situation; hand to mouth was. Or rather, mouth to mouth.

The woman was gorgeous. Movie-star gorgeous.

Playmate gorgeous. Even in a fencer's outfit—which was about as asexual as you could get—with curves straight out of his most vivid erotic fantasy, eyes the shimmering silvery-gray color of the sky before a storm that promised every bit as much of a wild ride, and a long golden curtain of hair that Zane wanted to sink his fingers into and never let go, the woman was absolutely stunning. And he was most definitely stunned. But not only by her looks.

"*Ungaro*," she muttered. "Not *en garde*." She shook her head, mumbled something else, then looked up at him. "Good day, um…?"

Zane would hate to see what she called a bad day if a good one was ending up on the wrong end of a sword. "Who are you, and what the hell is this?" He shook the sword.

She licked her lips—more centerfold fodder. They were plump and pink and now wet.

Hmmm, maybe it *was* a good day.

"I'm Vana, and that's a scimitar." Her expression was crestfallen and her sigh heartbroken. "I couldn't even manage a rapier."

Which made about as much sense as anything else.

Not that anything made sense.

Zane took the somewhat daring action of taking his gaze from her to glance around the room.

Circular, and ringed by stained-glass window, it had no door that he could see—unless it was behind him and he wasn't about to risk turning around, both for what she might do and what he might see—the room looked like something out of the old Hollywood movie set of *Lawrence of Arabia*. Overstuffed sofas covered in pillows filled the room with pastel silk panels draped from the ceiling like the inside of a harem tent.

He was as human as the next guy and, sure, every guy had harem fantasies, but he was fairly certain he wasn't dreaming, if only for the fact that the knot on the back of his head hurt like hell.

9

Rubbing it, Zane winced. He must have really conked it when he'd ended up on the floor.

A floor covered in hot-pink mosaic tiles. In the shape of a flower.

He shook his head, trying to clear the fog from it. How had he ended up on the floor? He could have sworn he'd just been in his great-grandfather's home, and while floral wallpaper abounded in that monstrosity of a Victorian mansion his family had owned for three generations too many, this flower was a little too "out there" for the puritans he'd descended from. Merely one of the reasons he'd decided to sell the place.

Another was to cut ties with the legacy of lunacy that came with the house. But given the contents of this room and the scimitar-pointed-at-his-chest thing, he wasn't so sure he'd be successful with the second one. "So... Vana, was it?"

The woman nodded and the curtain of hair cascaded over her shoulder, then down over breasts that were outlined quite spectacularly in that costume.

He must have hit his head *really* hard if that was what he was focusing on.

"Do you mind telling me where I am?"

The crestfallen expression turned pained. "Um... You're in Pennsylvania."

"Yeah, I get that. I mean, where in Pennsylvania?" He sure as hell wasn't in any part of the state he'd heard of.

"In Harrisonville. Peter Harrison's home, to be exact."

Zane winced again, and it had nothing to do with the egg that was fast forming on the back of his head. "This isn't the Harrison home."

"It's not?" Legitimate surprise lit up her face. God, she was beautiful.

Zane gritted his teeth. She'd pulled a sword on him; what was *wrong* with him to still be bowled over by her looks? As a pro football player, he'd seen his fair share of beautiful women. Had slept with plenty of them. But not one had tried to kill him. Not even when he'd broken up with them.

"No, this definitely is *not* the Harrison house. I was just there, and I lived there for the first twelve years of my life. I would've remembered a room like this."

She put a hand on his arm. "You lived here? I don't remember you."

Considering she looked at least ten years younger than his thirty-two, and he and Mom had moved the year he'd turned twelve after Dad died, there was no way she *should* remember him.

"Look, I just want to know where I am and how I got here. Or better yet, where's the door? I'll get out of your hair"—bad word choice because his fingers were itching to get into her hair—"and leave the sword outside." He hadn't conked his head hard enough that he'd give her the chance to skewer him.

"I'm afraid that's not possible." She tucked a swath of hair behind her ear. She even had adorable ears.

"Sure it is. I'll just lay the sword beside the door."

Her hair shimmered as it swung in counterpoint to the movement of her head. "No, I mean it's not possible for you to leave through a door. There isn't one."

This time he did look behind him.

Damn if she wasn't right. Windows ringed the entire room. "I'm not picky. I'll climb through a window."

"Except that they're for show."

"Show?"

She nodded. "They don't open. Watch."

Then she… blew him a kiss?

Well, okay, he'd already established that he was as human as the next guy, and if she was offering, he was taking.

He pulled her to him, intending just one nibble. One taste. But when his lips met hers, the first turned into a

11

second, then a third. A fourth. A fifth. And then he gave up counting and lost himself in the taste and feel of this beautiful woman in his arms. She was soft where a woman should be, her curves meeting the hard—and hardening— lines of his body, her lips perfectly shaped for his, her taste an ambrosia he'd never tasted, and—

Zane pulled back. *Ambrosia*? What the hell? Since when did he spout Shakespeare?

He looked down at her, so much smaller than he was, her lips still pursed, her eyes fluttering open, their silvery gray depths sparkling like moonlight, her cheeks pink where the stubble he hadn't shaved this morning had grazed them, and he leaned in for one more taste—

"Holy smokes!"

Until she said that.

Her eyes lost their sparkle as they flew open, and she spun around. "I said 'show!'"

Zane looked over his shoulder to where she was staring.

Something white poured from the windows and crept toward him.

Zane took a few steps back as it approached, stopping only when he bumped into her.

The white stuff began covering his feet. Shit, it was cold.

The woman nestled against him, muttering something foreign-sounding and blowing more air kisses. He'd had women make moves on him before, but this... This was beyond strange and he couldn't make any sense of it. He couldn't make sense of *any* of it; not how he got here, not the room itself, certainly not her, and now this... this... *snow*?

She started hopping. "Bop, cop, fop, hop, lop, mop, pop..."

The snow kept coming.

Zane was sure his mind was going. It was July, for

Christ's sake. At least, it had been when he'd arrived three hours ago. He *thought* it'd been three hours ago, but with the conk on his head... Had it been another day? Why didn't he know? And how had he gotten here, who was she, what was with the sword at his throat, and why was it snowing?

"Stop!" She yelled so loudly that the term "ringing in his ears" made sense because it felt as if a gong had exploded, stopping up his ears like a change in cabin pressure.

He was working his jaw and jiggling fingers in his ears to get them to pop when he realized that not only had she stopped hopping against him, but the snow had stopped rising, pausing at crotch level which, with her breasts pressed up against his back, was the perfect level to stop at, as if the Universe knew he needed some cooling down in that area.

Zane kicked at the snow and put a few inches between himself and the woman before turning around to see her brushing the snow in wide circles away from her.

"Uh, miss?"

She licked her lips again and brushed the snow away.

"Miss?"

She looked up, her eyes now a dark gray. "Sadly, I didn't miss you. I'm sorry. But in a circular room, it's kind of hard to when it's coming in from all sides."

"What?" She was speaking English, but that was the only part of what she'd said that made any sense.

She stood up and brushed off her hands. "I said I was sorry for not missing you."

"With the sword?"

"That, too."

As if that made any sense.

A chill ran up his spine and it had nothing to do with the snow. Well, yeah, the snow was part of it. So was this poor, beautiful, confused woman. And him being in this

13

room and the snow and the windows and the sword…
"Look, Vana. Can you just point me to the way out? I have
someone coming by this week and have a lot of work to do
beforehand." As well as find some place to take her where
she could get the help she needed.

He just couldn't get away from the stigma of his
great-grandfather's mental illness that had pervaded every
generation since, could he? Zane had tried to counteract it
by moving away and making something of his life and he'd
thought he'd succeeded.

Yet, with his mother's death, he'd inherited this place
and apparently all of its craziness. He hadn't even been back a
full day, and lunacy was rearing its ugly head—well, not ugly;
quite beautiful actually, but lunacy was still lunacy. Maybe she
was a distant cousin he hadn't heard about, which gave new
meaning to the term "kissing cousins."

Zane shuddered. It'd been an awesome kiss, but now
that he knew the truth—that she was crazy (and probably
some distant relation)—there'd be no more of that.

"The way out?" She nibbled on that bottom lip that
had been designed to tempt men into lusting after their
cousins, no matter how distant. (It was working, dammit.)
"Um, well, I guess you could leave the same way you came
in." She pointed a finger upward.

Zane looked up. The ceiling tapered into a long,
chimney-like structure that ended in darkness. "What do
you mean?"

"You can go out through the…" She looked up. "Holy
smokes!"

Zane was coming to dislike that phrase. "What now?"

"The stopper's in."

Zane jiggled a finger in his ear again. What she'd -
said made no sense—like everything else she'd said,
including the foreign language she was muttering again and
the fluffy white *snow* she was kicking… and the curly-toed
slipper she was kicking it with.

A fencing harem girl. Yeah, this poor thing had gotten the entire family tree's share of crazy.

"Look, sweetheart. I'll just leave through one of the windows and you can go back to doing whatever it was you were doing."

He slunk through the snow, keeping his gaze on her, his pace slow but steady so he wouldn't spook her.

"I was only trying to whip up a party dress." She slid her hands to her hips.

A whip dangled from one -.

She looked surprised to see it there and flung it away as if it were made of fire. Too bad it didn't melt the snow.

Snow. Right. He still hadn't dealt with that issue. But if he could just get out of this place, he was sure the snow would be a non-issue because he wouldn't have to deal with her. He'd get her to a nice facility, leave her in the care of trained professionals, and unload this place as fast as possible.

Maybe then the Harrison name—and his ancestors— would *finally* rest in peace.

Except she muttered something else and Zane was afraid that peace was something he'd never find.

"*Stuck?*" He froze in place and it had nothing to do with the snow. "What do you mean we're *stuck?*"

Chapter 2

Vana stared at the man in front of her.

The man who'd kissed her.

She put a hand to her lips. It'd been far too long since anyone had kissed her, let alone kissed her like *that*.

Towering over her somewhere in the six-foot range, with jet black hair just shy of curling and blue, blue eyes fringed in long, dark lashes that were at odds with a jaw that could handle a few punches—above shoulders that could throw even more—the guy could be an Olympian god, able with just one touch to make her feel as if she were merely a shimmering mass of magical Glimmer tightly coiled in a sandstorm of sensation, about to whirl apart if not for the force of his desire holding her together.

Not that she'd tell him any of that. It'd been her experience that gods—mortal or actual ones—knew their effect on women and relished the adoration.

She touched her lips again, unable to help herself. The last man to kiss her had been Wilhelm and, well, his kiss was only memorable because it'd been the last. The only men she'd seen since Peter locked her away had been on the television she'd ordered through the Genie Supply System about forty years ago. And, even that hadn't turned out well. when she'd tried hardwiring the television set to the toaster to sample one of those new-fangled TV dinners and had ended up *hotwiring* them instead, frying everything but what she'd been planning to eat for dinner.

He looked good enough to eat.

She was going to ask him why he'd kissed her, but he also looked angry enough to bite her head off, so she decided to keep that question to herself because the answer she had to give him was not going to go over well.

Especially when he tried to move.

Vana didn't even bother trying; she knew what the outcome would be. They *were* stuck. In every sense of the word.

"I can't move my feet."

She winced. "Try wiggling your toes." She did the same inside her curly-toed *khussas*. Yes, toe-wiggling was possible; it was just forward momentum that wasn't. Or backward. Or sideways.

"What in God's name is going on?"

She wished he wouldn't bring the gods into it. She was desperately trying to stay off their radar.

"What's happening here?"

Actually, she'd like to know that, too. She'd have to check the *Djinnoire* for an explanation because she had no idea what he was doing inside her bottle. Obviously her magic had gone wonky yet again. Usually when a mortal opened her bottle, the cosmic pull of The Service whisked her up and out into their realm in a plume of pink smoke, but she hadn't felt even a smidgen of cosmic energy before he'd been on the other end of the scimitar.

She glanced at it in his hand. Genghis's. She didn't need a panicky mortal swinging *that* thing around.

Unfortunately, however, The Code that governed all djinn mandated that she couldn't take it from him. Other than seeing to their masters' comfort and safety, genies weren't permitted to do anything magical to their masters

17

without their express permission. Well, do anything to them *on purpose.* Gods knew (and, sadly, they did), that over the centuries, she'd done plenty of things accidentally to her masters that they hadn't wished for.

But still, the more the guy tried to move his feet, the more frustrated he became, and guys and frustration and swords had never really worked out well, as history showed. So, with a dearth of magical options available to her, she tried pulling a trick out of the mortal hat—

Only to have a top hat float down behind the man and land on the snow, sinking in until half of the satin band was covered. Then a bunny hopped out. Luckily, it was white so it blended in with the snow, which hopefully would prevent the mortal from freaking out.

"Why can't I move?"

Well, freaking out more than he already was.

Normally, she'd try to whisk the snow and bunny away, but she didn't want to tempt Karma by attempting too much. Instead, she went with something light and easy. A little puff of a kiss managed to transport her pendant off the *pouffe* beside her bed and into her hand. She dangled the pink tourmaline in front of her, swinging it side to side. "You're getting sleepy. Verrrry sleepy."

"Are you serious?" At least that got him to stop struggling. The sword, however, was still swaying. "Who do you think you are, Freud? Snow White?"

She dropped her arm. If she was Snow White, that must make him Grumpy. Which wasn't helping matters.

She kissed the pendant into a shimmer of pink Glimmer and sighed. "I told you. I'm Vana. Short for Nirvana."

"Nirvana? Seriously?"

She didn't kid about her name. Nirvana Aphrodite. It was a mouthful—and a lot of pressure. As if her parents had set her up to fail. Poor DeeDee, her twin, had the unluckier name of Aphrodite Nirvana, but *she* certainly hadn't failed. No, DeeDee had the winning thing down pat.

Enough for both of them, which balanced the cosmic scales.

At least, that's what Vana kept telling herself. She'd tried telling it to her parents, but they hadn't bought it. Not *their* daughter. No sirree.

"Ahem. Yes, my name is Nirvana. Nirvana Aphrodite, and, before you say it…" She held up her hand, knowing what he was going to say the minute his mouth opened. Over the past eight hundred years she'd heard it more times than she cared to count. "I do know I have a lot to live up to." Her name was only one of a long list.

"Your parents were either hippies or Greek scholars."

"Something like that." The fact that her mother actually *had* been a scholar in Greece—ancient Greece—would probably fall on the TMI list, should she choose to reveal it.

She'd learned a long time ago not to. People tended to believe the genie thing once she *poofed* a couple of items into existence—gold typically being the first choice—but the whole immortality issue usually freaked them out.

Go figure. It wasn't as if *they* had to deal with immortality, since they tended not to live longer than it took her to age a few months, but when she started talking about Galileo and da Vinci as contemporaries, mortals looked at her as if she had two heads.

The one time she'd managed to duplicate her own head on her shoulders—not on purpose, of course—hadn't exactly been her best moment.

"So Nirvana—"

"I prefer Vana." Fewer expectations to live up to that way.

And fewer to fall short of.

He arched an eyebrow at her. It gave him kind of a rakish look, like d'Artagnan. That was a major compliment 'cause that guy had been a *babe*. There was a reason the story of the king's most famous Musketeer had been passed down through the ages, and without much fictionalization.

D'Artagnan had had enough charisma to fill a ballroom and the looks to go with it. She'd swooned into his arms like half the female population. What a time to have been in France.

"Fine. Vana. What's going on? Why can't we move? Where are we? Why is there snow?"

Vana fiddled with the knickers of her fencing uniform. Ugh. So far from Ungaro's designs it wasn't funny, and the uniform didn't even keep the snow off her legs.

Ah, snow. Cold. That could explain it.

"Well, um, I think, on account of the snow, that we're, uh, frozen in place."

His other eyebrow went north, too.

Okay, that wasn't going to fly—

Ah, but she was about to.

Her magic *kilim* glided out from under the snow, shook itself off like a puppy, whisked her off her feet, and zipped her over to him.

"Care to hop on?" First time today the magic had gone her way.

"What the hell? Hop *on*? A carpet? A *flying* carpet? Are you nuts?"

Well, *that* took the wind out of her sails.

And the magic out of the carpet.

She ended up sinking into the snow, which had the added benefit of now covering her legs, freezing her in place for real. Or maybe that was her mortification in the face of his accusation.

"I… I'm not nuts." She got the words out. Barely. They tended to get stuck in the back of her throat every time she had to utter them. "I'm a genie."

The guy sank into the snow next to her. "A what?"

She folded her hands in her lap and twiddled her fingers. "I'm a genie."

"A genie."

"Yes."

He didn't say anything for a few seconds, but the silence was deafening. She always hated waiting for their response. Sometimes it was disbelief; sometimes it was overly enthusiastic; and other times it was downright greedy.

"As in *I Dream of?*"

That was one she hadn't heard before. Mainly because she hadn't run into any mortals since 1898 and that television show had come sixty-some years later. "Oh, you watched it, too!"

The guy looked at her as if she'd done the two-head trick again.

She slid a hand to her neck, under the guise of scratching an itch, just to make sure she hadn't.

"So does that mean I get three wishes?"

She shook her head. "Actually, you can have as many as you want. I'm your genie for life. Well, unless someone steals my bottle. It's very important for you to safeguard it."

"My genie for life with unlimited wishes." He flopped his hands and the scimitar—thank the stars it was in the hand *not* beside her—onto the snow and shook his head. "Oh my God. It must be catching. Like the flu." His shoulders slumped and he looked at her, weariness etched around the bluest eyes she'd seen since Peter's.

He had Peter's eyes.

She did the math, but he couldn't be Peter's son; it'd been much longer than that. "What's your name?"

"Zane Harrison."

She clapped her hands together. "You *are* related to Peter!"

"My cross to bear."

"Oh, don't say that." She rested her hand on his arm. "Peter was a wonderful man. Maybe not like other people would have liked him to be, but he was wonderful to me."

"Hold on. What do you mean my great-grandfather was good to you? You can't be more than thir—uh, twenty-nine."

21

She couldn't help the chuckle. It was a good thing he was already sitting down. "Actually, it's eight hundred and twenty-nine, but thanks for the compliment."

"Eight... *hundred?*"

She nodded. "And twenty-nine. As of two weeks ago." DeeDee and the High Master had been the only ones who'd sent her any sort of acknowledgment. Mother and Father were still too embarrassed by her "little indiscretion" to even acknowledge publicly that they had another daughter.

Not that she minded. Well, not too much. But it worked for her because if the parental units weren't around to express their disdain, then she didn't have to remember that she was the cause of it. It helped alleviate some of the guilt she felt about smoking into that bottle way back when she shouldn't have. The day she'd played hooky and ended up in The Service without being qualified to do so had changed so many lives.

Not the least of which was Peter's great-grandson's. The guy was shaking his head again and pinching the bridge of his nose with the hand that had held the scimitar. Oh, good; he'd forgotten about it. Now if she could manage to zap it back to its scabbard...

A loud *bam!* and the sword shattered.

Zane jumped up, the momentum enough to free his feet.

Yay. One good thing to come from her screwy magic...

"Do you mind telling me what that was?" Peter's great-grandson asked, twisting around. "And where the snow came from? And what the hell you meant by genie? And... and—Jesus—a flying carpet?"

Vana took a deep breath and stood. Right; there was protocol to this. And after all these years of not having done it, she was doing it wrong.

Pretty much like everything else.

But that was going to change. She'd finally swallowed her visceral aversion to all things academic and had opened the famed *Djinnoire* her sister had written, the most comprehensive collection of djinn history, protocol, herbology, and magic since Maimun's mishap at the library at Alexandria. Luckily, Vana had had no part in that debacle—hadn't even been born yet—and none of her gaffes *quite* measured up to it, so she was gratified in knowing she wasn't the most inept genie that had ever lived. Merely the second most inept.

She was *always* second best.

Vana shook off the self-pity (for the most part), clasped her hands together, and bowed. "*Salam wa aleikum.* I am Nirvana, the genie of the bottle. What is your wish, master?"

She hoped he wished for her bottle to be unsealed.

A *pop!* like a champagne cork reverberated though the bottle and the ceiling opened up.

She heard the stopper hit the ceiling of the attic where her bottle had lain all these years and then *thwump* off a wall.

And then something crashed.

Sigh.

She didn't know how her wish had come to be granted (or she would have done it ages ago), and she didn't know why. But she did know that this was her chance, so Vana jumped at it—straight out of the bottle, dragging Zane along with her.

Chapter 3

Coming back to the family homestead had been a bad idea. Worst he'd ever had. He'd thought using the off-season to clean out the remnants of his past would be a good way to keep his mind off the mess going on with his career. But that past was not only catching up to him; it was overtaking him.

Zane rolled off the dress form he'd landed on, and a shaft of pain spiked from his right ankle to his knee. "Son of a bitch!"

"What does a dog have to do with anything?"

Zane looked up. Her question almost sounded serious.

He shook his head and tried to get to his feet. Damn it, that hurt. He hoped to God his leg wasn't broken. The coaching staff would crucify him. Or, after the torn ACL he'd just finished rehabbing, rescind his second-team contract altogether. Bad enough he wasn't going to start, but not get a contract at all? That could not happen. Jerry Rice had played for seven years after his injury; Zane was planning for two, maybe three more. But to do so, he needed to be in the best shape of his life to prove to the staff that he still had what it took.

He leaned on a sheet-covered old dresser and tested his weight. No way; he couldn't stand on it.

Zane gritted his teeth and worked himself into a different angle. Fire shot through his shin and sucked the air out of his lungs. Dammit. He needed to get to a hospital right away to have even a prayer of having a career left.

He shifted his weight, pain searing through the leg and radiating up through his entire body while he checked his pockets for his cell phone. He'd injured his right leg, so he wasn't going to be able to drive himself, and he'd rather not risk his Mercedes to this woman's next delusion.

But what about the snow? The pink smoke? Were they *delusions?*

Zane didn't know what they were, and frankly, didn't give a damn at the moment. The leg hurt like a son-of-a-bitch, and preventing the end of his career because of some stupid accident in his great-grandfather's attic needed to be his first priority.

The cell phone had no service, damn it. And the house didn't have a landline, which meant he was S.O.L. on an ambulance unless he could make it down the stairs, somehow manage to trek a good half mile or so down the god-awful long driveway to the closest house, and hope someone was home.

Or he could rely on *her*.

He had to be out of his mind with pain. No way was he going to rely on her. Nirvana Aphrodite.

Though she did look fairly goddess-like in that harem outfit. Or, more to the point, the genie that she claimed to be.

Wait. What happened to the fencing garb?

Zane stifled a groan. He knew things wouldn't have changed all that much in the twenty-two years since he'd been here, but he hadn't foreseen finding a cousin who thought she was Barbara Eden. Oh, God, if the press got wind of this…

He tried again to get to the doorway, grimacing when a loose floorboard clipped the side of his foot. This time the groan wouldn't be stifled.

"Are you hurt?" Vana took a few steps closer. Snow fell off the bangles on the low-riding belt on her hips.

Snow.

Pink smoke.

A harem outfit.

The utterly inexplicable fact that they'd been... somewhere... and now they were in the attic.

And that flying rug.

"You're... you're really a genie?"

She put her hands on her hips, which were curvy and naked enough to make him hope she was a *very* distant cousin. By marriage.

"Of course I am. That's what I said."

Blackness encroached, hovering just beyond his peripheral vision, and Zane was ready to give her the benefit of the doubt if she'd just get him to the hospital. "Please tell me you know how to drive."

"Drive what?"

He'd worry about that question later because not only was necessity the mother of invention, but pain was also the ignorer of bad options.

"Um, look." He squinted against the light of the lone light bulb and tried to keep from blacking out. "I think my leg might be broken, and I need to get to the hospital. Can you take me?"

She was nibbling her bottom lip again, and since that hadn't boded well for him in the short time he'd known her, he left off the part about maybe going into shock.

A good choice when she covered her mouth with her hands and uttered the now-infamous, "Holy smokes!"

He could swear he *smelled* smoke.

She made some more kissing noises and waved her hands in front of her face, her cough as adorable as she was.

He definitely was going into shock to be thinking like that at a time like this.

"Look, all I need is to get downstairs and then you can drive me to the hospital. My car's outside. You can drive a stick, right?"

"Only witches can do that."

She could be going into shock, too.

Zane leaned on his hands and worked his way through the attic among the forgotten minutiae of a hundred years' worth of stuff he had yet to sort through, maneuvering himself toward the staircase where coolness, his car, and—please God—some semblance of sanity remained.

"I could, um, fix that for you, if you want."

Her words stopped him. "Fix what?"

"Your leg." She nibbled on her bottom lip again.

Zane wiped his forehead on his T-shirt and, against his better judgment, asked, "You can fix a broken leg?"

She nodded and the bangles on her belt jingled. "Sure. Bones knit together easily."

He was out of his mind to even consider anything she said. And possibly even more insane to allow her to drive him.

"You know what? That's okay. I'll get myself to the hospital, and you can stay here and relax. Have a glass of wine or something. It's got to be five o'clock somewhere." He'd down an entire bottle of Jack if it'd take the pain away, but pain meds worked better.

Her shoulders slumped, and she started nibbling her lip again. Why did that make him feel as if he'd kicked a kitten?

Then his foot did kick something and he yowled.

"Oh, please. Let me help. I know I can."

Zane was trying to catch his breath and keep from passing out. He needed help. "Sure," he panted. "Fine. Whatever." He waved his hand, beckoning her over. If he could lean on her, he could cross the last five feet to the attic door. Why did this have to be the only spot in the attic where someone had moved all the furniture and knickknacks out of reach?

"Okay. Here goes. One knit bone coming up."

He opened his mouth to say "No," but what emerged was one long howl.

Right before he passed out.

27

Chapter 4

"Holy smokes."

Vana's heart was pounding like Crusaders' marching drums, drowning out the commands she was mentally screaming at her body, "Move!" being the primary one.

It took a good three seconds—not that there was anything good in them—for her feet to get a clue and rush over to him.

"Master?" She dropped to her knees beside his prone form where he'd crumpled to the dusty attic floor and shook his shoulder—the one now covered in a knitted sweater.

She nudged him again, then her fingers scrambled beneath the neckline to find a pulse.

There. Beneath the scratchy wool, his pulse throbbed. A little faster than necessary, but given the fact that he had a broken leg, that was understandable.

But she didn't think he'd understand about the sweater.

"Oh dear. Now what do I do?"

Duh. Fix his leg. Just like he asked.

Oh, right. He'd asked, so she could. That's the way the genie-master relationship worked, and if he hadn't quite said "I wish," surely it was implied. She might want to reread Chapter Six, though.

But she'd give it a shot. The opening of DeeDee's *Djinnoire* assured even the most novice of djinn that magic could be corralled—and she was not the most novice of djinn. (No matter what her magical ability said about her.)

She shook out her hands, then rolled her shoulders and neck to loosen them up. She could do this. Rule Number Two of Chapter One (right behind: "First, Do No Harm) was: Gather Your Confidence Before Gathering Your Magic.

She could do that. She just wouldn't use words like "knit" this time.

She pursed her lips, but this time in thought, not magic. Maybe she ought to leave the mending to the professionals. Transportation was more her forte. She could magick him to Peter's hospital.

Yes, better to err on the side of caution.

A *cushion* flew across the room.

Erring was definitely a good idea.

She scooted closer to Zane, leaned over, gingerly wrapped her arms around him, pictured Peter's hospital, then kissed the air.

Pink smoke swirled around them, and she braced herself against that rushing feeling she'd gotten the last time she'd traveled in this latitude when she'd tried to make blackberry brandy but, for some reason, had ended up with blueberries instead. That had started a berry battle, and she'd had to intercept the berries before they left the orchards and bombarded Peter's guests. Before that incident she'd loved to teleport, but not so much after. Blueberries might be tiny, but thousands of them had left her black and blue. Two shades of blue.

The pink smoke dissipated, her pink Glimmer falling onto a circle of hedges in front of the hospital like a cotton-candy snowfall.

She ducked and looked around. Probably not the best idea to think of snow. While mortals couldn't see her

Judi Fennell

Glimmer, they could definitely see snow, and since she was out among them, she had to be careful not to create any more havoc that would blacken Peter's—and now Zane's— name.

Zane materialized beside her without making a sound. Good, she hadn't lost her touch when it came to landing. And, thankfully, she hadn't even thought about not being able to do it right; it would have been just her luck to injure his shoulder or something.

She heard a shout and peeked over the hedge to the hospital's entrance.

Two men in white coats jumped away from the statue of Peter's grandmother there as the arm fell off.

Broken at the shoulder.

So much for not creating havoc. It'd been a long time since her magic had been out in the world. As long as she hadn't been. She was a little rusty.

And now so were the gutters on the roof above the hospital's entrance as a long line of copper shimmered across it as if a hand of a god were coloring it in.

Vana shook her head. Stress wasn't good for her magic. She had to get it and herself under control. Peter's reputation was in her hands, and now, so was her current master's well-being. She took a deep breath and folded her hands in her lap. No good. Her fingers started fiddling with each other.

Maybe she ought to resurrect the ol' count-the-hummingbird trick she'd used for calming herself as a child. It probably had something to do with the mobile of lifelike hummingbirds Mom had dangled above her crib. DeeDee's mobile had been of butterflies, but Vana would bet Dee never counted butterflies. Her sister was always in control.

A butterfly landed on Vana's fingers.

She clamped her eyes shut and imagined the h-u-m-m-i-n-g-d-i-r-b-s, counting twelve jeweled little birds, one for

30

each letter. Gold, green, teal, blue… shimmery bodies and fluttering wings, metaphorically hovering in front of her, their curved bills drawing the anxiety from her, only to whisk it away, taking her troubles with them.

When the last imaginary bird dissolved, she released her breath and opened her eyes. The butterfly was gone, too. That was better.

She looked at the hospital. It didn't look anything like when she'd last seen it. Now it was big and white and about three times as sprawling as before. The only similarity to what she remembered was the pomegranate tree in the middle of the front garden.

Thank that stars, *that* magic had worked. Pomegranates wouldn't grow in this part of the world otherwise.

Peter's name was above the front door, but in different lettering than before. And a different name. Harrison Memorial instead of Harrison Hospital. He'd be thrilled to see that; Peter had wanted big things for his hospital.

Who knew it'd come in handy a hundred and some years later?

And not a moment too soon. Zane moaned, an uncomfortable sound that dumped a ton of guilt onto her head. If only she hadn't whisked him out of the bottle with her. Or if she'd held on to him longer. Given him a chance to get his feet under him before she'd let go.

Vana stood up, putting a cork in those thoughts. Second-guessing herself had never worked in the past, so no sense doing it now. She had to get him help.

She waved the two men near the statue over and tried to find a way through the hedge, but there wasn't one. Vana pursed her lips. *Great*. Why wasn't there one?

Thankfully, the two men didn't see anything wrong with the brand-spankin'-new gate that spanked *her* in the back of the legs as they approached.

"Miss? Are you okay?" asked the heavier-set one.

31

"Yes, I am, but my friend..." She looked over her shoulder.

"Whoa!" The two guys rushed to Zane's side.

"What happened to him?" the black-haired one asked, whisking a stethoscope over his head and into his ears as the blond one did a rudimentary inspection of Zane's limbs.

Zane groaned when the doctor touched his left foot.

Wait. Hadn't he been favoring his right one? Gods, it showed how discombobulated she was that she couldn't tell his left from his right.

"I don't like the look of this leg. We need an X-ray."

Zane moaned when the doctor moved on to inspect his other leg.

"The right one, too." The blond looked over his shoulder at her. "Miss, what happened?"

Two broken legs? "He, um... fell. In the attic. At his grandfather's home. Peter Harrison. You know..." She thumbed the name above the door.

"He's a Harrison?" The black-haired guy flicked a small light at Zane's eyes. "We haven't had a member of the family here in decades."

Two of them, to be exact. And two years. Vana knew, to the day, how long it'd been since there'd been a Harrison living in that house because she'd kept track of every day since Peter had sent her to her bottle. Every moving day, every party, every slip of noise that had filtered up to the attic—which, sadly, hadn't been many. At least, until recently.

But she'd never been able to find out what had happened to Peter, had never known why he hadn't come back for her, until Faruq, the High Master's vizier, had ordered her a laptop, and she'd had the chance to read a local history book and learn about Peter's freak accident. One she'd had nothing to do with, thank the stars. Talk about the worst sort of irony.

Although, the fact that she'd had a lot to do with *this* freak accident negated the irony and just made it plain sad.

The blond flipped his cell phone closed and slipped it into his pocket. "Gurney's on its way." He looked at her. "Miss, if you wouldn't mind holding that gate open when they get here?"

"When did they put a gate on this side, Kirk?" asked the dark-haired one, shoving his stethoscope into his jacket pocket. The name "Corsey" was stitched above the breast pocket.

"Beats me, Hal. I've been off duty for a few days. Things can change in the blink of an eye around here."

Or the purse of her lips.

"Yeah, they say things happen when Old Man Harrison's ghost walks through town. And with Grandma losing an arm over there, the rumors are going to go haywire." Hal glanced at the statue and then looked at her. "Sorry if I offended you, miss. It's just that now that there's a Harrison back in town, well, you're going to hear the old stories. Best be prepared. Old Man Harrison was crazy enough for this town to keep telling stories into the next generation."

Considering three generations had passed since Peter's, that was a lot of stories.

The orderlies showed up with the gurney and transferred her master onto it with minimal moaning while she stood back and watched. One hour out of her bottle—not even—and she was already back to her old tricks.

Chapter 5

Vana sat in the waiting room, twiddling her fingers so fast and furious, she might actually be able to knit enough of the dust glinting in the sunlight into sweaters for everyone in the room. But then she'd have to explain it to them.

She sighed and tucked a hand under each thigh. Bad enough everyone was gossiping about the damage to the statue; she didn't need to give them anything more to talk about. Zane had been whisked through the double doors to the inner sanctum of examining rooms, and they'd been casting glances at her ever since.

"You one of Old Man Harrison's relatives, too?" the elderly man beside her asked.

"Me? Oh, no."

He tilted his fedora back and peered at her. "Good thing. I hear the apple don't fall too far from the tree, ya know? I mean, who wears a sweater in the middle of July? And *two* legs." He nodded toward the doors Zane had been wheeled through. "The stories my grandfather used to tell me about Crazy Old Man Harrison…"

He was one to talk about crazy. A fedora and a pair of stained overalls. Vana's lips twitched, and not with laughter. She so wanted to magick that hat into a toupee, but she wasn't about to feed the rumor mill.

Peter had been a great man. He'd tried to do so much for the town and its people; she was the one who'd goofed it all up... including his actual mill.

Vana winced. That gristmill was a sore spot for her, and if everyone was going to rehash Peter's "blunders," that fiasco was sure to come up. Best to steer clear of it.

If only she'd been able to steer the mill's waterwheel...

Vana sighed and plopped her chin into her palm. Nothing like having unintentionally created a haunted landmark. Peter had gotten a good chuckle out of it, but she... She'd wanted to crawl under a rock.

A rock popped into existence beneath the table behind Mr. Stained Overalls. Holy smokes! That wouldn't take long to discover.

Concentrating, Vana focused all her energy beneath that table to send the rock back to the quarry on the outskirts of town.

A table skirt *poofed* onto the table.

Well... at least no one could see the rock.

Vana buried her face in her hands. She needed to stop thinking.

Why wouldn't her magic work right? That question had been plaguing her ever since she'd gone to school. Before that, when she'd been experimenting with her magic just for herself, she'd done okay, but the minute she'd had to study theories and mechanics, things had gone awry. *Performance anxiety*, DeeDee had called it, which was as good an explanation as any Vana had come up with. But even now, when she wasn't being graded, she still couldn't get the hang of it. Broken legs, disfigured statue, snow... She was batting oh-for-ten.

A bat appeared, propped against her chair. Luckily, it was the baseball kind and not the winged kind. Vana slid it beneath the table with the rock.

"Miss? If you could come to the desk, please?" The

clerk at the front counter waved a piece of paper at her. "HIPAA prevents us from shouting patient information across the room."

Hippo? Vana clamped a hand over her mouth as she headed to the counter. She was *not* going to conjure a hippo.

"Patient's name?" asked the woman.

"Zane Harrison."

"Date of birth?"

Vana twisted a strand of hair around her finger. "I don't know."

The woman raised an eyebrow. "Address?"

That was an easy one. She'd lived there longer than he had.

"Any allergies?"

"I don't know."

"Insurance?"

"I don't know."

"Next of kin?"

"I don't—is he dying?" Thank the stars for the counter because Vana grabbed onto it when her knees buckled. "I have to see him." She turned to the right. Or maybe that was the left. No, it was the right. She was sure of that. But that was pretty much all she was sure of.

Oh gods, oh gods, oh gods, she couldn't have *killed* him. For Pete's—and Peter's—sakes, she couldn't have killed Zane. She'd never be able to live with herself if she'd taken a life.

"Where is he? Please. I have to see him."

The woman stood and put a hand on Vana's arm. "But, miss—"

Vana twisted away. She had to see him. Had to fix him. Okay, genies couldn't bring mortals back to life, but maybe the woman was wrong. Maybe there was something she could do—

"Miss?" A man stood behind her.

"Zane?" She spun around.

It wasn't Zane.

"No. Gary Huss. Harrisonville city councilman." The guy stuck out his hand.

"Um, hello." She gave his hand a perfunctory shake. "I… I'm sorry, but I really don't have time to talk. I have to find my mast—er, Zane."

"Zane Harrison, right? Peter Harrison's great-grandson?"

"Yes, that's him. I need to see him. Excuse me." She headed toward the double doors to the right (yes, it was the right) of the front counter.

The woman behind it stepped in front of her. "Miss, you can't go back there. Mr. Harrison is in X-ray."

"X… You mean he's not dead?"

"Of course not. I just needed the information for the forms. Standard procedure."

This time Vana's knees did give out. Luckily, Gary Whatshisname was there to catch her.

"Whoa. Let's get you a seat," he said, ushering her over to a bank of blue plastic chairs against the wall.

"I… uh… thank you." Vana closed her eyes and counted twenty-four hummingdirbs this time. Added a dozen dutterflies just to be safe.

"Feel better?" Gary was beside her with a can of soda in his hands. "Here. Not quite the kick you look like you need, but the fizz is refreshing."

Now why would he think she'd want a kick when she was already down?

"Thank you." But she almost spit the soda out when Gary sat next to her.

"You don't mind, do you?"

She did, but if he was part of the government of Peter's town, she didn't want to give anyone any reason to diss Peter's memory. She couldn't screw this up.

A screw fell out of the bottom of his chair.

Apparently, she could. "Um, no, of course I don't mind."

"Good."

He slid his arm behind her chair and faced her, effectively blocking her in because she was on the end of the row. Her next move, if she made one, would be onto her posterior, and that was a distinct possibility with wobbly legs.

"So Zane's back in town, is he? When did he get in? I've been wondering how he's been all these years. We were, ah, chums in school, you know."

"No, I didn't. But how nice for you."

Just the thought of school made her shudder.

"So, is this just a visit or is Zane planning to retire here now? I never thought he'd pick this place, but stranger things have happened, I guess."

Oh, she could tell him all about strange.

"What are your plans?"

Her plans were to get her magic working perfectly so she could end the children's enchantment, Peter's greatest wish. Unfortunately, today's events proved she wasn't yet up to that task.

"I'm not exactly sure what his plans are. You'll have to ask him."

"You mean you two aren't together?"

Was it her imagination or had Gary leaned a little closer?

And then his question registered.

"We're, uh… acquaintances. I just happened to be at the right place at the right time to bring him here."

"I see."

He was seeing a little too much. Vana glanced at him out of the corner of her eye and saw his gaze fixed on her breasts.

Never before had she felt uncomfortable in this outfit, but right now, she felt as if bugs were crawling all over her skin—

Or, actually, *his* skin.

A beetle peeked over Gary's shoulder, then crawled down to disappear into his shirt pocket.

She pulled her upper lip between her teeth and tried not to laugh. Or be horrified by what he'd do when he felt the second one on his head.

This probably wasn't going to end well.

"So do you think you might be interested in having dinner with me some time?"

He was asking her out? She could only imagine the nightmare that would be. "I, um... That is..."

Thankfully, it appeared to be mating season for beetles, and these two decided to choose Gary's nose for their rendezvous, effectively preventing her from having to answer.

Gary flew out of his chair, swatting his nose and his arms and his breast pocket and his waist and his cheeks and every other body part as if he were dancing *La Cucaracha.*

Okay, so they weren't cockroaches, but the image still made her snort.

She put her hand in front of her mouth to muffle it and blew an air kiss, sending the insects onto the pomegranate tree outside. Hopefully.

"See?" said the old man in the overalls. "I told you crazy don't fall too far from the tree. Yer hangin' out with a Harrison, yer gonna bring on the crazy." He thumbed to Gary. "And now it's spreadin' to Huss."

At that, Gary stopped jumping and waving his arms, and straightened his tie. He slicked back his hair, then clasped the man's shoulder. "Come now, Mr. Donohue. Crazy? It was just a couple of beetles. They startled me. I'm perfectly all right and so is Miss... Miss..."

He looked at her.

"Vana." She didn't mention a last name because djinn didn't have them.

"All's I'm sayin' is that if yer worried about yer

image for the election, ya might not want to be hangin' around crazy." Mr. Donohue tugged his fedora down and shook his newspaper. "Gives folks ideas. And not the kind you want. No one wants a tetched"—he tapped his temple—"mayor."

Gary stared at Mr. Donohue, then looked at her. "How about if we take a rain check on that dinner invitation? I'll call you."

She nodded, making no motion to give him her phone number (mainly because, *no way*, and also because she didn't have one). He made no motion to ask for it, either.

Then he turned and walked out of the doors.

Right into a spur-of-the-moment rainstorm.

***

Gary yanked his car door shut and wiped the rain from his face. Contact made. And what sweet contact it was. The woman was gorgeous, but then, of course she would be. Football players had the life: chicks, cash, and a job they loved. Beat the shit out of being a small-town councilman.

Gary gripped the steering wheel. Why'd Zane have to come back before he'd finished searching that house?

He started the car. The clutch protested when he rammed it into first. Yeah, well, the car could get in line with all the other issues in his life. He already had more demands than his limited funds allowed, namely two months of back alimony and the threat of more to come.

God, he hated his ex. She'd been a sweet piece of ass in high school that had turned into just a plain ass once he'd married her. And now the bitch was making his life hell. He needed a serious infusion of cash that even winning the mayoral race wouldn't cover.

If only he could find out what his great-great-grandfather Calvin had said he'd seen in Old Man Harrison's study during that last party, he'd have it made. Calvin had gone to his grave swearing that there were things in that house that people wouldn't believe, and if he could just get his hands on those things, he'd be rich beyond his wildest dreams. And Gramps's dreams had been pretty wild, with him swearing that there was magic in that house.

Now, Gary wasn't typically one to believe in magic or hocus-pocus, and he sure as shit didn't want to lump his great-great-grandfather in the same category as Old Man Harrison, but the bear that had shown up that day *had* lent credence to his great-great-grandfather's claim. And God knew, there were enough strange goings-on in town while Harrison was alive to open the door to any possibility.

So Gary had been sneaking into the Harrison house for years, looking for clues. He hadn't found anything out of the ordinary except for the old man's journals. He'd swiped one, thinking it would have something useful in it, but other than a bunch of coordinates, weather conditions, and some really boring meeting notes from some really boring meetings between Harrison and his fellow wacko treasure hunters, Gary had come up empty.

And *then*, June Ertel, the woman Zane had hired to clean the place, had discovered that the journal was missing and called the cops. How the hell she'd figured that out, Gary never knew. But it did make him more cautious about sneaking in. After he'd won his first political office, he'd had to curtail his search even more; it wouldn't do for a town councilman to be caught trespassing.

But he was desperate now. His opponent, Nickelson, was a successful businessman who'd sworn to bring jobs to town even if he had to create them in his own company. Gary *had* to win; the pay was more than he made now as a mere councilman, plus there'd been a Huss on the city council ever since Calvin's father had been the first mayor. Gary wasn't going to be the one to break that streak— *unless* it was because he was so freaking rich that he didn't have to work, which was where that old house came in.

41

His father had considered the story to be Calvin's teenage need for attention, but Peter had traveled the globe collecting oddities. Treasure, maybe. Who knew what he'd found in the far corners of the earth? There'd been talk of magic and witchcraft.

And Zane's friend was wearing a genie costume...

Gary turned left out of the hospital parking lot. Now *he* was being crazy. There were no such things as genies. Magical beings that lived inside lanterns, granting wishes. Zane sure as hell wouldn't be in a hospital with two broken legs if that chick really was a genie. Probably some hot-sex role-playing game that'd gotten out of hand.

One more reason to hate Zane. As he'd done for years, ever since the bitch he'd made the mistake of marrying had first looked at Zane in second grade. Back then, the hatred was because Lynda preferred Zane. Now it was because Zane *hadn't* preferred her, thereby setting Gary up for the torture that had been their marriage.

And now the lucky SOB had a porn star playing fantasy games with him.

Gary restrained himself from flipping off Tom Schmidt as the old guy cut him off at the intersection. Schmidty had seven kids and fifteen grandkids, all registered voters. And Gary needed every vote if he was going to beat Nickelson—unless he found something in that house to fund his early retirement.

Zane just *had* to come back, didn't he? Gary gripped the steering wheel. The SOB lived a charmed life, but this was Gary's shot at fame and fortune—albeit on a far less grand scale than Zane's. He was *not* going to let Zane fuck it up for him.

Or Gary might just have to return the favor.

Chapter 6

The first thing Zane saw when he opened his eyes was the beautiful brunette sitting beside his bed.

She ought to be *in* his bed.

The second thing he saw was that this wasn't his bed. And definitely not his room.

The third was…

A cast.

No, *two* casts.

Every foul word in the English language ran through his mind. His fucking legs were broken? More rehab. Just what he didn't need on top of the surgery. If the coaches got wind of this, he could kiss *ever* playing another game good-bye.

He dropped his head back onto the pillow, the antiseptic smell of the room making his eyes water.

Yeah. That was it.

"I'm really sorry." The brunette—what was her name? Ah, Vana—whispered, her voice sounding just as watery.

Now why in the hell would that be, and what was she sorry for?

"I thought I could fix it."

Nothing was making any sense. Least of all why she was sitting beside his bed and why she was apologizing to him. Why both of his legs were broken.

Zane opened one eye, and it all came rushing back. The sword, the snow, the kiss... the *genie*...

Ah, shit. His delusional cousin.

"Look, Vana. If you don't mind, I'd rather be alone right now. I've got a lot on my mind." And some kick-ass painkillers fogging it up.

"Oh." She fiddled with her fingers. "Okay. I'll just be out in the waiting room if you need me."

She touched his arm as she stood.

Zane shivered and covered her hand with his. "Wait."

She paused. "Yes?"

He had to know. If only for his own peace of mind. And considering how unpeaceful it was at the moment... "Are we... that is, are you a Harrison?"

"Me? Oh, no. Peter was my master, not my father."

Peter was a sick bastard if he was into BDSM with her and—wait. What the hell was he thinking? Peter had been dead for over a hundred years.

Oh, right. She was eight hundred and twenty-nine years old. The poor delusional woman—and that was the reason he should forget how beautiful she was, regardless of whether or not they were related. He pulled his hand from hers. "Well, thanks for coming by, but you don't really need to stay."

Her fingers trailed over his skin as she removed her hand and sat back down. "I don't mind. You might need some help."

From her. The woman in the genie costume. Right. *He* was not the one in the room who needed help.

He should have just hired someone to clean out the house. An antiques dealer, probably, because for all his eccentricity (or because of it), Peter had acquired a lot of interesting pieces in his travels before he'd founded the town and then promptly gone insane.

Zane struggled to sit up. Shit, his leg hurt.

Legs.

"What happened to my legs?"

Vana pulled a handful of silky hair over her shoulder and started to braid it. "They're broken."

"Yeah, I get that. Question is, how?" This was just fucking great. He was a wide receiver; he needed his legs in perfect shape. He'd spent months—intensive, pain-filled months—rehabbing the ACL. How the hell was he supposed to rehab two legs when they were both out of commission?

"Well, um, technically, you didn't break them."

"Then why are they in casts?"

"Oh, no, they *are* broken. It's just that you didn't do it."

Which made about as much sense as the rest of this nightmare. "I'm not following you."

She grabbed another chunk of hair and started braiding that one. "Well, I kind of, you see…"

No he didn't see. And he had a sinking feeling he didn't want to.

"*I* broke them."

Of course she did. Because she was a genie.

Jesus.

Zane looked around, half expecting mankind's Savior to appear in the room—or someone who *thought* he was the Lord and Savior, and you know? Zane wouldn't complain about that right now. He needed someone to save him. And his sanity.

"Vana, it's okay. Whatever you think you did, you didn't. Look, I really appreciate you coming here and everything you did at the house"—because she had to have been the one to call the ambulance, right?—"but you've done your good deed. I'm a big boy. I can take it from here."

"But if you're in pain, I could try—"

"Don't try anything." The words shot out of his mouth before he'd even thought them.

Unfortunately he couldn't take them back before she heard them.

45

She dropped the braid.

Man, he really felt as if he'd kicked a kitten.

Hmmm… He'd thought that exact thing in the attic. When he'd been standing on his feet. The ones that were now in casts.

His gaze slid over her. Over the gauzy transparent pants. The bangles at her hips. The flare of her hips and the slope of her waist up to the full breasts tucked into a tiny half shirt and vest… She looked like Barbara Eden's dark-haired cousin in full-on genie garb, and it wasn't anywhere close to being Halloween.

"Tell me again why you think you're a genie."

"I don't think; I know. I *am* a genie and I was in Service to Peter, your great-grandfather. I've been locked in my bottle in the attic since he died, waiting for a new master to open it."

"New master? Me?" He'd opened that bottle. Had landed inside of it, too.

That was ridiculous. No one ended up inside a bottle. At least not literally. Figuratively? Hell yeah. He'd been there a few times. October sixteenth, to be exact. The day he'd torn the ACL and put an end to his season. Possibly his career.

"Yes, you. You became my master when you opened my bottle. I'm not sure how you fell inside it, though. I need to check the *Djinnoire* for that."

Whatever a "djinnoire" was… He flung his forearm over his eyes. "I wish I could start today over."

"Oh, you can! Well, actually *I* can do that for you. Time travel is one thing I've never had any problem with. Well, once I perfected it."

Now why didn't that reassure him? Oh, maybe because she was going H.G. Wells on him.

He lifted his arm. "You know what? That's okay. I'm good. No big deal. Don't tax yourself."

"Really, it's no trouble. At least let me take you back to the attic. Before you—I mean, *I* broke your legs."

"God, if only you could."

"Which one?"

"Which one what?"

"Which god are you talking to? Is there one here in the room? I don't see any, and I've never heard of one who's invisible to the djinn."

He hiked himself up on the bed, his head swimming. And he didn't think it was because of the pain meds. "Vana, I have no idea what you're talking about." He meant in the general sense, but when she went with the specific, he went along for the ride.

It was quite a ride with Vana.

Wait. Ride. Hadn't she been riding a—

"I'm just wondering which god you're talking to and wondering what he or she is doing here. Usually they don't interfere in djinn business."

He gave up. He probably didn't even want to know what she was talking about. All he wanted was his life back. "I really wish you *could* fix my legs and end this nightmare."

"But that's what I'm trying to tell you. I can." She fiddled with his IV tubing. "By taking you back to before it began."

"Before what began? Time?" There had to be mold spores or something in that house that made crazy contagious. Instead of selling the place, he ought to burn it to the ground and save everyone from perpetuating this insanity. Starting with poor Vana.

"No, time *travel*." She shrugged her shoulders, and scads of gorgeous hair cascaded over them.

"Like *Back to the Future*?"

"No. Not the future. Only The Fates know what will happen then, and I've heard those sisters guard that information with thunder and lightning and a pair of nasty knitting needles."

Fates with knitting needles. God, it was such a shame

the woman was delusional. But he was lying here listening to her, so what did that make him?

"… one of the easier aspects of magic, going from place to place. That's because the locations are concrete. I know where I am and where I'm going. I just picture it in my mind's eye, and off we go. All you have to do is wish it, and your legs will be good as new in no time. And I think I can even make it so you'll remember, if you want." She looked at him. "Some people would prefer to not know."

He couldn't imagine why. Zane shook his head. The situation just screamed for sarcasm, but the reality was, he really did want her to be telling the truth. He'd love to find some way to get back into the game. "Man, I really wish you *could* fix this, Vana."

The smile that crossed her face almost took his breath away.

And when she leaned over and kissed him, she completed the job.

Chapter 7

The attic looked the same.

Zane, however, didn't.

He stared at the antique oval mirror in the corner and saw his left leg without a cast. The right one, too.

He shifted his weight between them.

No pain.

No break.

Son of a bitch.

He fell onto his ass—atop the same dress form he'd fallen on earlier.

Holy shit. She *was* a genie.

And she was looking pretty pleased with herself.

Now, normally, Zane was as grounded as the next guy. Well, as long as the next guy wasn't from his immediate family tree. But this… Hell, there'd been a flying carpet at one point, too; he *hadn't* imagined it.

"See? I told you I could do it."

He could only nod.

"I should have thought of this first. Of *course* fixing a bone would be more difficult than manipulating time. I need to reread that chapter. But I did get the remembering thing right."

Hey, there was a plus. He had no desire to have her go messing with his memory--she'd done enough to his mind as it was.

Time travel. Genies. Magic.

The world spun worse than it had after the tackle that had shredded his knee and his season. Zane had a feeling his world would be spinning much longer this time.

"Do you need a hand up?" She held hers out as if it were the most normal thing in the world.

Her world maybe.

"Master?" She shook her hand a little.

Zane looked at it, trying to process that She's A Genie.

"Fine. Sit there then," she mumbled before bending down to rummage through an old box. "Masters. You all like to do it your way."

His way? Was she nuts—er, bad word choice. But seriously… She thought this was *his* way? Being on the wrong end of a sword, having both legs broken, and being whisked around by *magic*… Add in the mess with his playing status, and *nothing* was going his way these days.

"Aha!" Vana spun around, holding out an old, tarnished lantern.

"Please don't tell me there's another genie in there."

She rolled her eyes. "No, silly. Only one genie per master. That's in Chapter Two. Or maybe it was Three." She scrunched her face, then shook her head. "No, this belonged to Peter's grandmother. It's why Peter was in Turkey in the first place. He was on his way to India because his grandmother used to tell him stories of when she'd lived there under British rule with her family and how she'd searched for a genie lantern in every marketplace. She was sure this was one and kept it by her side until she died. It sparked Peter's interest in finding a genie."

"And he found you in Turkey?"

"Yes."

That was all fine and good, but that past had no

bearing on his present. Nor his future either, apparently, since those pesky Fates weren't into sharing. Which meant he was right back where he'd started from. With two unbroken legs, thank God.

Zane stood up, amazed again that there wasn't even a twinge of pain or any aftereffects from the meds. Too bad she hadn't been around for the ACL tear.

"Are your legs okay?" She nibbled one side of her bottom lip. Probably because her fingers were wrapped around the lantern so she couldn't fiddle with them. Which was a good thing since bad things happened when she fiddled with her fingers.

"About that." He nodded at his legs. "You want to explain how time travel works?"

Her gray eyes twinkled. "Um… magic?"

Yes, he had asked that ridiculous question, and no, he shouldn't have. But in for a drachma—or whatever they used in Turkey—in for a pound. "Seriously, doesn't time travel mess with the whole time-space continuum?"

"The what?"

Obviously she hadn't seen that movie. "This… There were doctors and nurses and probably babies being born and people dying, and you just…" He waved one of his hands around. "Just whisked us out of there. Isn't that going to affect other people?"

Lord knew, it was affecting him.

He couldn't believe he was actually on board with the whole genie thing. But unbroken broken legs and pink smoke and the here-one-minute, there-the-next thing couldn't be explained away. Not logically, anyhow. Unless he'd inherited Peter's madness. Frankly, he'd prefer magical genies to that nightmare.

She tucked some of her hair behind her ear and hopped butt first onto a sheet-draped old dresser behind her, her feet in those ridiculous curly-toed slippers swinging as if she didn't have a care in the world.

51

"Actually, this isn't all that uncommon," she said. "If you've ever experienced déjà vu, then you've already experienced magic because that's someone else playing around with time. It's like a thread. You've heard of The Fates?" She didn't wait for his answer, but Greek mythology had been a class he'd enjoyed. "Three sisters as old as Time itself, which is why, I guess, they can manipulate it."

"But so can you. Otherwise I wouldn't be standing here." And he meant that in the most literal sense.

"True, but genies don't have the same ability as The Fates. Otherwise, there'd be pure chaos. We're limited by being able to return you to a place where you could be but aren't, and as long as I don't return you to a time where you might run into yourself, your current thread will never cross with the past one and everything will be just fine."

"So right now there's another me living somewhere in an alternate universe with two broken legs?" In this one he had a massive headache.

"Of course not. When we materialized here, that thread was cut. The Fates then weave this thread into everyone else's. My sister actually unraveled the how-tos and wherefores of time travel and recorded them in the *Djinnoire*."

"You have a sister?"

Her smile disappeared. "Um, yes. I do."

Zane wasn't touching those sibling dynamics with a ten-foot pole. And female dynamics at that. No way.

"So, okay, I'm living in the here and now. What about the people who saw me at the hospital? What about the doctors? Did you have to erase their memories, too?"

"Oh, no. I didn't have to do anything to them because, to them, none of this ever happened. Oh, but you know what?" Some of her hair fell forward, and she tossed her head to send it behind her back. A few strands didn't quite make it, their ends curling on her breasts.

Zane had a tough time getting that image out of his

head. Apparently, while time travel could scramble one's brain cells, it did nothing to one's libido.

"You're going to want to stop in and see your old school chum. Gary someone. He was at the hospital and very worried about you. Though I guess he won't be worried now, since it hasn't happened for him, but he did seem awfully glad to know you were in town."

"Gary Huss? That prick? He was no friend of mine. Made my childhood a living hell. He was a bully, always taunted me about my family." But no one had believed that because good ol' Gar, teacher's pet and only son of the school superintendent, had had them all fooled.

Gary had called Zane "chum" more as a reference to shark bait than to any kind of friendship and had teased him about the dementia that was sure to set in when he got older.

Zane had never discussed that worry with his father, and since Dad had died in a car accident before showing any signs of mental illness, Zane had no idea if he'd inherited the gene.

But he had inherited the *genie*.

God, the irony. Especially since *she* was the reason for the stories.

"Peter wasn't crazy, was he?"

"No."

It *had* been her. "Did you ever break his legs?"

"Of course not," she answered quickly.

Too quickly. There was a "but" on the end of that sentence. He could hear it.

"But there was the incident with a pot and his black eye."

He knew that story. "My grandfather told me he saw the pot fly across the room and hit his father in the eye." No one, of course, had believed either of them.

She shrugged and looked away. "Yes, well, Peter said something about my sister, and, well…"

"What'd he say?"

She set the lantern down and intertwined her fingers in her lap. "It was right after the blackberry incident."

He hadn't heard about a blackberry incident.

How many incidents had there been that he hadn't heard about?

"Peter said he'd wished my sister had been in my bottle instead of me, and well, words were said, and the next thing I knew, 'pot calling the kettle black' popped out, and, well, you can guess the rest."

He sure could. Which meant those old stories really were true and Peter's mental incapacity hadn't been in being delusional, but in thinking that people would believe him.

Zane had lived the first twelve years of life with that stigma hanging over his head. Crazy old Peter who hadn't been crazy.

"So why didn't my dad ever know about you? And why are you here now?"

"Peter put my bottle in that box where you found me. No one's ever looked." She gripped the edge of the dresser and leaned forward. "Why *did* you find me? How did you know where to look? I thought I was going to be stuck there forever."

Zane kneaded the back of his neck. "The box was behind that." He pointed to a painting of Peter. "I wanted to see what he looked like, and when I moved the painting, it knocked the lid from the box and the stopper from your bottle."

She smiled. "And the rest is history."

No, "the rest" *explained* history. Unfortunately he couldn't explain it to anyone else. Not without parading Vana in front of them, and did he really want to do that?

Marlee, his publicist, always said that there was no such thing as bad publicity, but after what he'd gone through with the media speculating that his injury was career-ending and the big controversy of him not being signed as the starter, he didn't believe her. Vana hitting the news would be a really bad idea—

And then a bird—a hot pink bird that looked like a cross between a turkey, a peahen, and a flamingo—popped in out of nowhere like a firecracker, with sparks and flames shooting in all directions, cawing out Vana's name.

Zane didn't think that would go over well, either.

Chapter 8

"Vana, you're never going to believe what happened!" Merlin, the phoenix who'd been keeping her company throughout the past centuries, *poofed* onto the mirror with his usual burst of sparkly orange fire, though this time he'd paired it with fuchsia feathers, his colors as changeable as his moods. "There's a Harrison back in town."

Merlin did *obvious* in so many aspects of his life.

"Yes, Merlin, I know." She let go of Zane's arms (reluctantly) and held out her hand as Merlin's perch. "Master, allow me to introduce you to Merlin Pendragon. Merlin, Zane Harrison."

"A talking bird?" Zane's mouth fell open. "You're kidding, right? And Merlin? I thought merlins were smaller, and as for Pendragon,,, Delusions of grandeur much?"

"Where do you think your kind got the story?" Merlin fluffed his breast feathers and a shower of pink sequins fell like *peri* dust onto her arm. "And no, I'm not a merlin, though I must say, I do appreciate the honor of having a species named after me. I'm a phoenix, you know. And not just *any* phoenix, mind you. I'm the First Lieutenant of the Third Order of Pyre. Pretty spiffy stuff, if I do say so myself.

"You should be thanking your lucky stars—which are Vega and Rigel, by the way—that you're meeting me. Do you know how many mortals go their entire lives without seeing a phoenix?" He struck a pose, one orange and red-striped leg stretched out beneath an open wing. "So, Mr. Negativity, are you sufficiently impressed?"

Zane looked anything *but* impressed. Disbelieving, stunned, maybe even a touch angry... And, with his gaze on the ceiling, praying.

Great. She did not need him invoking the gods. One word from Saraswati to the High Master and it'd all be over. She'd be whisked right back to Al-Jannah, the djinn capital city, to be reprimanded for all her transgressions (of which there were plenty) and possibly stripped of her status.

And that could *not* happen because not only would she be a failure in the (overly critical) eyes of her parents, as well as a joke in the djinn world, but she'd let Peter and the children down. And none of them deserved that. The children had been so innocent in their transformation and Peter had been so kind to her, believing in her when no one else had.

"Uh, what's the matter, big guy?" asked Merlin. "Cat got your tongue?" He nodded Zane's way and said behind his raised wing to her, "Why is it so hard for mortals to believe in us? They're all for aliens and loch monsters and conspiracy theories, but show 'em a real, live talking bird and they dumb up."

"I'm not 'dumbing up,'" said Zane, shaking his head and glaring at Merlin.

Good. Vana always preferred mortals who accepted magic; it gave them a starting point for conversation instead of the mortal merely staring at her as if she had a big wart on her chin like some witches she knew.

She'd have to hold off mentioning the children, though. Merlin was enough of a surprise for now. She'd release them when Zane wasn't around. Children could be quite exuberant, especially when they'd been tucked away nice and safe and Invisible in the armoire in the attic for a hundred years. When she'd caught them dancing in Peter's study during that last party, where anyone could have found them, she'd magicked them to the attic, planning to let them out once the party was over. Only, the bear had shown up and, well...

"Merlin and I have known each other for about five hundred years," she said to get her mind off that fiasco. "He kept me company while I was hanging out in my bottle."

"Actually, Van, it's five hundred and sixty-seven," said Merlin, tossing back the moussed-up pompadour on his forehead that was starting to droop in the late-afternoon humidity. "Remember the years in Rio?"

Merlin had inspired the themes for Carnival when they'd been there.

"Wait. Hold on." Zane held out his hands. "How much am I supposed to put up with today? A genie isn't enough? Two broken legs don't cut it? Time travel? No?" He raked his hands through his hair. "Now I have to buy into a talking myth named after a myth?"

"And what, exactly, would you call Vana, then, oh Great Bestower of Nicknames?" Merlin propped his bent wings on his flanks.

Vana shushed him. The bird never could tell when mortals were on overload. When *he* got like that, all he had to do was burst into flame and rebuild himself, but no other creature on earth (or off it, for that matter) had that same stress reliever. Sometimes Merlin, who was almost as narcissistic as Narcissus, forgot that.

Vana turned toward the attic doorway. "How about we go downstairs and I'll make us something to eat? I bet we could all use some food, and it's been eons since I've had someone to cook for."

She tossed Merlin into the air, the beads woven into

the ends of his tail extensions clattering on the hardwood flooring as he took flight, and she tugged Zane's arm. "Come along, master. I promise you, Merlin doesn't bite."

Not with his beak, anyway. His words, on the other hand, were a whole other story.

***

Zane brushed the corner of his mouth in case he was sporting some of the potato latkes Vana had whipped up with the lamb stew for dinner. It'd taken her three tries before the bullwhips had stopped showing up with the food, but the effort was worth it.

"So why were you in the bottle, Vana?" He tried ignoring the talking phoenix perched on the chair beside him. He wasn't sure which freaked him out more: that phoenixes were real, or that the bird could speak. "I would've thought Peter would've wanted to keep you with him at all times. A lot of people would be after you if they knew."

She finished the last bite of her latke and washed it down with some sweet mint tea. "Well, after the incident with the stairs—"

"Incident, Van?" asked the phoenix. "That was a bit more catastrophic than an 'incident.'"

Yeah, it was the fact that the bird talked.

"Go on, Van," Merlin chortled. "Tell your new master about the stairs. It's one of my favorite stories."

She turned a shade of pink softer than the color of her smoke and Zane wanted to hurt Merlin for hurting her. He reached for her hand to keep from punching the feathered bully. "That's okay, Vana. You don't have to if you don't want to."

"No, it's all right. It's not as if everyone doesn't already know it. Well, everyone back then."

Right. *Then.* Zane still hadn't wrapped his brain around the fact that she was *eight hundred* and twenty-nine years old. As of two weeks ago.

59

"I was trying to repair the bottom of the staircase because of an, er, earlier mishap—"

"I tried to tell you 'bear claws' were a kind of pastry, but you didn't listen," said Merlin, bolting back another latke.

Vana pursed her lips but kept going. "As I was saying, I was trying to varnish the stairs, but instead, they vanished. Peter was understandably upset with me."

"Understandable? Really?" Merlin shook himself so hard he started molting. "Seriously, Van, you deserved better than that. For all your shortcomings, it wasn't as if you did it maliciously. Not like Mr. Hornswager, or whatever his name was. Hunting that bear down during the party... Thank the gods I was in Antarctica that day or I would have fried myself to a crisp. It still burns me up."

Zane stuck a latke in the bird's face. Vana was feeling bad enough already.

"Hey, thanks." Merlin scarfed it down.

"Yes, well." She fiddled with her fork. "Peter suggested I take a break inside my bottle, and he put it out of the way for safekeeping. Unfortunately, he died shortly thereafter and I ended up stuck. I used to hear the family, though. The parties, the holidays, people stomping up and down the stairs." She had a soft smile on her face, and for a moment Zane forgot that she was a genie.

Until the bird ruffled his feathers, sending sequins cascading into the stew, and the whole illogical reality of the situation returned with a rush.

"So you were here all along when I was growing up?" he asked, scooping the floaters out of the dinner and onto a dish towel Vana handed him.

She nodded. "I remember hearing the birthday parties in the backyard. I used to try to imagine what it'd be like to know Peter's family. He was a good man. Had everyone's best interests at heart."

"They said he was delusional. A crazy old man." Zane

60

couldn't keep the bitterness from his voice. Bitterness... and self-recrimination. Because he'd bought into those stories. He'd condemned Peter along with everyone else, when all along Peter's genie had been the one wreaking the havoc.

And now she was his.

His.

The word sounded hollow. Zane didn't want anything from Peter. Not this legacy and definitely not a genie who could royally mess things up for him if the press ever got wind of her.

Zane winced. Like Merlin said—and he couldn't believe he was actually agreeing with the feathered menace—Vana didn't mean to be a mess; she just was. Zane couldn't condemn her for it, but at the same time, he *could* want to keep her out of sight.

Jesus. All he'd wanted to do was come home, pack up a few things, sign some papers, and the family homestead would be no more. He'd never seen a genie coming—who could have?

Peter, that's who. His great-grandfather had actually gone on a quest for one. And Zane supposed most people would be thrilled. After all, she could grant his every wish.

Hmmm, he'd forgotten that in the ensuing insanity. Maybe he should use it. See if she could do something to make him a starter again. She could put his body back in the shape it'd been in ten years ago, make him catch the ball every time and outrun every opponent. He could be MVP. A Pro Bowler again. Win a Super Bowl. Vana could do all of that for him.

Except he'd feel like shit about himself the whole time. Winning was nothing if you didn't do it yourself. And yet, one fucking play could change the entire game, both on the field and off.

Sighing, Zane picked up the cast-iron salt shaker in the shape of a little girl Vana had set on the table earlier. His grandmother's. "I remember this." He turned it around.

The dent that had made him laugh as a boy was still in the girl's backside. When his grandmother had finally figured out what he'd been laughing at, she'd shoved the shaker into the cabinet and had never pulled it out again.

"Peter got that in Germany," said Vana. "It made the trip back with us. The motion of the ship would clink it against my bottle, kind of like a song to put me to sleep every night of the crossing."

Zane looked at it. The piece had been a joke to him but a nice memory for her. "Here." He held it out. "You should have it."

"Really?" She licked her lips and took the shaker. "Thank you. This is one of the nicest gifts anyone has ever given me."

"Be real, Van," said Merlin. "It's the *only* one anyone ever gave you. Most of your masters were single-minded in pursuit of their hearts' desires. This one's different." Merlin arched his eyebrows. "Jury's still out on whether that's a good thing or not, Romeo."

Vana clamped the bird's beak shut. "Hush, you. It's very thoughtful and I'll treasure it always. Thank you, master. I don't know how I can ever repay you."

"You can start by calling me Zane. 'Master' is a little much."

She bowed her head. "Zane, then. Thank you. And I hope you don't find this condescending, but I think Peter would have been very proud of you for that kindness."

That made him shudder. Sure, okay, he knew the truth now, but still… thirty-plus years of stigma didn't go away in one afternoon.

He glanced at the Swiss cuckoo clock on the wall, Mom's pride and joy. Ah, dead. It'd probably been a long time since anyone had wound it. "I wish that clock worked."

Vana perked up and sat straighter in her chair. "Oh, I can do that, master. I mean, Zane."

She aimed a kiss at him again, and suddenly the pendulums started swinging wildly and the little wooden bird shot out of the tiny door to chirp the hour—except that it was twenty-three minutes after five. And the bird didn't stop at the end of its perch; the momentum flung it off the end.

Then the minute hand went haywire, followed shortly thereafter by the hour hand. And the pendulums started swinging not only faster, but out of sync so every couple of seconds there was a clash as the two disks smacked into each other.

"Holy smokes."

He was seriously coming to hate that phrase.

"Can you fix it?" He had to shout over the din because Merlin had ducked his head beneath one wing and was making some weird, keening noise.

"Um… yes." She cleared her throat and sat up a little straighter. "If that's what you wish, I can."

He could have sworn she muttered, "I hope," when he said, "I do," but she puckered up and blew a kiss.

The bells and whistles stopped. The pendulums stopped. The clock hands stopped. And the little bird flew backward from the floor onto its perch, which then zipped back inside, and the door slammed shut.

"Ah, peace at last. Never a dull moment with you, is there, Van?" Merlin scratched his beak with a talon—that was painted teal blue.

"I wouldn't mind a dull moment, actually." Zane pinched the bridge of his nose. "Listen, Vana. I've got a real-estate agent coming out this week, and I can't have wacko clocks or talking birds," he glared at Merlin, "or flying carpets or… jitterbugging willow trees."

"Now *that* would be something to see," said Merlin. "They do look pretty when they waltz, though."

Zane glared at him again. "You know what I mean. I need Vana to keep her magic under wraps."

63

Judi Fennell

"Why do you have a real-estate agent coming here?" She walked to the sink and started cleaning the dishes.

Zane carried his over, then propped his hip against the counter. "I need to find out what the house is worth so I can put it on the market."

"Market?" A curtain of her hair shielded everything but her upturned nose.

"It's a building with products for sale," said Merlin. "But that's not important right now."

Vana flipped her hair back, her silver eyes sparking with surprise. Or maybe that was the glint of the late-afternoon sun through the bay window above the sink. "You mean you're going to sell Peter's house?"

"Not Peter's house, Vana. Mine. And, yes, I am."

"But why? This is your home."

"My home?" Zane reached for the dish towel and handed it to her because she was dripping suds on the floor. "This isn't my home. It wasn't even when I lived here. I have a life somewhere else and it's not practical to keep the house. It makes more sense to sell it."

She twisted her hands in the towel with more force than mere drying merited. "Not to me it doesn't."

"Uh, Van?" Merlin leaned toward her and spoke out of the side of his beak. "I don't think you get a say in the matter."

She stopped mangling the dish towel. "But Peter wouldn't want you to sell it."

"Peter's not here." Zane took the dish towel from her and spread it out over the back of the ladder-back chair.

"But I can't leave here, Zane."

That didn't exactly strengthen her argument. He could lose the house, the legacy, and the cause of it in one shot.

"Vana, while I get that you cared about him, I can't keep the house."

"But the ch—the chores. I could help you with them. I could even fix the house up for you. You'd love it. I can

64

make it look just like it did when Peter lived here. It was the most beautiful home in town. And the parties... ah, the parties. Everyone wanted to be invited, and there was music and dancing and food..."

"And uninvited bears," said Merlin. "You know they only wanted to come to see what Crazy Pete would do next, Van, right?"

Vana's exuberance deflated like a balloon.

Zane glared at the bird and mouthed one word. "Barbecue."

Merlin gulped.

Zane didn't know why he cared, but he did. She looked so forlorn. He guessed that was understandable, though, given that this place had been more of a home to her than it'd ever been to him. "What was the house like back then, Vana?"

"It was lovely. All the rooms were decorated just so and the gardens... Peter had such lovely gardens, and I didn't even have to use my magic on them. Nature has her own magic, you know. How else could there be such perfection in rose petals? Such symmetry in daffodils? Such perfume in jasmine—"

"Such poison in oleanders," said Merlin out of the other side of his beak. He then looked up at the clock, whistling an off-key tune.

She pulled her hands free and clapped them together. "Oh, Zane, please let me turn it back into what it once was. I promise you won't want to sell it. You'll want to stay."

No he wouldn't. But he'd kicked enough kittens for one day, and she looked so darn hopeful he couldn't kick another. Besides, he'd been planning to do some work around here, and the better the condition the house was in, the more he could get for it.

"Vana, I am going to sell, but if it means that much to you, sure, you can help me fix it up."

Silver flashed in her eyes just before she jumped up to

plant a kiss on his cheek--but one small turn of his head and that kiss was everything it'd been before: hot, delicious, sexy—and over entirely too soon.

"Sheesh, you two," whistled Merlin. "Get a room."

There were a dozen and a half of them in this place, and Zane wouldn't mind christening every one.

Which could pose big problems in the days to come.

Chapter 9

S o what's the plan again?" asked Merlin. "You lost me."

Zane would like to lose him. The damn bird hadn't shut up since they'd stepped off the porch, bitching the entire walk around the property. Zane had offered him the opportunity to leave, but the bird felt some crazy compulsion to stick to Vana like glue, as if he expected Zane to try something.

Yeah, he might be thinking along those lines after that teaser of a kiss in the kitchen, not to mention the one in the attic when he'd thought she was a figment of his imagination. But she was a genie, for crying out loud. One didn't lust after a genie.

Then she walked a few steps ahead of him, her see-through outfit leaving nothing to the imagination, and, yeah, maybe one *did*.

"Isn't this where the lawn-bowling court used to be?" Merlin clacked his beak, and midflight, his wings turned purple and gold.

"Yes. By the fence beneath that mimosa tree," Vana answered.

"I'd rather *have* a mimosa than go lawn bowling near one." Merlin landed on Zane's shoulder. "You don't mind, do you, buddy? My wings were getting tired. Just flew in from Baghdad, you know." The bird cracked only himself up with the joke. "Geez, talk about boring. What is it with you mortals? Can't take a joke."

"I have you on my shoulder, don't I?"

"Hey, good one!" Merlin nipped his ear.

"Do that again, bird, and we'll go for the deep fryer this time."

"Sheesh. There you go, back to the no-humor thing."

"As I was saying…" Vana reached up to Zane's shoulder and shifted Merlin onto her fist. "The court was here, and over there was one of Peter's rose gardens. You can still see the brambles. I bet the bushes will spring back once I clear it out."

"You gonna do it now?" Merlin asked.

She stopped. "I could. If it's okay with you, mast—I mean, Zane?"

Zane checked their immediate vicinity. The closest neighbor was half a mile beyond the driveway. A dozen acres surrounded this manicured—as it were—portion of the property, and the Vlad the Impaler iron fence, complete with gargoyles, wasn't letting anyone in. They were all alone.

"Sure, go ahead." He wouldn't think about being all alone with her.

And then Vana puckered up and blew a kiss.

If the brush hadn't burst into flames, he might have.

"Oh no, oh no, oh no!" Vana wrung her hands as Merlin flew onto a mimosa branch. "I said 'tame,' not 'flame'!" She made some more kissing noises.

The flames shot up higher.

Shit. He didn't have to worry about someone strolling the property to get an eyeful. The bonfire was big enough to alert the entire town.

"Vana, we have to put it out!" He looked around for… what? A fire hose? Extinguisher? Waterfall?

Not a damn thing in sight, which shouldn't be

surprising, given the rest of the nightmare he'd encountered since arriving here.

"I'm trying to!" She made another kissing noise, and two giant flames—one red, one blue—shot up the middle. "No! Not red-blue! *Res*-cue! Res-*cue*!"

It was no use. The more flustered she got, the more her magic went haywire.

Zane ducked. They did *not* need a bunch of hay appearing out of nowhere—Jesus. Now she had him thinking crazy things, too.

And then she started fiddling with her fingers again. Puckering her lips.

Yeah, that hadn't worked out so well. So Zane did the first thing he could think of. He tugged her to him and kissed her.

Those flames licking at the brambles were child's play compared to the ones between him and Vana. One touch of his lips and Vana practically went boneless against him, melting into the kiss so that he had to catch her, which only made the heat between them that much hotter. With every one of her pliant curves fused against him, this kiss packed more of a punch than the attic and kitchen ones combined.

He wrapped one arm around her waist and cupped her cheek with the other, then threaded it through the hair that had been driving him crazy, no, nuts, no, insane—*whatever*—the hair that had been begging him to run his fingers through it ever since he'd set eyes on her. And oh, how happy those fingers were to oblige.

She moaned when his lips shifted slightly, and the sound raced right through him, conjuring images of harem-girl fantasies and hot, sweaty desert nights.

Zane traced the seam of her lips with his tongue and slipped inside when she parted them on another moan.

And then he moaned, too. God, she tasted amazing. The mint from the tea mingled with her very own flavor, and Zane wanted more. He stroked his tongue over hers, flicked it along her teeth, and crushed her against him, changing the angle so he could savor more of her. Could feel more of her. Could want—

"Uh, guys? Yoo-hoo. Lovebirds? How many fires are you planning to start out here anyway?"

Hell. Merlin.

Zane took one last kiss and pulled his lips from hers. She had a half smile on her face, and he felt one cross his own. He'd put that smile there.

"Yeah, yeah, you do good work," muttered Merlin. "Have her weak at the knees for you, Casanova, dontcha? You put that fire out, but you guys started two more over there. Whatcha gonna do about them?" Merlin added a squawk on the end of that, just in case Zane hadn't been paying attention.

Oh shit. "Vana." Zane had to shake her a little. "Vana, the fire."

Her eyes opened, a dark pewter this time, and, honestly, they took his breath away. *She* took his breath away.

"Fire?"

He knew the moment reality flooded back in.

"Holy smokes!"

"I wouldn't exactly say there's anything holy about them, Van," said Merlin from his branch, preening his now-teal feathers. "Unless you've got some holy water to douse them with."

"Oh dear." She started to link her hands in front of her, but Zane knew what that would lead to, so he grabbed them instead.

"Vana, you can do this." He said it softly, and she lost a little of her deer-in-the-headlights look. "You can. Just concentrate."

She *was* concentrating—on his mouth. And Zane was vain enough to enjoy it.

Then the fire crackled behind her. "Come on, honey, you can do this."

She licked her lips. Zane was aroused enough to enjoy that.

"I don't think so, Zane. What if I make them worse?"

Merlin flew above them, the beads on his extra-long tail feathers bouncing over their noses as he skimmed above their heads to land on an old trellis that looked like it'd been there since Peter's time. "Uh, Van? I don't think you could do any worse than this wind."

Zane looked behind her where a sudden hot summer breeze was swirling the flames upward. The bird had a point. Kissing her had worked on the first one. The key was to not let it get out of control.

The fire crackled again as it ate through a lawn seared dry by the summer sun.

He didn't have a choice. He tilted her chin up. "Close your eyes."

"But—"

"Close them, Vana."

She did.

"Now, what do you want to do?"

"I want to put out the fires."

"Okay. So kiss me."

Her eyes flew open and he put a finger on her lips. "Close your eyes, say what you want to do, then kiss me."

It worked beautifully. In so many ways.

"Well, well," cackled Merlin. "Looks like ol' Zane here has figured out the key to your magic *and* a way to get himself some."

"You, bird, are foul." If he were in range, Zane would throw the phoenix for a line drive right into the row of hedges.

"Oh sure, *you* get to make jokes. Of course I'm fowl." Merlin held up his wings. "Duh."

"Not amusing."

Merlin flung his wings down. "I give up." And with that, he disappeared in a burst of flames.

Which Zane had to swat to keep them from igniting the trellis.

"It worked, didn't it?" Vana hunched her shoulders.

"Yes. Both fires are out."

The one she'd ignited inside of him, however, was still raging. Fast, hot, furious. Which made no sense, considering what she was.

Or maybe it did...

"Vana, did you put a spell on me?"

"A spell?" She nibbled her bottom lip again. "I don't do spells. Only witches and warlocks and the occasional gypsy do. Genies don't need spells. Our magic comes organically from us. As easy as breathing."

Or kissing--*not* that he needed the reminder.

"Zane? Are you okay?"

No, he wasn't, but grumbled a "yeah" anyway. He'd wanted to blame it on her magic but couldn't, and he didn't need the complication of a woman right now. Especially her.

And then she licked her lips. Again.

He spun around and headed to a nearby garden shed. Good, old-fashioned manual labor was the perfect way to work off frustration. He rummaged through the assorted tools and grabbed two shovels, a rake, and an ax.

On second thought, he put the ax back. Her magic was dangerous enough.

As was the shovel she almost brained him with when she rested it on her shoulder to head to the garden.

Everything about Vana was dangerous: the way she affected him, the magic she couldn't control, and the threat of what the press would do if they ever found out about her. He'd be labeled a laughingstock, insane, or a fraud, none of which would help contract talks.

He dug into the mess of brambles, figuring the concentration he'd need to keep the thorns from drawing blood would keep him from thinking about her, but every little grunt she made while digging, every puff of breath when she flung the dirt, every "ouch!" when a thorn snagged her was as loud as a ref's whistle, and he found himself watching her more rather than less.

Maybe he should just put her back in her bottle, stop it up, and store it in a safe deposit box for his heirs to open in another hundred years or so.

Or, better yet, toss it into the ocean so it could wash up on a beach somewhere and turn someone else's world upside down because, on top of everything else going on in his life, the last thing he needed was to not be able to stop thinking about an inept and utterly adorable do-good genie who could twist his life inside out with just a twist of her lips.

Literally *and* figuratively.

***

Gary shoved the mail into the hall drawer. Bills and more bills. A letter from the bitch's attorney. All shit he didn't feel like dealing with at the moment.

He dropped his keys onto the table and yanked off his tie. He was done stomping for votes for the day, an activity that was on par with dealing with Lynda's attorney.

He popped the cap off a beer from the fridge, stretched out in his recliner, and turned on a college game. He'd been halfway through his first season of college ball when Lynda had shown up with the news of the pregnancy.

To this day, he still didn't know if she'd really been pregnant. The miscarriage had happened right after the honeymoon. It'd taken them seven years to have another— not a point in favor of that earlier pregnancy.

But it was what it was. And it'd been hell. Even now, he only saw Marshall, his son, on Lynda-decreed days. Bitch.

He swiped a hand over his face and looked at the book on the table beside his chair. Old Man Harrison's journal.

He picked it up, peeled back the worn leather cover, and flipped through the pages. He could practically recite each one by heart, he'd been through it so many times.

If only he could get his hands on the rest of the journals. There *had* to be something there about whatever Calvin had seen. There'd been too many stories from more people than merely his great-great-grandfather.

Gary sighed and put the journal in the drawer. There had to be something in that house. He needed to get back inside it and soon.

Chapter 10

Vana had felt so good in Zane's arms that even an hour or so of gardening couldn't undo . She could still feel his kiss on her lips and the effect it'd had on her magic. Like quicksilver, the magic had flowed through her, and it was as if everything were right with the world, her, and, most especially, her magic. It was such a pity that mortals weren't immortal. She'd love nothing better than to spend the rest of her days kissing Zane. The rest of her nights, too…

She shook her head, trying to clear the fog. She was getting way too caught up in this moment. And that's all it was. This entire meeting with Zane was merely a moment in time. A blink of an eye to her in the span of an immortal life, and she needed to get over it and move on.

But still, she was careful not to brush past Zane when he opened the back-porch door for her, focusing instead on something safe, like the little wobble of the hinges. Things she could control, because how she felt around Zane… that was definitely *out* of control.

Once inside, she kissed the air, setting the door straight on its hinges, then looked at the cuckoo clock and tried her magic on it. An air kiss had the pendulums gently swinging and the hour and minute hands slowly advancing to seven-fifty-three.

"Hey, don't you want this?" Zane held out the salt shaker, and something more than mere awareness sizzled through her when their fingers met.

"Oh... of course I do. Thank you." She hadn't been lying to him; not one of her masters—Peter included—had ever given her a gift. Most had assumed that since she was a genie she could conjure up whatever she wanted, but the reality was, it wasn't the salt shaker itself that touched her; it was the thought behind it. The generosity. The fact that Zane had listened to her story and realized what the memory had meant to her, and he'd given her a way to always keep that memory. Was it any wonder that he should affect her on so many levels?

And that scared her. With that kiss and his gift and his calm faith in her, well, she didn't know how many more levels he'd touch before it would become a problem.

She headed into the front parlor. And it would be a *big* problem. Because if a genie fell in love with a mortal—and lost her heart and head enough to tell him so—it'd be the death of both her magic and her immortality, two things she'd never want to put in jeopardy. *Couldn't* put in jeopardy. She'd worked too hard and too long to give it all up now. And she still had to change the children back, so she couldn't even consider falling in love with him— anyone—until that was accomplished.

"Vana, about earlier—"

"Don't worry, Zane." She didn't want to discuss that kiss with him. Was trying to not think about it. "There's nothing to talk about."

"Actually, there is. Let me get my sleeping bag and other things out of the car, and then we'll talk. Hang out for a few minutes, okay?"

"You're staying here?" She hadn't expected that, though she should have. It made sense, after all. But it was just going to make things harder.

"Better here than in town. I don't need the paparazzi showing up."

"Paparazzi?"

"Oh, right. You don't know." He smiled. "I play professional football for a living. I guess, with being in that bottle for the last century, televisions and professional sports teams are probably off your radar. Radar probably is, too, right?"

She knew condescension when she heard it, and it didn't sit any better with her coming from Zane than it had from her parents. She put her hands on her hips. "I'll have you know, Zane Harrison, that while I might not have been out and about in the world, it hasn't passed me by. The djinn world has all the advancements you do. Matter of fact, I have a plasma screen in my bottle. Running water, too. Indoor plumbing, and even an iPad and Wii. Wanna see?"

"You're kidding."

"I don't kid about being a genie. Ever."

He studied her, and it was the first time he'd looked at her that her hormones didn't start sighing. She might not be the best djinni her world had to offer, but she was one nonetheless. He couldn't insult her and get away with it. She raised her chin. "So, are you coming, or what?"

"No snow this time, right?"

The smile didn't take the sting out of that question. He might think it was funny, but to her it was one more mess she hadn't wanted to cause. "Trust me, Zane. Everything will be just fine."

She crossed her fingers behind her back, tossed her hair over her shoulders, summoned her pink smoke, and magicked the two of them inside her bottle.

And this time, she wasn't the one who yelled, "Holy smokes!"

77

Chapter 11

They'd landed in an Arabian Nights whorehouse.

Zane knew his mouth was hanging open but could do nothing to stop it. Everywhere he looked was sheer fantasy.

It was as if someone had gotten hold of every sheik porn flick ever made and splashed the sets all over the inside of Vana's bottle. Or as if that person had taken a peek inside his brain when he'd been kissing her because he'd be lying if he said he hadn't thought about this. And now here it was, in Technicolor.

Her bottle had *not* looked like this the last time he'd been here. If it had, they never would have left.

The bed, sprinkled with rose petals and covered in mounds of pillows and silks and pink satin sheets, turned slowly on a raised dais. Gauzy curtains draped from the ceiling, amazingly unscorched by the hundreds of candles flickering around the bed. An ice bucket with champagne and a plate of grapes were on one side, bottles of oils on the other. Soft music and incense filled the air, the perfect set-up for seduction.

His or hers?

He didn't care.

"I, um… oh dear." Vana darted to the bed, brushing

rose petals onto the floor and snuffing out candles as she went, shaking the heat from her fingers after each one. If she kept that up, she wouldn't have any skin left. And that'd be a damn shame because, God knew, he liked Vana's skin.

"This wasn't supposed to be here, Zane. It's not what I was planning—ouch!" She popped a finger into her mouth.

He was not immune to that utterly sexy image, and from the look of this place, she didn't want him to be.

"Sssh, Vana." Four strides, that's all it took, and he was beside her. "This is considerably more than fine. You really went all out, and all I can say is… thank you."

Her finger slid from her mouth with a soft *pop*. "Thank you?"

"For making this so perfect."

"Perfect?" Her grey eyes darkened to pewter, silver flashes in their depths, and the smile that lit her face was as perfect as the rest of the place.

He touched her temple with the backs of his fingertips. "Just like you," he whispered. Because the moment called for whispering.

She took a tiny step closer—tiny, because that was all the space that separated them.

Zane threaded his fingers through her hair and let the silky strands flow through them, draping them over her shoulder and watched them slide along her skin before tracing his fingers up the column of her throat, where her pulse beat quickly, and then over the soft curve of her cheek.

Candlelight flickered in her eyes. Or maybe it was the same heat that was racing through his blood at being so close to her. The scent of the rose petals wafted around them, a sweet scent that reminded him of the combination of the mint tea and the heady scent of her arousal.

"Seems a shame to let all your hard work go to waste," he whispered, trying to slow the pounding of blood through his veins.

79

Judi Fennell

"W… waste?" She looked at him from beneath her lashes and licked her lips.

He cradled her head in his palms and flicked the corner of her mouth with his thumbs to get her to open for him. She was so much smaller than him. So feminine. So utterly gorgeous. And if she licked her lips one more time, he wasn't going to be responsible for his actions.

As if she'd read his mind—and seconded it—Vana licked her bottom lip.

Zane groaned and covered that moist, beckoning lip with his own, cupping her head with one hand and raking the other through her hair, then down, lower, over the tight mound of her ass. His fingers strayed, cupping her there, the sensation so much more vivid now that he didn't have to worry about Merlin stopping them.

She moaned into the kiss, and Zane forgot the damn bird and tugged her closer.

God, what she did to him. Every tiny hitch of her breath was a gong crashing in his brain. The crush of her breasts against his chest, that thin fabric that hid nothing from him, especially the fact that she wore no bra, turned him on. He'd noticed in the garden that he was feeling all woman against him, and he wanted the chance to taste every inch of her. And he would, if only he could pull his lips from hers.

He would.

Soon.

Her scent surrounded him, captivated him, spun a web around him better than those sheer curtains did as the bed rotated among them.

He nipped her bottom lip, needing to mark her, if only a little, and she nipped him back, sliding her hands beneath his shirt, her fingernails scraping his back.

Her fingers dipped below his waistband, brushing the sensitive skin above his ass, and Zane felt his knees tremble.

Had to be some residual from the broken legs she'd fixed because no woman had ever buckled his knees. None. And certainly this small slip of a genie wouldn't be the first.

He shoved the genie thought out of his head. Right here, right now, she was a woman and he was a man, and the most elementary communication their species ever had was all they needed.

He twisted a hank of her hair around his fist, tugging her head back at just the right angle to drop kisses along her jaw. She tried to turn her head, but her hair held her captive. *He* held her captive. He could take his time and explore every hollow and curve and scent and taste for as long as he wanted.

And how he wanted...

He traced the beating pulse from beneath her ear down along the column of her throat to the base of her neck. Over to the hollow, her collarbone so pronounced yet delicate that he had to nip at it gently.

She gasped and her fingers clenched against him. God, what he wouldn't give to be naked.

And, hey, she was a genie.

His genie.

"I wish we were naked," he muttered between kisses.

It was amazing she heard him, his words were so thick with desire, but she did, and before he knew it, they were naked. Just like that. No fanfare, no sensation of clothes being ripped from his body—they'd explore that option later—but one wish and it'd come true.

He put a knee on the bed, trapping her between it and his other leg, letting her feel everything that he felt and wanted from her. "Vana..." He groaned as her belly fluttered, stoking the rush of blood in his groin. "Tell me you want this."

She didn't tell him; she showed him, sliding against him, breasts to thighs, and Zane hardened almost to the point of pain.

81

It hadn't been more than six months since he and Stephanie had cooled things off, but right now, he felt as if he had years' worth of desire bursting to get out.

Cupping her backside again, Zane lowered her to the bed. Rose petals mingled among the silky strands of her hair and slid across his fingertips.

He grabbed a few and traced them over her skin, all the while laving kisses and licks along her collarbone and the valley between her breasts.

She sighed and slid her arms free from beneath him to cradle his head when his tongue found her nipple.

"Oh, yes," she whispered, her sigh singing along his nerve endings.

There was the permission he'd sought, as was the tight bud pebbling for him. He rolled his tongue around it, eliciting gasps from her with each circle. He sucked her then and her fingers gripped his hair, her pelvis matching the tugs he made, rising with each, then falling back when he released. Tiny, short movements, almost nonexistent, but Zane felt each one with every cell in his body.

His erection was hard against her thigh, aching to be buried inside her, but Zane couldn't go that fast. He wanted to draw this out, make it last. Give her the pleasure she wanted. That he wanted.

His tongue slid down to dip into her belly button and her stomach fluttered. The musky scent of her arousal called him lower, but he took his time, exploring. Each flutter of her muscles deserved its own kiss, each ragged breath a long, drawn-out lick. She tasted of salt and roses, of mint and that special something that was all her, and Zane knew he'd never forget it.

His teeth nipped at her hip bone, and his lips played along the concave recess below, drawing ever close to the heart of his desire and hers.

Her fingers slid to his hair and she widened her legs, and the soft curls there caressed his cheek as he placed a kiss right above where they both wanted him to be.

"Zane, please."

"I will, sweetheart. I will."

He knelt on the floor by the bed and lifted her left leg over his shoulder, raining kisses from knee to the inner thigh. Her foot flexed against his back with each one.

He turned to the other leg, repeating the same maddeningly slow, tantalizing trek upward again.

She clasped the sheets and crumbled the rose petals, which only released their oils, and the scent turned him on that much more.

He had to taste her. Had to find the aching part of her to fill that ache inside of him.

His lips feathered along her inner thigh, drifting ever closer, and she opened her legs wider. Pulsed down toward him, the sleek aching part of her swollen for his pleasure.

And he took it.

Vana gasped when he touched her. Gods, the sensations. It'd been so long—too long—and this was beyond what she'd ever felt before with anyone. Including D'Artagnan.

She clasped the sheets, crushing them in her grasp, her fingernails tearing through the delicate fabric. Each lap of his tongue made her catch her breath, each gentle rasp of his teeth making her tremble.

She needed to touch him but couldn't. All she could do was be a slave to her body as each wave of feeling grabbed her and swirled her around in a vortex of color blossoming behind her eyelids, the anticipation overpowering everything but the thunder of her heart in her ears, the magic whirling through her veins and racing along her nerve endings. She felt as if she could not only touch the stars, but create them, too.

"Zane… I can't…" She didn't know what she couldn't. All she knew was that if he ever stopped this, for even one tiny second, she'd fall apart.

His tongue slid inside her, and Vana felt the end begin. Felt the first shudder wrack her body.

Judi Fennell

He did it again and she moaned. Loud and keening. And she didn't care. She pulsed against him, gasping when his fingers replaced his tongue, and she clenched around him.

"That's it, Vana. Come for me."

The candles flared and she could only thrash her head as his tongue once again worked its magic upon her.

She came then, against his mouth, open and aching and holding nothing back. He wouldn't let her; he was relentless in his pursuit of her pleasure, drawing out each wracking, shuddering tremor to its most painfully exquisite finale. Shimmering pink Glimmer rained down upon them until, at last, there was nothing left to give. Nothing left inside her but the knowledge that nothing would ever be the same again.

Vana caught her breath. What did that mean? What wouldn't be? *Why* wouldn't it?

She struggled to clear her mind of the utterly sated sensual haze he'd given her. She had to think. Had to figure this out.

But then he moved over her, above her, as sleek as a panther and as determined as a man could be, kissing his way up her body, and desire rose up again inside of her. She'd think about it tomorrow.

"I want you, Zane." She kissed him, tasting herself and him and the rose petal he'd rubbed across her lips.

"And you'll have me," he growled softly into her ear. "Where are the condoms?"

She smiled against his cheek. "You're with a genie. We don't need condoms. Magic takes care of everything."

"Ah, God, I love magic." He kissed her then, all tongue and lips and uninhibited desire.

As his tongue slipped into her mouth, his erection slid inside her, the combination of the two invasions thrusting her right back into the throes of orgasm. She wrapped her legs around his waist and set a rhythm she hoped he could match, but really couldn't worry about. She needed to feel him move, needed to wrap herself around him and accept whatever he wanted to give. She'd been so starved for human contact, mortal or djinn, that this... this was amazing. That it was him was beyond all her hopes and dreams and wishes.

As Zane moved inside her, matching her rhythm, she knew she should be worried about that last thought... but he took her last thought.

He pounded into her, the sweat on his back making her hands glide over his skin, seeking and grasping over the sleek taut muscles there. She latched onto his firm, perfectly shaped butt to keep herself in place.

"Yes, Vana... that's it," he huffed with labored breathing. "Touch me there, baby."

She kissed his throat, the muscles there straining as he thrust into her, then dragged her lips down over his hard, defined pecs, tasting him, savoring the scent of their lovemaking on his skin.

"Oh, God, Vana... Can't hold on... Come with me..."

She found his nipple then and flicked her tongue over it. He groaned, shuddering his release inside her.

Vana felt every movement in slow motion, every contraction of her body, every surge of his, reveling in the utter connection she felt with him at this moment. One she'd never felt with anyone before. More than a little frightening, the realization was also utterly thrilling.

At last he collapsed partly on top of her, the majority of his weight sinking into the mattress beside her, his breath warm on her shoulder.

She turned her head. His blue eyes were barely open, the smile barely on his lips.

But it was there.

He wrapped an arm around her waist and pulled her against him, placing soft kisses along the curve of her shoulder until he couldn't reach farther.

She tilted her head and smiled when he kissed her cheek before burrowing into the curve of her neck. "I could stay like this forever," he whispered.

So could she.

She stiffened. She actually *could* stay like this forever, but Zane... He had fifty, maybe sixty more years at best, but for her, eternity yawned out in an endless line. An eternity without this.

Without him.

The thought plagued her throughout the night in the sweet aftermath of every time they made love. She'd tried to forget it, tried to rationalize that it was just the sex talking, but every time he took her out of herself, every time they rode the wave together or they tried something new/different/exciting/poignant, Vana knew that what she felt with Zane was way beyond what she'd ever thought she'd feel with and for anyone. The ramifications of that scared her.

Forever.

With Zane's soft snore and warm breath on her cheek, Vana stared at the one candle still burning.

She brushed her fingertips over the arm he'd wrapped around her, too softly to wake him but enough to feel the texture of his skin. Zane wasn't like other people, mortal or otherwise. He'd held her hand when the fire had gotten out of control. He'd calmed her panic and, in doing so, had given her the means to get her magic back in sync. He'd *noticed* her and listened to her and had cared enough to help her. He'd thought about her. Had considered her feelings and given her a gift merely because it had meant something to her. He'd wanted her, and that all was a dangerous mix.

She could get used to this. Get used to falling asleep next to him. Making love with him. Waking up with him for the rest of his days.

But every day would bring her one day closer to losing him. One day closer to being alone with only the memories. One day closer to feeling that emotion she shouldn't.

But how in the stars was she going to prevent it? She knew herself; he'd gotten under her defenses as much as he'd gotten under her skin. She could put on a smile and pretend all she wanted that there wasn't some deeper emotion fluttering around her heart, but she couldn't lie to herself. He was so different from any of her other masters or men she'd met through the centuries that it wouldn't take much to tip what she was feeling to the side of something she shouldn't. And once that happened, well, she'd never been able to mask her feelings, a failing numerous masters had pointed out to her. And if she couldn't hide it, he'd know, and then…

And then she'd lose everything: her powers, her life, her family.

All genies knew it was a risk to become involved with their masters. It was such an intimate relationship, being able to fill another's deepest desires, and this had been the most intimate of all.

She shouldn't have let tonight happen. Regardless of wanting to prove herself to him, she should never have invited him back here. And she certainly shouldn't have done *this* to the inside of her bottle. What had she been thinking?

Okay, it was obvious what she'd been thinking, but that had been her subconscious. Which made this attraction way too dangerous, if her subconscious could override her common sense and self-preservation.

If only she could turn back the clock and make it so that it'd never happened--well, to him. She would always remember, but it would just be a reminder of what couldn't happen.

But, the irony was, she couldn't turn back time. Not for this. Because a genie could do something to her master's person only with their express wish. He'd never agree to her wiping this from his memory and what was the point of undoing it if she didn't undo the memory as well?

He murmured something, his breath tickling her, and Vana scooted away from him. It wasn't the best idea to stay snuggled up in his warmth, surrounded by his scent, his breath, his touch. It brought on too many "what if" thoughts. Too many dreams and wishes she shouldn't have.

With a pit in her stomach, Vana slid farther away from him until she was perched on the edge of the mattress. There had to be *some* way out of this predicament. She couldn't be the only genie who'd fallen for her master—

There, she admitted it. She was falling for him. But she couldn't be the only one. If only she knew what those others had done about it, but she couldn't very well go on the Djinn Network and spout out that question or ask DeeDee. Oh, her sister would answer her; that wasn't the problem. The problem was, she didn't *want* to ask DeeDee about this. She didn't want to have to go crawling to her sister yet again. DeeDee had always been there for her, helping, teaching, catching her when she metaphorically fell… But this kind of falling? No, Vana couldn't ask DeeDee how to prevent becoming more of a failure in their parents' eyes than she was right now.

Besides, DeeDee was away at a study retreat, preparing for the biggest test of her life. So she'd have to consult the next best thing: DeeDee's *Djinnoire*.

Vana slid out from under the sheet and tucked it around Zane. His fingers clenched the spot where she'd just been, and she held her breath to see if he'd wake up.

He didn't. His fingers released and went slack. Just as well.

Maybe.

With one last lingering look, she pulled on her robe and tiptoed to the desk tucked in front of the palm trees that had replaced the windows ringing the changeable interior of her bottle. She opened the top drawer and removed the griffin-hide-bound tome.

Calligraphic artistry decorated each page in a move

right out of a monks' school of publishing. The book was a work of art in so many ways, and Vana acknowledged a tug of pride that her sister was the author. DeeDee had never made a big deal about it; it'd just been one more sign that her sister had excelled where Vana had failed.

She touched the ivory-framed picture of DeeDee on her desk before turning it around. The portrait had comforted Vana during the time she'd been shut up in her bottle, but researching solutions for falling in love with her master while her twin looked over her shoulder was anything but comfortable. Her family had had such high hopes for her; a discussion of this sort would end those more completely than all of her magical mishaps combined.

She opened to the Table of Contents. Written in Phoenician, those little squiggly drawings were tough to tell apart and Vana had to concentrate to make out the words. She'd never gotten the hang of the language, merely one of the many reasons she'd hated school.

She read each chapter heading, knowing she wouldn't find one entitled, "How *Not* to Fall in Love with Your Master and What to Do If You Do," but the one titled, "Explanations of the Master-Djinni Relationship" looked promising.

The drawing of a big red scythe adorning the upper left corner of the page, however, did not.

Phrases and familiar passages of the Genie 101 mumbo-jumbo (a term borrowed from the Witches' Ruling Coven) jumped out at her: the logic behind sealing each djinni's bottle or lantern (transferring from the magical realm to the mortal one required a large expenditure of magic that could do great damage to the mortal realm unless it was released one djinni at a time); how the seal was broken (hope was always a big factor, but mostly it was dumb luck—those Fates liked to give Karma a run for her dirhams); how often a djinni could change masters (every time someone opened the bottle; theoretically meaning that a genie could have one person as a sequential master for as long as that mortal lived); what to say upon meeting one's master (a mantra every genie knew by heart after the first day of school); and what qualified a master to be a master.

Vana was about to skip that section when one sentence caught her eye.

The master-djinni relationship begins when the djinni materializes from smoke in front of the master.

Vana reread it twice—and then a third time—letting the implications sink in.

She hadn't materialized in front of Zane at any point. He'd shown up in her bottle. Then, when they'd smoked out of it, she'd gone first, leading him out. That was why he'd broken his leg in the first place; she hadn't thought to hold on to him for the landing. And even at the hospital, she'd materialized first.

Which could mean…

Vana's knees gave out. Luckily, she thought quickly enough to air-kiss a chair beneath her. And luckily, Zane's kisses were still working their magic on hers.

She wasn't in Service to Zane.

He wasn't her master.

And that meant that she actually *could* time travel with him back to before they'd made love and, if she didn't give him the ability to remember it, he'd never know. It would be as if it had never happened.

Very few things could kill a djinni, but she had no doubt that a broken heart was on that list.

Her fingers fiddled with the papyrus pages, but she'd look for that list later. When tears weren't threatening to make reading impossible.

Zane wasn't her master.

Vana took a deep breath and tried to figure out what to do next because, with no one laying claim to her magic, she could now go wherever and do whatever she wanted.

The irony was that she wanted to stay right here with him. Whether or not it was a good idea.

Vana closed the book and stood on her own two legs, literally and figuratively. She was going to stay. She owed it to Peter and the children, but most of all, she owed it to herself. Just because Zane wouldn't remember tonight didn't mean she had to forget. She would carry the memory with her for the rest of her immortal life, but she didn't have to deprive herself of being with him in the interim. And if her feelings for him ever did become a problem, she could always leave.

Though it might kill her to do so.

Vana inhaled. She was a djinni; first and foremost. She had a duty to her people, her family, and herself. Zane was just a momentary respite in the vast expanse of her life.

A couple thousand years and she'd come to believe that…

Before she lost her resolve, Vana walked back into the bedroom, drinking in the sight of Zane in her bed. This would be the last time she'd ever see him there. The last time anything could happen between them.

She walked over to the bed and leaned as softly as she could across it. She drew in a deep breath, her lips so close to Zane's.

And kissed them back to seven-fifty-two that evening.

Chapter 12

Vana preceded Zane into the kitchen and, for the second time that evening, fixed the hinges on the kitchen door and the cuckoo clock on the wall. The hour and minute hands circled around to land at seven-fifty-two, that one-minute difference keeping Zane from running into himself and giving the whole thing away.

Zane handed her the salt shaker again and she felt that same frisson of awareness sizzle through her. Only this time, she knew how much hotter it could become.

She led the way into the front parlor, put her ego on hold when he brought up the radar and satellite info, and skipped the invitation into her bottle. She only had so much self-control.

"Zane, why don't you get your things out of your car? You've been through a lot today." More than he knew, and that secret weighed heavy on her heart.

"Yeah, okay, but I'd like to talk. Hang out for a few minutes, okay?"

Her heart broke as she changed their future. And their past—the one only she could remember. "Can we do it in the morning, Zane? After all of... *that*... well, I'm rather worn out." She couldn't even look at him as she headed toward the stairs and began climbing them.

Worn out was one way of putting it.

"Vana."

She stopped two steps from the top. So close. "Yes?"

"Does your bottle have to stay upstairs? Can you bring it down here and keep me company?"

Her heart broke a little more. He thought he was her master, and it'd be best to keep that charade going. "Is that what you wish?"

"It is."

Which only dug the knife a little deeper. She really should have brought them back before the kiss in the garden and stopped it from ever happening. Or better yet, she should have just started their whole time together over.

Except… she was selfish enough to want him to have *some* memory of her. "I'll meet you here in five, how's that?"

"Sounds good."

It sure did.

***

She was inside her bottle on the mantel when he returned. Close enough to hear (and want) him, yet far enough to keep temptation at bay.

She'd purposely brought the stopper inside with her. Finally free, she intended to stay that way. If her bottle wasn't sealed, no one could open it and lay claim to her Services. And by *no one*, she meant Zane. She needed the option of being able to leave if staying became too painful.

"Are you comfortable in there?" Zane asked as he removed the dust cover from Peter's sofa and laid his sleeping bag on it.

"All the comforts of home." Which was true. Except the one thing she couldn't have.

He pulled his shirt over his head.

Vana's mouth turned to sand. She had firsthand knowledge of how every ridge and plane and hollow and muscle tasted and felt and moved. How each one worked in tandem with the others to give her the most exquisite pleasure. Her body started to burn with the memory.

Then he shed his pants. She should probably tell him she could see out of her bottle, but... why?

"I'm going to get up early tomorrow," he said. "There's a lot of work to do to get this place ready to sell. I'll try not to wake you."

Unable to face sleeping in their—*her*—bed, Vana had parked herself on her divan. She scrunched a throw pillow beneath her arms. "That's okay. I'm always up with the sun. I'll probably have to wake you."

"I doubt it," he said, looking right at the bottle as if he knew exactly where her face was. As if he could see her, and for a moment, she wanted to remove the silvered surface that protected her privacy.

But then reality and a certain memory crashed in, and she was thankful he couldn't see the effect it had on her, from heated cheeks to her pulse throbbing at the base of her throat and her nipples pressing against the fabric of her shirt.

It was going to be a long night.

"Zane, why do you want to unload this place so badly? It's part of the town's history. It's Peter's legacy that he wanted for his family. For you. You can't sell it."

Peter had loved having his parties here, with pony rides in the pasture, a barbecue in the fire pit, music and dancing in the parlor, and sweethearts strolling through the rose garden. Seeing them enjoying what he'd been able to provide had been a source of pride to Peter, knowing that he'd had enough to share.

"Look, Vana." Zane climbed into the sleeping bag commando, which shouldn't surprise her because he'd been commando in bed next to her.

Yes, a very long night.

"I know you cared about my great-grandfather, but people today, they don't. As long as this place stands as an empty eyesore at the edge of town, it's always going to be known as his house, and people will continue to talk about him. The best way to put the stories to rest is to sell it and let another family make memories here. Spruce it up and make it a home for the town to be proud of instead of an object of gossip and derision."

He left off the whole subplot about the reason they gossiped being her fault, and she would kiss him for that if she didn't know how dangerous kissing him could be. But she'd certainly never forget that he didn't lay the blame at her feet.

"But you could change their perception, Zane. I can help you."

"Even if I wanted to, Vana, I can't. I have to go back. Training camp starts in another month, so everything needs to be done by then."

"Your career can't be a substitute for your family."

"You don't know what you're talking about." He punched his pillow and repositioned it under his head. "There's no one left of my family, and I sure as hell don't call this place home. It's been an albatross around my neck ever since I was a kid. I can't unload it quickly enough."

She tried to understand, but his issues weren't hers. On the plus side, however, the threat of a sale would keep her from focusing on what she couldn't have.

"Vana?"

"Hmmm?" She tucked some of her hair behind her ear, trying to figure out what her next move was.

He was propped on an elbow, the sleeping bag barely covering his hips, that magnificent chest on display, and she knew what she wanted her next move to be.

"Is it… that is, are you comfortable in there?"

Nope.

"Yes." One word. Terse. Strained. For a host of reasons.

He sighed and ran a hand through his hair, rippling the washboard abs she'd kissed a half hour ago. "Okay, then. See you in the morning."

Vana was right; it was a long night and she didn't sleep a wink.

95

Chapter 13

"Y"ou better get out of here. I've called the cops."

Vana jumped out of bed and swiped the sleep from her eyes. Only about ten minutes' worth, which was obviously ten minutes too long if a woman could slip into the house undetected and aim a spray can at Zane.

The woman took a step back when Zane stood up, hiking the sleeping bag around him.

"Who the hell are you?" he growled, the muscles in his shoulders tensing.

"Get back." The woman brandished the can.

Vana squinted to see what was written on it. *Mice*? Mice came in cans nowadays? What did the woman think a mouse would do to Zane, bite him?

Vana readied her lips. She was so going to kiss those rodents good-bye. Well, in the figurative sense.

"Look, lady, I don't know who you are, but you're trespassing."

The woman shoved the can in front of her in case Zane had missed it. "I'm not the one squatting in an abandoned building. You better get out of here before the cops show up."

"Good. Let them. This is *my* house so you're the one who'll go to jail."

"Nice try, but I happen to know the owner hasn't sold it yet. I'm here to take the listing." The woman wrapped her other hand around the can as if she were getting ready to fire. Vana hoped she didn't have an itchy trigger finger. "Now I suggest you leave."

"You're Cameron Williams? The real-estate agent?"

The woman swiped at her nose and her eyes narrowed. "Who are you?"

Zane's shoulders relaxed. "Zane Harrison."

The mice can dropped. As did the woman's mouth.

Vana's heart dropped, too. *A real-estate agent.* He really was serious about selling the place.

"*You're* Zane Harrison?"

"In the flesh." Zane hiked the sleeping bag up again. "Er, so to speak."

At least he could speak; Vana was still stuck on the fact that this woman was going to help Zane get rid of Peter's house before she had a chance to un-Invisible the children, not to mention set them free.

"I'm really sorry. I walked in and saw you and thought, well…" The woman tossed shoulder-length auburn hair over her shoulder and tugged the hem of her blouse over her figure-hugging skirt. "I wasn't expecting you."

Zane gathered the sleeping bag tight around his waist with one hand—reminding Vana that he was commando under there—and extended the other. "Hey, it's okay. I'm glad you were looking out for the place. And that you didn't use the mace."

There was no way a mace fit inside that can. That made even less sense than mice.

The woman shook his hand. And didn't let go. "Well, a woman does have to be careful."

"Your name helps." Zane was the one to break contact. "I was expecting a guy."

"Most people do." Cameron knelt down to pick up her mice-mace thing. A good four inches of thigh showed through the slit on the side of the skirt. "You can't be too careful these days."

She better be careful…

"But what are you doing here so early?" asked Zane. "Our appointment isn't until one."

Cameron stood up and smoothed the skirt down her legs. Zane's back was to Vana, and while the play of his muscles there was very nice, it didn't allow her to see his reaction.

"I wanted to take a look around to have some suggestions for you when we meet. I know what attracts buyers."

And she obviously thought fiddling with the neckline of her blouse attracted Zane.

Vana smiled. She knew *exactly* what Zane found attractive.

"Actually, it turns out there are a few, ah, issues I want to clear up before I list it. Plus, as you can see," Zane shook the top of the sleeping bag, "I'm not exactly dressed for our meeting. So, how about if we postpone until next week? I promise that both the house and I will be in better shape."

It was *so* not possible for him to be in better shape.

Ms. Cameron Williams gave Zane a lingering once-over, obviously thinking the same thing, which made Vana want to claw her eyes out for more than just selling the house.

And, yes, she knew she was being totally irrational, but hey, she was going on fifteen minutes of sleep. Irrational was the best any of them could hope for.

"That's fine. Or, better yet"—Vana highly doubted it would be—"there's a charity dinner Saturday night to benefit the high school. Everyone in town will be there. You can come with me and I'll introduce you around. Set things in motion." Selling the house wasn't the motion *chicky* was talking about. "After all, word of mouth is the best advertising."

Vana stomped her foot. Both feet. Twice. The woman was asking Zane out on a date Over Her Dead Body. *Cameron's*, not Vana's.

"Hey, is that a football trophy or something?"

Holy smokes! Ms. None-Too-Subtle Williams was staring at her bottle. Vana must have moved it with her temper tantrum—um, foot stomping.

And, great, *Cameron Dahling* was walking her way.

Vana's fists curled at her sides. The woman did *not* want to get any closer.

Yet still she approached.

Luckily, Zane managed to intercept the woman and scooped up the bottle. "Or something."

Vana smirked, knowing full well that Cameron couldn't see her but still reveling in being the one in Zane's arms. Again, irrational, but who cared?

"Oh. Well, okay." Cameron tossed her hair over her shoulder again, then tilted her head to the side.

Oh come on! Did she *really* think that would work?

Vana wished she could've figured out how to restore the children to their human form already. Ms. Williams would so not be coming on to Zane if she knew he had a passel of kids living here.

Of course she still had to tell Zane about them.

"So *will* you come to the dinner with me? I really think it'd be a good idea."

Vana just bet she did.

She pursed her lips. One little wart. That's all she wanted to conjure. Right on the end of Cameron's nose.

Instead, a rose popped into bloom in front of the window.

Vana sighed. Thank the stars it'd only been a rose. And that it was outside. Zane was right. No magic where anyone could see it.

Zane shook her bottle enough to let her know *he'd* seen it. "I think dinner would be a good idea."

He did?

"My date and I would love to come."

His *date?*

"Your date?"

Heh. Ms. Cameron hadn't seen that one coming, had she?

Of course, Vana hadn't either.

"That's not a problem, is it?"

"Um, well, no. Of course not." Cameron brushed some hair off her forehead. "That will be lovely. The, uh, the dinner starts at seven. I'll put your name on the list. What, um, what's your date's name?"

"Vana. Peters." Zane didn't miss a beat, but Vana's heart certainly did. "Great. We'll see you then."

"Yes. I'll look forward to it."

Not half as much as Vana would.

Chapter 14

Vana managed to make breakfast on the first try. Sure, she'd done a lot of air-kisses while doing so, conjuring ingredients and cookware, but her magic had seemed to be working just fine for the past twelve hours.

Zane didn't know what the difference between today and yesterday was, but he wasn't going to question it. He was just thankful the rose hadn't been on fire when it'd popped up in front of the front window. And that Cameron hadn't seen it.

He wondered why, though. Why the rose. That didn't seem to be the work of a jealous woman, and, yeah, he'd kind of been hoping Vana had been. Subtle Cameron was not, which would have been a problem if he hadn't volunteered Vana as his date for that dinner. He hadn't come back to town to start anything with anyone, especially not his real-estate agent. Better she knew the score from the beginning.

"You don't mind, do you?" he asked Vana.

"Mind?" Vana asked over her shoulder as she poured the batter onto the griddle.

"About coming to dinner with me. I probably should have asked before I volunteered you."

"Being asked would have been nice, but I still would

have said yes, so there's no problem. Besides, I kind of had a feeling that woman was railroading you. No one likes that."

Was it his imagination or had there been a little sneer when she'd said *that woman*?

Probably not. More like wishful thinking on his part. He'd hoped that she would have come out of her bottle last night and they could have examined this attraction between them, but at the same time, he'd wanted to find the stopper and keep her locked in so they wouldn't.

In the end, she hadn't, and he hadn't, and he'd spent a night tossing and turning on the sofa instead of being entwined in satin sheets and her.

God, he'd imagined it so much during the night, it was as if it had actually happened. But if it had, there was no way he would've ended up sleeping alone on an old sofa.

And it was just as well they hadn't. No need to complicate matters, especially now that he'd outed her as his date.

"So what are your plans for today, Vana?"

Vana grabbed a plate from the drainboard beside the sink and started stacking pancakes onto it. "I thought I'd paint the back of the house. I don't want to start on the front and draw attention to it. With no work vans coming or going, plus with that woman knowing you're back, I'm guessing you'll have visitors soon, and it won't look right for you to have just arrived yesterday and all of a sudden the house is finished." She kept stacking.

"Vana."

"But I can work on the upstairs rooms instead if you want. Paint and furniture and whatnot. Maybe some knickknacks. I'm sure Peter's are still packed away somewhere. Though, we are going to have to make the timeline look believable for all of that, too." One of the pancakes slid off the spatula into the sink.

"Vana."

She grabbed the soggy pancake and tossed it into the trash bag he'd hung on a drawer pull. "I mean, people will probably talk, and just you being back is enough to keep them going. We don't need to add fuel to the fire—"

"Uh, speaking of fire—" Zane jumped out of his chair, grabbed the dish towel off the counter, sending the plates clattering onto it, and started beating the flames that were licking at the cabinets.

That finally got her attention.

The entire time she'd been talking, things had been popping up behind her: paintbrushes, a decorative pillow, some rope—must be the hanging-out thing she'd mentioned—and now the toaster was on fire. So much for her magic working properly.

"Holy smok—" She dropped the plate of pancakes onto the table, then ran to open the back door.

A cloud of gray smoke flew out as Merlin flew in, choking.

"Hey, you two, what's cookin'—um, burnin'?" The phoenix landed on the back of a chair and cocked his head.

"Broiler," threatened Zane, glaring at the bird before dragging the dish towel into the sink and turning on the faucet. Merlin had impeccable timing when it came to Vana's messed-up magic—impeccably *bad* timing.

"Okay, then, how 'bout this? I just flew in from LA, and boy, are my wings tired."

Vana didn't say anything. Zane just rolled his eyes and sat down to help himself to breakfast, trying not to make a big deal out of the fire. She'd feel bad enough for the magical mess, let alone almost burning Peter's house down, and unlike the phoenix, he hated to kick people when they were down.

"Nothing? Still? Geez, what is wrong with you two? *Everyone* laughs at that joke."

"I think they're laughing at *you*," muttered Zane. The bird rubbed him the wrong way.

"Funny, Ace. I'll have you know I kill 'em at the Tiki Bar."

Zane didn't ask where, didn't want to know when, and definitely had no plans to give the bird the opening to explain why.

"Okay, whatever." The bird clacked his beak, and his feathers changed to a powder-blue-and-white diamond pattern. All he needed was the face makeup and he could pass for a mime. "So, Van, what are we doing today?"

"Well, I was going to—"

The cuckoo clock interrupted her, chirping the hour.

Merlin almost fell off his perch. Eyes wide, he righted himself on the back of the chair, ruffled his feathers, then checked the watch on his wing. (Zane wasn't about to comment on *that* anomaly.) Merlin looked back at the clock, shook his wing, put his ear to it (did birds even have ears?), then glared at Vana.

"Van, did you—"

"Make breakfast?" she asked with her bright smile.

Despite everything, the woman was sunshine on two legs. Well, when she wasn't breaking *his* legs.

He still couldn't get over that and rotated an ankle just to remind himself.

"Yes, I did make breakfast, Merlin. And you'll be happy to know I didn't use eggs."

"You used something, all right," the bird mumbled as it hopped onto the edge of the table and sniffed at the pancakes. "So, cowboy, how was your first night in the old homestead? Everything you were hoping for?"

Thank God, Vana's back was turned because the bird's waggling eyebrows left no doubt as to what he was talking about.

Zane didn't know which to react to first: the fact that the bird had eyebrows or that he'd voiced the same thought he'd been having.

Zane shoveled a helping of pancake into his mouth.

He needed to get a grip; he couldn't be thinking about making love to her all the time or he'd drive himself insane.

And he was back to that.

"The house is fine, Merlin."

"Good thing. I heard you had a visitor. And so did your ol' pal Gary."

"Really? Did a little bird tell him?"

Merlin struck a pose, one wing outstretched, the other touching his breast. "*Moi*? Surely you jest." He held up the wing, the feather on the end extended. "Wait. Don't say it. I know. 'Don't call me Shirley.' I saw the movie."

A movie-quoting bird, a genie who kept him up at night (but not in the way he wanted), and the high-school bully. Three things Zane could do without.

"Would you like some pomegranate juice, Zane?" Vana held out a glass pitcher, her hair still in disarray from whatever it was genies slept on in their bottles.

Well, maybe there were only two things he could do without.

Zane shook his head. He must have inhaled too much smoke.

He held out his glass. "Thanks." He gulped half of it down. "As for painting the house… Why don't you just leave that to me, Vana? It's not easy."

"But you said I could help."

Shit. He had. What had he been thinking?

He'd been thinking he didn't want to hurt her feelings. For all her ineptitude, she wasn't doing so on purpose.

"Okay, Vana, you can do it, but without magic. I'll grab some more brushes, and we can throw on a couple of coats of paint."

"Oh, good! Let's paint it yellow."

"White's better. More neutral for potential buyers."

"But the original color was yellow. With blue and white trim, like Merlin's wearing. Can't we return the house to its former glory?"

105

"Uh, Van? Babe?" Merlin cocked his head so far to the side it was almost upside down. "Do you remember the so-called glory that came with this place? I'm with Zane. Use the KISS principle. Keep It Simple, Stupid."

Vana pulled out a chair and sat. "I know all about the KISS principle. That's actually how I figured out my Way of doing magic. See?"

She kissed the air, conjuring another rose, and Zane was riveted to his chair at the sight. Of her lips, not the rose.

Merlin groaned. "Seriously, Van? Anyone can see through that. You might want to try some subtlety."

Vana's eyes widened, and Zane had half a mind to wring the bird's neck. Nothing like tossing the sexual tension right out there for all to enjoy.

"Don't pay any attention to him, Vana." Zane tossed the biggest pancake to the bird. That ought to shut him up for a while. "Tell me how that principle helped you discover how to do magic."

She sniffed the pink flower, then offered it to him. "I came across the concept in my readings and figured I'd give it a shot. Other Ways hadn't worked. Snapping my fingers, crossing my arms, waving my fingers... I even tried that blinking thing, but nothing worked. Then I learned about the KISS principle and figured it was worth a shot, and *voilà*! Magic."

It certainly was.

Zane shook his head. *Focus.* He was here to deal with the house. Not a genie.

He took the rose from her, the scent striking at something in his memory... But, no. It was gone. Yet when he set the flower on the table, he had the strangest feeling of missing something. Something important.

"I'm glad that worked for you, Vana, but let's try painting without any kisses today, okay?" And he meant of any kind.

She exhaled. "Okay. I guess I can do it your way."

"Good. That's settled then." He wolfed down the rest of the pancakes. No eggs explained why they didn't taste like what he was used to, but Zane wasn't going to complain. For someone with unlimited power at her command—well, theoretically anyway—Vana's feelings were extremely vulnerable. "I have supplies in my car so you can get started, but I need to go into town for a few others. Will you be all right by yourself?"

"Oh, but I could whip up those supplies for you, Zane. No one will know and it'll save you the time."

He shook his head, both at the idea and the oversized whisks now hanging on the peg board over the oven. Probably a good idea not to mention them or the fact that her magic was on the fritz again. "If word's out that I'm here, going into town will curb people's curiosity and hopefully prevent them from coming out to see for themselves."

"Would you like company?"

Oh sure. He could see her waltzing around town in that getup. Or worse, conjuring a flying carpet. It was one thing to let her out of her bottle here, away from everyone, but in town? The stories about Peter would be nothing compared to the ones the residents would come up with about him.

"I thought you wanted to start working on the house. It's going to take a lot longer doing it my way than with magic."

"Oh, okay. Well, take your time in town. No hurry. I'll just get to work, and you don't have to worry about a thing."

True; he had to worry about *many* things when it came to Vana.

But, again, he wasn't about to curb her enthusiasm. "You might want to change your clothes. If anyone does show up, I don't think that outfit is the best idea. We want to dispel the rumors, not create more." It was on the tip of his tongue to ask her if she had that outfit in every color and was he going to be subjected to seeing her in the sexy thing every day?

What about out of it?

Zane shook his head. What was wrong with him? He wasn't usually such a horny bastard. The trip downtown would be good for both of them.

"Hey, I'm free if you want company, Shaggy." Merlin nudged him in the abs with the puff on the top of his head. What bird did that? What bird *could* do that?

Zane shoved his chair against the table. "Yeah, sure. A phoenix in the middle of suburbia. What part of 'dispelling rumors' does that fall under?"

"Geez. Grumpy, aren't we?"

Right now, that was better than horny.

***

Vana leaned against the sink, watching Zane through the kitchen window with a heavy heart as he climbed into his car.

He had no clue.

She rolled the salt shaker around in her hand. She'd really hoped that he'd have *some* idea. That last night had meant enough that *some*thing would stick. Because, seriously, it wasn't as if she was such a whiz with her magic that she couldn't have made some error for him to remember something. She'd thought, for a moment when she'd given him the rose, he might have… but nothing had clicked. Why was the *one* time she didn't want her magic to work the only time it did?

But perhaps that boded well for the children. Maybe she'd be able to turn them back now.

She turned to head up to the attic to do just that, but Merlin wouldn't let her out of the kitchen, hovering in front of her like an oversized hummingbird. His throat was even red— for all of about ten seconds. Then he clacked his beak, turning his feathers black, and drilled her with his now-orange eyes.

"Okay, Van, give it up. What'd you do?"

"What do you mean?"

"The clock. It was working fine last night when I left here, and this morning, it's off by sixty-three seconds."

Vana turned around and conjured another dish towel. She started drying the already dry pots so she wouldn't have to face him. And see? Her magic was working fine. "I don't know what you're talking about, Merlin."

"In a manticore's eye you don't. What'd you do?" He landed on the drainboard and put a talon on the griddle she was about to pick up.

She worked up her best glare. "The clock is old. Is it so inconceivable that it isn't working properly? Why does it have to be something I did? In case you hadn't noticed, my magic is working fine." She waggled the dry dish towel in front of him.

He pointed to the charred one in the sink. "So I see." He hopped onto the faucet, eye level with her. "The clock is a precision Bavarian timepiece. If it was working correctly last night, it should be working the same way this morning. Five hundred and sixty-seven years I've known you, Van. I can tell when you're up to something."

"I'm not up to anything, Merlin, so keep your beak out of it."

"Ah-ha! Out of what?"

"What?"

"You just said to keep my beak out of it, therefore, there has to be an 'it' to keep my beak out of. What is it?"

She threw the towel at him. And, of course, when she wanted it to burst into flame, it merely fell into the sink. "Get over yourself, bird."

Then she spun on the heel of her *khussa* and headed out back. This was not the mood to be in to test her magic on the children. Human beings couldn't be put back together with glue—even if they were in dish form. Maybe painting would work off her frustrations and help her ignore the bird.

But she knew Merlin. When he got a bug in his beak, he didn't let go until he'd pulled every appendage from its torso. He wasn't going to let this go.

Which meant she had to come up with a believable story because it was bad enough that she'd wiped Zane's memory, but for Merlin to find out about it...

The bird might be a phoenix, but he did like to crow.

***

Gary locked his car door and had to refrain from skipping down the street.

A real-estate agent. Zane had had a real-estate agent at the house. God, he loved the wildfire effect of small-town gossip. Well, when he wasn't the object of it, that was.

So Zane wasn't moving back in. And even more importantly, the place would have to get cleaned out for the sale. In that ensuing chaos, no one, not even eagle-eyed Ertel, would notice some missing journals. And if Zane held a yard sale, all the better.

Or, wait... Maybe he could convince Zane to leave the journals to the town archives in Peter's honor. Part of their history. He'd have to find some sickeningly sweet, unrefusable way to convince Zane that Peter would have wanted him to leave them for posterity and stress how much the town would appreciate the gesture. He had to play this right because he didn't want Zane to have any reason to keep those journals.

Gary grabbed the pamphlets from the trunk and tucked them under his arm. Today's PR campaign had just become more than a means to win the mayoral paycheck because the town archives fell under that office's jurisdiction.

Mrs. Mancini, the Spanish teacher who'd made his senior year hell, smiled at him, and, for the first time, Gary could give her a sincere one in return. Those journals and their secrets were all but in his hands.

Chapter 15

Zane had expected the looks. Even a few questions. What he hadn't expected was the utter silence as people stared at him as if he were his great-grandfather reincarnated, strolling down the middle of the road stark naked.

He glanced down. Still dressed, but he was going to check with Vana to see if she could read his mind because he had the oddest feeling that he'd been naked around her.

Wishful thinking.

Yeah, it was.

How did one ask a genie what the protocol was for sleeping together? *Could* she sleep with him?

That was a stupid question. All her parts had certainly responded the right way when they'd kissed. He couldn't believe that they wouldn't in bed.

He tripped on the curb and almost twisted his ankle as he landed in the gutter. Served him right. He needed to get his thoughts out of the metaphorical one and on to the reason he was here.

Carl's Hardware was in the middle of a long row of brick-front stores. The same bench that had been there when he'd been a kid was still beneath the awning out front. His father used to buy him ice cream at Patty's Parlor six stores down and they'd walk up to Carl's to enjoy it. He'd told Dad he'd wanted to sit in the shade, but that was because Gary or one of his fellow bullies had usually been hanging out at the ice cream parlor. It'd been easier to avoid the confrontation than suffer through it.

Yeah, he enjoyed the irony of coming back as a professional athlete. No one would bully him now.

Something good had come from the bullying, though. Zane now gave speeches to school kids about the dangers of bullying to help others end the sort of the hell he'd gone through.

"That's right, little lady. Step on over here."

Speak of the devil. Gary stood outside Marsh's Bakery accosting patrons, er, handing out some sort of pamphlet and schmoozing with a reporter.

"Come election day, all you have to do is push the button for Gary Huss for mayor, and this town will have all it needs to move into the twenty-first century."

If they wanted a dictatorship. Zane doubted the guy had changed all that much in two decades. His middle name ought to be Napoleon.

"Zane Harrison!" Gary hollered when Zane made the mistake of catching his eye.

He should have brought Vana along and let her turn Gary into the rat that he was.

"Welcome back to your hometown!" Gary just wasn't going to let it go. His tone was loud enough that the old men playing chess in the park across the street heard him, which would now link Gary's name to the whisper-down-the-lane effect of the story of Zane's return, an opportunity no politician would pass up.

Marlee, Zane's publicist, would relish the PR op, but he had no intention of being part of Gary's campaign.

Gary, unfortunately, had other ideas. He came over, clasped Zane on the shoulder, and shook his hand as if those twelve years of crap hadn't happened.

"Local boy makes good. Our star athlete's returned. What a great day this is for the town." Gary had yet to let go of his hand, and, yeah, the photographer beside the reporter snapped a picture. "Did you come downtown to help out the local economy, Zane?"

Much as Zane would like to tell the prick off, he wouldn't. He did, however, yank his hand away. "Thanks for the welcome, Gary. It's nice to be back."

The reporter flipped a page in her notebook. She looked young enough that the stories of his great-grandfather would only be urban legends to her, which was fine with Zane. "Hi, Mr. Harrison. I'm Cathy Lindt, reporter for *The Harrison Daily*. Can I ask you some questions?"

"Sure." He'd rather have said no, but turning her down would be as bad for his image as endorsing Gary.

"Did your family really move away because of the ghosts haunting your home?"

He needed a new publicist if Marlee thought this was a good idea. "We moved because my father died and the place was too big for my mother to keep up."

"So you never saw any of the ghosts?"

"There are no—"

"Of course he couldn't *see* any ghosts," said Gary, stepping in front of Zane. Not unsurprising because Gary hadn't liked sharing the limelight on a normal day. Now that he was running for office, he'd be even less inclined to. "They're *ghosts*."

The reporter took a step sideways so she was again facing Zane. "What about other phenomena? Things that moved by themselves, disappearing staircases, bears charging through the house?"

Zane withheld his wince. Man, he hated that story. "I don't have any stories. I was young when we moved away. I got involved with football soon after and never had the chance to come back, especially once I was drafted."

"So, are you back to stay now? Are you planning to retire here?"

Either the kid was utterly clueless or she was destined to become an investigative shark. His retirement, injury, and contract were all things he didn't want to discuss. "I'm back to get the house in shape to sell."

"You're selling?" asked the reporter. "But a Harrison has owned that house for over a hundred years."

"And no one's lived in it for the past twenty. I think it's time." Zane edged toward the hardware store. "If you'll excuse me."

"Oh, but—" The reporter hadn't quite honed her stealthy side to the point it'd need to be, so Zane was able to slip inside the store before the rest of the question was asked. He'd let Marlee do damage control on this one if necessary.

"Well, look who it is! Zane Harrison!" said the blue-haired woman wearing a blue-and-white checkered vest behind the old-fashioned cash register. Zane glanced at her back to make sure she wasn't sporting a tail on the off chance that Merlin could change his form like he could his feathers. "I'd know you anywhere. You look just like your father."

"Thank you, Miss…"

"*Missus*, my dear boy. Mrs. Winters. I don't suppose you remember me. I went to school with your father. Both me and my Johnny did."

He did remember her. She'd been one of the few who'd believed him about Gary and the bullying. "Of course I do, Mrs. Winters. How are you?"

"Ah, well, my rheumatism keeps acting up when the weather gets damp, but I guess that's to be expected. A tad lonely, too, now that the old gang is moving on, as we like to say. So much more positive than *dying*, you know?"

He *hmmmm*ed his reply. This place was a real party. Ghost stories, gossip, rheumatism, and death. Things hadn't changed at all. "I need a few supplies to fix up the old home, Mrs. Winters. Can you point me to the paint, please?"

My Fair Genie

"In the back there. I can mix up any color you like. Carl's son—he took over when Carl passed six years ago, you know—well, he finally broke down and bought one of those new paint-mixing machines since people were willing to drive forty miles to The Home Depot to get their colors made, which was just silly. Now they get them here, and the machine has paid for itself three times over. See? You *can* teach an old dog new tricks. Or I guess it's an old dog that can teach you new tricks." She chuckled, her ample bosom heaving beneath the blue-and-white-checked pattern.

"I believe you have a rather interesting shade of pink in one of the rooms in that house of yours, if I'm not mistaken, Zane," she said when she'd recovered her composure.

Unfortunately, her comment nicked his composure. The empty bedroom on the third floor. He'd forgotten about the paint in that room. Dad and Mom had painted it at least once a year, and every year the pink would bleed back through. Weird.

Or… magic?

He'd have to have Vana fix that. He couldn't sell the house with a self-painting room; the rumors would never go away.

"That color is long gone, Mrs. Winters."

"Is it? I could have sworn June said she saw it the other day when she checked the place. She and Jack really appreciate you paying them to take care of the place. Ever since Jack hurt himself at work, well, the money's been a godsend."

"She must have meant the color of the curtains. I'm going to change those, too." As soon as he had Vana un-magick the walls.

Zane headed down the closest aisle toward the paint. He didn't want to get into any hero-worship discussion. He'd paid June and Jack Ertel because they were the closest neighbors and the house had needed the upkeep. The monthly check-ins he'd made with them had given him peace of mind and allowed him to stay away.

He should have sold the house right after Mom died, but it'd been easier to write the check to the Ertels than come back and deal with it. But life was now pushing him toward a slew of decisions he didn't want to deal with. Coming here had been about getting things done instead of sitting around and stewing about things he couldn't change.

Zane made quick work of the supplies and managed to hear only two stories about the eccentricities of his forefathers before he left the store. Mrs. Winters was a veritable font of information when it came to the Harrison reputation. Thank God, there weren't too many of that old crowd left to remember all the stories.

He'd always been bummed that his parents had been older when they'd had him, a theme among Harrison men. Peter, Jonas, and his father had all married later in life, then had a child—just one, a son—even later. His father had been old enough to be his grandfather, and his age used to bother Zane a lot.

"Zane, you're really serious about selling your home?" Gary grabbed his arm the minute he stepped outside of Carl's.

He wrenched his arm away. "Yeah."

"That's too bad. Harrisonville won't be the same without the Harrison homestead."

That's because it'd be ridicule free, but Zane didn't say that. No one needed to think that he was getting rid of the house for any reason other than money. Not because the stories and the ridicule would never stop as long as a Harrison owned the house. He'd like to get married some day and have a family. He certainly didn't want to saddle his kids with this infamy. He'd promised himself years ago that the Harrison stories would stop with him.

But then he drove home and opened the door, shooting that theory to hell.

Chapter 16

He'd walked into a real-life *Fantasia*.

Zane ducked under the vacuum-cleaner hose that was dancing along the curtain rod, then sidestepped the mop and bucket that were splashing water all over the hardwood floor, gaped at the small rug that was polishing the chandelier, and stared at the squirrels that were using their tails to dust the banister.

But he came to a full-on, mouth-dropping stop at the sight of Vana. She'd changed from the harem outfit into a pair of pink shorts and a lighter pink tank top, but she still wore her genie slippers. Nothing overly outlandish in that, but what nailed him to the floor was the fact that she was *hanging upside down by those slippers* from the top of the frame around his great-grandfather's picture, which was now gracing the second-story wall.

Meanwhile, she just licked the edge of a rag and wiped a smudge of dirt off Peter's shoe as if what she was doing wasn't anything out of the ordinary. The gossipmongers would have a field day with this.

Zane dropped his bags with a *thud*.

"Uh-oh. Company." Merlin flew from the sconce on the wall and landed on Vana's heel. Which he pecked.

Vana shook her foot and was now hanging by one—

count it, *one*—curled piece of fabric. "Knock it off, Merlin. You know I'm ticklish."

"Yeah, well, he's puckish."

Vana bent backward as if she were a ribbon acrobat at Cirque de Soleil. Without the ribbon. "Zane! You're back!"

She did a half-kick move that would have had her taking a header onto the first floor if the chandelier-polishing magic carpet hadn't flown under her feet to float her gently down in front of him.

She hovered right at eye level. "What do you think?"

What did he think? What did he *think*? He couldn't think. Well, actually he could. About what would have happened if anybody but him had walked through that unlocked door. About trying to explain her slipper trick, the mop, the squirrels, the vacuum, and oh hell, were those rabbits sweeping dust bunnies off the floor with their tails?

This place was insanity.

He'd been out of his mind to come back. Utterly loco to open her bottle in the first place, and completely out of his mind to have even entertained the idea of allowing her to do anything around this house.

"That's it. This is over." He grabbed the mop, ignoring its squeal of protest—he wasn't even going to go *there*—and started shooing the rabbits and their dust counterparts out of the foyer, flicking the vacuum switch off in the process. Which had zero effect on the vacuum.

Neither did pulling the plug from the wall; the vacuum kept sucking dust mites as if everything were fine.

Everything was *not* fine.

"Zane, what are you doing?"

He scattered the squirrels with a sweep of the mop along the spindles as if he were playing a harp. "I'm putting an end to this craziness."

She shoved her hands onto her hips. "It's not craziness. It's magic."

"In your world maybe. In mine, it's crazy. Insanity.

118

Foolishness. And the best way to get me committed, never mind all the bad press I can't afford." He shooed a raccoon out of the storage space under the stairs. "Vana, this has to stop."

She clasped her hands in front of her chest, her eyes sparkling. "But it's *working*, Zane. My magic is working! And I did it without kissing you."

He didn't find that cause for celebration.

God, just shoot him now. He either had to knock down her happiness or put up with... *this*. And as for no kissing, well, he'd already decided kissing was a bad idea, so maybe it was a good thing that she'd gotten a handle on her magic and was finally in control.

An image of her *out* of control flashed through his mind. Vana, naked and writhing beneath him, her hair fanned out on a silk sheet beneath her, sprinkled with rose petals.

Where the hell was this coming from?

He shook his head—and the mop. The one whistling, "Whistle While You Work," if he wasn't mistaken. Or out of his mind.

"Vana, look. I'm sorry. This..." He waved his hand toward the vacuum that was now playing cobra to a snake-charming squirrel. "Is *not* working. I wish you'd make it stop."

Vana glanced at the vacuum, her bottom lip caught between her teeth, and when she looked back at him, it was as if the sun had turned in on itself and sucked all the life from the room. "If that's what you wish."

"It is." Wasn't it?

Vana blew a half-hearted kiss and the vacuum fell to the ground, undulating as gracefully as a ballerina at the end of a performance. Only instead of applause, there was a deafening silence.

Nothing had ever sounded better. Until he realized the room was too silent.

Vana and Merlin were staring at him. So were the bunnies and squirrels. Maybe even the vacuum, too.

Oh, no. They didn't get to make him feel guilty. He had a right to call the shots in his own home. And for now, that's whose it was.

Zane grabbed the stuff he'd bought and strode toward the kitchen to get away from the looks. "What happened to just painting the back of the house?" he muttered, then slammed to a halt on the threshold of the kitchen.

Forget the foyer; this room was a disaster.

He dropped the bags and braced himself in the doorway, trying to take in the scene in front of him. A fine coating of flour decorated the walls, every cabinet door hung lopsidedly off its hinges, the drawers were pulled open, and a flock of pigeons had made nests in them.

"What. Happened. Here?" He hadn't been gone long enough for birds to make nests in kitchen drawers.

"Holy smokes!" Vana bumped into his back. "I... I don't know. I didn't do this."

"And the leprechaun who lives under the front porch did?" Zane pinched the bridge of his nose. He had a hellacious headache. "Think, Vana. What magic did you conjure while I was gone? Besides the menagerie out in the foyer, that is."

Vana ducked under his extended arm and shuffled around the kitchen, tapping her teeth with a fingernail.

"I didn't use any magic to paint, just like you asked. I did as much as I could with the paintbrush, but painting that way isn't as easy as I thought it'd be. Nothing like painting a canvas. There are bugs and mildew and broken siding, not to mention climbing a ladder..." She dusted some flour off the edge of the table. "I was going to paint the front-porch spindles, too, but figured working on the inside would be easier. I found Peter's picture in the attic. Since you weren't here and neither was anyone else, I figured magicking it onto the wall wouldn't be that big of a deal since he would love to have it hanging up in his favorite place in the whole town. And then there was all the dust your cleaning lady couldn't reach, and well, I could get it done before you got home.

"No one would be suspicious of a clean foyer. That'd be the first thing you'd touch up to make the house warm and inviting to prospective buyers, right? So I be-wished the vacuum to get the job done. Such a handy device. We didn't have them the last time I was out of my bottle, and I've been dying to try one. Faruq would never fulfill that part of my requisitions list."

With good reason. Zane could just imagine the thing getting clogged with rose petals.

What was it with him and rose petals? That damn image of her on a sheet surrounded by them rolled like a movie through his mind.

The one he was losing.

Vana picked up a dish towel and the rose from earlier rolled off, its petals cascading over the counter. That had to be what had gotten him thinking about rose petals.

"But, Zane, I don't have any idea what happened in here."

"Never mind, Vana. It doesn't matter. Just… can you clean it up? Get rid of the birds?" And the dish towel.

"Oh, sure." Merlin flew into the room and landed on the open door of the old-fashioned iron oven. "Blame it all on the birds. Surely it can't be the genie's fault. That 'bird-brained' term hurts, you know. And you know who came up with that? Obo. A cat. Tossed that into the lexicon centuries ago, and it stuck. And now you're playing right to the stereotype, Tarzan. Did it ever occur to you that maybe, just maybe, we birds are victims of circumstance and not the instigators you and Hitchcock are so ready to brand us as? Besides"—he nodded at the pigeons—"do *they* really look capable of attempting something this grandiose, let alone actually pulling it off?"

"Vana, I wish the phoenix would be quiet."

"Oh, no, you di-in't." Merlin was in the middle of a head waggle when Vana kissed the air, and his swagger turned into mimed sputtering.

Zane enjoyed watching the bird's head undulate back and forth in direct counterpoint to the wing feather he was waving in Zane's face.

"I'm sorry, Zane." Vana spun around, her long hair fanning out behind her and brushing over his skin in one long sensuous movement that brought those rose petals and silk sheets and scented candles to mind again, this time with her hair no longer fanned out behind her but trailing down over his chest, his abs… lower…

God, he could almost feel it. Her lips, too. He swore he could taste them. Feel them against his. Feel them tracing down his neck and over his chest in delicious torture.

Zane scratched his chest for a second, then his head. What was wrong with him? Maybe he *had* taken one too many hard hits on the gridiron. Hanging out on the bench half the season might be a good thing.

Okay, now he really *was* going nuts.

He grabbed a set of steak knives from where they'd imbedded in the wall and dropped them into the closest open drawer. "Let's just get this place cleaned up." That was his focus. Not the woman in the clingy, pink tank top.

He sucked in a breath when she bent over to sweep up the rose petals.

Clingy pink shorts, too.

He blew out that breath and looked for something to straighten. There. The basket of apples that had overturned on the floor. When had he gotten apples?

Beneath the apples he found raisins. Thousands of them scattered on the floor like ants.

Which were also all over the floor.

This was going to take forever.

Merlin hopped off the oven door and onto the drainboard, knocking all the pots onto the floor in a loud mess, the only good byproduct of which was that it startled most of the pigeons into making a beeline out the open screen door.

The phoenix then started tapping his beak against the window, the staccato pings damaging to not only the glass, but also Zane's eardrums. And then Merlin began sweeping his wings together like a giant bellows, sending the flour swirling in a mini tornado.

Zane sighed. Heavily. "Fine. Okay. Vana, I wish for Merlin to have his voice back. But one more nasty word," he pointed to the bird, "and it's the meat smoker for you."

Merlin stuck his tongue out as he landed back on the oven door. Zane hadn't even known birds *had* tongues.

Vana opened her hands, freeing a pigeon into the backyard. "I don't understand what could have brought this on. All I'd wanted to do was get the foyer finished before you came home. I said nothing about the kitchen."

"The whirlwind part of your wish might have had something to do with it, Van," said Merlin, working his beak as if he'd been punched. Zane could only hope... "'Cause it sure looks like one came through here."

"I'll, uh, get to work on cleaning this up." She scooped a pigeon out of a drawer. Holy smokes. This one had laid an egg. She released the bird outside, wishing she could take flight as easily. She *had* used the term "whirlwind" in hopes that what had happened in the kitchen would have happened in the foyer, swirling all the dust outside and making clean-up easier. She wished she knew why her magic was so haphazard; she'd thought she'd had it all figured out.

Then Zane bent over and Vana realized she didn't have anything figured out. Including last night.

Especially last night.

Gods, if only he could remember it...

Yes, that was completely irrational, given that she'd

123

done what she'd done specifically so he *wouldn't* remember. And there were no *if-only*s for genies.

Zane stood up and his T-shirt stretched across his broad shoulders and tapered to his waist, slipping beneath the band down to his—

Vana tucked that *if-only* away and walked further into the kitchen, accidentally banging her knee on an open cabinet door she should have been looking out for instead of remembering what was beneath Zane's waistband.

The slamming door startled Merlin into lurching backward on the countertop, his talons scattering the flatware behind him, and he smacked into the open sack of flour, which went cascading over the edge in a cloud of white. Then he stumbled onto a pair of onions, backpedaling atop them like a circus performer, barely managing to take flight as the onions rolled off the counter and smashed all over the floor, the splattering juice causing Vana's eyes to tear up.

"Holy smokes." The onion was *so* not the reason her eyes were teary.

"Vana, don't get upset," Zane said, his voice all soft and concerned. Which only made her screw-up worse. He shouldn't be nice to her; he should be cursing her. Locking her back up in her bottle like Peter had.

"We'll take care of it. But my way. You have to stop trying so hard to use magic." He took a deep breath, those blue, blue eyes of his staring into hers with such intensity that she could tell the words were as hard for him to say as they were for her to hear. "It's too rusty."

"Not use my magic? But I'm a genie; it's what we do." Well, it was what she was *supposed* to do and why she was working so hard to perfect it. She was a member of one of the foremost djinn families, all of whom were among the most powerful and knowledgeable members of their world. Without her magic, who would she be?

That was a question Vana had shied from for centuries because she had a feeling that, without magic, she'd be an even bigger nobody than she was with it. And in her family of superstars, being mediocre was worse than being dead.

"Her magic is *rusty*? *That's* what you came up with?" Merlin snorted as he shook the flour off his now-eggplant-purple wings. "You go ahead and believe that, Big Daddy, and while you're at it, why not take a look at a bridge I wouldn't mind unloading. You interested?"

She could have sworn she heard Zane mutter, "Grilled," but when she looked at him, he was looking at her, not Merlin.

"We'll do this together, Vana."

"Kiss me, Zane."

"What?" Zane looked as startled as Vana felt.

Oh, gods, she'd said that out loud. "I, uh, well, that is…" Vana took a deep breath. That was the only way to get her magic to work right, and by the gods, work right it would, the consequences of what it'd do to her heart be dammed. "Kiss me."

"Vana, we agreed. No more magic."

"But I can fix this. It's too much of a mess to clean it all up the mortal way, and with one little kiss, it'll disappear, saving us hours of time and effort."

She was running a fine line between begging and being logical, although, really, there was no logic involved in asking him to kiss her. If she were being logical, that would be the *last* thing she'd want.

Zane wasn't saying anything. He was looking into her eyes, his fingers tightening on her upper arms. "Fine. But this is the last time, Vana. The magic has to stop."

That was so not happening when his lips touched hers. Soft yet firm, insistent yet undemanding, Zane's lips were utterly perfect, and she felt the magic flow through her again in a way it didn't when he wasn't involved.

Vana stood there, fighting with herself not to lean into him. Not to wrap her arms around him and let this feeling sweep her away and make the kiss so much bigger than

125

what he thought it was. But to her, this was the world. It was every fantasy she'd ever had, every memory from last night, every wish for things she couldn't have, all rolled up in one delicious package of the man she'd slept with. One she couldn't have again.

Right. Vana sighed and broke the connection.

"Go ahead," he whispered, his lips inches from hers. "Try it."

It? Try *it?* What *it?* So many possibilities were whirling around in her brain that Vana couldn't do anything.

"Oh swee… tie…" Merlin sang. "You wanna try getting that magic to work?"

Magic. Right. Vana brushed a pair of metaphorical sleeves up her forearms, put her hands on her hips, puckered up, and blew.

The kitchen was clean in an instant.

Zane, however, was a mess. Every particle of flour was on him as if glued there, the flatware stuck to him as if he were a giant magnet, and an onion made the perfect beanie cap on his head.

"Don't say anything," he said, the weariness in his voice so like Peter's. "Just pray the shower is in working order. I'll take care of this."

Vana winced with every white-powdered footprint Zane left across the hardwood floor.

"Look at the bright side, Van." Merlin hopped onto her shoulder and pulled something from her hair. "At least it wasn't pepper."

Vana glared at him. "That's not helping."

"Yeah, well, you know what else isn't going to be helpful? The fact that there's no hot water. Dude's going to be taking a nice cold shower."

That, actually, wasn't a bad idea.

***

126

Gary could barely contain himself. He'd followed Zane home to try to talk him into donating the house to the town. Never in his wildest dreams had he expected to find the answer to his prayers.

A genie. The woman was a magic-wielding genie.

His great-great-grandfather *had* known what he was talking about, and who the hell cared about the journals now? A talking bird… a self-vacuuming vacuum… a flying carpet… and the woman who controlled them all.

Oh no, Peter hadn't been crazy. Well, other than staying in this shitty little town when he'd had the riches of the world at his fingertips.

Gary wouldn't mind having *her* at his fingertips. Just think about it: whatever he wished and *her* at his command. The hell with the journals; he needed to find her lantern or bottle or whatever kept her bound to a master.

He had the momentary thought of rushing in there and grabbing her while Zane was showering, but she could just zap herself out of his grasp and he would've tipped his hand. No, he had to take some time to think about this and find a way to make sure she ended up his.

Chapter 17

Vana had just finished whipping up a couple of BLTs—without magic and without the whisks this time—when Zane returned from the shower, his hair slicked back, the hint of stubble he hadn't shaved giving his face a more defined, masculine look. Not that she really needed him to look more masculine. The green T-shirt, faded jean shorts, and an old pair of running shoes only helped matters. Or didn't help them, depending on your take on the situation.

"Everything okay in here?" he asked, looking around the perfectly clean kitchen.

"Just fine." If she didn't count the burn mark on her palm, a first for her. Sucker had hurt, but the cold water she'd heard Zane cursing in the upstairs bathroom had been a godsend in her case.

"Thanks for making this, Vana. It looks great." Zane stretched his long legs out to the side of the table she'd set for lunch and took a bite of the sandwich.

"Sure does." Merlin's tongue was doing circles around the outside of his beak as he eyed the sandwich.

Vana was trying hard not to eye Zane the strength and power and muscles in those legs she remembered so well from last night as he'd thrust inside of her.

Why was she torturing herself? She'd been doing it the entire time she'd made lunch. Last night was over. Done. Shouldn't have happened, and she had more important things to think about than what he'd looked like as he'd held her in his arms and taken them both to completion.

She took a big bite of her sandwich, using the concentration required to talk without choking on it to keep from saying what was really on her mind. "So how did your visit in town go?"

Zane tossed a piece of bacon to Merlin. The bird gulped it down without taking his eyes off the rest of the sandwich. "Saw some people I remembered. Gary, that 'chum' you mentioned, was there. He's campaigning to be mayor."

"Are you going to vote for him?"

"The election is four months away. I don't plan to be here then. And hopefully the house will be sold so I won't have any ties to the town."

"I know you said you don't want it, Zane, but Peter wanted you to have it. He wanted to leave a legacy for his descendants. That was all he talked about."

"I'm sure Peter would understand, Vana. We all have our own lives to live." He tossed Merlin another piece of bacon. That was one way to keep the phoenix quiet.

"No, Zane, *you* don't understand. This house, this town, they were what he'd worked so hard for his entire life. He'd been raised by his grandmother, you know. Emeline. That statue by the hospital is in her memory." Vana winced. The statue she'd broken the arm off. Luckily, by going back in time to fix Zane's legs she'd also undone everything else, so Emeline was still in one piece.

She cleared her throat. "Peter's grandmother married against her family's wishes and when her husband died, leaving her alone with a baby, they wouldn't welcome her back into their home. She had to struggle to make a life for her daughter."

"I don't see what any of this has to do with—"

129

She held up her hand. "When her daughter, Peter's mother, died in childbirth, and his father, who hadn't been much of a father to begin with, took off, there was no one but Emeline to raise him. Peter was forever grateful to her, but his father's desertion and the resulting poverty and hunger greatly affected him.

"He told me about a time he had to beg for potato peelings. He vowed then that he'd never be poor again. He'd been five at the time. Five. Can you imagine what that must have been like? How scared he must have been? How worried his grandmother was?"

She didn't give Zane a chance to answer. She'd gotten teary-eyed whenever Peter had told her this story. She must have heard it a hundred times; he'd been so proud that he'd had his fortune and this home to leave after him.

"Peter worked so hard to build his fortune and this town, Zane. He was one of the first people to start a soup kitchen, did you know that? It wasn't called that back then, but toward the turn of the twentieth century, there'd been some bad harvests and fearsome winters, and Peter opened up the house to families who didn't have enough food. His cook never stopped grumbling, but she never stopped cooking either, and that was the start of the Sunday parties Peter insisted upon. He was quite the hero."

Until Vana had tried to get involved. Oh, Peter had wished for her help; the only way he could feed the people once his stores had run out was for her to magick up a larder full of supplies. The proverbial three fishes.

Unfortunately, she'd conjured up pomegranates, tabouli, and baklava. Not exactly normal fare in this part of the world.

Talk had started immediately. But the exotic food hadn't kept people away. They'd been more than happy to partake of Peter's generosity, even while talking about him. But Peter hadn't minded. He'd been happy to be able to help so many people.

Zane pulled his legs in, sat up straighter in his chair, and tossed Merlin the rest of his sandwich. "Vana, I appreciate what my great-grandfather went through. But that was his life. His choices. They're in the past. This place isn't my home and I don't intend it to be. My life is elsewhere. With friends, teammates, a condo... I don't need this place. You've seen how often I've come here."

"But what about making it a vacation home? You could come up every once in a while, right?" He couldn't sell the house. He just *couldn't*. It wouldn't be right. She couldn't let him. Peter, who'd been through so much and had done so much good for so many, deserved better.

And she deserved another chance.

Vana swallowed that argument. A woman needed to have some sense of her own dignity, and admitting to Zane that failing Peter was the biggest regret of her life would be too painful. It was too painful admitting it to herself.

But she had to find some way to make things right. Some way to make Peter's greatest wish come true. And the children. What would become of them? If Zane did sell and she somehow managed to turn them back, she'd have to confine them to her bottle and that was no place to raise children. Especially after they'd been confined for so long as dishes. Children needed to run free.

Speaking of which... She pursed her lips. She needed to let them out of the armoire and un-Invisible them soon. Henry and Eirik and the rest, too.

Of course, that meant she'd have to mention them to Zane.

She blew out a breath. Okay, maybe that could wait—

"Hello? Anyone home?" The back door rattled.

Zane grimaced, Merlin *poofed* out, and Vana glanced down at the twenty-first century outfit she wore. Other than her slippers, she could pass for mortal.

She toed off the *khussas* and shoved them as close to the wall as she could, deciding against magicking them into the spectrasphere on the off chance—okay, not so off, but definitely chancy—that her magic wouldn't work properly, then turned around to see who it was.

The guy from the hospital stood in the open doorway. Another plus to time travel was that he hadn't had the chance to leer at her.

"What do you want, Gary?" Zane practically growled.

"I tried the front door, but I guess you guys didn't hear me." Gary looked at her. "Well, hello there. I heard Zane had a beautiful friend with him."

Scratch that. The guy had perfected his leer.

"Mind if I come in?"

"Would it matter if I said no?" Zane leaned onto his elbows.

"Aw, come on, Zane." Gary might be talking to Zane, but his eyes never left her face. Well, maybe to travel a bit lower. Vana was glad she'd changed clothing. "It's been years. Surely we can bury the hatchet?"

Vana could have sworn Zane muttered, "In your skull," but it got lost in the screech of his chair being pushed back from the table.

He strode out the back door past Gary, letting it bang behind them. Hmm, she thought she'd fixed that.

Vana walked over and tested the door. The hinges worked perfectly.

"Gary, let's not kid ourselves," said Zane, leading him off the back stoop. "There was never any great friendship between us and I don't plan to be around long enough to start one, so whatever you've got in mind, don't include me."

"Now, Zane, hear me out." Gary put a hand on Zane's shoulder, flashed a practiced grin with just the right amount of conciliatory in the tone, and lowered his head so as to be non-threatening—or condescending, as the case may be—but that was thwarted by the fact that Zane was two inches taller.

132

Still, the man had political posturing down pat. "We both want what's best for the town. And that's preserving the history of Harrisonville. I just want to talk to you about that. "

"Not interested." Zane slid out from Gary's hold.

"But—"

"Gary." Zane could do conciliatory, too, though the squinting of his eyes belied the schmoozing tone and went right to calculating. Vana was going to have to watch some of his football footage; she had a feeling he was a very effective player. And he probably looked really good in those tight pants, too.

"I get that you need to look good for your campaign, but this isn't your civic duty. It's time the stories about my family were put to rest, and hopefully unloading the place will finally do the job."

"But, Zane, those stories have kept up the interest in this town. We can't lose a vital part of our heritage. I've got plans, big plans, once I'm mayor. I want to bring in tourism, and to do that, we need to keep our history alive. It's what sets us apart from other towns in the area. It's our draw. The quaint homespun town built upon the ideals and efforts of one man."

"You're forgetting the stories, Gar. Those will never die if you hype Peter's efforts in this town."

"I don't want them to die, Zane. Think of it. Tourism means jobs. Transportation, hospitality, retail. Instead of selling the place, why not donate it to the town? People will come from miles around to see the house and its contents. To see if they can see any of what Peter claims he saw. We'll do tours: the blackberry incident, the old mill, the church window. It'll be a gold mine for the town and for you. You'll get a cut, of course."

Zane looked like he wanted to cut Gary.

Vana had forgotten about the church window. Shortly after Peter had brought her here, he'd wished for a rose window for the church, so she'd conjured one for him.

133

Never having been to Paris to see the one he'd wanted it modeled after, she'd fashioned one made from pink glass. And that was it. Square instead of the circular one he'd been expecting, there'd been no design, no stained-glass effect, nothing. Just a block of pink glass.

Poor, unsuspecting Peter hadn't been prepared for the giant gasp that had gone up when he'd removed the covering with grand fanfare at the church's dedication, and, afterward, there'd been no way to fix her gaffe, short of destroying it. She and Peter had discussed that possibility, planning an accidental lightning strike during a bad storm, but Peter had died before a suitable storm had shown up. The window was probably still on that church, a giant billboard to her incompetency and yet another blight on Peter's name.

"So you want to make a public spectacle of my great-grandfather's eccentricities to bring in tourists?"

"A spectacle?" Gary unknowingly mimicked Merlin's "moi?" "Zane, please, you wound me with your assumptions. There will be no spectacle. We want to honor Peter. Make this place a museum. His legend will bring people in to see the wonderful place he's built and revitalize the town."

"No way, Gary. I want no part of this, and if you even try, I'll sue you."

Vana wanted to applaud. For all that she liked the idea of honoring Peter, she didn't want him to be remembered for her mistakes. He deserved better than that.

"Zane, Zane." Politician mode was back in full swing. So was the leering when she looked out the back door, which really bugged her. "Just think about it. I'm sure we can come to a mutually satisfactory agreement."

Zane opened the screen door, his back to Gary. "Trust me, Gar, what I have in mind you wouldn't find satisfactory at all."

She, however, got great satisfaction from the dozen or so beetles that followed Gary into his car.

Chapter 18

Zane had slammed the kitchen door on his way back in, apologizing to Vana for both breaking the hinge and Gary's asinine ogling, but the anger hadn't stopped clawing at him.

The guy still knew which buttons to push, and Zane was royally pissed off for allowing himself to get pulled back into that shit by reacting while Gary had played him. Twenty years ago, he hadn't had the life experience or self-confidence to handle Gary, but he was a grown man now with a good career, not the scrawny, meek kid that prick used to torment.

Needing to diffuse his anger, he spent the next few hours working up a hellacious sweat removing the sheets from the furniture and giving the pieces a thorough vacuuming. Then he headed up to the attic to clean that out, too. He was getting the house ready for sale by next week's appointment with Cameron if it killed him.

When he lifted a rug in the attic, it almost did.

Pain seared his shoulder. Christ. He didn't need to tear his rotator cuff on top of everything else.

He backed up and leaned against an old armoire, willing the shoulder to stop throbbing. Hell. He was only thirty-two, not seventy-two. Too young to be thinking of his body failing him, but as a professional athlete, he knew it was one of the hazards of the job. But he wasn't *that* old; others had played longer than him. Look at Rice. Owens. Stallworth. They'd played for years.

The genie could allow you to play as long as you like.

The thought had him checking his other shoulder to make sure there wasn't a little devil sitting there because, with Vana around, anything could happen.

He could think of a lot of things he'd like to have happen with Vana.

He repositioned the rug on his shoulder, welcoming the pain to get his mind off her. She'd been occupying it too much lately. He'd been ready to curse the cold shower until he'd pictured her in it with him, and he'd been thrilled to have something other than his hand to cool him off.

He needed to get laid. But since that wasn't happening until he got the house up for sale and got the hell out of town, manual labor would have to do the trick.

He hoisted the rug again, then stood up, and—son of a bitch!—banged his head on a rafter. Shuffling his feet to keep his balance, Zane angled the bulky rug toward the doorway.

The rug smacked into the doorframe, and pain ricocheted through his shoulder again. Son of a bitch!

He'd been saying that a lot lately. Maybe he ought to ask Vana for help. Just with the bulky items, like the rug. And that armoire. He had no idea how he was going to get that thing downstairs.

No, he'd said no magic and that's what he had to stick to. This might be the tortuous route, but at least he wouldn't have to worry about the armoire magically sprouting wings and flying out the window.

He glanced uneasily at the armoire, then chided himself for being ridiculous. Of course the thing couldn't fly. He was going to have to find a neighbor to ask for help.

Yeah, and then watch Merlin show up, or Vana would make the coat rack dance, sending said neighbor screaming from the property. Zane sighed and hiked the rug back into place. He was on his own with this.

Four steps from the doorway, the rug hit the doorframe again and bent in half across it.

What the—? Zane backed up, hiked the rug again, and aimed it forward.

This time, the rug angled down, slid out of his hold, hit the floor, and flipped over and sideways, ending up lying perpendicular to the threshold.

"Zane? Are you okay up there?"

"Yes." No.

What the hell was going on with the rug? He yanked it around. The thing was as cumbersome as a blocking sled on the practice field.

"You sure?" Vana's voice sounded a little closer now.

"Fine."

He pushed the rug toward the doorway.

It didn't budge.

"I can help, you know." She poked her head around the doorframe. "Without… um… magic."

She couldn't help even *with* magic.

Zane didn't answer, just walked to the far end of the rug, sat behind it, braced himself against an old steamer trunk, put his feet on the rolled end, and shoved.

The rug moved, unfurling just enough to catch on the doorframe.

"Help? Is that what you call *that*?" Zane pointed to the rug fringe that was gripping the doorframe like… like… like *fingers*. "I thought we agreed. No more magic."

Vana took her sweet time looking at the fringe. Then she looked at the rug lodged in the doorway. Then she looked at him and climbed over the rug into the attic.

"I'm not doing that, but I guess I should've warned you."

"You think?" *Warned* him? Oh, Jesus. Did he really want to know?

"I'd forgotten about her."

137

"You'd forgotten." He didn't bother making it a question; he wasn't asking one. Because he was afraid of what the answer would be.

Vana nodded and knelt beside the rug. She tapped it in the middle. The damn thing rolled up like a cartoon scroll. All that was needed to complete the mockery it'd made of him were slot machine-like bells and whistles.

"I'd honestly forgotten, Zane. Peter brought her here only a short while before he put me back in my bottle, so it's not like she was on my radar."

"How does one forget a magical rug—oh God, please tell me it doesn't fly."

Vana shook her head. "If she did, I highly doubt she'd still be up here."

"Oh, I don't know. It's doing a damn good impersonation of something that doesn't want to leave."

"I think that's because she thought you were going to throw her in the trash and she didn't want to go."

"Hold on." Zane pulled himself off the floor and onto an old ottoman. "You're personifying this thing? Giving it feelings and a brain? Logic?" Although... Vana kept calling the rug a *she*, so logic was questionable.

Vana stroked a hand across the rug. "She's actually not a rug."

"She's not." Again, he didn't make it a question. Because, again, he was scared of the answer.

"No." Vana leaned a little closer. "She's someone who annoyed Faruq."

"Faruq?" Shit. He'd asked.

"The High Master's vizier."

"I see." No, he didn't. He didn't see one damn thing. Who and what was a vizier? What could possibly annoy him or her to the point of turning someone into a rug? Who was the rug? And why was he not freaking out at that question, let alone the entire idea of someone being turned into one in the first place?

Jesus. Why couldn't this just be a normal clearing-out of a house? He'd expected odds and ends. The occasional nest of spiders and a bunch of mice. But genies and cross-dressing phoenixes and anthropomorphized rugs?

"Faruq is in command of Djinn Compliance. Or, rather, he was before he was put on lantern arrest." Vana sat back and intertwined her hands in her lap.

Zane scraped a hand over his face and blew out a breath. He was going to go with the question most relevant to his situation. Forget whoever the rug was or what lantern arrest was and why Faruq was on it. "So what am I supposed to do with it now?"

"Well, I—"

The rug stroked its fringe along her arm.

"What's it want?" he asked, marveling that he could ask that question so nonchalantly.

"You have to understand about this rug, Zane." She brushed the fringe off her arm as softly as it had stroked her. "Faruq wanted Fatima as part of his harem, but when he caught her in the arms of one of his head guardsmen, well, he wanted everyone to walk all over her as he'd felt she'd walked all over him."

"Uh, okay. Understandable." If one were a genie.

"But, the thing is, Fatima wasn't cheating on him. She'd fallen into the river and couldn't swim. Ghazi saw her flailing around and rescued her. Faruq, however, saw what he wanted to see and had her imprisoned in the threads of this rug."

Zane didn't ask what Faruq had done to Ghazi. He had a feeling he didn't want to know.

"So now Fatima has to wait for a thousand and one people to walk over her—"

"A thousand and one? As in *The Arabian Nights*? Are you kidding me?" Zane mentally kicked himself. He needed to stop asking irrelevant questions and just be on a need-to-know basis so he could *know* what he *needed* to do to remove this craziness from his life. It was a wonder Peter had actually been sane.

"Of course I'm not kidding. That number is very auspicious in djinn culture." She cleared her throat and straightened her shoulders—which drew his eyes to her breasts.

Christ. He really did need to get laid if he was thinking about breasts while dealing with rug people and screwy genies… though the images he'd been having of Vana and him in bed together were as real as if it were last night.

But that was ridiculous. Of course they weren't. He'd spent last night awake and aching on the uncomfortable couch, hearing every tap of the branches of the old oak against the house. It didn't matter how hard he'd knocked his head on that rafter, he definitely wouldn't have forgotten having sex with Vana. His libido, imagination, and ego were quite certain of that.

"Fine. Okay. Whatever." He scratched both hands through his hair. "So what am I supposed to do with the rug, Vana?"

"Well, you could put her downstairs so she can fulfill her sentence. She's already had seven hundred and forty-eight people walk on her."

"You want me to put a magical rug, one that's capable of moving itself, where she can pop up in a cloud of pink smoke and a harem costume when she reaches the magic number? What if it's in the middle of a walk-through?"

"Fatima's smoke is green."

He'd had to ask.

"But of course she won't, Zane. Fatima will be able to transform at any time once that number is reached, so she'll wait until the coast is clear. And you'll even get to keep the rug once she's back to normal."

Such a bonus.

"Please, Zane. She's been locked up here for such a long time." Vana's voice was soft.

And the rug was sitting up with one unrolled edge wagging like a dog begging for a bone.

Kittens *and* puppies. Hell. He was toast.

"Fine." He put his hands on his knees and pushed up to standing, managing yet again to knock his head on a rafter. You'd think at some point some sense would be knocked in with the bumps and bruises, but apparently not. "But no funny business while there are mortals around. Understood?"

The rug shook the fringed end—Fatima's head?

Zane shied away from any kind of thought like that. If he started imagining a woman's body being woven into the threads of a rug…

Vana jumped to her feet and clasped her hands. "Oh, Zane, thank you! Thank you! Fatima won't be any trouble. You'll see. You won't even remember she's there."

Zane wouldn't bet on it.

He hefted the rug again and started walking toward the door. "Fine. Let's get her downstairs. I've had enough magical beings in the attic for one day."

And then the armoire tripped him.

Chapter 19

After waking from *that* conk on the head when he'd hit the floor, Zane learned that he was the, um, *proud*? owner of not only a personified rug, but a haunted armoire, a bewitched coat rack, an enchanted lady's compact, and several stacks of animated dishes, making this a cartoon worse than the earlier *Fantasia* debacle.

Zane gawked at Vana while she rattled off the list beside him.

"Henry Fitzsimmons wished to hide himself inside his lover's armoire when her husband came home, but his genie, Eirik, had been imbibing a little too much absinthe and, well, now Eirik's the coat rack over there."

The piece of furniture in question leaned out from where it was partially hidden behind a pile of boxes and waved an upper limb just slightly enough that Zane could have imagined it but, sadly, hadn't.

"Since Eirik's Way of doing magic is to cross his arms, you can see why he's unable to change either of them back." This time there was no imagining the heaving sigh the coat rack gave.

Vana pointed to the compact on an old vanity. "Lucia's genie didn't speak Italian, so he didn't understand her wish to have a mirror that reflected her inner beauty to the world instead of *being* a beauty *in* the mirror."

A burst of sparks blinded Zane for a few seconds. Oh, joy. Merlin had showed up to complete the fun.

"Yeah, that one still has me scratching my feathers," said the phoenix—who was wearing leopard. Someone needed to have a serious talk with the bird about his fashion sense. "No offense to Lucia, but a beauty she wasn't, so I don't get the mirror thing."

The mirror rattled on the tarnished silver tray.

"That's why she made her wish, Merlin," said Vana. "She might not have been beautiful on the outside, but she was on the inside, and she thought that if people could only see that part of her, they would find her delightful and charming, and she'd then be able to find *her* Prince Charming."

"Stupid Grimm brothers," said Merlin. "All a ploy for more tail. Those guys were dogs, let me tell you. They'd go around spouting sappy, happy stories of true love, prince charmings, and happily-ever-afters, and end up with women falling at their feet. Thank the gods a genie fixed that." He brushed his feathers together.

"One of the brothers decided to hit on the wrong guy's wife. The king, of all men. And being the ultimate in treasure hunters and hoarders that all successful kings are, His Majesty just so happened to have had a genie. One wish. That's all it took to kill two lovebirds with one big downer of an alteration to their stories and ruin the guys' MO. What a day it was for the rest of us, I'll tell you."

Zane didn't want to know. He didn't care what the Grimm brothers did or who they did it with or what had turned their happily-ever-afters into the dark, depressing stories they were known for. He just wanted to get out of this attic with his sanity and body parts intact.

Unfortunately, neither looked promising. Zane sighed and shook his head—and, son of a bitch! It hurt.

"So what about the dishes?" He had to ask. Sometimes not knowing was worse than knowing—though he'd reserve judgment in this instance until he heard their story.

"A group of children," said Vana sadly, caressing the box she'd taken from the armoire.

Henry. Sheesh.

"Would you like to meet them? They're cute little imps."

"Not real imps," interjected Merlin. "Just saying. If they were real imps, there's no way they would've stayed nice and quiet in that cupboard this long. Real imps would have broken themselves all over the place the minute the doors had closed. And good riddance I would have said. Imps are royal pains in the tail, let me tell you."

"Vana." Zane directed the conversation back to her because there was only so much insanity he could take.

"The children were visiting the home of a dowager countess as part of her charity work," said Vana. "Peter had heard about them during our trip through Hampstead when all the locals were talking about loony Lady Lockshaven. They laughed at her talk of dancing dishes, but Peter always paid attention to those kinds of stories."

"How did they come to end up as dishes?" Cheating adults and non-multilingual genies were one thing, but Zane was concerned about the transformation of a half dozen or so children who were now under his care.

"One of them had broken a piece of her china and she cursed them, wishing they knew what it was like to be so delicate. Her husband, a fellow explorer associate of Peter's, had just given her the genie he'd found. It ended up being her first and last wish. She was so distraught over what she'd done that she threw the lantern—and the genie—into the fire.

"Now, we djinn normally live forever, but we can be killed, and fire is a nasty way to go. The woman was doubly horrified by that so her husband begged Peter to take the children with him, hoping I'd be able to turn them back someday."

"Is there a chance you can?"

Vana tucked her chin to her chest and fiddled with her fingers again. "I... don't know..."

"Wrong answer, Van." Merlin looked at her pointedly.

Zane raised her chin with his finger. "What does he mean?"

"Well..."

Merlin stuck his beak between them, his beady black eyes boring into Zane's. "What I mean is, she *could* have changed them back *if* she'd stayed in school just a wee bit longer. But not our Van here. No sirree. She had to jump feet first into the first bottle to come along and missed the lesson about a dying djinn passing on an obligation. In this case, the children.

"But that's not the part I'm talking about. Oh, no. Van now has to figure out how to undo the enchantment all on her own. There was a reason she skipped school and a reason the kids are still the way they are. Isn't that right, Van?"

"You know, Merlin, for someone who's supposed to be her friend, you're not exactly on her side."

"I'm more of a friend to her than you'll ever know, Lover Boy."

"I hear rotisserie's pretty good, bird."

"Guys." Vana shooed Merlin out of arm's reach. "Since we know how to get my magic to work, maybe now I can turn them back."

"Uh, Van?" interjected Merlin over the excited clatter of dishes. "Not to be a party pooh-pooher, but you haven't exactly been hitting home runs with Studmuffin's kisses. You really want to risk the kids on a maybe?"

As much as he'd like to fricassee the bird for pointing out Vana's lack of success so harshly, the bird was right. They couldn't risk the kids until her average was one hundred percent.

Practice makes perfect...

Zane stood up and smacked his hands together.

"Okay, so that's it, right? There aren't any other magical beings around here I should know about?"

"Um…"

"Um" did not bode well for his peace of mind. And of *course* there were others. Peter couldn't do crazy in a small way now, could he? "Who are they?"

Her fingers twiddled in her lap. "A pair of enchanted wind chimes. But they're not in the house, so you don't have to worry about them."

"Being out in the open where anyone can see them is supposed to make me feel better?" He pinched the bridge of his nose again. Much more of this and he'd have a bruise. "It's not going to work, Vana. I'm sorry, Fatima." He looked at the rug, then shook his head. He was conversing with a rug… "One, maybe two magical beings are do-able, but all of these? It's just not feasible. I can't have them here. It's too much. How do I get rid of them?"

Vana jumped to her feet as the rug wilted like a flower to the floor.

"Oh, but you can't get rid of them, Zane. They belong here. This is their home."

"Vana, I can't have a rug with a mind of her own sliding across the hardwood floors. What if someone wears stilettos or something on her? I can't afford for her to yank herself out from under that person. What happens if the coat rack sneezes and hats go flying across the room?"

Zane heard himself asking the questions and found them surreal. He'd lost his mind. One day back and he'd broken with reality. Sliding rugs? Sneezing coat racks?

"They'll behave if you bring them downstairs, Zane. They did for many years until your father put them up here."

"My father knew about them?"

Vana shrugged. "I can't say for certain since I was in my bottle during his lifetime, but I do remember the day he hauled all of the pieces up here. It was right after your grandfather's

My Fair Genie

funeral. That afternoon, actually. He told your mother to stall the guests until he'd gotten Fatima up. Eirik was easy enough, but he had to have a few of his friends help him with Henry. He waited until later that evening after everyone else had left. They'd been drinking. I guess he wanted an excuse if Henry did something out of the ordinary. But Henry didn't. He behaved exactly like a real armoire."

Zane almost asked how a real armoire behaved but kept it to himself. He'd probably break out in hysterical laughter before he got the whole question out. "So how can I see the dishes now if they're supposed to be invisible?"

Vana nibbled her lip and looked away. "I don't know. I must have done something to undo their Invisibility."

Of course she had, and of course she didn't know how she'd done it. Thank God his father had put Henry—the *armoire*—up here. But too bad he hadn't just gotten rid of everything. "I have to do something with them, Vana. No one is going to want to buy a house with haunted furnishings." Well, some might, but he didn't need that kind of publicity either.

"Why not put them back to work? They've been bored up here."

The fringed end of the rug raised her head and nodded.

Zane rubbed his eyes, trying to quash the headache that was starting. "I don't know—"

"Please, Zane. I promise you they'll behave. Right, everyone?"

The dishes clattered in the box, the rug waved her fringe, the armoire thumped its doors, the compact opened and closed like a clamshell, and the coat rack waved its arms.

He shouldn't. He knew he shouldn't. But Vana's hopeful expression tugged at his heartstrings.

"I know I'm going to regret this," he muttered, hefting the rug once more onto his shoulder.

147

Vana popped up and clapped her hands. "Oh Zane, you won't. I promise you won't."

Merlin, meanwhile, cackled. "I certainly hope you know what you're doing, big guy."

So did Zane.

Chapter 20

Vana was so happy for Henry, Lucia, Fatima, and the children. Eirik, too, though, as a genie in The Service, he should have known better than to imbibe alcohol. It did bad things to the djinn, which was why it was forbidden. But she wasn't exactly the poster child for proper djinn behavior, so she'd cut him some slack.

Henry and Eirik had walked down on their accord once she and Zane had cleared a path for them, and the children clacked against each other in their box, the closest thing to excited chatter they could manage in their current state. The poor things had been locked away after that last infamous episode to await the day she felt competent to free them.

They were all still waiting for that day. Maybe if she played on Zane's sympathies he'd give in and kiss her again.

Vana shook her head and decided to consult the *Djinnoire* instead. It was the safer option.

"Hello? Zane?" someone called from the foyer. "Are you here?"

Another female voice. Singsong-y this time. Vana knew *exactly* what that meant.

With a quick "hush" to the dishes to stop their

149

clanking, Vana set the box on the second-floor landing, then peered at the front door where Eirik snapped to attention like a sergeant-at-arms. He always did have delusions of grandeur.

So, too, apparently, did the woman at the front door. Cute red high heels tapped the porch planks on the other side of the screen door. Shiny red high heels. Shiny, fire-engine red high heels. With peekaboo toes. And shapely legs and a clingy black skirt just long enough not to be called a belt above them. Tiny waist and boobs that Vana would bet her last dirham had cost more than some of the treasure in The Cave of Great Unknown.

The face wasn't anything to write home about, but with that body, that didn't really matter.

"Oh, Za-a-ane! I know you're in there!" The woman's knuckles rapped on the wooden screen door.

Vana wouldn't mind *her* knuckles rapping on the woman's—

"Hello?" Zane strode into the foyer with a quick glance up the staircase, his expression saying all he didn't have to.

Vana pulled back out of sight.

"Lynda?"

He knew her? Oh, no, no, no. This was not good.

Vana peeked back around the stairwell, the view of Zane's back nothing to complain about. *Lynda*, however, was.

"Oh you remember me!" One of the cute, red high heels cocked sideways. "I heard in town that you were back."

Vana couldn't see the top half of the woman on account of Zane's broad shoulders, but she'd just bet the woman's hip was cocked, too, and a fingernail was making it to the corner of her glossy, fire-engine red, lipsticked mouth to be nibbled *oh-so-delicately* between just a hint of teeth.

Yes, Vana was jealous. And with good reason—that Zane could never know about.

Sigh.

"Yes, I'm back," said Zane, opening the door. "Word travels fast."

"Always has in this town." The shoe moved a little closer, bringing the body with it. "Mind if I come in?"

Vana minded. A lot. She took another step forward, forgetting that this part of the landing creaked until it did.

She hopped back, chastising herself. She'd always been so careful when Peter had been alive.

Zane glanced over his shoulder, a knowing arch to his right eyebrow. "I'll come out there. The place is a bit of a mess." He pulled the mahogany door closed behind him.

Vana gnawed her lip. She wanted to know what was going on.

The dishes started clattering again and now she couldn't even hear.

Well, she'd always been good at Invisibility.

Merlin showed up right after she'd shushed the kids and kissed the air to disappear. "You so did not just do that."

"Mind your own business, Merlin," she whispered harshly as she climbed toward the stairs, going slowly over the creaky area so it wouldn't make a noise.

"This *is* my business, Van." Merlin landed on her shoulder. Phoenixes were one of the few beings able to see through Invisibility.

She shooed him off and glided down the stairs. Well, not literally. She was still trying to manage Hovering. "I don't see how. Now, hush. I want to hear what she's saying."

Merlin landed on the newel post at the bottom of the stairs and spread his bright orange (for now) wings across the staircase, his talons scraping on the iron-ball post topper like nails on slate. Peter's son, Jonas, had had all the spindles made from iron at some point. Probably to prevent any more collapses, but nothing stopped Vana's misguided magic.

"I'll tell you what she's saying," Merlin rasped back, sounding like a crow with a sore throat. "She's probably inviting him to dinner with full hopes of getting him into bed and having her wicked way with him—what?"

Vana ducked her head, knowing her face was as red as Lynda's shoes at the memories of the wicked things she and Zane had done. No way was Lynda going to get that same chance with Zane.

"Oh, no. You didn't. Vana, please tell me you didn't." Now Merlin sounded like a crow on the verge of a nervous breakdown.

Her cheeks flamed hotter and she didn't look up.

"Nirvana Aphrodite, tell me you did *not* sleep with him." Merlin stuck a wing—now as black as newly forged iron—in her face and raised her chin. "Oh, gods, you did." His feathers fell in a slump, effectively blocking her from reaching the foyer floor.

Meanwhile, Lynda was saying whatever it was she was saying to Zane and he was talking with her out there on the porch where Vana couldn't know what was being said. She wanted out there now.

She ducked under Merlin's wing and tiptoed to the door, careful to step over the creaky third floorboard from the stairs. She didn't know if anyone had fixed it when they'd replaced the spindles, but now wasn't the time to find out.

"Hold on, Van." Merlin landed on Eirik beside the front door.

The phoenix's feathers were a soft apple-green color now, but Vana wasn't buying the conciliatory measures. She'd seen Merlin at work when he'd wanted something. He was trying to play her.

And Lynda was out there doing the same thing to Zane.

"So when was this? Last night?"

Vana pressed her ear to the door and refused to answer when she was trying to eavesdrop.

"Of *course* it was last night." Merlin answered himself. The bird always thought he knew all the answers. That he did this time didn't mean Vana had to give him the satisfaction of confirming his high opinion of himself. "But I don't see you two acting all lovey-dovey. Unless... Oh, gods. It wasn't bad, was it?" The bird whistled. "Man, that's disappointing. A big guy like him and no mojo to back it up. Wow, Van, that's got to suck."

"Of *course* it wasn't bad." Vana covered her mouth.

"Aha! You *did* sleep with him! So...? How was it?" The bird clacked his beak and his feathers turned fuchsia, one of his favorite colors. "Well, *duh*. What am I thinking? It had to have been awesome if you're keeping the news to yourself." The bird raised his eyebrows, appraising her.

"Nice work, Van. But how come you two aren't all over each other? I'd think if it was that good, there'd be some pretty spectacular PDA here all by your lonesomes. Or at least some longing glances, a few more blushes, and he sure as *scheisse* shouldn't be on the front porch with Little Red Ride-Me Shoes when he's got his own little slice of heaven right here..." Merlin's voice trailed off and he stared at her. "Unless—"

"Hush, Merlin. I can't hear what's going on out there." She flipped her head so her other ear was to the door, covering Merlin beneath a fall of her hair.

"Oh, no." Merlin's voice dropped an octave.

"Oh, no" was right. Lynda's voice had gone all sultry, making the words difficult to understand, but not the intention behind them. Vana wanted to go out there.

And do what?

That was a problem.

"You *did* play with time again, didn't you?" Merlin spit out her hair. "And he doesn't remember any of it."

Vana held up her hand, pretending she wanted to hear what Lynda and Zane were discussing. Well, she did, but she wanted Merlin to stop his train of thought before he arrived at the right station.

Judi Fennell

Of course he didn't pay any attention to what she wanted. "Vana, you can't do that to him," Merlin whispered hoarsely. "Mortals hate to have big chunks of memory missing. I'm assuming it was quite *big*, right?"

She pressed her ear closer to the door and put her other hand over her other ear, wanting to ignore the fact that Merlin had figured it out. The bird was too smart for her own good. Vana's heart dropped into her stomach. Bad enough that *she* knew what she'd done; it'd be so many more times worse for someone else to know, too.

She closed her eyes, trying to imagine the scene on the other side of the door instead of the one from last night that she couldn't seem to push out of her brain, thanks to Merlin. Well, and Zane, too. First sight of him over the breakfast table this morning had brought all the memories back. In living, breathing, panting, gasping, growling, vivid color.

"*That's* why the clock was off, wasn't it?" Merlin landed on her shoulder and wiggled the tip of his beak beneath her palm. "You are going to be in so much trouble. You do know that, right? You cannot keep playing with Time, Van. The Fates aren't going to like it."

She turned around and leaned against the door, forcing Merlin to take off or risk crushing his cornrowed tail between her shoulder and the door. "You don't know what you're talking about, Merlin."

He hovered in front of her. Oh, sure; *he* could hover.

"Like Hades I don't, Van. Clotho doesn't like people messing with her job. You might get away with it the first time, but twice in the same century, let alone the same day? And sleeping with him? Puh-leez. How clichéd can you get?"

"You're just jealous because it wasn't you." Oh... *frankincense*. She shouldn't have said that. She'd just given him all the ammunition he'd need to get her in a world of trouble—or never let her live it down for the rest of her immortal life.

154

Merlin opened his beak to say something, then snapped it shut. His wings turned peacock blue. "Van, you can't just go around removing guys' memories after you *boink* them. That breaks at least five of the Codes of Conduct for Masters."

"It would if he were my master. But he's not."

"Huh? Say what?"

"It's in the *Djinnoire*, Merlin. Now hush. I want to hear what they're talking about." She turned back around and pressed her ear against the door again.

All she could hear was a soft masculine murmur and Lynda's oh-don't-be-silly giggle that really meant "I want you to think that I think you're the funniest, smartest, brightest, hottest man in town so you'll let me take you home tonight and have my way with you." Mortals hadn't changed all that much in the hundred years she'd been out of commission.

"Okay, so I get that you never earned the gold bracelets that mark you as being in The Service, but if he's not your master, what are you doing hanging around?"

She sighed, then opened her eyes and looked at Merlin. "You're not going to let go of this, are you?"

"I don't get it, Van. If you're free, out in the world with no master, able to go anywhere you want, do whatever you want, why are you hanging around this dump, sneaking around like a shadow? And look at you." His wings fluttered over her body. "You *are* a shadow."

Vana looked down. Oh, right, she was Invisible.

She kissed the air and her body melted back into view. "I can't let Zane sell the house. It was Peter's greatest wish to keep it in the family and I failed him at so many others. I have to do this for him. And the children."

Merlin tapped his head with his wing. "You're staying here for a *dead* guy? What part of 'dead' don't you get, Van? Peter will never know. And the kids stack up nicely, in case you hadn't noticed. Some bubble wrap, packing tape, and you're free to go."

"I can't do that to any of them, Merlin. This is their home."

The doorknob turned.

Holy smokes! Vana shooed Merlin away, kissed herself back into nothingness, and plastered herself into the tiny space between Eirik and the doorway just as Zane backed through the door.

"Yes, Lyn, it was great seeing you again. I'm glad you stopped by."

"Are you sure I can't tempt you out to dinner? I really do make a good steak."

Vana rolled her eyes. Seriously, how hard was it to grill a hunk of meat? The woman was doing it with right now with her eyes as she looked at Zane.

Vana curled her fingers into fists to keep from scratching those eyes out.

"Thanks, Lyn, but I have to pass. Too much to do."

"Why don't you just have your assistant take care of it? Isn't that what assistants are for?"

"My what?"

"I heard you were bringing someone to the dinner on Saturday. I assumed she was your assistant." A peekaboo toe shoe worked its way into the doorway. "If she's not here yet, I'd be willing to help with whatever you need."

Vana just bet she would.

"If you don't want my home cooking, we could order pizza while we do whatever it is that needs to be done around here. Paint the porch, air out the bedrooms… whatever." Her blonde head was next in the door.

Zane didn't budge.

Vana, standing inches beside him, didn't either. His *assistant*? Couldn't the woman come up with anything else? Talk about no subtlety…

Vana had a good mind to give the woman a *piece* of her mind. Except she was Invisible, and suddenly materializing where she was would only create problems. Materializing from the kitchen, on the other hand…

Vana kissed herself into the kitchen, brought her body back to the visible plane, whipped up an apron and an apple pie out of thin air (literally), and headed back toward the foyer.

"Whoa, whoa, whoa!" Merlin showed up in a shower of silver sparkles and matching feathers, and plastered his wingspan across the opening. "What do you think you're doing?"

"She thinks I'm his assistant."

"So you want her to think you're the housekeeper? Why not just give the tart a leather teddy and concede defeat?" Merlin looked her over.

"Oh." Vana set the pie on the table. "I see what you mean."

"Come on, Van. You want him, you gotta fight for him."

She yanked the apron off her head. "I don't want him, Merlin."

"Yeah and Arthur pulled the sword out all by himself." Merlin rolled his eyes. "Look, Van, it is what it is. And you got first dibs. So whip yourself up something femme fatale and show that man-killer out there that you're anything but Zane's assistant."

Chapter 21

Lynda wasn't the only one who could wear red, and Vana intended to let her to know it.

And rue it.

"Zane, what do you think of this dress for our dinner date?" Vana walked down the front stairs in a killer red evening gown. "Too revealing?"

She reached the bottom stair and twirled around, giving both Zane and *Lynda* the full show. A spaghetti-strap bodice with a full scarf sleeve over one arm, the fabric swirling with splashes of gold and orange that wrapped around and gathered at her waist, the flowing jumble of chiffon allowing one leg to peek through, ankle to thigh.

Zane's mouth fell open.

Lynda's became a thin, tight line that smeared lipstick just above her lip.

"Oh, hello." Vana stuck out her hand oh-so-innocently. "And you are?"

Furiously angry, but Vana wouldn't expect the woman to admit it.

"Lynda Hus—er, Wattrell." Lynda played the game well. If Vana hadn't been privy to their earlier conversation, she would have thought the tight voice Lynda used was her natural one. Or maybe it was and the baby-doll breathlessness was fake. "Zane and I, uh, well, we go back a ways."

Oh, the woman had innuendo down, too, but, again, Vana knew how old Zane had been when he'd left here. Twelve-year-olds' crushes—if he'd even had one on the girl this woman had once been—were nothing compared to what *she* and Zane had shared.

Too bad he didn't remember it.

Vana kept the smile plastered to her face and took the *teeniest* step closer to Zane. "Isn't that nice, Zane? All of your *old*"—that word stressed, of course—"school chums are stopping by. I guess they couldn't wait until we went to the dinner to see you. You and your husband will be there, won't you, Lynda?"

She put just the right amount of inflection on the "we" and just the right amount of sincerity in her smile. After being around mortals for eight hundred years, out-innuendo-ing Lynda was a piece of cake. Preferably of the Marie Antoinette kind because she'd like to lop off this chick's head.

Especially when Lynda turned a slyly calculating gaze toward Zane. "I'm assuming he'll be there, but Gary and I are divorced."

Ah, touché. Letting Zane—and Vana—know she was available. Good play. Too bad Vana had the ultimate hand—*if* she told him about last night. Which, of course, she couldn't.

Vana's smile faltered. What was she doing? She wasn't here to make nice with Peter's grandson. (Though it had been *very* nice.) She was here to make Peter's wish come true by turning the children back, and if Lynda could make Zane happy and keep him in town and living in this house, then maybe Vana had no business trying to outdo the woman. Instead, she should embrace Lynda's feelings for Zane and step aside to let Nature take its course.

Except she'd never been too good with that. Patience

was not one of her virtues, which was how she'd ended up in her bottle to begin with.

Vana took a step closer, practically plastering herself against him. Gods, he smelled so good. The tiniest tang of perspiration mixed with his natural scent, along with the same soap Peter had used.

And it probably *was* the same soap; she'd conjured up enough to last until Doomsday. Unfortunately, Peter had said "until Tuesday."

She shook her head. Why was she thinking about Peter with Zane mere inches away? Peter had been an old man when she'd become his genie and had held no physical attraction whatsoever for her. Zane, on the other hand, was anything *but* old. Hot, sexy, fun, nice, funny, good with his hands...

Lynda was checking out those hands. And the rest of him, too.

Vana wanted to blast a wart onto the woman's nose. A big hair on her chin. Bags under her eyes. But she'd never had good luck with that magical specialty, and with her luck, she'd...

On second thought, screwy magic could come in handy.

She took a little breath. One wart coming up. She puckered her lips and—

Zane planted a kiss on them. A quick peck, but enough to surprise the magic out of her. And wipe the smile off Lynda's face.

"The dress is beautiful, Vana. I think it'll be fine." He left a stunned Vana standing there as he worked his own magic, spinning Lynda around and guiding her back to the door. "It's been great catching up, Lynda. We'll see you at the dinner. Thanks for stopping by."

Just like that, Lynda found herself on the other side of the door.

And when Zane turned around, Vana found herself in hot water.

"What was that?"

"What?" she squeaked.

"That." Zane pointed to the door. "I thought we were going to need a referee in here."

Vana smiled weakly, still trying to get her hormones under control from that one little kiss. The man pecked, er, packed a mighty wallop. "I don't know what you're talking about. And I thought you didn't want to kiss me anymore."

"Don't try to distract me from the issue here, Vana. That kiss was the only way I could prevent you from doing whatever you were going to do to her. You might be hundreds of years older than me, but I wasn't born yesterday. Care to tell me what's with the attitude toward Lynda?"

"Her?" Vana swished the dress around her legs. She'd worn her own version of peekaboo-toed red shoes, with ribbon ties around her ankles that made Lynda's look like something one would wear to the supermarket. "Could you not tell that she had one thing on her mind?"

"And what the hell's wrong with that?"

Okay, wrong answer…

Vana flung the skirt behind her. How dare he! After all they'd done—

Oh, right.

She took a deep breath. "Oh, please, Zane. You show up out of the blue, a rich, successful athlete with this inheritance, in this little town that looks as if it's still stuck in the 1800s, and she comes over dressed to kill at three in the afternoon, and you're wondering what *I'm* up to?"

"What business is it of yours? Or are genies supposed to monitor their masters' love lives, too?"

It was on the tip of her tongue to tell him that love was not what Lynda had in mind, but then she'd have to address the master thing and her innate sense of self-preservation wouldn't allow her to go down that route.

161

"Look, Vana, do me a favor. Stay as far away from my love life as possible, okay?"

"Uh… sure."

Unfortunately, it was a little late for that.

***

Zane strode into the kitchen. Good God. Vana talking about his love life. She'd walked down those stairs, her bare legs playing hide-and-seek with the silky fabric, and his dick had gone straight to attention. Thank *God* she'd engaged Lynda in that little pissing match. It'd given him time to get himself under some semblance of control, but holy fuck, a guy could only take so much. Now she wanted to *talk* about it?

He'd known what Lynda was up to the moment he'd heard that singsong way she'd called his name. He'd been around the block with sports-team groupies for years. Had partaken a few times, but there'd never been even the slightest chance that those encounters would lead to anything.

Same deal now. Especially with Lynda being Gary's ex. That alone would put her on the Do Not Touch list, regardless of the fact that the crush he'd had on her had fizzled out the day Mom drove them out of town.

But Vana, on the other hand…

He glanced at the cuckoo clock and opened the fridge. Too bad it was still two hours until five. Although that didn't matter anyway since he hadn't brought beer for this trip—which was turning out to have been a really bad decision. But then, he hadn't exactly counted on meeting *her*.

Swiping the orange-juice carton over his forehead, Zane willed the chill to cool his heated blood. He didn't understand it; he knew what Vana was, and he still couldn't get over this attraction he felt toward her. He'd think the fact that she wasn't a mortal would wipe it away, but apparently hormones only responded to sexy.

And, God, was she sexy. She'd sashayed down those stairs, her hips swaying, her breasts bouncing, her fingers trailing lightly along the banister, and all Zane could imagine was them trailing over him. Her breasts sliding against his chest, her long, toned legs wrapped around his waist… his shoulders…

He closed his eyes, almost feeling the sensations. But like a whisper in a dream, they were just beyond reality.

The tightness in his groin, however, wasn't.

He chugged the OJ, then tossed the carton into the trash can on his way out the back door. A cold shower was out of the question with her and that dress between him and the bathroom, and rather than flinging her over his shoulder and going all caveman on her to ease this frustrated ache, Zane opted to head out the back door. Nothing killed a good dose of lust like a ton of grunt work, and the outside had it in spades.

And if he could keep his mind on the actual work and not what other activities he'd rather consider grunt work, the afternoon could turn out for the better.

***

Well, that hadn't gone over so well.

Gee, you think? Vana set the box of dishes on the back of the sofa and kissed her red dress into the closet inside her bottle upstairs. No sense in letting a perfectly good outfit go to waste in the spectrasphere. After all, she'd been trying to conjure that exact Ungaro creation when Zane had shown up there.

Why *had* Zane shown up inside her bottle? She had yet to figure that out. She'd never heard of any mortal doing that—though, she had *kinda* missed out on some genie-training essentials.

Judi Fennell

Vana adjusted her lavender T-shirt to lay flat over the matching shorts and pulled her hair into a ponytail. The children were bound to be rowdy when she freed them from the box after spending so much time cooped up.

"So now what? You want to go after him?" Merlin, wings outstretched, coasted around Vana with a bit of a breeze on his second pass around the parlor.

"No." She opened the box lid, the muted blue-and-green leaf china pattern belying the energy vibrating from the eight children. She'd hated to magick them from the study during the party, but they'd known better than to be out and about when Peter had guests. She was going to have to talk to them about that.

"You sure you want to unleash them?" Merlin poked his beak into the box. "You do remember why they're like that, don't you?"

"Hush, Merlin. They think you're serious." She removed Anthony.

Merlin's feathers changed color to the black-and-white-striped pattern of a referee's shirt. "I am."

She flicked his beak away from the children. "No one's asking you to stay."

"Good. Have fun with that. I'm outta here." He left in a flash of flames that looked like little tongues sticking out at her.

She shook her head. Merlin always said he didn't like children, but he obviously liked *acting* like one.

She took out Hannah, then Dahlia. Eloise was next. Each one ruffled their fluted edges and Vana could almost hear them inhaling the fresh air, which, of course, wasn't metabolically possible, but it was the closest approximation for what they couldn't do in their altered state.

Colin practically leapt out of the box by himself, but then, he'd always been the most exuberant. He was the one who'd broken Lady Lockshaven's china, though none of them ever reminded him of that. He hadn't done it on

164

purpose, and if there was one thing Vana totally got, it was the feeling of utter dejection when you did something you hadn't wanted or planned to do. Especially if it turned out wrong.

Francesca was next; then Benjamin and Gregory, the twins, rounded out the set.

"Hello, everyone." Vana brushed a hand across the line of them along the back of the sofa—everyone liked human contact. Even if they were no longer human.

Their fluted edges rippled against her skin.

"No, I'm sorry. I can't turn you back yet. But I'm working on it. I promise." She wished genies could make their own wishes come true because she'd gladly give up her magic if only to be able to do this one thing. But that wasn't an option. The only thing genies could give up their magic for was love. And thinking about Zane in that capacity was out of the question.

"Come along, everyone." She summoned her flying *kilim*, and the dishes slid on. "Let's get something to eat. Wait until you try the new flavors of ice cream that have come along in the last century!"

Luckily, the gods, Karma, and probably even The Fates were on her side for the next hour. Nothing untoward happened while the children glided in puddles of peppermint, toffee, mint chocolate chip, butter pecan, strawberry, and rootbeer ice cream she'd flawlessly conjured across the table, countertops, and floors looking like exactly what they were: children at play.

It was one of the most perfect afternoons Vana could remember.

Which meant that it was bound to go wrong.

Chapter 22

Zane kicked the brambles from his legs, cursing both the pain of torn flesh and the disasters of the afternoon. First Lynda, then the hurt look he'd put on Vana's face, and now the wind-chime debacle.

The first round of grunt work hadn't even taken the edge off his frustration, so he'd gone searching for the bewitched chimes.

They'd had been easy enough to find, but convincing them to relinquish their place on the shepherd's crook in the middle of a bramble garden had been another thing entirely. Mother Nature, Father Time, and the chimes that Zane now swore were demons (or at the very least, those imps Merlin had described) had conspired to slash his skin to the point where he'd probably shed more of his blood in the muddy earth than he had left in his body. But in the end, he'd persevered and gotten the chimes out of the so-called garden.

That he also had had to remove the shepherd's crook that'd been cemented into the ground was just an added workout bonus.

Zane propped the heavy chunk of concrete with the crook sticking out of it against the back-porch roof support, but there was no way he was leaving the chimes out here unattended. Amid the brambles, they'd swung out of his reach every time he'd tried to grab them, aiming for his head on the backswing so many times that he'd ended up using a stick to twirl the leather straps they hung from around each other so they didn't knock him out. They'd struggled the entire walk back but hadn't managed to get untangled or do any more damage. Well, much. Every so often one of them would get a good enough swing going that it'd smack its metal end into the back of his hand, and son of a bitch, that had hurt.

Grabbing the chimes, Zane pulled a pocket knife from his shorts and flicked the blade out to slice the leather from the crook.

The chimes shrank back in his hand as if he were some sort of ax murderer.

He exhaled. He'd had enough of magical beings today. He raised his hand to slice through the straps and—

"Zane, no!" Vana came flying out the kitchen door (only figuratively, thank God) and would have tackled him if he hadn't caught her, dropping the knife and the chimes in a discordant jumble against the side of the house in doing so.

"Oh Zane, you can't," she said, breathlessly, as she smacked against his chest.

Oh yes he could.

Wait. What was she talking about?

He closed his eyes for a second. She was still there when he opened them. Still plastered against him, his arms still wrapped around her tight little body, her lips right there for the taking.

Time stood still for the space of three heartbeats. He knew because he counted them tolling in his head like a bell.

"I… that is…" She braced her arms against his chest, then looked into his eyes, her silvery ones darkening.

He knew what that meant. Somehow he knew her passion when he saw it. Maybe it was because he was feeling it himself. And, hell, she couldn't fail to know he was feeling it, too, not with her abdomen where it was.

Apparently, wrestling with bewitched garden accessories hadn't dampened his frustration as much as he'd thought. One touch. That's all it'd taken, and he was wound up tighter than the chimes.

"I... I didn't want you to hurt them." She made a movement to slip down his body and Zane let her, if only to torture himself.

"*Hurt* them?"

Vana tucked some hair behind her ear and took a step backward. "The chimes. You can't cut their straps. Those are literally their life lines."

"I don't understand." So many things.

"The chimes need to be attached to the shepherd's crook to be able to make music. If they're not, they turn into inanimate objects."

Of course they did. "Vana, I *want* them to be inanimate objects. I can't have people seeing them like this." He waved his hand their way and the chimes shrank back as if he was going to strangle them—which actually wouldn't be a bad option if she wouldn't let him cut the straps.

"Look, Vana, just do something with them so they won't be a danger to me or the sale of this house." He picked up the knife and shoved it into his pocket, then raked a hand through his hair. A couple small bumps had sprouted where the chimes had hit. "I need a beer. I'm going into town. "

"Can I come with you?"

Her words stopped him mid-step onto the porch. He spun around, the word "no" on the tip of his tongue, but she stood there, looking utterly delectable and utterly hopeful, and well, it was that kitten-kicking thing again.

He was insane to even consider it. But then, given what he'd learned in the past twenty-four hours, insanity was the natural progression. "Fine, but remember: no funny business. I don't need any more stories to add to the rumor mill."

She cocked her head, and her lips puckered up in a sexy way he was sure she hadn't intended but that looked sexy as hell nonetheless.

"I'm not trying to be funny, Zane." Her eyes flashed with specks of steel as she crossed her arms. "And it's very insulting for you to say so. I haven't done anything wrong on purpose, you know. Haven't you ever tried to do something that didn't turn out the way you'd hoped?"

"Yeah, the entire last twenty-four hours."

Her arms fell by her sides, and the flash in her eyes fizzled out. Shit. Apparently he hadn't finished kicking kittens.

Zane took a deep breath, acknowledged the futility of trying to turn her down, then held out his hand. "You're right and I'm sorry. Sure, come with me."

"Can the children come? They're so longing to get out."

That's what worried him. "Vana, I don't know—"

"Oh, please, Zane. I promise they won't be any trouble. It's just that they've been cooped up so long and they've never ridden in a car. They'll love it. And just think of how good the fresh air will be for them. I promise you they won't be any trouble."

Famous last words.

But when she smiled at him like that, so full of hope and happiness, he just couldn't say no to her.

He just hoped he didn't come to regret it.

***

Gary checked the balance in Marshall's college account. Both sets of grandparents had been more than generous to their only grandchild; there was enough there to put a serious offer on Zane's house. But how long would it be before Lynda noticed the money missing?

If he got the genie out of this, that wouldn't matter.

A genie. Zane had a fucking genie. No wonder the guy seemed to live a charmed life; he actually did. The son of a bitch.

Well, the jig was up. Gary ripped the withdrawal slip from the back of the checkbook and shoved it into his pocket. That fund had been set up to secure Marshall's future; no one could argue that having a genie wouldn't do that.

Not that he was going to tell them. Oh, no. This— she—would be his little secret. And so was this money. After all, once the genie was his, she could make the paper trail disappear.

Make Zane and Lynda disappear, too.

Chapter 23

Zane regretted his decision the minute they'd pulled onto the main road.

Vana had introduced him to the children—and the fact that they fluttered their edges like sea anemones, the pattern and direction changing like some sort of Morse code that Vana understood, freaked him out no end.

She'd introduced him to each one, and he had no idea how she could tell them apart. Well, except for the one with the chip missing. Anthony? Or was it Benjamin? Zane couldn't—and didn't want to—remember, because as long as the children and the armoire and the phoenix and Vana existed, his life would never be the same.

They'd made it to the first stop sign before the dishes proved beyond a shadow of a doubt that they were children: power plays to see who could be in the middle of the back window, who could sit on the front dashboard, who got to sit on Vana's lap, who tried to climb onto his arms and drive the car—that one was Colin. Children were children, no matter what their form, but unfortunately they couldn't use seat belts in this one.

"Vana, they need to go back in their box. It's too dangerous for me to drive with them jumping all over the car. If they were"—he'd almost said "normal," but, really, what could be more normal than a bunch of kids bouncing around the backseat?—"That is, if they want to go for a ride, they have to behave themselves or I'll have no option but to put them away."

It was almost comical how they responded with military precision, and it spoke to the premium they placed on being out of the box, as all eight of them lined up across the back window and didn't move one rippled edge for the rest of the ride into town.

But when they got there, Zane decided he didn't want to take any chances because all he needed was one round of "he's touching me" or "she's looking at me" and the insanity would be right there in his back window for the entire town to see. So, foregoing the desire to hang out in a bar, Zane grabbed a couple of six-packs to go.

It turned out to be a good decision because he'd no sooner gotten back into the car when something—not a dish—popped up in the backseat.

"Hey, guys!"

"Damn it, Merlin. What the hell are you doing here?" Zane yanked his seatbelt on and looked in the rearview mirror. The dishes hadn't moved, thank God. "Anyone could see you."

"They wouldn't know what they were looking at."

"Until some scientists got hold of you and took you apart feather by feather." Bright orange feather by cherry red feather. "Is that really what you want?"

"Plucking? Really?" The bird shuddered. "Barbaric."

"Why are you here, Merlin?"

The bird shuddered again—and started molting red and orange all over the backseat. Frickin' perfect.

"You've got company. And if you think *I* scared you, you're going to be totally freaked out when we get back to your place."

"Hell." Zane's stomach twisted as he tried to remember if he'd left anything magical lying around.

Just a set of dishes in his backseat...

He should have gotten a case of beer. A keg, even. All for himself. He had a feeling he was going to need it.

"Oh, yeah." Merlin shook his head—and a slew of beaded braids whipped around his head like a lasso. "It's a real party back there. A couple, their real-estate agent, and a pair of hot tamales. Quite a scene going on, and not in a good way."

Fifteen minutes later, Zane pulled the car into his drive to find people everywhere: the front lawn, the porch, heading toward his car...

"I thought you said there were only five people here." Zane gritted his teeth as he had to slow down to drive through the news vans stationed along his driveway.

"There were when I left," Merlin mumbled from beneath the seat where Zane had banished him.

Cameras surrounded the car when Zane parked it. "Vana, put the children in the box while I do the talking. Merlin, you stay here until it's safe for you to leave."

"No arguments there," said Merlin. "Any chance you want to leave the AC on?"

"That'd look a little funny, wouldn't it?" Zane turned off the car and undid his seat belt.

"Wait until you see what I look like after fifteen minutes in this heat. That *won't* be so funny."

"I'll leave the window open enough for you to get out. Give me five minutes to get everyone away from the car."

"Leave me a beer and you can have ten."

"Forget it." That was all he needed: a drunk, Liberace-wannabe mythical bird meeting the press. He'd never be able to show his face in any locker room anywhere ever again. And while he might not be thrilled to be playing backup, it beat not playing at all.

Zane put his hand on the door handle. "Okay, here we go. Wish me luck."

Vana stopped him with a mere touch of her hand.

She blew him out of the water with a kiss on the cheek.

"Luck," she whispered as she climbed out of the car, but "luck" was not the four-letter L word he was feeling.

***

Vana wasn't sure if she'd actually managed to conjure some luck for Zane or if The Fates were on her side (they must not have gotten a report on her time travel escapades yet), but it took only five minutes to get rid of the real-estate agent and her clients, and another ten to field the reporters' questions.

But unfortunately, it took a half hour and two beers for Zane to wrestle his temper under control after they'd opened the door to find Eirik, Henry, and Lucia plastered against it, eavesdropping. Vana had had to round them all up and march them into Peter's study to help ease Zane's ire. Then she made herself scarce as well, heading out to the front porch to paint the spindles she hadn't gotten to earlier, using a brush to paint them the mortal way because there was only so much magic Zane could be expected to take in one day and his quota was pretty much filled.

Which was why when Merlin showed up—his feathers now looking like a bad '70s lime-green shag rug— Vana asked him to leave.

"You can't be serious," he said. "You want me to leave you sitting out here all alone doing manual labor? Oh, and by the by? There's a reason it's called that. You should get him out here to do it. That way you could kill two gremlins with one stone: get the porch painted and get your hooks into him. You're going to have to put a little effort into it if you want him, Van. No one's going to drop him in your lap."

"I told you, Merlin. I don't want him. I can't."

"Yeah, that's what Juliet Capulet said."

174

"And look how well that turned out."

"Oh. Good point." Merlin sniffed the paint can. "But seriously, Van. I can't leave. Who's going to be your voice of reason if I do?" He stuck his beak into the paint and came up sputtering. "Blech! What is this stuff? I thought it was a batch of piña coladas."

"It's paint, Merlin." She slid the can away and held up a drop cloth while he shook his head, sending paint spatters everywhere. "And now you really do need to leave."

"Not without you."

She sighed and finished painting the spindle. "Give it a rest, Merlin. I'm not going anywhere. I can't."

"Because you're the only one who can paint the porch?"

"No. Because Zane needs me to stay."

"Really." Merlin swiped his feathers across a row of spindles so that they ended up looking like barber poles. "The only reason a mortal would need a genie is to have his wishes granted. How many has he asked of you? Besides fixing the legs you broke, I mean."

Ouch. Vana dipped her brush in the can and took her time wiping the excess paint off. It didn't matter that Zane hadn't done the typical thousand-and-one wishes most new masters spouted off. He needed her to stay, and so did Peter.

"See? You don't even have an argument. You say you don't want him, so that must mean you're staying for you and a dead guy. Seriously, Van, I think you might have conked yourself on the head getting out of your bottle."

"I didn't ask for your opinion, Merlin. Besides, it's my life."

"Exactly. It *is* your life. And you're just hanging out here wasting it. What'll you do if he just ups and asks you to leave, hmmm? All this time wasted. And he doesn't even *know* about last night. When he does…" The bird whistled. "He's gonna *order* you out of the house."

"No, he won't."

Merlin flung his wings again. "What—find out about last night or ask you to leave?"

"Both." She grabbed the phoenix's beak and clamped it shut. "You're getting paint on the floor." She was *not* having a life discussion with Merlin. Merlin had zillions of lives, being reborn whenever he upped and flamed himself into a pile of ash, and while hers was an immortal one, it was the only one she had. He couldn't relate. "And you're not going to tell him, either."

Merlin shook his head until his beak was free. "Oh, don't worry. I was done interfering in mortals' lives with the whole Arthur-Guinevere-Lancelot debacle. Learned my lesson on that one."

"Good." She started painting the next spindle. Four down, seventy-six to go.

"But that doesn't mean I can't advise you on yours."

And she thought The Fates were on her side? They were probably laughing their collective patooties off on Mount Damavand right now that she was held captive by a determined phoenix. Why didn't he just poof himself up in a ball of flame and go bug someone else?

"Just because you're immortal, Van, doesn't mean every day isn't precious. It is. And you need to remember that, instead of hanging out here hoping for some—I don't know… romance, maybe?—from Studly in there instead of focusing on your magic and freeing the children and everyone else. Isn't that what you say you've been trying to do for a hundred years?"

She threw her brush at the bird. And didn't care that it left a two-inch-wide streak on not only his back, but the porch, too. "Merlin, you know nothing about it. I *am* trying to free them, but it's not as easy as you or my parents or my sister or half the djinn world think it is. These are *children*. Flesh and blood. Who are only immortal because of the enchantment. I can't go magicking them back until I'm

176

absolutely certain I can do it. Otherwise I could end up killing them. And whether you understand this or not, I *owe* Peter. I caused him enough trouble, and this is my chance to fix it. So don't go thinking you know anything about me or my life until you've lived in my bottle for a while."

Merlin held up his white-tipped wings. "Hey, don't shoot the messenger. I'm just here to give you food for thought."

"I don't need another conscience. The one I have is enough. And it's telling me I need to stay not only for Peter and the children, but also for Zane. He doesn't know it, but he's searching for something.

"Uh, sweetie? I don't think so. If he were searching for something, he wouldn't be selling the place."

"That's exactly *why* I have to stay, Merlin. Zane thinks he wants to get rid of this house, but there's something here he needs. Peter used to tell me what it'd been like for him growing up without any security, any place he could call his own. Zane has financial security and a condo, but his father died years ago and, more recently, his mother. That's it for him. All he has in the world. Oh, he talks about his teammates being his family, but his job is up in the air, and players get traded or injured all the time. Coaches move to different teams. Owners sell their franchises. Nothing's stable. Zane doesn't have a grounding spot. A home base. This place could be that for him."

"But what if he doesn't see that?"

"Then I have to show him. It's the least I can do for all the pain I caused Peter, pain that has trickled down to Zane."

"Huh?"

"If I hadn't screwed up and gotten the townspeople talking, Zane wouldn't have gone through what he'd gone through and—"

"But he also wouldn't have turned out to be the man he is today. Do you think he'd want to be any different?"

Vana shrugged. "We'll never know. What happened is in the past and can't be changed."

Well, okay, it could, but if The Fates weren't yet on her case, undoing the last twenty years of Zane's life would have them out in full force. With two Time alterations already under her belt, she'd be doing more than tempting them; she'd be in full *bring-it-on* mode, and one shouldn't do that if one didn't want her own Life Thread snipped. "I'm doing this for future generations."

"Okay. Fine. Whatever. Sounds like a plan." Merlin hopped onto the edge of the paint can. "I guess you don't need me since you've got it all under control. I'll see ya around."

With a flap of his wings, Merlin took off—and flung zillions of tiny paint droplets everywhere: the porch floor, the railing, the steps, the spindles, even the siding on the house. Great. One more mess she had to fix.

Vana sighed and stepped off the porch to survey the damage. Besides paint being everywhere, the shutters were lopsided, two chimneys needed repointing, a section of fence had been knocked out of whack by a falling tree limb, and the overgrown shrubs had been trampled by the earlier mob of people.

This place would take forever to fix up. And while that could be a good thing to keep Zane here, she didn't want him to see the house as an obligation. A time-sucking money pit. He'd definitely want to get rid of it then.

She fiddled with her fingers. She could try to fix this…

She looked in the front window. Zane wasn't in the parlor anymore. He wouldn't have to know—*if* she got it right. If she didn't… Well, that was *not* an option.

Closing her eyes, she conjured up the memory of their first kiss. The taste, the feel, the intensity, the way her magic had flowed through her like a fine symphony. Then she puckered up and gave it a whirl—

Only to open her eyes and see the porch spinning around the house like a merry-go-round.

Chapter 24

Zane was just about to step onto the porch when a paint can went sailing by.

Then the old rocking chair his mother used to sit in during the evenings.

Then a drop cloth. Two spindles that had rotted out and fallen onto the porch. Several old newspapers, an assortment of dead leaves, and a squirrel running in the opposite direction like a hamster on a wheel.

Zane now knew what that felt like.

And there was Vana, standing across from him on the other side of the spinning top, staring in horror.

He tried to keep a mirror image off his own face. The only way to fix this was for her to gain some control, and preventing her from panicking was the first step.

Zane grabbed the lintel above his head and leaned out over the whirling floorboards. "Something wrong?"

Her gaze shot to his. "You don't see it?"

He had to laugh. Either that or cry. "Oh I see it. It's the reason I haven't stepped out the door. Question is, what can you do about it?"

"Um, well..." Vana closed her eyes, clutched her fingers together in a death grip, and puckered up.

The image socked him in the gut and twisted his insides with desire.

He really did need to get laid if he was thinking with his dick at a time like this. Maybe he'd clear out tonight and head back to the city. See if Stephanie was still unattached, take her out for dinner, then a night of mutual pleasure. It'd worked for them in the past.

Yeah, and that was why he hadn't spoken to her in over six months, had no idea if she was seeing anyone, and had come up here on his own.

"Holy smokes!"

God, he hated that term.

He opened his eyes slowly. "What now?"

"Um, nothing."

The wide-eyed stare she had while looking up toward his roof didn't say *nothing* to him.

"What's up there, Vana?"

She didn't answer him because she'd closed her eyes again and puckered up. This time his libido was wise enough to shut up so his gut could churn with dread instead.

The squirrel lapped the front door again.

Vana opened one eye, which she slammed shut.

Then she puckered up again.

"Vana, please, no more." Zane was eyeing the width of the porch. If he started in the kitchen, he should be able to work up enough speed to jump it. If he didn't, he might break his leg on the landing. Again.

When Vana emitted another "holy smokes!" Zane was willing to take the risk. She'd already proved that she could heal his legs.

Of course, she'd already proved that she was good at breaking them, too.

Zane backed up into the kitchen, took a running start, yelled, "Don't move, Henry!" before he ran past the armoire, kicked off at the threshold, and managed to land on the top step with a huge crescendo.

Crescendo?

Zane ran down the stairs. Each one played a musical

note. It sounded like the opening of Beethoven's Fifth Symphony.

Vana's eyes flew open again and her mouth dropped. If she said "holy smokes" one more time, Zane didn't know what he'd do.

Another "holy" had just made it past her lips when he kissed her. Hell, it'd stopped her mixed-up magic before.

She gasped when their lips met, grasped his wrists when he held her face, and melted into him when he couldn't help but slip his tongue inside.

She felt so good. Tasted better. Fit against him perfectly and drove him half out of his mind when she tentatively flicked her tongue over his. Her fingernails curled into him as she kissed him back.

Something flew off the porch and smacked into the backs of his legs.

"Ow!" he muttered, yanking his mouth from hers.

"Oh, no. What'd I do now?"

She said it so forlornly that Zane immediately lost any anger he had. She hadn't done it on purpose. But why had she done it at all?

"Vana, why did you use magic? Didn't we discuss this?"

"Well, yes, but the mess… And it works when you kiss me, Zane. It even worked when I *remembered* you kissing me, so that's what I tried to do just now."

"Well, it's obviously not working now. You need to stop."

"I know, but what about… them?"

He didn't like the way she said that, really didn't like the way she stared at the roof, and pretty much dreaded turning around to find out why.

Gargoyles were dancing on his roof.

The slate roof tiles were disintegrating under their feet, the pieces sliding over the edge and crashing onto the metal porch roof below. Combined with the stairs, he had one hellacious symphony going on in his front yard.

And then a car pulled through the gate at the end of the drive.

"Quick! Get rid of them!" Zane spun around. Like his porch was still doing.

"And stop the porch! And the steps! For God's sakes, turn off the steps! And what about the gargoyles?" He should be doing something. Running around picking up far-flung paint cans or collecting the brushes—one was stuck in the bark of the oak tree's trunk—or chasing the gargoyles who—oh, God!—*jumped off the roof* and were now turning into Tasmanian devils all over the side lawn. Thank God for the overgrown rosebushes that shielded them from the driveway, but how long would that last? One whirling dervish on the front lawn, and this whole thing would turn into an even bigger circus.

"Vana!"

She hadn't moved. Except for her hands. She was wringing them as if she were trying to unscrew her fingers from her body.

And her lips. They were moving, forming a pucker—

He kissed her again. Anything he could do to boost her powers for good.

"Go for it, Vana," he whispered when he released her. "I know you can do this."

Her smile was like a beacon of light that would turn into a spotlight on this craziness if she didn't fix it *now*. The car had just rounded the last bend.

Zane sucked in a breath, his gaze darting between the approaching car and the gargoyles.

Then the car stopped.

"It's fixed," said Vana.

Two words. Such relief. Zane exhaled and glanced over his shoulder.

The gargoyles were gone, the roof was back in shape—better actually, because the gutters were no longer listing at the top—the porch had stopped moving, and the paint cans were back in place. She'd missed the paintbrush on the tree, but he could pull that off when she wasn't looking.

"The stairs?"

She nodded. "Muted."

"Thank God."

The car door slammed, ending further conversation.

Gary was back. Jesus. Didn't the guy ever learn?

"I know, I know," he said striding toward them, his hands in the air. "You don't want to hear what I have to say, but you have to listen to me, Zane."

"I don't have to do anything, Huss. You, however, have to get off my property."

"So here's the thing. What if it were my property?"

"What are you talking about?"

"Hear me out. I've given this a lot of thought and it makes perfect sense." Gary, the sleazy, smarmy politician was at work again. "I want to buy the place."

"In what universe?"

Vana sucked in a breath and looked at Zane sharply. Great. Did that mean there were other universes? He didn't want to know.

"Seriously, Zane. You want to sell; I want to buy. It's perfect. Just name the price."

Part of the reason Zane was an effective ballplayer was that he analyzed the play while it was in motion and came up with countermeasures when it didn't go well, but what the hell was he supposed to do with this bomb? *Name the price*? Since when did politicians make that kind of money?

Although… Gary was probably counting all the money he was going to make with those damn tours of his. Tours set up at the expense of the Harrison name.

"I'll have to think about it." The words surprised him as much as they did Gary.

"What's there to think about? I thought you couldn't

wait to get rid of it. I'm giving you the answer to your problem. I'm even prepared to give you a nonrefundable deposit right now." He waved a stack of hundreds in front of him.

The thing was, it wasn't just about the money. Sure, it'd be a nice chunk of change, but selling the house was about more than that, and Zane couldn't shake the feeling that Gary was up to his old tricks.

"Let me sleep on it, Gar."

Gary looked at Vana, who was having a hard time keeping the smile off her face. "Can't you get him to see how perfect this is?"

"Me?" Vana splayed a hand on her chest and gave up trying not to smile. "No, I don't think I can."

"I said I'll think about it, Gary. I haven't even considered what I'm asking for the house, but when I do, I'll let you know."

"You're not going to find anyone else around here who'll want it, Zane. Not with its reputation."

It was that reputation he was thinking about.

And wondering why he cared.

***

"Oh, Zane, I knew you couldn't sell the house! I just knew it!" Without thinking about it, Vana flung herself into Zane's arms the minute Gary's taillights disappeared around the first bend.

When his hands gripped her arms and held her where their faces were inches apart, she thought about it. She couldn't *not* think about it.

"Vana, I didn't say I'm not selling. I said I'd think about it."

"But he was giving you the perfect opportunity. If you'd wanted to sell it, you would have. There's something making you hang on to the place." She'd like to think it was something she'd done, but she knew better. If anything, what she'd done should have had him *giving* the house away.

She glanced over his shoulder, but the gargoyles were still waiting for her to find them since she was "it." A game of hide-and-seek was the only way she could keep them from running all over the place. Gargoyles loved parlor games.

"Vana." Zane scrubbed at the side of his face. "Let's table this discussion for now, okay? I just want to call it a day and go into town to get something to eat."

Tabling it was a good idea. It'd keep her here another day.

And another night.

Chapter 25

Gary waited for Zane's car to pass his hiding spot behind the Ertels' shed. Good, the genie was in there with him. Talk about perfect timing. That'd make this much easier.

When the taillights disappeared around the bend, Gary got out and ran to the trunk for the supplies he'd rounded up after his errands this afternoon. He'd set several wheels in motion in case Zane hadn't gone for his offer, but at least now he could put Marshall's money back. With any luck Lynda wouldn't find out. Nah, make that, with a genie Lynda wouldn't find out because the woman was like a hawk. He yanked the tarp over the car. Overkill probably because the Ertels' eyesight wasn't what it'd once been, but Gary didn't want to take any more chances than he already was.

He checked around the edge of the shed, slung his supply bag over his shoulder, and set off along the wooded path toward Zane's house. He'd prefer to do this in the dark of night, but they'd be home then and who knew how light a sleeper a genie was? Did genies even sleep?

Gary shrugged. He'd find out soon enough.

Carefully, he watched every step. That talking bird might be flying around, and if that was the case, the jig would be up. He clenched his fingers tighter around the mesh bag he'd bought to contain the bird.

All in all, though, it was ridiculously easy to get into the house. He should probably warn Zane about the dangers of leaving old screens in open windows, but… why?

He popped one out, climbed in, and *voilà*, instant access to unlimited power—

Holy shit! The idiot had left the thing right on the table. There, in tarnished brass, stood the oddly fluted thing that had to be the genie's bottle. Heh, Hollywood had gotten it wrong back in the '60s; the bottle wasn't glass, but brass.

Gary scooped it up and shoved it into the bag. Now on to find those journals because who knew what else Old Man Harrison had found and this was the perfect opportunity to snoop.

He was halfway to the kitchen when he stopped. Had that armoire moved?

Hell. He was imagining things.

He took another step, keeping a sharp eye on the furniture.

Nothing. Though… he thought he'd seen some movement out in the foyer.

He spun around quickly. Nothing but a coat rack and the vacuum cleaner, neither of which was so much as breathing.

Normally a comment like that would be ridiculous, but with a genie around, anything was possible.

Like the tackle from the… coat rack that dropped him to the floor.

Or maybe it was because the armoire *tripped* him.

Gary smacked his forehead on the floor and twisted, the bag with the genie bottle skittering away. But he had bigger problems: that coat rack could throw a punch. He was trying to dodge the wildly swinging arms, kicking it in what he hoped were its nuts, while he half crab-walked away from the armoire that was stomping across the floor like a giant.

This was Fucked Up.

So was the rug that started undulating beneath him.

Fighting with the fringe that was wrapping around his fingers, Gary scrambled out from beneath the psychotic hunk of wood, scooped the bag, yanked the genie bottle out, and brandished it in front of him. "Get back or I'll melt this. Then where will your genie be? Where will *you* be?"

Either they couldn't hear, or they didn't get the concept of smelting; they kept coming. And now the armoire's doors were flapping. That would hurt more than the spindly arms of the coat rack if it caught him, and, man, these guys could move.

And then something small, shiny, and metallic flew across the room, just missing his nose and clacking like a bad set of chattering teeth. What the fuck?

Gary headed toward the kitchen since the coat rack stood shoulder to shoulder (figuratively speaking) with the armoire, blocking his escape route.

And then he stumbled into the kitchen to find… dishes. Standing on their edges. Lined up like a field of linebackers—with their ruffled edges fluttering in the breeze. Except there was no breeze. And these were *dishes*. Inanimate objects.

Or were they?

Oh, ho; this was his lucky day. Enchanted dishes. Things he could easily transport. The genie would definitely want her magical, dancing dishware back. Women always liked this kind of stupid shit.

Then one of the dishes went whizzing by his head like a Frisbee. Followed by another—and another—forcing him toward the back door.

He was not leaving without one of them.

When another dish went sailing through the air toward him, Gary grabbed it. Its edges whirred around like a saw but luckily were too smooth to do any damage. He, however, could do a lot of damage to it.

He shoved the bag with the lantern under his arm and held the dish out in front of him with both hands. "One more step and I snap it in half."

Every inanimate animated object in the room stopped moving. The chattering-teeth thing stopped clacking. Thank God.

"That's it, big guy," he said to the armoire. "Back it up. Right into the living room where you belong. You, too, Ichabod." He could swear the coat rack shivered.

"You." He nodded at all the dishes who'd landed on the dish towel on the drainboard. "Wrap yourselves up in that towel. One layer each." He grabbed another towel from the cabinet knob and tossed it to those on the table. "The rest of you, too. Hurry up. One flex of my wrist and this guy's history if you don't."

The dishes drooped their edges as they worked themselves into a stack, each one divided by a layer of towel. He grabbed a pair of grocery bags and stuffed the bundles inside, tying the ends securely, then shoved them inside the box on the counter, just squeezing them in. Good. They wouldn't be able to move at all.

Then he shoved the box inside another couple of bags and tied each one tightly, trussing them up enough that they wouldn't be able to alert Zane or the genie while he got away. He'd like to take them all, but that would alert Zane immediately that someone knew his secret. Gary wanted some time to plan how to use this to his best advantage.

Now to see to the thugs in the living room.

He shoved the remaining dish into his supply bag with the bottle, picked up the package of dishes, then walked back into the living room.

The furniture was having a powwow, leaning against each other as if they were planning something.

"I'm not kidding, you two." He held up the box of

dishes. "Separate or I start breaking these one by one until you do."

He could almost feel the animosity emanating from them, but who the hell cared? He just needed some way to stop Zane from finding out what he'd been up to. Since kidnapping an armoire was out of the question, the next best thing would be to knock them out... Hmmm.

Before the coat rack had a chance to realize what he was going to do, Gary grabbed it and swung it at the top of the armoire with all his might. Luckily, the thing didn't break as it made contact, but he felt the reverberations all the way up his arms.

He also felt the coat rack go slack. And saw the armoire's door fall open.

Aha!

Gary grabbed the fishing line he'd packed and made quick work of tying their legs together in a crisscross pattern. He did the same thing with the armoire's door latches after shoving the box of dishes inside. That shit was stronger than twine and had the added benefit of being nearly invisible. Zane and the genie wouldn't be able to see the binding unless they were looking for it, buying him more time.

The rug was a little tougher, but a couple of thick nails from Zane's toolbox—ah, the irony—nailed it to the floor and some tape on the fringe kept it immobile. The little clacking compact, though easy to transport, was too vicious to risk it getting free in his home, so Gary taped it shut and stuffed it between the sofa cushions after it came at him one more time. Hopefully no one would find it for a long time.

Gary picked up his bag and saw the lone dish trying to escape. He gave it a nasty flick and it flinched. Good. It needed to know who was boss.

He made sure the bottle was still in there, smiling as he imagined the cash he'd have the genie zap all over him with his first wish. He'd wallow in it. Bathe in it. Sleep in it. And then he'd spend it. Every freaking dime, and have her conjure more. Gold the next time. Jewels. A Ferrari— no, a Bugatti. No. A Bugatti *and* a Ferrari. And a Porsche, too. Or three.

One quick glance around the room showed that everything looked the way it had before. He ran across the living room, climbed back out the window, put the screen in place, and hightailed it back to his car.

Like taking candy from a baby.

Chapter 26

In spite of everything, Vana was excited to head back into town to Watson's Diner. Peter had loaned the original owners money to get it started, and she hadn't been in since the ribbon cutting.

Surprisingly, the diner hadn't changed all that much. Well, the technology was different and the sepia photographs on the wall had faded, but the gingham décor and the smell of Catherine Watson's homemade pies were still the same.

The townspeople, however, had done a complete one-eighty from their predecessors.

Peter had been accustomed to stony silence, but the minute she and Zane took their seats in a booth by the window and ordered two sodas, the chatter started.

"You're Peter's great-grandson, aren't you?" asked an older gentleman who spun around on his stool at the counter to stare at them.

"Of course he is," the man's wife chided, spinning her stool around. "Who else is going to be living in that house?"

"Who else would *want* to," muttered the woman on the other side of the counter.

"I remember your parents," said another woman in the booth behind Vana. "I never understood why anyone cared about those old stories when your parents always did such nice things around town. Like the scholarship your mom created in your father's name. My son won it his senior year. It really helped with college. I guess she was just carrying on both families' legacies, huh?"

"She was," said Zane. "That scholarship was important to her. Thank you for telling me and congratulations to your son."

Vana cleared her throat after they'd opened their menus. "What did she mean by 'both families'?"

Zane exhaled and set the menu down as a teenaged waitress put their sodas on the table. After they'd given their orders he answered in a low voice, which, considering she was the only one in the place who didn't know what the woman was talking about, probably had nothing to do with being overheard.

"Civic duty. It's on both sides of my family, though Peter was way ahead of my mother's father on that front. Probably why the old guy busted a gut when Mom decided to marry into the Harrison family. He was a judge in the next county. Old school. You know the type: stern, disapproving, thought he was better than everyone else. Especially Peter Harrison's grandson. And because of that, I never saw my grandparents. Even after my father died, we didn't move in with them. Mom took me to a distant cousin in Philly. I was just happy to be away from all the gossip where no one knew anything about Peter or the stories. Thank God the Internet didn't exist in those days. I wouldn't have had the same anonymity if it had."

"Yet you chose a high-profile career."

"But it was *my* choice. Where *my* accomplishments earned me what I wanted. Where my drive and my talent and my ethics and my hard work allowed me to decide who I wanted to become. If I'd stayed here, I'd have been defined by everyone's opinion of who I should be. That's why I have to get rid of the place, Vana. It's not who I am anymore."

193

"But you don't have to sell it."

"Look, I appreciate how much you care, but let's change the subject. How about you tell me about you?"

"Me? I'm a genie. What more is there to know?"

"Well, for starters, do you have a family?"

She started choking. She never handled talking about her family well.

Zane thrust her soda into her hand, but, holy smokes, that fizz burned when it went the wrong way. She coughed it out. "Of course I have a family, Zane. Genies don't just spring from a fairy ring, you know."

Zane put up his hands. "Okay. I get it. Backing off."

Frankincense. Bad enough she kept sabotaging his house; she didn't need to bite his head off, too.

The waitress returned then with their meals, giving Vana another couple seconds to get herself under control *and* summon the shell she metaphorically plastered around her shoulders when dealing with anything having to do with her family. "Sorry, and, yes, I do have a family. My parents are somewhere in the world when not in Service to anyone—which is most of the time. They're probably rescuing a ram off the Matterhorn or retrieving a cow out of the Ganges as we speak."

"They're genies, too?"

"Of course. We're a race, not an occupation." Though her parents had treated djinn life as a vocation. Educated to the nth degree on every subject there was, her parents were experts in every field—and they'd expected the same from their daughters. DeeDee was on her way to fulfilling their wishes, but Vana? She might as well wish for Zane to fall in love with her because she had a better chance of pulling that off than living up to her parents' expectations.

Hmmm… apparently fairy tales weren't just for mortals.

"So genies can use magic for whatever they want?"

Her brain had gotten stuck on that little happily-ever-after scenario for a second, and she had to pry it back to their conversation. She picked up a French fry, then dropped it onto her plate and licked her fingers. Sucker was hot. They'd always been soggy and cold by the time they'd gone through the necessary channels to make it into her bottle.

"Technically, genies in The Service are only supposed to use magic for their masters' safety and comfort, unless they're high enough on the proverbial food chain that the rules don't apply. My parents are that high." And she never forgot it.

"What about your sister?"

"DeeDee?" Vana nodded. "She's that high, too. She's the complete opposite of me, even though we're twins. She's the perfect daughter who can conjure a flawless diamond on the head of a pin with the bat of an eyelash. Granted that *is* her Way of doing magic, but still. Her magic is as flawless as that diamond." Hers, on the other hand…

"Where are they now? Aren't they wondering where you've been for the past hundred years?"

Vana shrugged and shifted on her seat when the knot that always formed in her belly when she talked about her family started acting up. "They know where I am." The entire djinn world knew where she was. And why. "We Skype occasionally."

Very occasionally and only very recently. The iPad they'd given her for her birthday two years ago had made that possible—but it'd also brought on more "life lessons." And *should-do*s and *read-these* and *practice-this*…

She was tired of being treated like a child. Yes, she'd made a boneheaded decision when she was younger by jumping into the bottle before she was ready, but she'd figured it out in the interim. She shouldn't have to pay for that mistake forever, but even when she'd mentioned that she'd picked up DeeDee's *Djinnoire*, her parents hadn't been appeased. She'd hate to think what they'd say about the magic she'd been doing lately.

Unfortunately, she *knew* what they'd say, so she was keeping it to herself.

"Are you sure you don't want to visit your parents, Vana?"

Absolutely sure. "It's no big deal."

"You could go now. I don't have a problem with it." He bit into his hamburger. "Well, after we get home, obviously. I'm sure the health department would have something to say about pink smoke all over the diner."

He was trying to make her laugh, but she was getting hung up on the image of that word. *Home*. It conjured up images of hearth and home and snuggly big chairs and warm hugs and cookies baking in the kitchen—none of which she'd ever had. Mom and Dad's idea of home had been a mausoleum filled with sculpture and libraries and works of art. Marble and gold, cool and beautiful. Sterile. Just like her parents.

"Seriously, Vana, you should go see them. Once your family's gone, they're gone. You'll wish you could have spent more time with them."

His voice was soft and hoarse. He wasn't talking about *her* family.

"You miss yours, don't you?"

Zane cleared his throat. "Well, doing this, visiting the house and stirring up old memories... This place, in spite of everything, is where the three of us were a family. Dad taught me to throw a ball in the backyard. He cheered me on when I climbed to the top of the willow by the creek. Then Mom would yell at the two of us for risking my neck." His voice had gone soft again. "There were a lot of good memories."

Vana didn't have any memories like those. Her earliest ones were of books. Hundreds and hundreds of books. In every language imaginable. Now, there was nothing bad about books; but all that mandated reading and memorizing and studying... All she'd wanted to do was learn how to use her magic, but her parents had insisted upon learning the history and ways of the world before she was unleashed in it.

In retrospect, their idea had been valid. But not the execution of it, stifling to a little magical girl unsure of her powers and all that came with them, one who only wanted to test her abilities and find her limitations.

Well, she certainly had.

Just then a young boy walked up to their table with a piece of paper and pencil in his hand. "Mr. Harrison, can I have your autograph? You're my favorite player."

"Sure thing." Zane smiled at the boy, slid to the end of the booth, and took the pen and paper. "But call me Zane, okay? What's your name?"

"Tommy. I mean, Tom."

"Do you play ball, Tom?" Zane didn't sign the paper, instead focusing his attention on the boy.

"Yeah. Receiver, just like you. But I'm not as good."

"I wasn't good when I was your age. It took a lot of practice and hard work."

"I'm on three teams. One at school, one for infermertels, and one with my buddies. We play all the time."

Zane didn't even crack a smile at the child's mispronounced word; he talked to Tommy in the same serious tone that Tommy used. A real man-to-man football discussion.

"It sounds like you have the practice thing down. Good job. But you know what else you have to do? You have to keep your grades up so that they'll let you keep playing in school."

"I do. I got all As on my report card last time."

Zane clasped him on the shoulder. "Hey, that's great. If you keep that up and pay attention to what your coach tells you, you'll have a good shot at playing for a long time."

"I want to play pro like you. My dad, he told me he

used to be in school with you, and you didn't even play back then."

A flicker of something crossed Zane's face, but he quickly masked it as he set the paper on the table. "That's right. I didn't start until I was thirteen. How old are you?"

"I'll be eleven next week."

"Well, see? You're starting even younger than I did. And if I can do it, you can, too." He quickly wrote something on the paper. "Here you go, Tom. Good luck. I hope you get to play pro ball someday."

Tommy looked at the paper, his lips moving as he read it. Then he smiled from ear to ear. "Thanks, Mr. Harrison, I mean, Zane! You're the best!" He took two half-skips, then stopped and turned around. He walked back and stuck out his hand. "And good luck to you, too, next season. I hope this time you get to win the Super Bowl."

Zane shook his hand but didn't respond for a few seconds. Then he cleared his throat and nodded. "Thanks, Tom. Me, too."

They remained like that for a few seconds, Zane with an expression on his face that Vana couldn't quite figure out, before Tommy ran back to his family, waving Zane's signature as if it were a winning lottery ticket.

Zane watched him go, then nodded an acknowledgment to Tommy's father.

"You really love it," Vana said when he slid back to the middle-of-the-bench seat.

He cleared his throat again. "I do. All of it. The fans, training camp, off-season workouts, the camaraderie, the rivalry, and, of course, the actual game itself. I love it all. And I'm good at it. Like I told Tommy, I was a late bloomer, but I worked my tail off and earned a scholarship that paid for college. I worked even harder there and was lucky enough to get a shot at the pros. Football is my life. The team, the coaching staff, even our competitors; they've all become family to me. It'll kill me to leave it."

198

And again he brought up family. For all his not wanting to be part of Peter's, he obviously wanted one.

So then why…? "You're planning to leave football?"

His fiddled with his own fry. "Planning to? Hell, no. Facing the possibility? Yeah."

She covered one of his hands with hers. "But why, if you love it so much?"

"They've got me on second team. I'll see some playing time, but not like I'm used to. And for all that I'll still be playing, it won't be on my terms." He went on to talk about injuries and age and up-and-comers and stats and a bunch of other things she didn't fully understand about the game, but beneath it all, she heard the sadness.

"What else will you do if you don't play?"

"There's always network commentating."

"That's good, right?"

He laughed, but there was no amusement in it. "Let's just say that sports reporting is where players go to die. Where we fool ourselves into thinking we still have something to contribute to the game, but, in reality, we're merely reliving our glory days. Trying to keep the illusion going that we're still what we once were." He folded her fingers into her palm and enveloped her fist in his, his thumb tapping her wrist, his smile bittersweet. "The truth is, ex-jocks are a dime a dozen, and we can be replaced in the booth as easily as we can on the field. This latest contract offer has proved that loud and clear."

If he could only hear himself. He was looking to belong. To be valued. But he was looking in the wrong place. Like she and Merlin had talked about, coaches left, owners sold teams, things changed. If Zane wanted somewhere to belong, all he had to do was look across the table.

Vana fell back against the padded vinyl behind her, pulling her hand from his.

Oh, gods, it was true. He *did* only have to look at her

because she wanted to fill that hole in his heart. She wanted to belong to him and wanted him to belong to her and not in a genie-master relationship. She wanted to be his home and his family and that part of himself he was missing. She wanted to love him.

No, she *did* love him.

Zane sat back then, too, and went on to talk about other options: coaching, agenting, teaching. Vana tried to pay attention and comment, but her mind was reeling.

Gods, she *couldn't* love him. What about getting her magic right and making her parents proud? About proving that she wasn't the screw-up they thought she was?

She barely knew him.

No, that wasn't true. Time didn't matter; she knew what was inside his heart. Knew his hopes and dreams and fears. Heard the loneliness in his soul and the lingering pain of Gary's childhood taunts. She saw the beauty of the person he was inside: his compassion for Fatima, the children, and the rest of them; knew the way he'd handled her magical mistakes without berating or blaming or belittling her; witnessed the kindness with which he'd spoken to Tommy; heard the loving way he spoke of his parents.

And she'd experienced firsthand the way he'd made her feel.

No one had ever made Vana feel like he had, and she wasn't talking about the sex. She'd been alive for over eight hundred years; she'd had sex with plenty of people. Good sex. Hot sex. But none of it had been like last night. No one's kisses had ever spread through her with such sweet warmth and light, as if the sun were dawning each time they touched. No look from anyone else had ever made her feel as if she were the only person in the room. No simple touch had ever made her want to stay in that one spot for all eternity so she'd never lose the moment.

She'd never felt this need to be there for anyone. To

be something more than a genie granting a wish for her master. All her life, ever since she'd found herself mistakenly locked up in that bottle, that was all she'd wanted to do.

But now, Zane wasn't her master and she still wanted to give him everything. Make everything right for him. She wanted to conjure up the contract he wanted and kiss away the painful memories of his childhood. She wanted to give him that family he wanted, that sense of belonging. She wanted to be the one to care about him for more than just the next play or season.

"Vana? Are you all right?"

She had absolutely no idea.

"Um, sure." She tucked her hair behind her ears, then picked up her fork and fiddled with it. She wanted to look at him, but couldn't. It would only take one word from him, one question, and the words would spill from her lips.

And that could never happen. If it did, she'd fail to master her magic, and that was *exactly* what everyone expected of her. And even if, by some cosmic miracle, she knew he'd say *I love you, too*, she couldn't give up her magic and prove everyone right.

"Is there anything more I can get you?" Their waitress showed up with perfect timing.

Vana shook her head while Zane asked for the check.

"I was thinking, Vana," he said as if her world hadn't been turned upside down, "when we get back, how about building a campfire? My dad and I used to do that. It was fun. What do you think?"

On one hand, she needed no further temptation around him and shouldn't take him up on his invitation, but on the other, after that trip down memory lane, maybe he didn't exactly want to be alone. And on the other, *third* hand that she didn't have but was going to count anyway because this reason would strengthen her overall argument, *she* didn't want to be alone either.

"It sounds great. It's been a long time since I've done that. One of my previous masters was interested in ancient Egypt and we used to go on expeditions. We did a lot of camping at the base of the pyramids."

"Let me guess. He wanted you to find treasure for him?"

"Sir John? Oh, no. You didn't know him. The only thing he wanted from me was to tell him about what the olden days were like. Unfortunately I wasn't around during the time of the pharaohs, so it wasn't much." And she'd been afraid to try to find out. Conjuring misbehaving gargoyles was one thing; animating a mummy was something else entirely. Those things scared her.

"You weren't around during the time of the pharaohs." Zane shook his head. "Man, sometimes I forget what you are."

She wasn't a *what*. But the fact that he saw her that way put her in her place as quickly and firmly as Peter had by locking her in her bottle all those years ago.

"Vana. About earlier. When I kissed you." Zane leaned in and lowered his voice. "I don't want you to get the wrong idea."

Oh gods, her face zoomed to overheated faster than she could say "holy smokes." "Wrong idea?"

"I wasn't coming on to you."

"Of course you weren't." Because she was a *what* to him.

She'd always been a *what* to everyone: an untrained, capricious child to be managed; a sister to be protected; a rotten student in the shadow of her genius sister. A genie to make everyone's wishes come true. She'd been Vana the misfit child. Vana the behavior problem. Vana the incompetent. Never just Vana. Loved and wanted for who she was, instead of put up with for *what* she was.

"It's just that you said that your magic works better when we kiss, and I needed the house to stop spinning—"

"Only the porch was spinning." That was a very important detail to her; she'd managed to maintain some element of control amid the chaos. In years past, the whole thing would have gone up into a tornadic funnel cloud, so she was making progress and she was all about celebrating the victories. However small.

"Right. Okay. The porch. The point is, I had to get it to stop somehow, and that was the fastest and easiest way I could think of."

So she was fast and easy. Her parents would be so proud.

She couldn't even manage to fall in love right.

"I understand, Zane." And she did. She didn't necessarily like it, but she understood.

She also hurt like hell. The only reason he thought he'd kiss her was to turn off bad magic.

The image of him sliding his tongue down her torso and dipping into her navel last night poked its naughty head out from the dim recesses of her mind. He hadn't been trying to turn anything *off* with that move.

But maybe tampering with Time had altered what he'd felt for her. It certainly was feasible; anything was feasible with her magic, or lack thereof.

Hmmm, maybe she should tell him how she felt. She'd say those words, lose her magic, and end the madness once and for all.

But there was Peter. And DeeDee. The children. She didn't want to let any of them down. And Merlin would never let *her* live it down.

"So you're okay with this?" Zane asked. "Everything's okay between us?"

No, she'd keep her thoughts and her feelings to herself. She'd had a lot of practice doing that. "Of course it is. We're fine."

And *they* were. *She*, on the other hand… She'd get over it.

203

Judi Fennell

So she tucked her emotions into a safe, little cushioned box in her brain as she'd done every time she'd let someone down, pasted on a smile, and grabbed some Happy from somewhere in her soul. After all, she'd won a little bit of the battle by getting him to put a stay of execution on selling the house, even if only for a few hours.

Like she'd said, she was all about celebrating victories, no matter how small.

Now all she had to do was convince her heart to get over him.

Chapter 27

Vana stood on the top of the hill that overlooked the creek bed, with the smell of crackling wood from Zane's fire filling the air. She wrapped her arms around her waist and stood there, drinking in the perfection of the moment before darkness stretched over the sky. It'd been so very long since she'd experienced a sunset outside of her bottle, and the changing of day into night held its own kind of magic.

"A penny for your thoughts." Zane said from behind her. "Or maybe I should offer a dollar. Inflation, you know."

She glanced at him when he stood next to her, inches yet worlds away. Yet still her heart fluttered. She needed to get it to stop doing that.

She wrapped her arms tighter around her waist. "I was just thinking of how perfect this moment is. These last few seconds before the sun slips away. Where the sun and the moon are both visible on different ends of the spectrum. Yin and yang. Night and day. For this one moment they're equal, just in a different place."

The metaphor for her relationship with Zane wasn't lost on her.

No, there was no relationship. He wasn't her master

and he couldn't be her lover. As for anything more, well, that wasn't in the stars either.

Venus, the first star of the evening, winked at her. It figured that the goddess of love would think that was a play on words.

Vana took a deep breath, the cleansing sort. What-ifs and could-bes were for mortals with genies, not the other way around. "The fire's wonderful, Zane."

"I can make one mean fire. Eat your heart out, Merlin."

She smiled at his joke, but really, the joke was on him. Or maybe it was on *her* because he certainly could make a fire—in her. Like now, with that smile.

Vana tried to look away.

She did.

But the moment changed.

She didn't know how or why. It was nothing she did. Nothing *he* did, but it subtly slid into something more, and time stood still with no help from her.

She saw it then in his eyes. The memory of last night was just beyond his consciousness, but he was looking at her as if he did remember. As if he wanted to remember.

As if he wanted her.

He couldn't. They couldn't. *She* couldn't. She couldn't go through wanting him again. It was too much. Too deep. Too... something.

"I think there are some marshmallows in the kitchen." She interlocked her fingers behind her back, out of temptation's way, and took a step back. And another. "I was going to make an ambrosia salad tomorrow. We can use them now instead. I haven't had toasted marshmallows in a while. Have you? Oh, and you should probably find some long sticks so we don't get burned." She was babbling, which was odd. Usually, she kept her mouth shut in awkward situations—mainly because most were her fault and mortification made her clam up.

A basket of clams appeared beside the fire.

Great.

"Vana."

"I'll be right back, Zane. Just stay here and I'll get them. I think we have chocolate and graham crackers, too. I'll bring them out."

She couldn't get away from him fast enough, practically tripping over her feet to get into the house.

Zane grimaced. What had he expected after telling her that kiss hadn't meant anything? He was an ass. No woman liked to hear that.

Especially when it wasn't true.

He walked back to the fire, finding a pair of sticks just right for toasting marshmallows, then grabbed a bigger one to move the logs around with. Sparks crackled upward as the fire danced from log to log, the flames as restless as he was.

Today had been... He didn't know the word to explain what today had been. Enlightening, maybe. In a lot of ways.

He hadn't known about his great-grandfather's childhood. Hadn't realized exactly what this house had meant to the man. But there were *people* in his furniture. He still couldn't get over that. And phoenixes. And magic. He kept coming back to the magic.

He kept coming back to Vana.

It was a good thing she'd ended that moment back there. She was a complication he didn't need. He'd always been able to block out whatever he'd needed to keep focus on training camp, the game, whatever. But no matter that he kept telling himself to forget Vana, he'd been aware of her every second of the day.

Maybe he ought to take it to the next level. Apologize for that asinine comment and own up to wanting her so he could get her out of his system.

A log hissed and sparks popped onto the grass. Zane stamped them out, the symbolism in putting out a fire making him shake his head.

His indecision made him shake it again. Since when had he ever had to second-guess how he acted around a woman? Since coming here, that's when. Since meeting Vana.

No, if he were honest, he'd been second-guessing himself since the moment he'd come out of surgery after he'd taken that hit. Football had shaped who he'd become; being part of the team defined him. Now he was no longer a superstar, but an aging player whose failing body was forcing him to be second best. Who the hell was he supposed to be if he was no longer the player he'd worked so hard to be?

The screen door slammed shut and Vana walked toward him with her arms full, looking utterly gorgeous in the fading light. As before, his body went on instant alert.

"Vana," he said, dropping the marshmallows sticks on the table, then walking over to help her. "I heard Merlin asking you earlier why you won't leave, and you said you couldn't." He took the chocolate and the graham-cracker boxes, and his fingers brushed hers, making him swallow as his nerve endings roared to life. "You can, you know. I won't hold you to whatever rules you're supposed to follow as a genie. As your master, I can do that, right?"

She snatched her fingers back as if she'd burned them, and her smile became strained.

What the hell had he said wrong now?

"Isn't it lucky that I'd planned to make pies so we'd have all of this?" She walked to the other side of the table, dodging both him and his question.

What was it she'd said about equal but on different sides?

He wasn't so sure about the equal part. For all that her magical ability wasn't reliable, Vana knew exactly who she was and didn't make excuses for it. She owned up to her shortcomings and tried to make the best of them. He admired that about her.

"Vana—"

"I think all the strenuous exercise of the last two days caught up to Henry and Eirik and everyone. They're all sound asleep in there. The children even put themselves to bed somewhere."

Good. He didn't need prying eyes tonight.

"Vana—"

She stopped ripping open the bag of marshmallows and looked up at him from beneath her lashes. "Yes?"

Zane forgot what he was going to say. He could swear she'd looked at him like that before. He'd swear that he knew the softness of those lashes fluttering against him. Knew the feel of her cheek, the sound of whispered longing at the back of her throat, the softness of her curves pressing against him, the slide of her skin on his.

He blinked and the image faded. He was imagining things. *Fantasizing* things. Things he had no business fantasizing but didn't ever want to stop.

Flames hissed and flickered, sending the fire's bluish smoke wafting between them, making her seem... Otherworldly. Ethereal. Magical.

"Vana, how come I never knew you existed?"

She finished ripping the bag and dumped the marshmallows into a bowl. "I've been in my bottle, and since Peter never passed down that information, there's no reason you could have."

"No, not you specifically. You as in genies. And magic. And Merlin."

"Oh. Well, genies aren't meant to be known to anyone but their masters," she said, opening a bar of chocolate. "Can you imagine if everyone knew about us? Your race would never have accomplished anything. They'd always be in pursuit of a genie for themselves." She picked up the two sticks he'd found and stuck a marshmallow on each.

"Most people like to keep us hidden. Have us at their beck and call for wish granting. Not everyone is like you, Zane, asking very little of me. On average, mortals rattle off 53.2 wishes within the first half hour of meeting their genie. Most for money and power. Several for revenge. A bunch of greater-good ones that we, unfortunately, can't grant, and then there are the random ones unique to each person. Part of the thrill of having a genie is knowing what others don't."

Zane set down the package of crackers he'd opened. "So what about you? Do genies ever have their wishes granted?"

"Us? No. That's not how the system works."

"Yeah, I can see why. Why have someone else grant it when you can?"

She handed him a stick. "Actually, we can't fulfill our own wishes."

He headed to the fire with her. "So what would you wish for if you could? What's the one thing you'd love to have more than everything else?"

She held her marshmallow over the flames so long, Zane wasn't sure she'd heard the question.

But then he heard her answer. Whispered, as if she didn't plan for him to.

"Competency."

The marshmallow hissed when it hit the log as Vana dropped the stick into the fire and clamped her hands over her mouth. She blinked at him with those big gray eyes that sparkled silver and gold in the firelight.

Sparkled with tears…

Zane set his stick down on the rocks ringing the fire pit and tugged her fingers from her lips. "Don't, Vana. Don't cry. You're competent. More than you realize. And you deserve a hell of a lot more than that for your wish. You are who you are, and there's absolutely nothing wrong with you."

Fat lot he knew. But Vana blinked back the stupid tears anyway. Gods, how could she have blurted out her deepest desire—and her deepest embarrassment?

And then Zane had to compound her misery with his utterly sweet reply.

She'd done the absolute best thing last night in turning back the clock because, with those few sentences, he'd crept further into her heart. If there was even the slightest chance that he remembered what they'd done, she had no doubt they'd be doing it again right now. The moment was ripe for it; the emotion, the attraction, and, for that one sliver of humanity and understanding he'd just given her, she might be willing to utter those three words she so wanted to say.

But he didn't. And she couldn't.

"Are you okay?" Zane asked, his fingers still holding hers.

She nodded, her composure having flown off somewhere.

"Good. I'll get you another marshmallow. I hate eating s'mores alone." His smile took away some of the tension, and by the time they'd finished making the snacks, the rest of it was gone.

And then Merlin showed up.

"Hey, kids, how's it shakin'?" asked the phoenix, proceeding to do just that, flinging feathers—striped zebra ones—all over the place. "Hey, s'mores! Cool! Love me some of those. Anyone up for toasting one for me?"

Zane swung a flaming marshmallow toward him. "Is there a reason for this visit, or are you just always around to annoy?"

"Sheesh. What rotten apple did you eat today? Snow White's stepmother hasn't been by, has she? They swore she wouldn't be able to get out of the new nursing home, but I wouldn't put anything by that old broad. She's only gotten craftier in her insanity." He snapped the marshmallow off the stick.

211

"Speaking of insanity." Zane twirled the stick above Merlin's head. "How much longer are we going to be graced with your presence? And your feathers?"

"Chill, will ya, big guy? I got some news you're going to want to hear."

Zane glared at Merlin but put the stick down. "What is it?"

"Seems like your buddy Gar is planning a surprise for you."

"What kind of a surprise?"

"Sheesh, let me tell it my way, already."

"I don't have time for all the grandstanding, bird. Just get to the point."

Merlin sighed loud and long and put-out. "Fine. You really are a killjoy, aren't you?" He looked at Vana. "Just like his great-grandfather, ain't he?"

Zane like Peter? Aside from the color of their eyes, they couldn't be more different.

"Anyhow, here's the Cliffs Notes version. Your buddy Gar has been meeting with the city inspector's office, trying to slip this house out from under you any way he can. Eminent domain, getting it condemned, running title searches and probably even your credit history for all I know. He's calling in all sorts of favors. Seems the guy's kept a checklist since high school and a lot of people are in his pockets."

"Son of a bitch."

"Yeah, well, you'd *think* his mother would be if she birthed him, wouldn't you? But, poor thing, she's a mouse of a woman. Her husband on the other hand... Gary is definitely a chip off the old blockhead."

"He's not going to get away with this."

"Actually, I think he kinda might. Question is, which head honcho is going to cave first? For such a sleepy place there sure is a lot of cheatin' and snortin' and embezzlement going on around here. And your man, Gar, knows about it all."

Zane swiped a hand through his hair. "What the hell am I supposed to do now?"

"You might want to take him up on his offer to buy you out. After all, he did say you could name your price."

"No!" Zane answered at the same time she did. Vana didn't care that they did so for different reasons; it was the first time they'd agreed about something having to do with the house.

Merlin held up his wings. "Hey, don't shoot the messenger. I'm just telling you what I know. It's up to you two to figure out what you're going to do, but I'd suggest you come up with something quick because if I know Gary—and unfortunately I do—that guy is going to have more than a couple of tricks up his sleeve."

Chapter 28

Zane had spread drop cloths on the floor and moved the furniture to the center of the room by the time she'd materialized from her bottle the next morning. He was already rolling primer onto the second wall.

The first one was almost back to pink.

He dropped the roller with a curse when he saw her. "Vana, please. Can you fix this?"

She linked her fingers and took a deep breath. She was going to miss that color. It was the same color as her gemstone. Bright and happy, and it had always made her smile. "I can try." She puckered up.

"Wait."

She stopped mid-pucker. "What?"

"What'll happen if, you know… it doesn't work?"

She lost the pucker. Nothing like instilling confidence. "I don't know."

"Do you think, that is… should I kiss you?"

After the night she'd spent last night? Aching and lonely and frustrated? Vana shook her head. Forget what his kiss would do to her magic; she had to think about what it'd do to *her*. "No, this should be fairly straightforward."

He didn't look convinced.

Truth was, she wasn't either. But what was the worst that would happen? The gargoyles would turn to stone?

Speaking of which, she should probably look for them at some point. They could stand as still as statues—*duh*—but she didn't want anyone accidentally bumping into them. Both the gargoyles and their finders would get the shock of their lives.

She blew out a breath and put that on her mental to-do list. Then she closed her eyes, puckered up, and kissed the air.

The walls were still pink.

Zane was looking out the window. "Well, the good news is that the porch isn't moving."

In any other household, that sentence would make no sense.

"Okay. Fine." She flung her arms to her sides. "You can kiss me."

That was her, team player. Taking one for the team.

Liar extraordinaire.

Zane took a step toward her. Hesitant. As if he didn't quite know what to make of her—a far cry from how he'd looked at her two nights ago.

Yep, she must have really changed the way he felt about her during that last time travel. She was going to have to check the chapter again to see if DeeDee had mentioned that side effect.

"I'm not going to turn you into a toad or anything, Zane. Only fairy princesses can do that, and we're all agreed that a fairy princess is one thing I'm definitely not." No, she spent her time cooped up in a bottle while those chicks flounced around castles and gardens with handsome princes and unicorns and fairy godmothers. She, lucky lady that she was, got Merlin, the sarcastic firecracker.

"I seriously do not want to know about any of that," Zane said, closing the gap between them to mere inches so their toes were touching. Until his breath was warm on her cheek and her breasts were barely grazing his chest. Close

215

enough that she could feel each breath he took—each shallow, shaky breath—yet far enough away for her to ache with wanting to be pressed against him.

She tilted her head back. She couldn't help herself. Her mind might be shying away from this, but her body was one hundred percent on board.

She watched his lips descend until he was so close she had to close her eyes or go cross-eyed.

And then he kissed her.

Soft, gentle, the kiss still reached deep down into her soul and tugged every bit of love out of it, drawing it through her veins and up around her heart, tying it up in one big bow before passing through her lips into his, giving him every bit of what was inside of her.

She was in so much trouble.

His lips lingered a few more seconds. Just long enough to make her knees wobble.

"Go ahead, Vana," he whispered against her lips. "Work your magic."

He'd certainly worked his. She could feel it, the quicksilver tumbling and flowing through her, carrying all her magic with it.

She puckered up, kissed the air, then opened her eyes.

The walls were sunshine yellow.

"Wow," Zane whispered, and it was absolutely the best word for what had just happened.

He gripped her arms a bit tighter and smiled into her eyes. "You did great, Vana."

She could only smile back while she searched for her breath.

"Now what about the rest of the house?"

"What?" That kiss must have rattled her brain. Or his.

"The rest of the house. With your magic working, you can fix it up now. Floorboards, paint, trim, the appliances, any cracked windows. Everything."

"But I thought you didn't want to use magic."

"That was before Gary got involved. I need you to do a general 'make the whole house perfect' spell because I'm not giving him any ammunition to condemn this house. I've been thinking about it all night."

Pity, she'd been thinking of something completely different. "I told you, Zane. I don't do spells."

He waved his hands. "Incantation, mumbo-jumbo, whatever it is that you do."

Whatever it is that you do. As if it were the easiest thing in the world to do magic. Aside from the gods who could do it without thought, magic required concentration. Knowledge and know-how and an inherent ability she didn't have.

Vana tamped down the utter dejection that thought brought, focused on what he wanted, and kissed the air.

Nothing. No quicksilver, no magic, no feeling.

"Well?" Zane's smile was hopeful.

Hers... not so much. "I can't."

Now his faded, too. "What? Sure you can. You just blow a kiss and..."

She shook her head. "It's not working again."

"Oh."

Yeah. *Oh.*

"I should kiss you again, shouldn't I?"

No, he *shouldn't* kiss her again. She wanted him to *want to* kiss her again. To need to. Not do it for the end result. The best part about a kiss was the journey.

Vana almost stamped her foot in frustration, but the poor guy wasn't responsible for her stupid heart and feelings. "I think... well, it'd probably be a good idea."

He nodded as if it were his solemn duty, while she stood where she was, bracing for his touch. She closed her eyes and got lost in his kiss all over again.

Zane held her away from him. Only inches, but each one was killing him. He wanted to wrap his arms around her and pull her against him and do a hell of a lot more than kiss her.

217

But he wouldn't. It'd taken every ounce of control to stop the last kiss, and somehow he needed to summon that control again to keep this one from getting out of hand.

But, man, he did not want to.

Her lips trembled beneath his and her breasts quivered against his chest, so softly he might have imagined it, but the tightness in his shorts argued that he hadn't.

What was his argument for not wanting to do this again? Oh, right. Magic. Genie. Opposite sides of the house issue. A complication he didn't need. Life throwing him enough curves.

But it'd also thrown him *her* curves and he wanted them plastered against him, filling his hands, wrapped around him as if there were no tomorrow.

He slid his arms around her shoulders; he couldn't *not* hold her.

Her chin dipped slightly, and her lips parted. He couldn't *not* slip his tongue inside.

And then she moaned softly, and he couldn't *not* deepen the kiss. Couldn't *not* slide one hand down her back, tracing all the curves. Couldn't not twine his fingers in her hair and tug her head back just a little more, open her mouth a little wider, taste her a little deeper.

Her fingertips brushed his rib cage, and Zane couldn't not crush her to him.

And then all bets were off. The kiss turned hot and sexy and steamy as all hell.

He fanned her hair around them as her breasts tightened and swelled against his chest. His cock did the same thing against her abdomen, as his knees tightened when hers wobbled. He took her weight in his hands—yes, holding her by the ass, but it fit so damn perfectly he just had to.

She shifted just a bit, and there, sweet Jesus, her hand slid beneath his shirt, the warmth of her palm searing his back like a branding iron. He wanted to take off every stitch of his clothing and hers and lay her down on the drop cloth and pound into her to the rhythm of the blood pounding through his ears.

Wait.

That wasn't blood.

Someone was knocking on the front door.

"Yoo-hoo! Hello? Anyone home?"

Vana stopped moving in his arms. Truly a sacrilege.

The door rattled again. "Hello?"

Vana pulled back, her eyes wide, her cheeks flushed. Her lips swollen and wet.

He couldn't not kiss them again.

"Mr. Harrison, it's Mrs. Ertel."

He couldn't not pretend the woman wasn't there. He pulled his lips from Vana's—reluctantly—and held on to her until he was sure she could stand. And that he could.

"She's not going to go away," he muttered.

Vana nodded.

He brushed a strand of hair from her bottom lip. "I'll see how quickly I can get rid of her."

He left her there. Felt her watching him walk out of the room. Tasted her all the way down three flights of steps to the front door—which he might have yanked open a bit too hard because Mrs. Ertel gasped. Or maybe she gasped because—

Zane looked down. No, his shirt was still buttoned and his cock was behaving itself better than his manners were.

He pasted a smile on his face. "Hello, Mrs. Ertel."

The woman recovered and held up a basket. "I wanted to welcome you home so I thought I'd stop by with my homemade cherry pie."

"Thank you. That's very nice of you. I appreciate you and Mr. Ertel looking after the place. I'll handle it now that I'm here."

"Well, I, that is, we, Mr. Ertel and I, we were wondering if you're planning to move back in because, you see, we've gotten used to our cable television and the

219

money you've paid us has helped out with that, and, well, if you're going to be taking care of things from now on, we'll just have to find another way to pay for it. I do love those real housewives, you know. Such entertainment."

Zane had no clue what she was talking about. He couldn't imagine a show about housewives being all that entertaining, but then he wasn't Mrs. Ertel. But he realized he hadn't thought how selling the house would affect her. Her husband had had an accident and was on disability. They obviously counted on the money he paid them.

"I'm not sure what my plans are at the moment, Mrs. Ertel. But don't worry. This month's check will still be coming. Next month's, too." And at least six more after that. Maybe a year. It wasn't as if it'd break him. Even playing second string.

"Aren't you a sweet boy! I told Jack you'd say that." She patted his arm. "Well, I best be going and let you get back to whatever you were doing."

Yeah, he wanted to get back to what he'd been doing, too.

"Oh, by the way." Halfway to the porch steps, she turned back with a finger against her bottom lip, a pose he remembered really well from his days of dodging the gossipmongers.

"Is there a reason, I mean, that is, do you know there's pink smoke coming from your chimney?"

Zane wanted to congratulate himself for not altering one iota of the smile on his face. "Yes, I am aware of that."

"Oh." Her finger curled into her hand and she laughed an insincere, inquisitive laugh. "It's just that I've never seen pink smoke before."

"It's a new way of cleaning out a chimney," he deadpanned.

"Ah." She nodded, her mouth twitching as if it wanted to disbelieve him but wasn't sure she should. "Well, then, I'll be going. I hope you and your lady friend enjoy the pie."

Lady friend. A term that could mean a whole host of things, and he wasn't about to clarify any of them for her. "We will. Thank you, Mrs. Ertel."

He stood in the doorway, watching her walk all the way down the path and get into her car. The woman was too curious for his own good. He didn't need her waltzing back in here on the pretext of wanting to ask him something else just to satisfy her curiosity.

He waved good-bye as she drove away and watched her make all three bends in his driveway, then closed the door, set the pie on top of an unusually quiet Henry, and ran up the steps to the bedroom.

"That was June Ertel," he explained when he walked back in to find Vana by the window. "I've been paying her and her husband to look after the house."

Vana nodded. "I recognized her voice. They come over every Saturday. She stays in the kitchen while he checks the rest of the house. He repaired the window in the attic once when a storm had sent a branch through it. I'd hoped he'd find the box I was in and open it, but that never happened."

"It must have been lonely in there, huh?"

She shrugged. "Part of the job."

The job. Genie. Right.

"So, um, how'd your magic work while I was downstairs?"

"I didn't do anything. I didn't want to risk something happening while she was here."

"Ah."

"Yes."

They were dancing around the kiss as if it'd never happened. As if it weren't hanging in the air between them, charging every look, every word, every breath with meaning. But it had and it was.

And, Zane wanted it to happen again.

"So any chance you want to try it now?"

"It?"

221

Crap. He was never like this around women. Uncertain. Unsure. Especially ones who were as into kissing him as much as Vana had been.

He walked over to her and stopped himself just shy of pulling her into his arms. He was sending her mixed signals again. "Vana, I know last night I said I wasn't coming on to you."

She walked around him and picked up a paintbrush. "I know. And you also said no more kissing and no more magic." She pointed the brush at him. "What's it going to be, Zane? I'm a genie, not a ping-pong ball."

He had to smile. He liked women who wouldn't take shit from him or anyone else. And he really liked Vana.

"I'm an ass, okay?"

"What?"

He'd surprised her. Good. Always good for a relationship.

Wait. They weren't having a relationship. A few kisses did not make a relationship. Hell, a few turns in bed didn't make a relationship. He'd been clear about that with every woman he'd slept with. Somehow, though, he had a feeling Vana would be different.

He brushed a hand over his face. "I'm an ass, Vana. You turn me on. I can't deny it. But this isn't the right time in my life to explore it."

She put her fists on her hips. "You were doing more than exploring a few minutes ago."

He liked that she wasn't letting him off the hook. Uncomfortable as hell, but he respected it. "I know. And I'd apologize, but I'm not sorry. You're gorgeous, you turn me on, and if the only way to make your magic work right is to kiss you, I'm man enough admit I'll do it."

"Is that supposed to be an apology?"

"Um… yeah?" He pulled out his charming smile.

"Seriously? You're going to kiss me because I'm here, I'm hot, and you have a convenient excuse? Pardon me while I swoon."

Okay, so the charming smile didn't work. He'd go for just charming. "I was paying you a compliment."

She raised her eyebrows. "Really? No wonder you're still single."

"Hey, I'm single because I've chosen to be single. There are a bunch of women who want to marry me."

"Good. So go kiss them and get them to fix up your house."

"I just might."

"Good."

"Good."

They glared at each other from opposite sides of the room.

He scrubbed his face again. He needed a shave. "I'm sorry. You're right. That was a lame apology. And I *am* sorry. For the lame apology and for sending you mixed signals and for acting like an ass." He held out his hand. "Please accept my apology?"

She glanced at his hand, nibbling her bottom lip. Besides fidgeting with her fingers, she also nibbled her lip when she was nervous. And thank God for it. He didn't like being the only one nervous here.

"All right. Apology accepted." She put her hand in his. The one with the paintbrush.

That had wet paint in it.

He laughed, glad he had a reason to not tug her the rest of the way into his arms and break the truce. "So, about your magic… Can we start this over? For the good of the house?"

She rolled her eyes and blew out a breath, but there was a hint of a smile beneath it. "The good of the house? Okay, whatever you say." She tugged her hand back (leaving the paintbrush), puckered up, looked at him one more time, and blew a kiss.

And the bottom fell out of his world—or rather, out of the bedroom.

Chapter 29

Vana waved away the plaster and dust, coughing to clear her lungs as she tried to figure out what had gone wrong this time.

"Vana! Are you okay?" Zane moved a chunk of floor—or maybe that was the ceiling of the room below them—off her calf and helped her stand.

She flexed her toes. Nothing broken, thank the stars. "I'm fine. Well, I would be if I could figure out what happened. I swear I was trying to fix everything." And now she had even more to fix. Gods, what was *wrong* with her? Even the most simple of things...

"Maybe it was too much at once."

"Come on, Zane. This is pitiful. It's not like you asked me to repaint the Sistine Chapel."

Vana clamped a hand over her mouth. Please gods, let her not have just destroyed that masterpiece.

"It's all right, Vana. We can fix this. The key is not to get discouraged."

She shoved her hands onto her hips. Leave it to a mortal to lessen the magnitude of an epic fail in magical ability. "Oh it is, is it? Do you *not* see this? Looks pretty discouraging to me."

"No, it looks pretty powerful to me."

Way to rub salt in the wound. "Powerfully destructive."

"So let's make it *con*structive."

"Huh?"

"Vana, look at all the power inside of you. Do you see those rafters?" He pointed to the exposed beams that looked like a giant had gnawed through them. "See how thick they are? Your magic has to be really strong to be able to do that. We just have to figure out how to reverse it."

"But how? And why? That's what I don't get. I've studied and practiced every chapter in DeeDee's *Djinnoire* for years. Centuries. I should be able to handle my magic. Do you know I once tried to make alfalfa sprout up during a drought to feed a starving town? Guess what happened. It rained falafel instead. Tiny balls of chickpeas bouncing around like manna from heaven. Luckily, that's what they all thought it was, but come on—falafel? *Falafel*? I just don't get it. I should be able to fix the paint and the floor and everything else without you having to kiss me. And now I can't manage to do it even when you do."

"But Vana, you *did* do it right."

She didn't bother responding. What was with Mr. Sunshine all of a sudden?

He raised her hand and intertwined their fingers, palm to palm. "You did, Vana. I asked if we could start over and then you blew that kiss. You were starting this—the room—over. From its beginning." He pointed at the rafters. "Just as I'd asked."

"What are you? A Dr. Phil wannabe? Mr. Life Coach?" He could take his brand of happy and peddle it elsewhere. She'd lived through this ignominy for centuries.

He arched an eyebrow at her. "Think about it."

Drat. She couldn't argue with someone who didn't want to argue. "You're stretching it."

"There's only one way to find out."

"And that is?"

He tugged on her hand.

She stumbled into him and, just like that, found herself where she really wanted to be.

Judi Fennell

"I'll kiss you again," he said, saying the words she really wanted to hear. "We'll make it right."

She really wished they could.

This kiss was tender. Soft. Gentle. Every bit as pervasive as the other one, and this time, the magic swirled through her again, bubbling up from the depths of her soul and spreading to every part of her. She opened her eyes to see if it was shining from her pores, so bright did it make her feel, but all she saw was Zane watching her.

The kiss turned erotic in an instant.

But an instant was all she allowed it to last.

She wrenched herself away and kissed the air, wishing to make everything right.

In the next instant they were back in the bedroom on the third floor with the floor beneath them—

Holy smokes, they were in bed.

Together.

"What the hell?" Zane jumped out of the bed. Thank the gods he was fully clothed. But his shorts did nothing to hide the effect their kiss had had on him. "*What* did you wish for?"

Vana scrambled out of the other side, flinging sheets—oh, gods, pink satin ones!—and pillows off. One hit him in the chest. "Not this! I wasn't thinking about this!"

"You weren't?" He sounded disappointed and hugged the pillow to him. "Wow. Talk about opposite sides. That was definitely what I was thinking about."

"You were?"

"Uh." He cocked an eyebrow. "I told you I was an ass."

She threw the other pillow at him. "You are."

"At least I'm an honest ass." He tossed a pillow back at her.

"What?"

"Admit it. You *were* thinking about this." He waved a hand over the bed. "I dare you to say otherwise."

226

Vana rolled her eyes. "Fine. Okay. I was thinking about it. But I wasn't wishing it. That's the truth."

"*Could* you wish it?"

"What? Do you mean could I wish you into mak—going to bed with me?" Now there was an interesting question. If he were really her master, then no, she couldn't because genies couldn't do anything to their masters without their express wish. But he wasn't her master, so theoretically, it should be possible. Whether it was ethical was another story. But then, she'd pretty much rewritten the ethics about sleeping with mortal non-masters, hadn't she? "You're saying that's the only way you would?"

Cocky gave way to flirty. And sexy. He leaned a hand against the footboard and cocked his hip. "Hell, no." Then he got serious. "But it might get complicated."

It was already complicated. And, really, this was for the best.

She'd remind herself of that in a thousand years. "You're right. It's not a good idea." She so lied.

"Good. Then we're agreed."

She glanced at his hand on the footboard. Time to get this temptation out of here. "Yes."

"Okay." He didn't move.

"Uh, Zane?" She waved her hand for him to move away from the bed, mentally pleading with him to move. Begging him because her resolve was only so strong.

It took him a few seconds, but then he stood up and stepped back. "Oh. Right."

And that, as they say, was that. Over. Done. All that was left was to get rid of the bed.

She tried to muster a smile—or at least keep the frown from her face—and pucker up. Somehow she managed it.

"There." She brushed her hands together. "That's done. And so is the room. Time to move on to the next one."

"It's another bedroom." He waggled his eyebrows.

She couldn't not smile at him. "You're right," she laughed, walking past him. "You *are* an ass."

Judi Fennell

"And I'm told I have a pretty nice one, too."

Cocky and flirty and funny and sexy. If she hadn't been in trouble before, she definitely was now.

***

Gary removed the dish and the bottle from his safe. He'd hated running out this morning, but getting the money back into Marshall's account before Lynda noticed had been tantamount. Now he could focus on getting the genie so that wouldn't be an issue.

But no matter how many times he'd rubbed this damn bottle last night, the genie had refused to make an appearance.

He tried rubbing it again.

Nothing. What the fuck could be preventing her from coming out—

Oh, hell. Zane. It was always Zane. First in school with teachers and parents and girls all loving the kid. Hello? Did they forget who his great-grandfather was?

Then there was his own father. Probably *the* biggest offender. Always putting Zane on a pedestal as a testament to what you could overcome with hard work and perseverance.

Not to mention, a genie. God, what Gary wouldn't give to drop that bomb in dear ol' Dad's disapproving lap.

Instead, he dropped the bottle back in the safe. Then he picked up the dish and pulled the duct tape off it.

The thing didn't even flinch.

"Come on, move." He shook it.

Nothing here either. Not even a wrinkle of those curly edges that'd been flapping like a bird last night as it'd flown across the room at him.

"I know you're in there. I know what you can do. You can't fool me. I was in that kitchen." He squeezed—and still nothing. Son of a bitch.

228

He tossed it back into the safe, too, smiling when it clinked against the bottle. He hoped that hurt. "Fine. Be that way. We'll see if you're so stubborn after being locked in my safe for days on end. No sunlight at all. And you'll never see your friends again." Unless he could trade it to the genie for her services.

Maybe even the ones Zane was probably enjoying…

Chapter 30

The house was completely restored to the way Peter had had it built and decorated, down to the last tassel on the furniture, and Vana had even added modern conveniences like air conditioning and a dishwasher. Even the old iron oven looked brand new.

She'd thought about trying to change the children and everyone back, starting with Eirik since his magic would, hopefully, mitigate any issues her magic might whip up. Unfortunately, a whip showed up on her first attempt, which didn't bode well for anyone. Plus Eirik, like Henry—like all of them, come to think about it—was still sound asleep.

"Zane, do you think we should wake everyone up?" she whispered as she peeked into the front parlor from the kitchen.

"Why would you want to do that? Let's enjoy the quiet."

"I don't know. Something just doesn't feel right."

"It's called freedom, Vana." He grabbed her hand. "Come on. Let's go outside. We still have work to do out there."

She glanced back once more, but when he tugged her hand, she went willingly.

As if that was ever in question.

"Okay, Zane, but we're going to have to pace ourselves. Mrs. Ertel will have a cow if anything happens like this." She snapped her fingers.

They both did a double take when a cow mooed in the doorway.

"Holy smokes!"

Zane, amazingly, laughed. "I guess it could be worse."

She'd like to know how because her magic being on the fritz again was pretty bad (as were most Fritzes—an angry family of gnomes she'd known once).

She looked around, praying she wouldn't see any of them while Zane grabbed the cow's halter and led it toward the back door. "Come on, Vana. Let's take Bessie outside before she wakes everyone up, and we can get to work."

"Do you think fixing up the outside is really going to help? You heard Merlin. Gary's gunning for you."

"Then I'll just have to outgun him, won't I?"

"How?"

"I'll think of something. Don't forget; I play offense, and the best defense is a good offense."

But this wasn't a game. She hoped he knew what he was doing.

When he led her to the shed in the backyard and handed her keys to something mechanical, she knew he didn't.

"Keys?" she asked, taking them as if they were coated in venom. "What for?"

"The riding lawnmower."

"A riding lawnmower. As in, something with blades? Sharp blades?"

"Good." He tied Bessie to a tree, then backed the mechanical monstrosity onto the grass. "I wasn't sure if you knew what one was. I didn't realize these had been invented when you were out of your bottle last."

"Not ones that needed keys." She took two steps back

231

from the vehicle, still dangling the keys as if they were dead mice. Actually, she'd rather they be mice. Mice, she didn't mind. Mechanical things with deadly attachments, however... "Just what do you expect me to do with the lawnmower?"

"Mow the lawn?"

"Funny." She enclosed the keys in her fist and held it out to him. "Seriously, Zane. I don't mow lawns."

"You also didn't do magic well, but you overcame that."

"That is so not a fair argument."

"You know that's an oxymoron, right?"

She'd tell him who the moron was... "Did you, or did you not, just experience the entire second floor of your house caving in? And that was without spinning blades."

He shook out a floppy hat and plopped it onto her head. "First of all, it was only the one room. Second, you fixed it. Third, we can't cut the grass by magic. I don't trust Mrs. Ertel not to come back because the woman is dying for something to gossip about."

Vana flicked the brim out of her eyes. It didn't stay there. "I thought her husband was supposed to do this?"

"Do you want him riding around with gargoyles on the loose?"

Frankincense. He had a point. "I could magic them back to the fence posts."

"Don't you have to find them first?"

Double *frankincense.* She blew out a breath that sent the hat brim flipping back on itself, gathered her hair, and fashioned it into one long braid down her back. "Fine. How does this work?"

Surprisingly, it wasn't all that hard once Zane showed her. And without magic, too. She had a feeling it was easier to work *because* of no magic, but she didn't want to test the theory.

Pretty smart of him, giving her something semi-dangerous that could blow into full-on lethal if she tried to get out of it the supposedly easy, magical way.

And she was actually enjoying herself. Zane was fixing things like the basement door, a crooked gate post, and the rotted floorboard on the back porch, but she was just riding around in pretty patterns on the grass and enjoying the birds darting around her as they swooped in to pick off whatever insects the cut grass gave up.

The weeping willows offered shade when the sun got too hot, and she stopped by the honeysuckle vines growing in profusion over the gate at the back of the yard to sip their nectar. Many years ago, Peter had run a carriage service in town and put the horses out to pasture on the land behind the fence when they were too old to work anymore. She'd have to let Zane know. It would be a nicer spot for Bessie than that tree she was tied to.

She caught a glimpse of two of the gargoyles. One was imitating the willows; he'd gathered some of the fallen branches and draped them over his flat head, which was pretty inventive for a gargoyle. He must be higher on the evolutionary scale than others she'd dealt with in the past, but his buddy? Not so much. That one was huddled by the creek, trying to pass for a stone. It might have worked if he hadn't kept flicking his tail.

Both gargoyles grinned when she drove by without "finding" them. No need to ruin their good time, and she'd be able to find at least those two when her magic was working again.

Vana couldn't remember the last time she'd had absolutely nothing to do but experience the world. Oh, sure, she was "mowing the lawn" (she put mental quotes around the phrase because, really, she was riding a piece of machinery; *it* was doing all the hard work and this was actually quite the cushy job), but no one was around and she didn't have to answer to anyone.

For all that her parents wanted her to become some *über*-genie like DeeDee, Vana was enjoying this autonomy... and the fact that the only person she'd be letting down with screwy magic right now would be herself. That had a lot to recommend it.

An hour after Zane had said she'd finish, Vana drove the mower back to the shed. It and she were covered in grass clippings and sweat, and she had a sprinkling of new freckles, but Vana felt great. She'd accomplished something all on her own. And without magic. She'd bet Mother and Father had never mowed a lawn that way.

"I was just about ready to come looking for you." Zane swatted her hat brim when she handed him the keys.

"Why? I was having fun."

"Glad to hear it 'cause I have more fun lined up for us."

She could only imagine the sorts of fun the two of them could have together.

Unfortunately, his imagination was quite different from hers.

***

Four hours later, steaks were on the grill (that they'd scrubbed) and beers in the cooler on the porch (that they'd washed). They sat in the rocking chairs (that they'd hosed down) from the shed (that they'd swept) and watched the sun kiss the horizon as the fireflies came out to frolic. Vana's muscles creaked with every motion the old chairs made.

She'd climbed ladders to de-bird's-nest the shutters. Had heaved on a creaky old pulley system to haul slate tiles to the roof so Zane could replace the ones she'd missed during yesterday's cleanup. She'd offered to magically fix them for him since a slanted tile roof wasn't the safest place to be, but Zane had looked both insulted and horrified.

She had to say, even with the aches, pains, seven out of ten chipped nails, and the chunk of hair that had gotten wrenched from her braid when it'd gotten caught on a protruding nail as she'd climbed down the ladder on one of many trips, there was a satisfaction in what they'd done that she hadn't felt when using her magic. Although, that might be because using her magic rarely went as smoothly as using her muscles.

"So what are we going to do tomorrow?"

Zane took another sip of his beer. "*We* aren't going to do anything. *You* are going to play lady of leisure. Your body is going to need it after today, and I have to take a little trip to deal with our friend Gary."

"You're leaving? Can I come along?"

"Not this time, Vana."

"You know, I *could* always turn Gary into a toad and save you the trip."

"I thought you couldn't."

"I can't *kiss* someone into a being toad, but *magicking* him into one is a whole other story."

Zane swished the beer around in his bottle. "Much as I'd like that, we'd better not. But thanks for the offer."

"I could make him mute like I did to Merlin."

Zane sat back in the rocking chair, rolling the bottom of his beer bottle in circles on the armrest. "It's tempting but I want to beat Gary on my own. There's no sense of accomplishment if someone does it for you."

"Now you sound like Peter. He always wanted to do things his way, too. He never really asked anything of me, other than trying to change the children back and conjuring food for his picnics." And the rose window…

Hmmm. Maybe that was why he hadn't made other wishes.

"Then what was with all the stories?"

"Well, I…" She pulled her braid forward and combed through the end. "I was… um, experimenting with my magic."

"You're not born knowing how to use it?"

"No more than you are."

235

He arched an eyebrow. "I think I have an excuse—I didn't believe in magic before I met you."

"And that's why it doesn't work." She tossed the braid over her shoulder. "See, every one of the gods' creatures is born with magic. Even mortals."

His feet hit the floor. "Morta—us? Me?"

She nodded. "It was there inside of them—you— thousands of years ago, but for some reason mortals moved away from it. That was before my time so I have no idea why. It was before your recorded time, too, but for some reason, your race didn't embrace their magic. Djinn, on the other hand, did and built a world that mortals can no longer see unless your eyes have been opened."

"By opening a genie bottle?"

"Among other ways, yes. But the magic is still there inside of you. It's buried deep, but you occasionally do have flashes of it. What you call intuition, for example. Fortune tellers and mystics and mediums have learned how to tap into it. And then there are people who somehow just know things without understanding how or why they do."

"Like psychics or people who talk to dead people?"

"Exactly, except those people aren't dead. They've just moved to a different plane by going into the Light."

"A different plane? The Light? You're telling me that my whole concept of this world is wrong? That there are planes and ghosts walking among us, and genies watching me when I shower and sleep? Birds can listen in on our conversations?" He downed the rest of his beer.

Vana winced. She wasn't doing the best job of fostering djinn-mortal relations.

"It's not as pervasive or invasive as you're making it sound, Zane. Everyone has their own lives. We don't sit around watching mortals on flat-screen TVs or anything. But yes, we're there."

"I guess that makes my pissing match with Gary over this house rather insignificant in this universal, plane-based world order."

"Not at all. Everyone has a purpose and a path. It's merely a matter of finding the right one to walk."

"Or fly?" At least he could joke about having his world turned topsy-turvy on him.

She smiled. "Or fly."

He set his empty beer bottle on the floor next to his chair and leaned forward, his elbows on his knees and his hands hanging between them. "What's it like?"

"Flying?" Vana had to think about her answer. No one had ever asked her before. Usually, they'd demanded a ride to find out for themselves. But not Zane. He hadn't demanded anything from her at all. That was half his appeal.

And she was not going to think about the other half.

"Flying is… freedom. Like you said earlier but not the you-can-go-anywhere kind because it's more about *how* you go. On land, everyone's confined by gravity. In water, it's by our lung capacity and buoyancy. But on a carpet… it's magic." She chuckled. "I mean, of course it's magic, but not *my* magic. Well, not totally. The rugs themselves are enchanted, and the combination of its magic and a genie's creates a unique experience every time.

"It's the feeling itself that is magical. You can go as high as you want or skim the ground or even hover. Go fast or slow, ride the wind like a roller coaster, or take it easy and fly straight. There are no boundaries. You can even fly upside down and you won't fall off. There's nothing more freeing, more alive than riding a magic carpet." She put a hand on his knee. "Would you like to try it?"

He sat up. "Go for a ride? Now?"

"It's almost dark. No one will see." Especially if she used Invisibility. She stood up and held out her hand. "What do you say? Want to give it a whirl?"

"Absolutely."

They coasted above the Pennsylvania mountains, dipping down into the canyons and skimming their toes along the surface of the creeks there. She banked the rug around the overhangs and soared over the tree line, wanting to give him the perfect first flying experience.

"I see what you mean about this being freedom." Zane leaned back on his hands, his legs dangling over the edge as they passed through a cloud. "I could get used to this."

"Then you'd be missing the magic. I never get used to it. There's something new every time." Vana steered the carpet beside a great horned owl out looking for dinner.

Unlike mortals, birds were fully accepting of genies and, like Merlin, able to see through Invisibility. The raptor stuck to his flight pattern while merely blinking his big yellow eyes at them as they coasted past.

Zane closed his mouth when she veered off into a cloud. There was nothing like the soft caress of a cloud—unless it was Zane's caress. Not what she needed to think about now. Or ever.

"I see your point, Vana. There really is nothing like it."

Actually… there was. Making love to him was every bit as thrilling and freeing and wonderful.

The carpet dropped out of the sky.

Luckily, they fell into a wandering rain cloud, thank the stars, because the denser water particles slowed their descent and allowed Vana to regain control of the carpet.

If only she could be that successful with her wayward, weak-in-the-knees thoughts—which weren't helped when Zane pulled her against him.

"What was that?" he practically growled, his breath coming fast and heavy against her cheek, his arms wrapping around her body, pressing her against that hard, muscular chest that was rising and falling with each heavy breath he took. None of which was helping with the weak-in-the-knees thing.

Then he tilted her head back. "Are we okay now, Vana?"

He was so close. The protective way he held her, the concern in his eyes. The way his lips parted just a whisper away from hers…

The ridge she felt against her thigh…

"Everything's fine, Zane. You can let go."

Please don't.

He didn't.

"What caused it?"

Being lovestruck.

Thankfully, she didn't say that out loud either. "We hit an air pocket." Which normally wouldn't have been a problem, but normally she wasn't thinking about having him inside of her when she hit one.

"Magic carpets are subject to air pockets?"

"Magic or not, aerodynamics are aerodynamics."

The cloud shifted then, revealing a night sky blanketed in stars, and what the proverbial "they" said was true: the stars had never sparkled so brightly as they did at this moment. The wind had never caressed her skin so softly. The swoop of the rug had never been so uplifting, the troughs never so tummy-tickling, the feel of his skin on hers never so magnetic, and the moment… never so perfect.

"Vana…" His breath was as soft as starlight, and the look in his eyes…

She licked her lips. She couldn't help it; her mouth had dried up.

His gaze zoomed right there, and a half second later… he kissed her.

Or maybe she kissed him.

She didn't know.

She didn't care.

It didn't matter.

Nothing mattered but this moment.

Nothing mattered but him.

And her.

And this.

His lips slid over hers, nipping, nuzzling, stroking, licking, nibbling, all manner of tasting and teasing that sent her tummy—and the carpet—twirling through the air.

But Zane didn't notice, and she didn't mind.

He slid his hands up her back, pressing her closer to him, and Vana twined her arms around his neck to hang on.

They stayed like that for a while—it could have been seconds; it could have been hours. All Vana was aware of was the man holding her, touching her, kissing her, *wanting* her, and it was all she could do to try to retain some hold—however small—on her sanity and remember who and what she was and what would happen if this got out of control. She would never become the genie she'd been born to be.

If only she knew who that was.

***

Gary paced his living room for the second night in a row. A second night he wasn't going to get any sleep. Where the fuck was she? What genie didn't notice their bottle missing? Hell, he'd been online all afternoon doing research on genies, and every legend, story, and fable said genies were bound to their bottle, so what was he doing wrong?

That stopped his pacing.

Of course! What he was doing wrong was waiting for *her* to come to *him*. *He* had the upper hand here. He had her bottle *and* the dish.

And *he* was now her master.

It was time he made her aware of those facts.

Chapter 31

Vana woke to an empty bed.

That wasn't a surprise because she'd gotten into it that way after their carpet ride. It was, however, a shame.

But it was safer this way.

The rest of the house was just as empty. Zane had left on his errands; the gargoyles were presumably still hiding; the furniture was still asleep; and Merlin was playing hard to get, which was fine with her. She didn't need his brand of sarcasm after the wonderful day she'd shared with Zane. The phoenix would show up at some point, she was sure, but until then, she was going to enjoy the peace and quiet. A genie rarely had that outside of his or her bottle.

She went into Peter's study. His chess set sat between the two leather chairs in front of the fireplace. Ah, the times they'd sat there to play a game. Mrs. Hamm, Peter's housekeeper, had been the first source of the "crazy" rumors. She'd thought the man absolutely batty to play chess by himself, but Peter had refused to give up his weekly matches with Vana. He'd compromised with the housekeeper by taking those naps he hadn't needed.

Vana positioned the pieces on the board as they'd been during the last match she and Peter had played. She'd been within one move of checkmating him when he'd called it a night to prepare for the luncheon the next day and needed his sleep, but she'd known he'd wanted time to come up with a way to beat her.

There hadn't been one. Then the fiasco with the bear and the stairs had happened, and she'd been banished to the attic, and well... they'd never had the chance to finish.

She made the only move Peter could have made, then nudged her rook into place, but sadly, there was no triumph in the victory.

She looked around the room. There'd been life in this house. Of all the masters she'd served, Peter had offered the most satisfying experience of her Service. He'd been her friend. He'd enjoyed talking to her and had taken her on those treasure-hunting missions where they'd found the others.

She'd been his treasure, too. And, for the most part, she'd felt it. Peter had wanted to have a genie only for the confirmation that they existed, not for what she could do for him. He'd been too proud of where he'd come from and how he'd made it all happen himself to take handouts from her, so he'd valued her for her company. And she his.

Those had been the best years of her life, and not because Peter had taken her on his travels, though they'd been fun. It'd been the ability to work on her magic for magic's sake, not his, and the lack of pressure to be perfect. Even when things had gone wrong, he'd been the father she'd wished hers had been: patient, kind, understanding.

She missed Peter. She missed what they'd had. What *she'd* had. And she wanted it again. Wanted to feel as if she mattered to someone. That she had a friend. Someone who accepted her for who she was.

Vana got out of the chair. If she sat there any longer, she'd end up a pile of blubbering mush and that was never productive. She wiped the two tears that managed to escape just as someone knocked on the front door.

Her first thought was "yay, company!" followed shortly thereafter by that dread she'd felt when that stopper had sealed the top of her bottle that first time. Trapped.

The rapper rapped again. Vana brushed her hair back over her shoulders and thanked the stars that she'd worn mortal clothing today. She tugged the hem of her T-shirt over her jean shorts and pinched her cheeks. (She wasn't quite sure why, but she'd seen movie characters do it so apparently it was what one did when mortals came calling.) Then she headed toward the front door.

"At ease," she mumbled before Eirik could do his normal snap-to-attention, not sure if she meant him or her. She opened the door.

A gaggle of women stood on the porch.

The term was appropriate because even though they weren't geese, the women resembled them: each one gabbing over the other, and the ones in the back craning their necks to see over the ones in front.

"We wanted to welcome you to town," said one.

"It's so wonderful to have a Harrison in this house again," said another.

"What are your plans?" asked yet another, none of them giving her the chance to answer.

"My Mikey wouldn't mind taking over from Jack Ertel when you leave. This lawn must be too much for him," said another.

"Oh, the place looks lovely." That intrepid woman had her foot over the threshold and her head around the door.

Thankfully, Eirik behaved himself.

"May we come in?" The question was moot because Ms. Intrepid, apparently the leader of the gaggle, was now standing in the foyer.

Five more followed her in.

"Um, okay." Vana shut the door after the last crossed the threshold.

"Is that Peter?" Intrepid asked, pointing to the portrait hanging there before picking up one of the perfume bottles Peter had collected on that trip to Istanbul. She lifted the stopper and sniffed the contents. Pomegranate and poppy: quite a potent aphrodisiac back in its day. Vana wouldn't be surprised if the fumes in the bottle still packed a punch.

"Yes, it is." She barely got her answer out before Miss Nosey Pants picked up a set of tintypes Peter had found in a little shop just before the visit to Lady Lockshaven.

"Is this him and his wife? Mildred, I believe her name was."

"Millie, but no. They're just some—"

"I must say, those drapes are in remarkably good condition." The woman didn't wait for an answer before leading the way into the parlor.

Vana managed to return the pictures and perfume bottle to the table in the foyer before following the flock into the room, her "Thank you" falling on deaf ears as their feet fell on a few strands of Fatima's fringe.

That counted.

Wow. Nice compact," said another woman, pulling Lucia out from the sofa cushions. "From the '40s, right?"

Vana just nodded. The *1*540s, but she wouldn't say so. What was Lucia doing there?

"And the furniture is as beautiful as if it'd been crafted yesterday." Another woman walked on Fatima, while yet another stroked her hand along Henry's side.

Vana thought she saw Henry sigh. She'd have to remember to do that—human contact, even when one wasn't in human form, was still important.

After introductions were exchanged, Vana was able to escape to the kitchen alone to conjure up iced tea and a batch of baklava, two things she had no trouble whipping up—and luckily no whips showed up.

She brought the tray into the parlor, only to find the children stacked up nice and neat on the coffee table. Once she got over the shock and panic, she realized they couldn't have done it themselves. If they had, the women would have run shrieking from the room.

She wasn't surprised to see Ms. Intrepid—er, Laura Hardins—surreptitiously slide the cardboard box around to the side of the sofa. "I hope you don't mind," she said, patting her pocket from which a piece of thread or something dangled, "but I just *had* to see what was inside that lovely armoire. These dishes are just exquisite. Quite rare, too, aren't they?"

The woman had no idea.

"This looks delicious." Laura put two pieces of baklava on the plate that was Anthony.

Vana held her breath. Anthony hated baklava.

Sure enough, one of the pieces started to inch toward the edge.

"Why don't we sit down?" Vana took the plate from Laura and managed to slide the baklava onto Francesca and put Anthony at the bottom of the stack with a sleight-of-hand trick that had nothing to do with magic that she'd learned from Ali in the *souk*.

"Where did you find the time to bake amid this extensive renovation?" LeeAnn Something-Something, a name full of Spanish articles that Vana hadn't caught during the introductions, set Gregory on the table. The youngest of the children fluttered one of his edges slightly.

Vana picked him up and set him in her lap, her fingers stilling the roving edge. Unfortunately, though, he had more of them to move, so she tucked him beneath her hands. "Baklava isn't really that hard to ma—"

"Who was your contractor?" Stella Johnsen set Benjamin on the table.

Benjamin loved baklava; Vana would have to keep an eye on him to make sure he didn't absorb any. In this heat, melting baklava wouldn't be hard to explain, but evaporating baklava would be. "Zane and I have been work—"

"Is everything here original to the house?" asked Lorelei Someone, examining the antique salt shaker Zane had given her.

"Yes—"

"I love this," said Terri—or maybe it was Tess—holding up Lucia. "Pity you had to tape it shut."

Tape it shut? Vana tried to keep her grimace looking like a smile, but her mind—and Gregory's edges—were reeling. What was going on?

"Did you have old photographs to copy from or did you hire a decorator?" Brenda Anderson helped herself (and Eloise) to another piece of baklava.

"Um, no. We just did what we thought looked right."

Laura ran her fingers over the scroll-worked lantern Vana had found for Peter in the Grand Bazaar in Istanbul. "I heard the original owner picked up some amazing things in his travels." The woman had *no* idea. "No one makes things like this anymore."

She was more right than she knew. Peter had been convinced that an ifrit had inhabited that lantern. Vana hadn't agreed; an ifrit would never have chosen something so plain, nor sat idly inside. Every ifrit she'd ever come across had been literally bouncing off whatever walls tried to contain it. Unless it'd been up to something.

Hmmm, maybe she should have kept that in the attic.

The questions continued, and while the women were polite, their interest in the house was anything but subtle. They were dying for a grand tour and only good manners prevented them from asking.

And thank the stars they didn't. Besides the fact that house was her home and not a tourist attraction, something was going on. Lucia with the tape and now Gregory was acting up in a way she'd expect of Colin when mortals were around.

Colin... Holy smokes! Where was Colin?

Sheer panic rose in a tidal wave over Vana. There

were only seven dishes on the table. Where was he? What was he going to do? Colin was enough of an imp that he might actually have some in his genetic makeup, but now was not the time to test that theory.

She had to get these ladies out of here. Gods, what if Colin decided to skate across the floor? Fling himself through the air like a flying disc? She'd promised Zane that the kids would behave, and if they decided not to in front of this gaggle, the story would be all over town faster than her magic could stop it. Thankfully, she remembered what Zane said about being offensive. Or something like that.

She tucked Gregory into the sofa behind her, then stood up. "Ladies, thank you so much for this visit. It's very nice of you to stop by, but, as I'm sure you can imagine, I still have a lot of work to do."

"Zane isn't here to help you?" That Laura woman didn't give up.

Vana started gathering the children, then picked up the plate of baklava. Couldn't be more on the offensive than that—or more offensive, probably, but Vana didn't care. She had to get them out of here. "He had business to attend to."

"About the house?" Laura asked again, both hands wrapped around the lantern. Vana needed to make sure it didn't leave with the woman.

"Oh, please ask him not to sell it to a developer." Stella handed over Benjamin right before a dollop of honey disappeared. "I know it must be worth a fortune, but someone will want to keep it as it is."

"Stella's right," said LeeAnn. "He can't sell to a developer. My son was just saying how his Future Farmers of America club had to get off the property they're leasing because a developer bought it to build a mall. More projects like that, and we'll lose that small-town feel that Larry and I moved here *because* of. A lot of people feel the same way."

247

"Which is going to play a big part in the mayoral race come November," said Stella.

"I hope he doesn't sell it at all," said Terri-Tess. "This house is part of our history. Where and how the town started. The City Council should preserve it as a historic landmark. Then no one would be able to buy it."

"That's a great idea, Tessa," said Brenda. "Think of all the possibilities. From the house itself to the grounds, to the surrounding land, we might really want to think about bringing that idea up at the next Council meeting."

"We could have the 4th of July community picnic here."

"Or summer camps."

"Oh, that'd be a great idea. It'd save me a twenty-mile drive to the closest one before going into the office in the summer."

Vana was more concerned with finding one wayward child than what the women were planning. She smiled at the right moments and nodded appropriately, but she was trying to figure out how to get them out of the house while trying to figure out where Colin might be hiding. Using magic was looking better by the minute, which illustrated exactly what Colin's disappearance was doing to her sanity. He could be anywhere. Planning anything.

"Thank you for all the suggestions, ladies. I'll be sure to pass them on." She headed toward the front door, wishing she could enchant the women like the Pied Piper had enchanted the mice and lead them out of the house.

Especially when Eirik started leaning toward her.

Great. If he fell over, that'd be another story to circulate around town.

She opened the front door, blocking him from their view. "Thank you all for coming, ladies. It's been a pleasure getting to know you."

Luckily, they took the hint, though with much hemming and hawing—and straining of necks to look

248

upstairs—leaving just before Eirik decided to thump against the door.

"What is wrong with you?" Vana yanked the coat rack back to upright. "All of you? You know you can't misbehave when mortals are around." She dragged Eirik into the parlor—literally dragged him because he would not walk across the floor.

"Colin, you come out here right this instant, young man."

The dishes started clacking. And Henry started thumping his doors. Eirik wobbled back and forth, and Lucia started jumping on the table while Fatima did some weird undulation thing that almost knocked Vana off her feet.

"Hold on, hold on!" She held up her hands, and like an orchestra waiting for the conductor's signal, everyone quieted down. "What's going on with you? And where's Colin?"

The noise started again, and Vana held up her hand again. "One at a time, please."

The story came out then in all its horrifying ugliness. Gary had Colin. He'd tied up Henry and Eirik—luckily Laura's curiosity had made her cut Henry's bonds, but the fishing line was still on his and Eirik's legs.

Vana cut it off, a sick feeling in her stomach. She'd let them down. She'd allowed someone to learn of her magic and use it against them. She was exactly what her parents expected: an utter failure as a genie.

But she couldn't sit and wallow. She had to rescue Colin. She had to make sure Gary didn't do anything with the knowledge he now had. And she needed to do it without Zane finding out because he'd *give* the house away before letting any of this taint his family name.

She untaped Fatima and Lucia, promised the children she'd bring Colin home, then magicked herself to Gary's house.

Chapter 32

Zane was definitely right: the best defense *was* a good offense.

And Gary was quite offensive.

Vana Invisibled herself into his house to find him sitting in his front parlor staring into Peter's grandmother's brass lamp with Colin duct-taped to the table next to him.

It took everything she had *not* to turn Gary into that toad she'd mentioned to Zane earlier. Too many questions would be asked if he disappeared, although she doubted that anyone would complain.

"I know you're in there, genie," he said, rubbing Emeline's lamp. "I also know I'm your master. Come out here and show yourself. I have wishes I want granted."

Oh, he did, did he?

Vana unInvisibled herself and levitated into the room in all her djinni glory: full-on harem garb in the most vibrant and sheer fabric, the richly embroidered, ceremonial high-curled *khussas*, and a veil straight out of the collection of the Seven Veils of the Dance. He was going to get the full treatment.

She stood right behind him, her magic making her entrance silent, then she tapped him on the shoulder.

"What the—" Gary jumped and spun around. Emeline's lantern went rolling beneath the sofa.

"Hello, Gary."

"You!" He was breathless with awe for all of about a second, then the leering took over. "It's about time you showed up. What kept you?"

"Your clues were a little too vague."

"I'll work on that for next time."

There would be no next time.

"So…" she said, keeping a tight enough rein on her temper that the grimace stretching across her face could be construed as a smile—until one heard the gnashing of teeth behind it. "I hear you have some wishes you want granted."

"You don't even care about the dish?"

She shrugged. "It's just a dish."

"But it moves."

"So?"

That took away his bluster. "You don't want it back?"

"Why? There are others." She couldn't look at Colin. She'd explain this to him afterward, but oh, how she hated for him to hear her say this. If she could be certain of her magic, she'd make him unable to hear it, but she didn't want it to backfire and ruin his ears.

"Oh." Gary lost more of his bluster. The jerk had actually thought he'd entrap her.

Poor, misguided man. The thing with the djinn was a djinni in control of her magic could be a formidable opponent. One *out of control* of her magic would be even worse.

"So what do you want?" Vana tapped one *khussa* in the air—and made sure he saw it.

He did. "That. I want to do that."

"Tap your toe?"

He snorted. "No wonder you're enslaved by mortals if that's what you come up with." He circled around her.

She let him preen. Let him think he had the upper hand. She was no more his genie than she was Zane's, which meant

251

she could do to him whatever she wanted—and there was a *lot* that she wanted to do to him.

"I want to be able to walk on the air like you do."

"No problem." She kissed the air, and Gary was hanging upside down from the doorframe. Wow, she'd actually done what she'd set out to do.

"Not like this, you idiot!"

She wanted to *tsk-tsk* at the name-calling, but she didn't want to overplay her hand just yet because the fun was only beginning.

She kissed the air instead, and this time Gary was upright. Well, if he could call being hunched over and trying not to bang his head on the ceiling since his feet were five feet off the floor "upright."

"Put me down, genie!"

"The name is Vana, if you don't mind." But she lowered him anyway. Maybe a little harder than she'd planned. Or... not.

"Your name is whatever I want it to be, genie. I'm the master."

She ground her back teeth together, trying to refrain from flinging him into the cold, dark fireplace. Where was Merlin when she needed him?

Merlin *poofed* into the room.

"Yo, Van, what's shakin', bab—Oh, ho! What have we here?" Merlin glided around Gary three times, his feathers changing color with each rotation. Right now they were ebony with the tiniest lick of flames on the edges.

"Seriously? You're wasting firepower on *this*?"

Gary's face got as red as those feather tips. "Get out of here, bird. This doesn't concern you."

Merlin nodded and stroked his chin with one wing while coasting with the other. His circles were getting smaller. And his flames were getting bigger.

"You know, that's true, bug guy—I mean, *big* guy." He narrowed his eyes. "This actually doesn't concern me. I have every faith Van is going to be able to handle you perfectly."

Merlin looked at her, saluted, and winked. "Have at it, babe. Enjoy." Then he burst out in one of the biggest fireballs Vana had ever seen.

It singed off Gary's eyebrows.

He glared at her, but the effect was ruined without eyebrows.

"I want riches. Right here. Right now." He even stamped his foot, the spoiled bully.

"Very well." She kissed the air and—

"What the hell did you do?" he screamed, staring at his forearms.

Where a long line of *stitches* practically bisected the length of both limbs.

"Um…"

"Get rid of these right now!" He flung out his arms.

That was too easy.

But it *was* what he wished for…

Vana kissed the air.

"What the fuck?" Gary stared at his shoulders—that had nothing hanging from them.

"You wanted me to get rid of them."

"Not my *arms*, you moron!" His eyes narrowed, mean and beady. Maybe she should turn him into a rat instead of a toad. "Put them back on, genie."

She raised an eyebrow and the room fell silent.

Finally, Gary exhaled. "Fine. Vana."

"That's better." She kissed the air, and he had his arms back.

Too bad they were on the wrong sides.

"What the fuck?" Gary flung them awkwardly—not that Vana could blame him. It must be difficult to gain control over backward appendages. "Put them back the right way!"

"Is that what you wish?" she asked, trying desperately

253

to keep the humor out of her voice. See how much *he* liked being bullied.

"Of course it's what I wish. That's why I said it! What—you need me to spell it out for you?" He still didn't get it.

"There *are* certain rules and protocol you need to follow, Gary."

"You're kidding."

"I don't kid about being a genie." Especially in this minute when she was in full command of all her djinn power. Was this how DeeDee felt all the time? It had a lot to recommend it.

"Fine. What are they? How do I get my arms back? And get my money?"

"You want money? That's what this is all about? That's why you're hounding Zane to sell the place? That's why you want to turn Peter's memory into a laughingstock?"

Gary crossed his arms—well, he tried to. "Do you mind?" With his palms up, he looked like he was pleading. A very good look on him.

Vana kissed the air; she'd had enough fun at his expense. Being a bully didn't feel good, no matter how nasty he was.

"It's about time." Gary shook his hands. Of course he didn't say thank you. For that, alone, Vana seriously considered replacing his legs with his arms and vice versa. "And I don't have to do a thing to turn Peter's memory into a laughingstock. He did that all by himself—or *you* did it for him. Right?"

She should have turned him into a toad. She didn't understand croaking. "Peter was a great man, and you need to remember that."

"Oh, sure. Peter was great. It was his all-powerful

being who couldn't get it right." Gary shook his head. "And now I'm saddled with you."

Okay, that was just way too easy.

She kissed the air and Gary was a donkey. An ass, to be specific. Wearing a saddle.

His legs fell out from under him, and he hit the floor with a *thud* hard enough to bounce the table where Colin lay. The smart kid twisted just enough that when the table hit the floor again, some of the duct tape gave way. He started working himself free. Colin always was resourceful.

"Oh, God, turn me back, gen—I mean Vana. Now." Gary stared at his splayed front legs.

"You don't like it, do you?" She took a step closer to him. He couldn't kick her from that position. "You don't like being at someone's mercy. Made to do things you don't want to. Having no control. It stinks, doesn't it?" Like he did. Donkey or otherwise.

He nodded, the big brown donkey eyes looking a bit teary.

"This is how you made Zane feel when you were children, you know. You were a bully. And you still are. Leave Peter's memory alone. Leave Zane alone. Matter of fact, why don't you leave this town alone? Everyone could use a break from you. If you promise to leave here, I'll turn you back." She tapped her *khussa* again. "No more bullying people, Gary. No more trying to wheedle them out of the votes or their inheritances or their possessions."

She held out her hand and kissed both Emeline's lantern and the freed Colin into her hands. "I am not your genie. I never was. And if I ever see you in this town again, you'll wish I'd left you a donkey. Do we understand each other?"

Gary bared his big, yellow teeth in an equine snarl.

Vana puckered up.

Gary lost his bluster and hung his head. "Yeah, fine. Whatever."

"And not a word to anyone. They wouldn't believe you anyway. And then the stories about Peter would stop and the ones about you would begin. Do you want that legacy? Because if you think today's demonstration was something, just wait until I put it on a grand scale in your dubious honor."

"Can I at least have something before I leave? Say… a couple thousand bucks?"

Talk about easy… She bit her lip. "Um, sure. I can do that."

And she magicked a herd of deer into his backyard as she spirited Colin home.

Chapter 33

Zane pulled into the driveway a little after nine. It'd been a long, frustrating day, and the gargoyle playing ostrich in the front yard didn't help matters.

He parked the car, his knee twinging as he got out. He'd put it through the wringer today to prove to the team's trainers—and himself—that it was back to a hundred percent. He'd worked his ass off rehabbing it in just eight months, and all the ladder-climbing yesterday had convinced him to set up today's appointment because he needed to show them he was better than second string. He wanted to start, dammit.

He hadn't gotten a "no,"—or a yes, actually, but at least the lack of a "no" allowed him to hope.

He'd then tracked down his attorney on the golf course in sweltering ninety-five degree heat to see if Gary's threat could pose a problem, only to be charged time and a half to get called an idiot for not accepting the offer in this tough real-estate market *and* to learn there was no way to prevent Gary from bidding on the house without facing a major discrimination lawsuit that could tie up *any* sale to *any*one for ages.

Then, to top it all off, his condo building was being fumigated so he'd had to drive three hours twice in one day to spend another night under the same roof as Vana. After the last two, he didn't know how many more he could take without taking things further, regardless of the complications that would arise.

The woman was one giant complication. She got under his skin in a huge way—to the point that he had to wonder why he was backing off. She was his genie; she wasn't going anywhere. How much longer could he fight the attraction—and, seriously, why did he want to? He turned to fire when she was in his arms and she melted in them. They were a match made in Heaven—or whatever constituted genie nirvana.

Nirvana… She was aptly named.

God, it was going to be another torturous night. He should have stayed in a hotel in Philly. But he hadn't and here he was, debating whether or not he'd tell the gargoyle with its head buried in the flower bed that he could see it.

Nah. He'd had enough of magical beings—except for the one he had a feeling he'd never have enough of.

He opened the front door to find Eirik standing beside Henry, who was fluttering his doors in what looked to be a heated discussion. They froze in place the second he walked in.

"Don't let me stop you." He plucked a note with his name on it that was floating in the air at eye level.

> *Zane,*
> *There is baklava in the kitchen and I'm in my bottle upstairs. Send Merlin to get me when you're home. I need to talk to you.*
> *~Vana*

If only she needed something else from him…

"Oh, honey! He's ho-o-o-o-me!" The bird flew into the foyer with a piece of—baklava?—balanced atop one of the children on his back, his cornrowed tail feathers

258

knocking three glass bottles and the old-time photos over. "Miss us?"

Zane plucked the plate off Merlin's back, then fixed the toppled items. "Where's Vana?"

Merlin rolled onto his back and crossed his wings on his chest, his feathers strumming his gold belly. "Guess that's a no."

"Merlin, is there a point to you being here?" Zane asked as he bit into a piece of flaky pastry. He loved baklava, and this was the best he'd ever tasted. One more plus in Vana's favor.

"Uh, no. But most people like having me around."

"I'm not most people."

"Okay. Fine. I can tell when I'm not wanted. But it looked to me—and Henry and Eirik and even little Lucia— like you'd walked out on her. Just when she needed you, too. We all did. We were about to send out the troops."

"Needed me? Why? And what troops?"

Merlin shook his head. "Nope, you're not getting the story from me. Ask her. But as for the troops, those gargoyles aren't as dumb as they look, you know."

"Then why is one standing with his head stuck in the ground in my front yard?"

Merlin smacked his forehead with his wing and landed on the sofa. "You know, you try to give them the benefit of the doubt and look what happens. I better go fix this." He disappeared in a cloud of gold flames, just as Vana ran down the steps.

God, she was beautiful. It didn't seem possible that he would have forgotten how beautiful in twelve hours, but he had.

"Zane, you're home!"

And just like that, with those three words, it all fell into place.

His life.

This house.

Vana.

He looked around. His great-great-great-grandmother's lantern on the side table. His parents' wedding picture hanging above the fireplace. His baby picture beside it. Peter's portrait in the foyer. His mother's thimble collection, his grandfather's pipe. The salt shaker he'd given Vana on the mantel next to his Little League trophy.

This was home.

Somehow, in a short period of time, Vana had turned this place from a dusty, dingy, sheet-covered bad memory into a place filled with life and warmth and memories.

She'd made it a home.

"Zane? Are you okay?"

He nodded. Because he couldn't speak.

He was *home*. For the first time, he had a sense of what that meant.

And he had her to thank for it.

"I'm so glad you're here." She took the plate from him and tugged him toward the living room, her smile taking his breath away.

That was something a man could get used to.

He cleared his throat. "What happened, Vana?"

She stumbled but quickly recovered. "Happened?"

"Yeah, while I was gone. Merlin said something about you needing me." Those words had a nice ring to them. Yeah, he could see the whole picture.

"Some friend he is," she muttered, setting the plate down before tucking some hair behind her ear, then fiddling with her fingers—very telling signs with her.

Zane glanced around. No cows, no bears, and the stairs were still in one piece.

"What happened, Vana?"

"Nothing really."

Oh, it was something.

"Tell me." He picked up her hands. "Please."

She nibbled her bottom lip and glanced at the table

before giving him a too-quick smile. "I took care of it. You don't have to worry."

Apparently he did. But he didn't pressure her, just sat there holding her hands and looking at her. She'd tell him when she was ready.

"It's Gary."

Shit. "What about him?"

"He knows about me."

Double shit. "How?"

"I'm not sure, but he knows. He… he took Colin."

"One of the children?" Zane stormed to his feet. "Where is he? What'd he do with him? Is Colin okay?"

Vana grabbed his hand and stopped him from running out the door after that mother-fucking prick. "Colin's fine. He's here. Unharmed. It's okay, Zane."

No, it freaking was not. On so many levels: Gary, the kids, how he was coming to feel for them, for Vana… and in one blinding instant he'd thought it'd all gone up in swirling pink smoke.

He needed to sit down because his knees were threatening to give out in a way that had nothing to do with his ACL. "What… what happened?"

Vana took a deep breath and pulled her hands back into her lap, her fingers twiddling madly. Zane covered them with his. "Vana, tell me. I'm imagining all sorts of horrifying scenarios right now."

"Okay, but remember, it all worked out in the end."

He tried to quell the desire to murder Gary as Vana relayed the story she'd pieced together from Henry, Eirik, Fatima, Lucia, and the children, as well as the parts only Colin had known.

"So while Lorelei was talking about using the yard for a community picnic, and LeeAnn was suggesting donating the property to the Future Farmers' Club, and Laura was thinking we should open a series of summer camps, I was trying to figure out where Colin had gone. It wasn't until the ladies left that Henry and the rest could tell me what happened."

"But how did Gary know in the first place?" And who else knew...

"I didn't find out. I was more concerned about getting Colin back."

"And he's back? He's okay?"

Vana's laugh relieved some of his tension. Well, his worry, but the desire to commit murder was still pretty strong. "Oh, he loves telling the story now. Quite the adventure."

"And you? How are you?"

Her tough façade wavered just as he knew it would. She'd been as terrified as he'd been when she'd first told him. He shouldn't have left her here alone. "You should have called me, Vana. Or magicked me back here."

"Which would have done exactly what I was trying to prevent Gary from doing. The whole world would have known about me if I showed up out of nowhere and whisked you away." She took another deep breath, and this time, her shoulders rolled back and her chin tilted.

"Besides, I handled it. *I* did it, Zane. And I could do it because Gary took something from me that was more important than my problematic magic. I had to get Colin out of there, and I had to keep Gary from going public with what he knew. I didn't have time to worry about what my magic would or wouldn't do. And it was actually better than I could've hoped. Gary won't be spreading tales about what he knows for a long time. Ever, if I have anything to say about it, and the beauty of it is that Gary thinks I do. So our secret is safe."

"I still think you should turn him into a toad."

"That's always a possibility if he tells someone something he shouldn't."

"But... that would mean you'd have to be around to monitor him. Here."

The idea no longer bothered him. Matter of fact, he liked it. It answered everything. The children and the furniture could stay here while Vana tried turning them back, and if they wanted to stay once they were changed, well, the house certainly was big enough—

No. The *home* was big enough.

She tugged her hands away and tucked hair behind both her ears. "I... I actually wouldn't have to stay here, Zane. Gary's leaving town. On threat of being turned into a donkey."

"I like that better than the toad idea. He's already an ass."

She smiled and Zane felt another piece of his life fall into place. He wouldn't leave her to face Gary or anything like that situation again. "But what if I wanted you to stay here? What if I..." He took two seconds to think it over and realized that he had to say it. Had to do it. "What if I don't sell the house?"

He counted to three before her mouth closed. Counted five more before any words came out.

And even then, they were breathless. "Are you... Really?"

He cupped her cheek. "Really. You've made this place a home, Vana. For all of us. Even the gargoyles and Henry and Eirik. When I walked in the door tonight, I felt it. That sense of homecoming I've never had."

"You did?" There was something in her eye. A tear, perhaps.

No, she shouldn't cry. Ever.

He brushed it away with his thumb. "Vana."

Shimmering silver eyes met his. "Yes?"

He caught another tear. "I want to kiss you."

She inhaled and her fingers flexed against his chest. They grasped his shirt and hung on. "Oh," was all she said.

That was all she needed to say.

He slipped his hands, so slowly, beneath that fall of hair, letting the strands glide between his fingers, igniting every nerve ending he had.

He tilted her chin up just slightly with his thumbs, feeling the steady thud of her pulse against them.

He watched the silver sheen in her eyes darken, the pupils dilate, saw her lips part to take in more breath.

"Vana," he whispered, her lips just out of touching rang.

She swallowed. "Yes?"

"I'm going to kiss you."

This time she said nothing. Not a gasp, not an "oh," not an "okay."

This time, she moaned.

It was Zane's undoing.

He pulled her into him and kissed her, her lips trembling beneath his as she sighed into his mouth.

It wasn't enough.

He shifted on the sofa to get closer, but his leg was in the way. So he leaned forward, urging her back. He lifted his knee to the cushion and raised himself above her, never once breaking the kiss.

Her fingers slid up his chest and around his neck as he slipped her legs beneath him on the sofa, every inch touching, and framed her face with his hands, tugging on her bottom lip with his teeth until she opened her eyes. Starlight shone in them.

"You are so beautiful." He stroked a strand of hair from her cheek. God, he could swear he'd been imagining her like this since the day they'd met. He wanted to tell her that, but the words wouldn't come. He stroked her cheek again in a caress that felt so right it was as if he'd done it before.

She lay there in the moonlight with the sweetest welcome in her expression, as if she were a gift from the gods. As a genie, *his* genie, she just might be.

But he didn't want the genie. He wanted the woman. Because, for all her magic, nothing had made this house a home more than Vana had.

"I want you, Vana."

There it was. No preamble. No dissembling. No games. Honest, raw, stark desire.

The same thing he saw reflected in her eyes.

264

Something *thwumped*, and for a moment, Zane thought it was his heart.

But then it *thwumped* again behind them.

Zane looked up. Eirik's limb was pressed against Henry's door, and both of them were staring at him and Vana. Not that Zane knew how they could stare, since they didn't have eyes, but he could feel their looks like a physical touch—or make that a physical "do not touch."

What were they—her guardians? "Don't you two have something better to do?"

Eirik made a big production—as big as a coat rack could—of lifting his limb from Henry and stomping back to his post by the door. Henry straightened his shoulders, er, frame, so he was two inches taller. The two of them radiated displeasure through every grain of the wood they were made of.

God, there were people—*beings*, whatever—in his living room. Gargoyles running amok in his yard.

And Vana in his arms.

That made everything right.

Everything except…

He wanted her.

In his bed.

No, hers. The one on the third floor that he'd forever think of as theirs.

"Say 'yes,' Vana. God, please say you want this."

He waited half a heartbeat. A desire-filled, anxious half of a heartbeat. With his blood throbbing in his ears, dread and hope warring in his gut.

No, not his gut. A little higher.

And then she looked at him beneath her long lashes and said the magic word—and it wasn't "Abracadabra" or "Open, sesame" or even the dreaded "holy smokes."

It was the one three-letter word that opened the door to every possibility.

"Yes."

Chapter 34

Vana didn't have to think about it. Of course she'd say "yes."

Aside from the fact that she'd wanted him desperately since she'd first set eyes on him, *he* wanted *her*. Despite everything, Zane wanted her.

And he wanted the house, too. Finally, they were on the same page, and Vana was so utterly happy she could cry. Was about to, actually, but then Zane jumped off up from the sofa, swept her up in his arms, and strode toward the stairs, taking them two at a time.

Rhett Butler couldn't hold a candle to Zane.

Candles covered every dresser, nightstand, and windowsill when he kicked open the door to her bedroom.

"Thank God," said Zane, kicking it closed behind him.

She was about to agree, but then he let go of her legs, and inch by maddeningly slow inch, she slid down his body.

"Zane, I—"

He kissed her then, and it was as if lightning arced between them with hot, intense, unmitigated desire. She forgot what she was going to say as her fingers fumbled with the buttons on his shirt.

Zane muttered something against her lips, then

covered her hands with his and yanked, sending the buttons flying.

Oh, gods, he was all planes and angles that her fingers wanted to trace; ridges and valleys her lips wanted to explore; sinew and muscles and the sexy line of hair heading down to his belt line and below that she remembered all too well. How it'd felt beneath her fingers, against her cheek, along the tips of her breasts.

His fingers fumbled with his belt, and it was her turn to cover his hands with hers. "Allow me."

He nipped her bottom lip and removed his hands—which he then rested on her waist. "Your wish is my command."

That was her line—

No, she wasn't going to think about the differences between them or her magic or the last time they'd done this… This was a whole new start for them, as if that other night had never happened.

She wasn't going to take this night from him. Not now, when he knew everything about her and who she was.

Well, not *every*thing.

"Kiss me, Zane." She needed to stop thinking of anything beyond tonight and just live in the moment. That's all genies could ever do.

Zane backed her up against the bed and bent her back over his arm. He leaned into her, taking her gently down to the mattress, his other arm bracing their descent.

He followed her down, that glorious chest mere millimeters above hers, his lips a hairsbreadth away, his gorgeous blue, blue eyes now the deep indigo of the sky just before night claimed the day.

"Be sure this is what you want, Vana, because if I kiss you now, I'm not going to stop."

"Thank the gods." Every single one of them.

Zane smiled. "I'll take that as a 'yes.'" He slid infinitesimally closer. How was it possible that he still wasn't touching her?

267

She arched off the bed. There. Her breasts came in contact with that warm, naked expanse of skin, and she breathed a sigh of relief that, in the next second, turned into a gasp as desire shot through her, as heady and quicksilver as magic.

Zane had to have felt it, too, because he dropped those last few inches onto her and kissed her senseless.

He dragged her hands above her head and intertwined their fingers, nipping at her jaw and her neck and just beneath her ear where his warm breath caused shivers that undulated out like a wave on the shore, everything in its path caught up and swirling and tumbling along the tide of desire.

Gods, she wanted this. Wanted him. Yes, she knew it was dangerous, but that danger only heightened what she was feeling.

And, oh stars, what she was feeling. It transcended the physical. This was love, a joining of two hearts and souls in an act so profoundly beautiful that it surely had to be magical.

See? Mortals still had their magic, if only they knew how to find it. Zane had found his and was wielding it so utterly perfectly that Vana willingly gave herself up to the enchantment, as exhilarating as a magic-carpet ride over storm-tossed clouds and as beautiful as the rainbow that followed.

She shifted when Zane's lips slipped from her earlobe to the curve of her neck, needing the pressure of his thigh against her, needing that ultimate contact that she knew would be all the sweeter for the wait, but wanting it now.

She wanted to touch him, to give him the same pleasure he was giving her, and she moved her hands. But Zane tightened his hold and nipped along the cord of her neck, then down to her collarbone, nuzzling the hollow above it, his tongue soothing the sharp little bites, each and every one heightening her pleasure.

She squeezed her eyes against the emotion he drew

from her with the utter perfection of his touch and the pleasure he wanted to give her, and she wondered... dear gods, she wondered how she'd ever live without this. Without him.

He licked his way down to her T-shirt's scooped neckline and paused there, looking up at her with hooded, sexy bedroom eyes that seemed to glow, warming every cell in her body while the rasp of his stubble invoked shivers down to her toes.

"Shall I continue?" He smiled wickedly.

She could only nod.

Zane grabbed the shirt's fabric with his teeth and scraped it down, catching it briefly on her tight nipple before releasing it beneath her breast. He then took the aching, swelling flesh into his mouth and worked his own brand of magic.

Vana shifted beneath him, the contact not enough. She needed to be naked against him. Needed to feel his skin against hers, that roughened hair bristling against each of her nerve endings.

She turned her head to kiss the closest part of him so she could summon her magic. That body part turned out to be his forearm, an area she'd never consider sexy on anyone but him, and she put every thought and hope and wish behind that kiss to magic their clothes away.

Thank the stars, it worked. Skin on skin, hearts beating together, they were finally, *thankfully,* as the gods had intended. Not genie and mortal, but man and woman. As elemental as Time itself.

Zane smiled against her. "Leave it to you to come up with just what I was wishing for."

Her wish was that she could tell him how she felt. That she didn't have to choose between her magic, the thing that made her who and what she was, and loving Zane, the man who'd showed her who she could be.

But who could she be? She'd been trying for eight

hundred years to find out and hadn't had any luck so far. Well, other than bad, that is. But here, now, with him... He gave her the ability to make her magic work. Among so many other things...

It wasn't fair, this choice she had to make. How could she make it? Why did she have to?

Vana swallowed, choking back the tears welling up inside her. She didn't want to ruin tonight.

Zane slid his lips up her neck and over her jaw and kissed the tears he found there. "Are you crying?" he murmured against her skin.

"No." *Yes*. "I don't know."

"Do you want me to stop?"

"Gods, no."

He smiled at her vehemence and kissed each tear away. "There. No more tears. This is supposed to make you smile."

She smiled.

"And moan." He flicked his tongue over her nipple.

She moaned.

"And shatter you into a thousand pieces."

He released her hands and skimmed his tongue down her body to swirl and tease and taste and torture that one part of her that had been denied his attention, and she shut everything out of her mind but this. This wonderful, exciting, perfectly devastating assault on her body and her mind and her heart and her senses, and she let herself ride each sensation.

He stroked her and kissed her; he teased her and gave in to her pleadings, only to stop at the last possible second, driving her wild with each half-finished touch, each too-light caress, playing her body and her heart like a virtuoso.

"Zane," she gasped time and time again—because it was the one word she didn't have to search for in the swirling beauty of color that burst behind her eyelids when his tongue found the one spot that was barely holding her together. If he just kept doing *that* a little longer, nothing in the universe would matter but him and here and this one moment of perfection.

Over and over, he brought her to the pinnacle only to leave her there, each new onslaught taking her higher until she was writhing on the bed, clutching his head, sliding her fingers into his hair, gasping, wanting, reaching for the final release…

And then he gave it to her. One long final stroke that had her shattering just as he'd wished. Into a thousand *and one* pieces.

And it was that last one that finally fit into the puzzle that was her life.

***

It was as if the stars had fallen from the sky to swirl around the room when Zane slid into her wet, tight heat. Shudders wracked her body around him, the slick sheen of arousal on her skin mingling with the taste of honey still on his tongue and the scent of rose petals that seemed to follow her around like a sensuous cloud of temptation.

She moved, the tiniest of movements, sending his blood thundering through his veins, and Zane had to grit his teeth to hold back when she clenched him.

He was so damn close just from watching her. And she'd tasted so amazing. And the sounds she made—God, the sounds. He knew each one as if he'd heard it before, as if it were etched into his mind and heart and soul for all time. As if they were a part of him. Each one had reached through his skin and wound around his heart, tugging and tugging until he'd found it impossible to breathe, yet somehow he'd found a way to push on, to take her higher and give her more pleasure, more of himself.

And now she was giving back. The demanding strokes over the skin of his back, her nails marking him as she locked her ankles around his hips.

"Gods, Zane, yes," she panted, and it spurred him on and drew out his pleasure like no other woman ever had.

Vana was unlike any other woman he'd ever been with. And he didn't mean her magic. It was as if their bodies had been designed for each other. As if their souls had found the lost half of themselves. He knew what she'd like. Knew what she'd want. And she knew him. Sometimes before he even knew what he wanted from her.

But Vana was always there. Giving, accommodating… her passion as greedy and needy as his, and Zane reveled in it.

There was a connection between them beyond the physical. As if he could read her mind, and she, his. When he needed her to move one way, she did. When he needed her to unclench, she released him. When he needed her to say his name in that soft, breathless way she said it, she did. And when he needed her, period, she embraced him and opened herself to him.

Home. Vana was home to him.

He didn't know how it was possible in so short a time, but if there was one thing life had taught him, it was to grab that one perfect moment before it disappeared.

And so he did, surging into Vana at her gasped urging, nipping her shoulder when she nipped his.

"Yes, Zane, that's it. Oh, there…" Her directives only turned him on more. He would have sworn it wasn't possible, yet it was, and he shouldn't be surprised, really. She had magic inside her. A magic that made him want to believe in everything. Believe in the possibility of hearth and home in a place he would have least expected it.

With a woman he would have least expected.

He reached for her hands, intertwining their fingers and tangling them in that glorious hair that was softer than any satin sheet could be.

Her eyes flared open, desire, want, need, all of it swirling with the starlight in their depths.

"Zane, I…" She closed her eyes and arched back, her throat offered, begging for his tongue.

So he obliged. And was rewarded with a tight hot grip on his cock that almost had him coming that instant.

God, the sensations were driving him crazy, and when she dug her nails into his backside and shifted just the tiniest bit, Zane sucked in a ragged breath and pulled out, resting his forehead on hers, trying to get his body under control.

"Zane? What are you—"

He kissed her. "Shhh. Give me a minute. Or I won't last even that long."

She smiled against his lips. "Do you need to?"

He needed so much… "I want to. Vana, I want to make love to you all night. And all day tomorrow. And tomorrow night. And the next." Maybe at some point—next month—he might think about stopping, but he doubted it.

Oh, God… On a groan, he surged back in, unable to deny himself even one more second of her heat, let alone sixty of them. She felt so good around him, skin to skin, every ripple of her inner muscles caressing him, and he felt his orgasm churning at the base of his balls. It seared through him, rocking him into her over and over, taking everything she had to give and then wanting more.

He arched back, the final moment of heaven, and images poured through his mind: Vana licking and kissing him while she rode him, the feel of her beneath him, the way her body convulsed and shuddered around him as she came, the beauty of her hair as it trailed down over his abdomen, the warmth of her mouth when she took him inside…

The last was so erotic he couldn't hold off, and he poured himself into her, every last sensation being wrung by her contractions as she came, drawing every last breath from his body, and oh, God, he could do this forever.

He fell forward with a ragged, shuddering breath,

catching his weight before he crushed her. He kissed the curve of her neck, inhaling that incredible, indelible scent of her skin, roses, and their passion.

They lay there, their breaths in time with each others', and still the images rolled like a movie reel through his mind as if it were déjà vu.

She mumbled something. He didn't know what, figured she didn't either; it was a mumbling sort of moment, this warm, sleepy, perfect aftermath.

He slid his weight from her, regretting that he had to pull out of her, but he slid his arm beneath her shoulders and tucked her against him while she mumbled something else. He nudged her nose with his. "What?"

"You didn't ask," she whispered, sleepily.

"Ask what?" He wasn't capable of forming anything more coherent than a two-word sentence at the moment.

"Protection."

His ego was gratified to know he wasn't the only one incapable of forming compound sentences. "You explained already."

Vana stiffened beside him.

Oh, no, she hadn't explained.

At least, not *this* time.

Chapter 35

V ana?" Zane asked, shifting slightly, and she could feel his gaze boring into her. "What's wrong?"

"Nothing." Everything.

She hadn't mentioned protection. Not tonight. She'd been too caught up in the moment, and besides, she'd already explained it to him once, and if it hadn't been her first thought then, it definitely wouldn't have been now.

Oh, gods, did he remember?

"If nothing's wrong, why are you shrinking from me?"

"I'm not. You're imagining it."

Oh, no, he wasn't. Vana squeezed her eyes shut. It wouldn't be the worst thing in the world for him to remember. They'd ended up here together anyway. And he'd wanted to, so he couldn't accuse her of taking advantage of him—

Except that's exactly what she'd done by manipulating Time for her own benefit, and Merlin was right. Mortals didn't like people playing with their minds, figuratively *or* literally.

"I'm not imagining it, Vana." He tugged her close. "Why is talking about protection freaking you out now? You were fine when you told me about it. Practically purred when… I…"

Had brushed a rose petal over her lips.

There were no rose petals on this bed. Not this time.

"There were rose petals."

Oh, gods, he *was* remembering.

"Where are the rose petals, Vana?"

She squeezed her eyes shut even more.

"We were on pink satin sheets."

Oh, gods.

"In your…"

She knew the minute he remembered all of it. His body turned to stone, and his arm fell lax against her waist.

"Vana, why am I remembering rose petals and pink satin sheets in your bottle?"

She opened her eyes, then blinked away the tears. There would be no more kissing them away. Not once he found out.

"Because…" She cleared her throat. "Because we did this before."

To his credit, he didn't yell at her.

To hers, she'd rendered him speechless.

"Holy shit."

Well, for all of about two seconds.

"What did you do?" He dragged his arm out from under her and propped himself on it.

Vana looked at the ceiling, unable to face him. "I… We… did this, and then… while you were sleeping, I…" She swiped a tear from her cheek and took a deep breath. Best to get this out in one long rush. "I took us back to earlier in the evening so it was as if it had never happened."

"But it did."

She nodded, not sure if he was asking a question or making a statement, but either way, the answer was the same.

"But *why*?"

Because she'd been so close to falling in love with him then and had been terrified of ruining everything she'd been working toward all these years by blurting it out.

And yet here she was, *definitely* in love with him and incapable of blurting anything out.

"Vana." It wasn't a question, but it—he—deserved an answer.

Unfortunately, she couldn't give him one. Because if she did, it would negate the reason she'd done it in the first place and she'd lose him twice. "I… I can't tell you."

"You play with my mind, yet you can't tell me why you did it? I remember every moment, each gasp, groan, and scent there was that night. Why now? Why let me in on the big secret now?" He got off the bed and grabbed his pants from the floor. "Is this some genie way of getting your kicks? Mess with the mortals' minds and bodies? Use me?"

She struggled up onto her elbows. "I didn't use you, Zane. You wanted me as much as I wanted you. Both times." He wasn't going to deny that.

He stormed across the room and grabbed his shirt off the floor lamp where it'd landed. "So… what? You always sweep your regrets under the magical rug?"

"I didn't regret it. I… made a mistake." She pulled the sheet around her, feeling exposed in so many ways.

"A mistake." He shoved his legs into his pants. "*I* made the mistake. Tonight was a mistake. From start to finish. Hell, these past few days have been a mistake. What was I thinking? I should have put you back in that bottle the minute you made the vacuum cleaner dance. I should never have let you talk me into bringing Fatima and Henry and everyone else downstairs.

"I should have just left you there for the next owner to deal with and grabbed a few things, signed the listing papers, and gotten the hell out of this town and gone back to my life. But no, you gave me a glimpse of something I thought I'd missed out on. Something I thought I might want. But it was all concocted by your magic. Is this how you treat all your masters? Or just the ones you sleep with?"

She sat up, still clutching the sheet. "That's not fair—"

"You're talking to me about fair?" He raked a hand through his hair and started pacing. "Do *not* talk to me about fair, Vana. I know all about what's fair and what's not. My life being decided for me by others isn't fair. Peter, Gary, the coaching staff, my fucking knee. Then I come here, trying to forget what's going on, only to have *you* make decisions for me about what I can and can't remember. How many times, Vana? How many times did you do this?"

He stopped and stared at her.

"Just… just the one night."

"That's one too many." He started pacing again. "Isn't there some rule in that book about doing this to your master? What about all the wish-granting—that I didn't take advantage of, by the way. I was considerate enough not to use you. You could have afforded me the same generosity. Or is it okay to treat your masters like shit just because we're mortal?"

"It wasn't… I had a good reason."

"What on earth could possibly be a good enough reason for you to tamper with my life and my memory? I want answers, Vana."

Oh gods, this was the moment of truth she'd been dreading. It'd seemed like such a small matter when she'd done it. He wouldn't remember and no one would be the wiser. Just a few hours that meant the world to her but could mean nothing to him.

And now it'd blown up in her face.

"Vana? I'm waiting. As your master, I demand—no, I *wish*—you'd tell me why you did it."

"But you aren't my master."

Zane stopped moving. Everything: his legs, his arms, his head… his breathing. Everything except a tic in his jaw. "What. Do. You. Mean. I'm. Not. Your. Master.?"

"I… well… It's complicated."

His silence said so much more than any words would have.

She clutched the sheet tighter to her chest with both hands. "You see, according to the *Djinnoire*, the genie-master relationship happens when a genie materializes in front of a master. But I never did that with you. You somehow ended up in my bottle and then I led you back to your plane. So, technically, you aren't my master."

"So you used me twice."

"It wasn't like that, Zane."

"No? What was it like? How do you explain manipulating me like that? Lying to me like that?"

"I didn't lie. I *did* think you were my master. It wasn't until after... well, until after..."

"After we had sex?"

She flinched at the brutal honesty of that question, because that was exactly what they'd done. She'd been the one to make more of it than what it'd been.

"Yes." She cleared her throat and willed the tears not to fall. Which was about as possible as asking The Fates not to cut someone's Life Thread.

"The sex that I only just now remember."

"Yes." Her throat got clogged all over again.

"Is there anything else I don't remember?"

She shook her head. "Zane, I'm so sorry—"

He inhaled long and deep, his eyes boring into hers, his anger palpable. "Did you do this to Peter? Is that why he sealed you in the bottle? Why me, Vana? Why *me*?"

She flinched and shook her head. They were all honest questions, but they belittled the reason she'd done this in the first place. If she hadn't manipulated Time that night, they would have continued sleeping together and she would have gotten to this point—feeling this way about him—so much sooner, which meant she would have had to leave to protect her magic. And if she'd done that, Zane wouldn't have had the incentive to stay and come to think of this as

279

home as much as she did, and he'd still be trying to find where he belonged.

If only she could show him the good her magic had done—

Nice try, Nirvana, but don't sugarcoat it.

She could almost hear her mother's voice, but it wasn't Mother; it was her subconscious. And it wasn't about to be denied.

This whole debacle is your fault. You couldn't accept your failings and were trying to justify your existence as a djinni in The Service. Trying to be something you're not. That's why you jumped into that bottle all those years ago; if you'd failed, you'd be able to blame it on that. You weren't ready to enter The Service eight hundred years ago, and you're not ready now.

You aren't DeeDee and you never will be, and as soon as you finally own it and demand that your parents see you for who you are instead of wanting you to be an exact replica of your sister, you and everyone around you will be a lot safer. And happier. Face the truth, Nirvana, and stand up for yourself. Or at the very least, stand up for the man you say you love.

She hated her subconscious. Almost as much as she hated the fact that it was right.

"Then why, Vana? Why did you do this? To me?"

She sniffed and took a shaky breath, then rolled her shoulders back and lifted her chin just a smidge.

Zane—and her subconscious—were absolutely right and everyone, including herself, would just have to deal with it.

"I did it, Zane, because... I love you."

And then she disappeared.

Chapter 36

C ut!"

   "Wrong!"

   "Are you *kidding* me?"

Vana blinked when the world around her slowed its spinning, but the cackling voices kept harping.

"You've really done it now."

"I told you she couldn't do anything right."

"This is going to be a nightmare to clean up."

Vana put out a hand to steady herself. Her fingers encountered a rock.

A rock?

She looked up in surprise—and got an even bigger one.

Three old crones were staring at her. And not just any old crones, but… Holy smokes! The *Fates*.

"Do you realize what you just did?" asked one, using their shared eyeball to glare at her. Lachesis.

"And now we have to fix it. Again," grumbled Clotho, the hunched one.

Atropos was sharpening her scissors on a strap, flashes of lightning glinting off the blades.

It was a dark and stormy night on Mount Damavand, portentous weather for being summoned by the three sisters.

Not that there was ever a good time to be summoned by the Fates.

Lachesis *thwacked* her staff on her palm like a metronome, and lightning punctuated each downbeat. A clap of thunder struck the air. "Would you care to tell me what made you do what you just did? You're not normally a stupid girl."

"Sure could have fooled me." Clotho leaned on her cane. Her knitting needles hung from a chain around her neck. A woven chain, as befitted the Weaver of the Threads of Life.

Atropos, the one who cut those Threads, kept sharpening her strap. "Well? What do you have to say for yourself?"

"You shouldn't have pulled me out of there. I need to explain it to him. Tell him why I did what I did."

"Look here, missy." Clotho grabbed the eye from Lachesis, popped it into her socket, blinked twice, then glared at Vana. "You have been nothing but a stitch in my side for the past four days." She stabbed the space between them with one of her needles. "First, I have better things to do with my time than unravel and reweave the Threads you're flinging all over the place as if it were bargain day at the mall." Stab, stab.

"You think it's easy, keeping everyone's lives running smoothly? You think it's a walk in the park to make sure I'm not doubling back on something that's already happened in someone's life because you got it into your pretty head to time travel an hour or two every few days?" Now she waved the needle around like a wand.

"Do you know how much people's lives are affected by choices other people make? Do you have any idea that those six steps to Kevin Bacon mortals laugh about are no laughing matter?" And now she was back to stabbing. "Weave and reweave, knit one, pearl sixty thousand. I've got enough on my plate without you acting as if Time were your own personal plaything, and I"—stab—"for one"—stab—"am damn sick and tired of having to clean up your messes.

"And as if playing with Fate and Time weren't enough—" She leveled the needle in front of her like a jousting lance. "Now you go and do something that not *one* of us decided for you. Hauling off and tossing an 'I love you' onto the playing field? That is so far beyond a foul, you're lucky we're not throwing you out of the entire game."

"Then why did you put him in my bottle?"

"What? Are you out of your mind? We would never do something like that, and don't you dare try to palm this off on us, you ungrateful wretch." Clotho went back to stabbing. "You are on my last nerve, Vana, and, with us Fates, that is *not* a good place to be."

Atropos caught that needle with her scissors. "Chill, Clotho." She plucked the needle from her sister's fingers and stowed it safely in her box of knives.

Which didn't make Vana feel any safer.

"Vana. Dear." Atropos tucked the scissors into the pocket on her cloak, then snapped her fingers and Vana found herself dressed in a *chiton*. The Fates did like to stand on ceremony, and white Grecian robes were about as formal as you could get. "What my sister was saying in that roundabout way of hers is that you are a member of the djinn and, as such, must adhere to certain protocol. Telling a mortal you love him? Big mistake. Huge.

"You are not destined to be mortal, Vana. It's only by the grace of *us* that we managed to pull you from that plane before the High Master sucked your powers dry. We all have a lot invested in you. Your parents, us, the High Master... you cannot continue to let us down. Your sister is on track to become the first female vizier in the cosmos's history. We cannot have her sister become... *mortal.*"

Atropos's tone seared through Vana as if she were

sixteen again and jumping into bottles she shouldn't. She'd paid for that sin for years, but loving Zane wasn't a sin. It was the first time—okay, second, counting the other night—that she felt as if she belonged. For these past few days, she'd found somewhere she fit. And if it meant she had to be mortal, so be it. It wasn't as if losing her magic would be any great calamity. And as for everyone's expectations, well, she was used to not living up to those.

"But I love him. Why is it so wrong to want to be with him?"

"Because you are a member of the djinn," said Lachesis. "You don't get to choose your destiny."

"I disagree." Vana clamped her hand over her mouth. One did not disagree with The Fates and live to tell the tale.

But her decision had been the right one. Giving up her magic and immortality was nothing compared to what giving up Zane would mean to her, and if he knew what it cost her to love him, he would understand. She needed the chance to tell him, and if that meant challenging The Fates, well, she'd already lost everything of consequence.

"You *disagree*?" The eyeball fell out of Clotho's socket when her mouth dropped open.

Vana removed her hand. "Someone wanted me to be with him, otherwise we would have met in the normal genie-master way." She was not going to back down. Not about this. Zane was too important.

Lachesis, however, grabbed the eye, then aimed her staff at Vana, and a bolt of magic knocked Vana off her feet. "Sit!" A stone chair shoved into the backs of her knees, catching her before she fell.

"This is unacceptable." Lachesis enunciated each syllable as her sisters joined her on the mountain's peak. "I don't care what theory you spout, you *will* return to the mortal and you will *not* say those words. This will be the *last* time we will ever manipulate Time for you, and I will inform the High Master that he must strike that ability from your genie card. Get your magic and your heart under control, Nirvana, and accept the role we have chosen for you."

Vana looked at The Fates, huddled next to each other to share the vision of the eye Lachesis held in the palm of her hand. The sisters' will was formidable.

But Vana's love was stronger.

"Fine," she said with resignation in her voice. "Send me back. I won't say the words."

She looked them in the eye.

And lied.

Chapter 37

Y ou're talking to me about fair?" Zane raked his hands through his hair—*again*—as he paced across her bedroom—*again*—while she sat in the middle of the bed with the sheet clutched to her like the *chiton* The Fates had put on her. *Again.*

Vana dropped the sheet.

"Do *not* talk to me about fair, Vana. I know all about what's fair and what's not. My life being out of my control and decided for me by others isn't fair. Peter, Gary, the coaching staff, my fucking knee. Then I come here, trying to forget what's going on, only to have *you* make decisions for me about what I can and can't remember. How many times, Vana? How many times did you do this?"

He stopped pacing and stared at her.

She saw the flash of awareness at her nudity. Felt the heat that had been there mere minutes ago—well, to him anyway—flare to life, and it gave her hope.

"It was just the one night, Zane."

He shook his head and resumed pacing. "That's one too many." He stopped at the dresser in front of her bottle and reached out to touch it, but yanked it back as if he'd been burned.

The analogy was too close for her comfort.

"Isn't there some rule in that book about doing this to your master?" He looked at her in the mirror above the dresser. "What about all the wish-granting—that I didn't take advantage of, by the way. I was considerate enough not to use you. You could have afforded me the same generosity. Or is it okay to treat your masters like shit just because we're mortal?"

She shifted her legs under her. "I had a good reason and if you'll just let me expl—"

"What on earth could possibly be a good enough reason for you to tamper with my life and my memory? I want answers, Vana."

Vana got off the bed and walked over to him.

Naked.

Yes, it was a ploy as old as The Fates themselves, but she needed to capture his interest. Whatever else he was feeling for her, he was definitely interested.

But she'd hurt him. Not on purpose, of course, but still. Zane, for all his alpha-macho toughness, was as aching. She shouldn't use her sexuality to fix this, because, really, it couldn't. Sex would only cause more problems if she wasn't completely honest with him. Look at what had happened so far. But she'd needed to get his attention. Now that she had it, she kissed the air, summoning the *chiton*.

And a couple extra gallons of resolve.

"Zane, I will grant your wish because I owe it to you, not because you're my master." She stopped next to him and met his gaze in the mirror. "Because you're not."

"I'm... what? You lied to me, too?" He gripped her shoulders. "I guess I shouldn't be surprised. Isn't that part of the whole genie mystique? Is this what you did to Peter? Is this why he sealed you in the bottle?"

She clasped her hands in front of her. "No. Peter put me in the bottle because he knew I was upset, and he wanted me to have the chance to calm down and get my

287

magic under control. Peter cared for me. And I cared for him. But not like I care for you, Zane."

He dropped his hands. "Don't give me that. You care about one person, and that's you. *You* wanted to grant Peter's wish about the house, even though I'm the one who's here now. *You* wanted me not to sell so you could get your happily-ever-after. What about what I want, Vana? This is my life. My only life. I can't manipulate Time like you do, with instant replays and do-overs. I get one shot. It's not a warm-up. Where do *my* wishes come into play?"

Vana flinched. She was trying to do the right thing, but why did it have to hurt so much? He was in real pain... and so was she.

She shook out her fingers. "Zane, I'm sorry. I did the wrong thing for what I thought were the right reasons at the time. I now know that they weren't, and if I could undo everything, I would. But I can no longer travel through Time to fix this, so all I can do is ask your forgiveness."

"Forgiveness?" He walked over to the bedroom door and turned the knob. The *click* had never sounded so loud. "Yeah, sure, Vana. I'll give you forgiveness." He opened the door and leaned against the frame. "As soon as you give me back the night of my life that you took."

If only she could.

She followed him to the door, wanting to touch him, but she didn't. "I wish I could, Zane. The gods know how much I wish I could, but maybe if I tell you why I did what I did, you'll understand."

"There's nothing that would make me understand how you could have made a decision about my life for me without discussing it with me."

He spun around and was halfway to the landing when Vana raced after him. "Zane! Wait. If you'd just hear me out, you'd understand."

He paused.

But he didn't turn around.

"What is it?"

"This whole thing, I did it because…" It was so much harder to say the words this time. But just as necessary. "Because I love you."

And once again, Vana disappeared.

Chapter 38

"S he did it again. *Again!*" Clotho threw the eyeball off the mountain peak.

Atropos shot out her hand and caught it before it fell past her. Such a pain in the ass to find the damn thing, and Clotho was forever throwing it around. Her sister seriously needed to work on her anger-management issues. Thank the gods—only the major ones, of course—that Lachesis wasn't there to see it. Clotho's short temper had been wearing on their sister for the last two millennia. Now, with Vana disobeying orders, there was enough tension in the air to disrupt weather patterns on half the globe.

"She can*not* just go around deciding what's best for everyone. This poor mortal has had his Threads played with so many times they're practically in knots." Clotho held up her knitting needles.

Atropos popped the eye in and peered at the numerous Threads Clotho needed to weave into one. Yes, they were all tangled around each other, his pale blue ones wrapped up and around each other and the pink one in the middle…

Atropos leaned over and lifted that one by the end. Zane's Threads came with it. "Look at this, Clotho."

Her sister held out her hand for the eye. Atropos gave it to her.

"I told you," said Clotho. "It's an utter mess."

"Look again, sister. When have you ever seen this?"

"A mess like this? Last time I can think of is when that pop singer took up with her back-up dancer, popped out a few kids, then chopped off all her hair and did such a number on her Threads that I wanted to check *myself* into a spa to have the time to sort through them."

"No, not the mess." Atropos raised the pink one higher. The blues came with it. "The fact that his are tangled so tightly around Vana's. How many times have you unraveled these?"

"Don't make me count. You know how I hate to count."

"But that's my point. Every time you do untangle them, they somehow come to be retangled, and always with hers."

Clotho popped out the eye, shined it on her cloak, and popped it back in. "So the guy has lousy taste. What of it?"

"I'm saying that maybe their Threads are supposed to be tangled with each other's. Something keeps drawing them back together."

"But we're the architects of Fate and Destiny. Us. No one else."

"Really." Atropos didn't even bother going for the eye. She just blinked. "We know the masses believe that propaganda, but you want to try running that train of thought by the High Master, Zeus, and the rest of the Ruling Board?"

Clotho shoved the needles into her cloak and chomped down on her dentures. Atropos was sure she heard them crack. Nothing new there; Clotho went through a set about every third day. Mortals seriously ticked her sister off.

"So what are you saying?" Clotho spit out a tooth.

"I'm saying that maybe there's more here than meets our eye." She stuck it in her socket. "I'm saying that Vana has dismissed our power and our wishes twice now, and that maybe we need someone else in on this situation. Someone who can really get through to her."

"You mean…?"

Atropos nodded. "Her sister. If there's one person in this world—and any other—who can get through to her, it's Aphrodite."

***

Vana came to in the stone chair Lachesis had blasted her into before, with Clotho poking her with the end of the knitting needle. The flat end, thank the stars.

"About time you woke up."

"Now, now, Clotho, let's focus on what's important here." Lachesis appeared in a flash of lightning between her two sisters. "I'm surprised at you, Nirvana. Most beings wouldn't dare tempt us twice."

Vana wisely kept her mouth shut.

"And I get the feeling that, were we to send you back, you'd do it again."

This time Vana nodded.

Lachesis exhaled and shook her head. "That's it, then. We wanted to keep this matter between us, but you leave us no choice. Once we summon her, that's it. This incident will be on your permanent record."

Vana had heard that threat all through school. She had yet to see any adverse effects. Probably something teachers used to threaten kids into obedience. Well, Zane was too important for Vana to cower at their manipulative tricks.

"We're hoping Aphrodite will be able talk some sense into you, Nirvana."

Vana winced. Lachesis didn't mean the goddess.

"She's not going to change my mind." Vana had to marvel at herself. She'd challenged The Fates *three* times and was still alive.

Though Atropos had taken her scissors out again.

No, Atropos wouldn't cut her Life Thread. If she were going to, she would have done it at the first sign of insolence.

"Aphrodite *will* talk you out of this nonsense if she wants that vizier position," said Lachesis, clapping her hands, which sent more thunder and lightning crashing across the sky. "This will be her final challenge to see if she is worthy of monitoring genie compliance."

With another blinding flash of light, DeeDee appeared on the platform in front of Vana.

"What—?" Her sister looked down at the *chiton* she probably hadn't been wearing three seconds ago, then looked at her. "Vana? Are you okay? Why are you here? Why am I?"

"You're here to undo the damage *she* caused," said Clotho, spitting out a... *tooth*?

"Damage? What did you do now?"

"Nothing."

"Nothing?" Clotho sneered. "I would think a declaration of love for a mortal wouldn't be considered 'nothing,' otherwise why bother to say it?"

"Love?" DeeDee gasped. "You told a mortal you love him?"

In years past, Vana would have tucked her chin to her chest and let her hair fall over her face as she would have grumblingly apologized and then done what everyone wanted her to. But not now. What she felt for Zane was too important.

She sat up straighter in the chair and tossed her hair back. "I do, Dee. And I don't care if it destroys my magic. I'm sorry for letting you down, but it's my life. I love him. It's as simple as that, and if you condemn me for it, well, that's your choice. But my choice is Zane."

"You don't get a choice!" screamed Clotho as she stole the eye from Atropos and threw it at Vana like a baseball.

293

DeeDee caught it. "I'll handle this, Clotho." She rubbed the eye on her skirt, then tossed it to Atropos before she knelt in front of Vana. "Explain this to me, Vee. A mortal? Really?"

"I love him." Vana shrugged. Three words summed it up, explained it, and couldn't be argued with.

"But you can love him and still not tell him. After all, his lifespan will be but a blink of an eye to you in the grand scheme of things."

Of course DeeDee would argue; her reputation was on the line if she couldn't make a shining example of her own twin. And while Vana respected that, she wasn't going to live her life to anyone else's expectations. Not anymore. Zane was right; this wasn't a dress rehearsal. It was the only life she had and she needed to be true to herself.

"I don't care, Dee. Being with him is magical. My own magic is just icing on the cake. When it works right, that is—which is every time he kisses me."

"So find some other guy to kiss you."

"I have and it's not the same. It's not his actual physical kiss. It's the feelings it creates inside me. The way he makes me feel. As if he sees me. *Me*. The woman. Not the genie who can grant his wishes. He asks my opinion, listens to what I say, values what I think."

"Everyone does, Vee."

"Really? Mother? Father?" She thought a moment before she said it, but needed to say it for herself. "You?"

"Of course I do. You're my sister. I love you."

"Then show it. Let me live my life as I want. I'm not hurting anyone by loving him. Mother and Father wrote me off years ago. I'm not their superstar, you are." Vana grabbed DeeDee's hands when DeeDee started to argue with her. "No, Dee, it's true. And I'm okay with it. I've never begrudged you your successes. *You* are the magical superstar in the family, and I love you for it and in spite of it."

She brushed some hair off DeeDee's face and tucked it behind her ear. "But I love him, too. I need him. And he needs me. He's lonely, Dee. So lonely. I understand that loneliness. I know what he's feeling, and I just want to make it go away for him. He doesn't even realize what he's feeling, what he needs, but I do. And I can give it to him. Tonight, before all of this, before we made love, his eyes had finally started to open. He's making progress. If I leave him, he'll never finish. He'll never become what he can become."

"What about you, Vee? What about who you're supposed to become?"

"I finally know who that is, Dee. Don't you see? I'm good at loving him. I'm good for him. Me. Who I am now. *That's* who I'm supposed to be. Just me."

"Your speech is pretty," sneered Clotho again, pulling another pair of knitting needles from her cloak. "But it's not going to work for two reasons. Number one, your sister's promotion is on the line, and number two, you took his destiny into your hands when you took his memory, and destiny is *our* business."

She held up the needles, gossamer Threads dangling from them, spinning slowly. "Undo what you've done or we'll play with his Threads so much and so often his brain will become scrambled. We don't know how much of that a mortal can take, but I'm willing to bet it isn't as much as you think. How much are you willing to risk?"

"Vee, please, do as they ask." DeeDee kneeled by the chair and grasped Vana's hands in hers. "And not for my sake. I'm not asking as a genie, but as your sister. Love him but don't tell him. I can't lose you. You're my other half."

And Zane was hers.

Vana was torn. Could she be so selfish with all that DeeDee had strived for? Zane had turned from her in disgust; there was no guarantee he'd ever come around. She could be giving up everything and end up with nothing. Could cause DeeDee to end up with nothing.

She looked at her sister, so earnest and worried. She looked at The Fates, angry and determined. Maybe even spiteful, if Clotho's look was anything to go by. She was holding Zane's Life Threads so tightly, Vana was worried the Fate was choking the life from him.

"Please, don't, Clotho." She nodded at the Threads. "Let him breathe. He's not at fault."

Clotho loosened her hold and held them up, a sly look on her face. "Maybe Aphrodite *wasn't* the incentive we needed. Maybe it's him."

She rattled the Threads, the pink and the blue jumbling together, reminding Vana of how she'd been wrapped around and by Zane—physically, emotionally, that shared bond of loneliness… It had been so perfect, as if it'd been predestined.

But it hadn't. Not if The Fates hadn't placed him in her bottle, so she really could end up with nothing if she gave up her magic.

But she'd have nothing even with her magic if she didn't have him.

Clotho shook the needles again. "Maybe you'll come to heel if Atropos takes out her scissors—"

"No!" Vana stood up. "You can't."

"Can't?" Lachesis raised an eyebrow. "I believe you're forgetting who we are, Nirvana."

"I'm not. I'm just remembering Chapter Forty from DeeDee's *Djinnoire.*"

The Fates looked at her sister with their collective eye.

DeeDee stood and smiled hesitantly at the three sisters. "Vee, what are you doing?" she whispered.

"Trust me, Dee. They might control my life, but they don't control my heart. I read your book. And I can't thank you enough for writing it." She lowered her voice. "Just promise me that you'll take care of the children when you get the job."

"Vee, are you sure—?"

"Promise me, DeeDee."

Her sister nodded.

"Thank you." She gripped her sister's hand, squared her shoulders, and faced The Fates. "According to my sister's research, you can cut the Threads of mortals' lives with impunity, but you cannot do so with the djinn. You need permission from the High Master."

"We aren't talking about your Threads, dearie." Clotho rattled them again. "See?"

"Whose Thread is the pink one? You can't cut his without cutting that one. *Mine*."

There was silence on Mount Damavand for one millisecond of a second, but it was perfect.

"No, no, no, no, no, no, no, no, no, no!" Clotho shook the needles as if they were poisonous. "You don't get to do this!"

Lachesis grabbed the needles from her. "Calm yourself, sister!" Thunder echoed her words.

"She *can't* get away with this!" whined Clotho.

Atropos dropped her scissors into her pocket with a half-smile on her lips.

DeeDee had a huge one on hers. "Vee, that's brilliant!"

"No, no, no, no, no, no, no, no, no!" Clotho wailed again.

Lachesis clapped her hands, and thunder roared across the sky. The mortals on the planet below probably thought the world was coming to an end.

"Very well, Nirvana. You have seen through our threat. But there is still one consequence of your actions that must be considered if you insist upon this foolish plan. Your sister will fail her test."

Vana had to hide her smile as she squeezed DeeDee's hand when her sister started to answer. DeeDee had really done her homework with the *Djinnoire*.

"Would you like to tell them, Dee, or shall I?"

"Go ahead, Vee. It's your moment."

"Thank you."

"You're welcome."

"Hello?" Clotho rattled the Threads again. "Any day now, ladies."

Vana intertwined her fingers in front of her and took a deep breath. "There's an entire chapter in the *Djinnoire* as to the process of selecting a vizier, and it specifically says that the High Master is the only one who can devise tests for the applicants. No one else. Otherwise different factions with different agendas could hold up the process for eons. DeeDee was quite thorough in her research."

Clotho threw the needles with Zane's Life Threads attached in disgust. Vana watched them fly off the mountain peak in slow motion, out into the thunderous sky.

She sucked in a breath, ready to leap after them because when they hit bottom, so would Zane, and she had to do something to prevent that.

DeeDee held out her hand and blinked. The needles ended up on her palm.

She gave them to Vana with a wistful smile on her face. "Here, Vee. I wish you'd reconsider, but I can see that you won't. You now hold his fate and yours in your hand. But just because they're entwined now doesn't mean they always will be. There are no guarantees, Vee."

"I know. But I love him, and as you can see," she lifted the needles, "my destiny lies with him. I have to try, Dee. I'll always regret it if I don't try."

Her sister smiled a tight smile. Her eyes were a little more sparkly silver than usual. But DeeDee never cried. She was always stoic and completely in charge of her emotions and any situation. It was who DeeDee was.

Well, this was who Vana was. And she hoped her sister could accept her for that person.

"I love you, Vee. I hope you find what you're looking for." DeeDee hugged her. "Now, let me send you back to whatever time you want so you can fix this."

Vana brushed the short hair from her sister's face. "Send me back to whatever day it is for him now, Dee. I don't want to turn his world upside down again. He deserves better."

"And he's getting it," DeeDee whispered. "Because he's getting you. I just hope he knows the gift you're giving him."

And with that, Vana left the mountain in a cloud of pink smoke.

Chapter 39

Half an hour later, Mount Damavand time
Three weeks later, mortal time
Zane *had been counting*

G et moving, Henry."

Zane should never have come back a second time.

He'd been crazy to think he could come back here and it wouldn't matter—not after that last night when Vana had welcomed him home and everything had fallen into place only to turn into a nightmare a few hours later.

He'd spent most of that night cursing her, Peter, Gary, himself, Merlin. He would have left if he hadn't already driven too many hours that day. He'd cooled down enough the next morning to make arrangements for a donation to the benefit. Then he'd left the mess in Peter's house behind locked doors.

But today was the picnic he'd donated and he had to go a few rounds of head-butting with Henry and Eirik, pack the children up for the trip to his condo, and round up the gargoyles before anyone else saw them.

"I saw you walk down the stairs, Henry. I know you can go back up them, so move."

Henry slammed his doors shut.

"I'm not above getting a lit match, you know." Or a flame thrower if that's what it took to get the big hunk of wood out of here.

But the armoire still didn't move.

Zane cursed. The past three weeks in Philly had been so normal, and now this.

Normal but lonely.

He ignored the voice in his head that had only made an appearance once he'd pulled into the driveway. He'd barely thought about her during the past twenty-one days.

Barely *was right—she'd looked good naked.*

He rubbed his eyes to get rid of the image.

That only etched it into his brain all the more. Not that his brain needed any help. Vana hadn't been far from it. Through the surprise contract talks with a team he'd never thought would be interested in him to start and the equally interesting call from the school superintendent here, to the possibility of a commentating job and dealing with the press about the upcoming picnic, Zane would have thought he wouldn't have time to remember every single detail about her: how tall she wasn't, how tiny she was, how her hair fell to caress perfect breasts, how her lips had trembled beneath his, the look in her eyes when she was happy, the nervous way she fiddled with her fingers. The compassion she had for this lug of an armoire and the children and Fatima…

He'd tried not to think about her. Or he'd tried to focus on what she'd done, and usually he'd succeeded—until it was just him and his thoughts: driving in the car, waiting for a meeting, standing in line at the grocery-store checkout, or coming home to his empty condo.

That had been the worst. That and those minutes before he'd fallen asleep when he'd lain there staring into the darkness. Then he couldn't *not* think about her. About why she'd done it--and it wasn't because of love. If she'd loved

301

him, really loved him, she would never have taken something so precious from him—his say over his own life and the memory of their first time.

Zane put his shoulder into Henry and shoved. The armoire moved about two inches. Which Henry promptly backpedaled over, erasing six inches of progress.

"Come on, Henry. I can't risk anyone seeing you. I'm not going to be here to cover it up."

Damned armoire took *another* step back.

"Fine. Be that way. I'll just take Eirik up to the attic and hang him from the rafters unless you follow me." The two of them had done nothing but huddle in the corner of the living room since he'd gotten here, concocting something or cursing him; Zane didn't give a damn.

But he had no guarantees they wouldn't pull this shit with witnesses and the press around. That he *did* give a damn about, so they *were* going to do what he said. This was, after all, still his house and they were still pieces of furniture.

"So..." Gold sparks sprinkled down from the chandelier in the foyer. "The prodigal has returned."

And Merlin was still a pain in the ass.

"Don't you have anything better to do, Merlin?"

"Obviously I can't ask you that." The bird floated onto the sofa and lay on his back, crossing his—oh, for chrissakes—*purple sequined feet* over each other and pulling matching sunglasses down over his eyes. "Because apparently you *have* had better things to do in the past twenty-one days."

Zane pulled the pillow out from under the phoenix's head. "Leave it alone, bird."

Merlin waved a wing. "Isn't that your line? I mean, we figured when you raced your fancy-schmancy import down the driveway—in some pretty slick moves, by the by—that we'd seen the end of you."

"That was the plan." And right after the picnic he'd be

gone again. This time for good. Let someone else deal with all of this. He shoved Henry again. Who wouldn't budge. Again. "You need to get out of here, Merlin. The Ladies Auxiliary will be here any minute to start setting up, and while I can bolt Henry to the floor and tie his doors shut, I can't explain you."

Merlin rolled onto his feet, the red mohawk on his head making him look like a rooster. "Hang on, hold your unicorns. Ladies' Auxiliary? Please tell me they're a dance troupe."

Zane gripped the back of the sofa. It was either that or Merlin's neck, and he didn't want to find out what the karmic retribution was for wringing a mythological bird's neck. "Of course they're not a dance troupe. They're part of the firehouse."

"I don't see any smoke. Or did those wind chimes get into the compost pile? I told them if they rubbed together enough they'd cause friction, but I hadn't meant in the literal sense."

The bird had a one-track mind. "The women are coming to set up for the picnic I auctioned off before I left."

"Vana came up with a good idea, didn't she?" asked the bird.

"Can we just leave Vana out of this, please?"

"Well, duh… She *is* out of this. You did a pretty good job of that. I guess congratulations are in order, but I'm not so sure you want them."

"Look, Merlin, just drop the Vana talk. She's gone and that's over."

"You make it sound so easy."

"Apparently it is. She disappeared in a puff of pink smoke and I haven't seen her since. And good riddance."

"Good riddance? Good *riddance*?" Merlin started hacking, and Zane, against his better judgment, whacked him on the back.

"Don't expect me to thank you for that," said the

ungrateful bird. "If you hadn't put on such an asinine production in the first place, I wouldn't have been gasping for my last breath there. Do you have *any* idea of what Vana did for you?"

"Of course I do, Merlin. She erased my memory and screwed with my life." Something he'd reminded himself of every time he'd woken up imagining her in bed next to him.

The bird spit feathers. "Not *then*, you mortal. The day she *poofed* out of your life. You don't, do you? You have absolutely no idea what she did and what it cost her."

"What are you talking about? You weren't even there. Unless—God, please tell me you weren't watching."

"Blech." Merlin shuddered, more feathers molting all over the carpet—Fatima. Crap. He'd have to get her out of the room, too, and he wasn't relishing the fight she'd put up.

"Puhleeeeze," said Merlin. "If you've ever seen your kind in the throes of passion… it's not exactly pretty. I leave bedroom doors closed—it was closed, wasn't it? You weren't whooping it up on the stairs or anything, were you?"

Zane glared at him. "Do you have a point?"

Merlin smiled and raised his chin. "Of course I do. Sharpest beak in the West. Or is it the Occidental? I can never remember the PC terms these days."

Just then the children started banging on the front window. Zane hurriedly gathered them up. He was going to have to find something to wrap them with. He didn't need clacking from the attic attracting anyone's attention tomorrow.

"The kids miss her," said Merlin. "They need her, too. A lot of people do."

Zane used doilies from the furniture to muffle the noise. "Leave it alone, bird."

"I don't understand what you're so upset about. It's not as if she took time from your life, and you certainly got what you were after in the end."

"*That's* your argument?" Zane had to remember he was holding children in his hand when he set the plates down on the table so that he didn't slam them. "She took my memory from me." And control of his life.

"Technically, she didn't. She manipulated time, and a piece of your memory got lost in the shuffle—you got it back, didn't you? And, if you think about it, she *added* hours to your life by repeating a few things, so you actually came out ahead."

"I am not going to discuss this with you."

"Well tough, because I'm going to discuss it with you." Merlin strutted along the back of the sofa like the Liberace version of a rooster. "I haven't looked after that girl for almost six hundred years for you to get a bug up your butt about a so-called mistake. She didn't have to stay here, you know."

"Yeah, I found that out. After she lied about me being her master."

"I'm not saying her methods were the best, but her heart was in the right place. I mean, she said those three words that every genie dreads."

"Yeah, I can see how 'as you wish' would cramp her style."

Merlin fell back onto the cushion with a wing over his eyes. "You seriously need a history lesson." He lifted a feather and glared at Zane. "Here it is in a nutshell. Genies *like* being in The Service. It's an honor. A privilege. Not every genie is Chosen to be. See the big picture?" He hopped to his ridiculous purple feet. "Let's put this in your terms. Say, you're playing in the World Cup—"

"Super Bowl."

Merlin rolled his eyes. "Whatever. Biggest game of your career, right? Not only do you want to win, but you want to be the superstar. We on the same page here, big guy?"

"Go on."

"Why, thank you. I think I will." Merlin ruffled his zebra-striped breast. "To Vana, that's what Peter's wish is like. It's her Olympic Games. She pulls it off, it'll be like

305

hitting it out of the park. She'll finally earn the respect no one's given her. You haven't seen her parents. Those two make Sophocles and Aristotle look like toddlers. And then there's her sister... Talk about a superstar. And then comes Vana. Struggling along to live up to the family name."

Zane didn't want to hear this about her. Didn't want to know it because it didn't matter when it came to *his* life. *His* choices. The ones she took.

"So you come along," continued the bird. "Big, strapping, nice guy, you. Not hard on the eyes, and well, the girl's been in that bottle for over a hundred years. Think what *you'd* be like in her situation. So, you turn on the charm and she falls. Hard. But she knows she can't because if she does, it's a slippery slope to losing the chance for redemption in the eyes of her family and the djinn world. *That's* the big deal. Are you following me?"

He *really* didn't want to know this about her. He'd heard "I love you" so often from so many women that he'd stopped believing them long ago. Actions spoke louder than words, and her actions...

He'd actually liked her. Admired the earnestness she'd put into every task. The unflinching optimism that had kept her trying. She'd made mistakes, owned them, and had tried to learn from them.

But she'd also used him. She could couch it in whatever terms she wanted, but by taking his memory, she'd made his decisions for him.

The familiar anger simmered, and in a move opposing teams had used on him too many times to count, including the one that had torn his ACL, Zane rushed Henry. He caught the armoire by surprise and shoved him two feet toward the foyer. An *armoire* was not going to stand in his way.

"What's the matter, Zane?" sneered Merlin. "Are you so used to fawning fans and an adoring public that you don't care what Vana gave up for you?"

"You, bird, are out of line." Anger gave him the strength to move Henry another foot.

"No, you are. You condemned her without knowing the facts, and you have no idea what's happened to her since. Do you even care?" Merlin landed on top of Henry. "That woman, that sweet, giving, hurting woman did something so utterly selfless and loving that you should be prostrating yourself before her, begging her forgiveness for the callow way you spoke to her. She didn't just disappear. Not of her own volition. She was yanked off this plane to face The Fates. You know them, right? Old crones from Greek history?'

"Mythology, you mean."

"Yeah, as mythological as I am. Good argument." Merlin clacked his beak and his feathers turned black. With orange bands around his legs. "Vana was summoned to face their wrath for meddling in Time—"

"Good. She ought to be held accountable for her actions."

"But mostly for telling you she loved you. They're up on their mountain trying to placate The Power That Is and fix this because genies don't say those words. To any mortal. Ever."

"Sure they do, Merlin. You just don't know about it because they're too busy rewinding time."

"Geez. Who would have thought you were this cynical? This jaded?"

"Life does that to you. And lying genies." Zane shoved Henry another ten inches. But then the armoire opened his door against the trim around the arch into the foyer and something rolled out.

Instinctively, Zane caught it.

Vana's bottle.

The memories of *that* night, that first night, came rushing back to him. He knew what the inside of her bottle looked like. Remembered the snow and the non-windows. The rose petals and the candles. Her bed. What they'd done.

How she'd looked at him. How she'd touched him—inside and out.

He'd thought he'd seen something in her even then. A kindred spirit, maybe. Something good and wholesome and right. A connection.

That's why he'd taken her to bed that night. Not because he was a young first-round draft pick with women throwing themselves at him for the first time. Ten years ago? Hell, yeah. But he'd matured beyond that and had seen something in Vana—*thought* he'd seen something in her—and had responded to it. To her.

Only to find out that he'd been wrong.

Zane sagged against Henry. "Fine, Merlin. Say what you want to say, then get out. I'm at my limit for magic these days."

Merlin flew onto the back of the sofa, brushed a feather over his cockscomb, and started pacing. "Here's the lowdown, Mr. Lowdown. When Vana said she loved you, it wasn't to put anything over on you. There was no ulterior motive. Matter of fact, it was because she *didn't* want to say those words that she manipulated Time in the first place."

"Yet she ended up doing exactly what you say she didn't want to do."

"Arrrrggggh!" Merlin squawked. "Will you listen to yourself? You're so blinded by that chip on your shoulder that you can't see what was right in front of your face. Genies can't tell mortals they love them or they are no longer genies. Get it? They lose their magic and their immortality. Can you think of one person who would willingly give those two things up? She gave up life everlasting, her family, and her magic by giving you the gift of her love. And you threw it back in her face."

"You expect me to believe that?"

"No, I expect you to sprout figs from your ears." Merlin stomped his foot and a spark shot out. "Of course I expect you to. It's the truth." He stomped his other foot and another spark shot out, flaring to life on top of his talon.

"*That's* why Vana rewound your night together. You'd gotten too close. You'd touched her soul." The flames mingled at the bird's knees. "Among other parts of her, I'm sure, but hanky-panky doesn't make a genie fall in love with you. It shouldn't make anyone fall in love with anyone because love transcends the physical."

The flames climbed up Merlin's belly. "The Fates will undo her saying it—they hate to have their collective Will thwarted—and she'll never be able to say it again, but she felt something for you that she's never felt before. I've known her for close to six hundred years and never have I seen her even be tempted by anyone else to say those words, mortal or genie." Now his wings were getting singed. "For her to go to such lengths for you, you ought to be feeling honored instead of pissed off."

The fire licked at Merlin's chin, but the bird went on as if nothing were happening. "When she said she loved you, she was sealing her own coffin, and unless you accept that," the cockscomb caught fire, "you're going to miss out on the best thing that could have ever happened to you."

The fire claimed Merlin with a *whoosh*, leaving behind a cinder image of him on the edge of the sofa which collapsed into a pile of dust that burst into nothingness.

Zane stared at the spot where Merlin had been so magnificent in his anger… his *righteous* anger?

What if what the bird said was true? Had he misjudged her? Or was Merlin playing mind games with him, too?

Zane looked at her bottle. It didn't matter if he'd misjudged her. She was gone. Back to her life, and he'd go back to his. He had options now; the future was looking brighter. He'd go back to Philly, pick up the threads of his life, make a decision about his future, and forget the four craziest days of his life.

Except… that didn't look like it was going to happen because, somehow, he ended up inside Vana's bottle.

Again.

Chapter 40

H oly smokes!"
Zane stared at the woman holding a scimitar to his heart.

Hadn't they done this before?"

"Zane?" Vana tossed the sword away and fell to her knees beside him. "I didn't know who it was—" She pulled her hands from his arm and sat back. "What are you doing here? How did you get here?"

"I have no idea, Vana. For the second time in my life I have no idea how or why I'm here." He got to his feet and helped her up. "The question is, why are you?"

"I live here."

"Ten seconds ago you didn't. Your bottle was empty." He looked around. It wasn't empty now.

He was in her bedroom. The one from the first night they'd made love.

This must be the karmic retribution for wanting to wring the phoenix's neck.

"Ten seconds ago I wasn't here." She licked her lips, and while Zane found that particular nervous habit of hers distracting, it was also very telling. Maybe Merlin was right and he had misjudged her.

"Vana—"

"Zane—"

"No, let me." He had to know. "That last time… that last night… Why did you say the words you'd gone to such lengths *not* to say?"

She licked her lips once, but then raised her chin. "Because I'd hurt you with lies and you deserved the truth."

"But at what risk to you?"

She inhaled and walked over to a desk where a large leather-bound book rested. She opened it. "The first rule of the djinn is to do no harm. But I had. And I had to make it right."

She linked her hands in front of her, but this time, she didn't fiddle with her fingers. "That night, when I realized what I felt for you, where it could lead, I'd thought only to protect myself. To ensure I'd have my magic so that I could become the genie everyone wants me to be—everyone but me."

She closed the book and leaned against the desk. "I'm not like the rest of my family, Zane. They're all master genies, and me… I'm a mess. Words get mixed up or left out, letters disappear or get transposed… my magic is all over the place. I read and read DeeDee's manual, and still I can't master it. I thought I'd get it if I only tried harder or read longer or studied more, but it never clicked for me."

She shoved off from the desk and walked over to one of the non-windows. "After so much intensive study, I should be able to manage at least the simple things besides travel and Invisibility, but something always goes wrong. Remember that falafel incident? I was one letter off. One letter! How hard is that?"

It'd be pretty hard if she were dyslexic.

The thought popped into his head as if by… no, not magic. Learning disabilities had been part of his curriculum for his education degree, and while he wasn't qualified to make that diagnosis, what she described fit the parameters. He'd have to do some research, but there were techniques that could help her.

311

She wrapped her arms around herself. "Every Chosen genie can master simple magic the first month of school, but I was still on the primer when everyone else had moved three levels ahead. I felt so stupid. And there I was that night with you, trying to protect something more important to everyone else than it was to me, while denying that you were—are—what's important to me. And when you remembered it, when I saw how much I'd hurt you, I had to tell you the truth. The magic didn't matter in the face of what I'd done to you."

He walked over behind her and covered her hands with his. "I think you're brilliant, Vana."

"What?" She turned in his arms and looked up at him with those gray eyes that could change like quicksilver. Warm and inviting when she was happy, brittle when unsure, glinting when wary, and liquid silver when her emotions threatened to get the best of her.

Her emotions were one of the best parts of her. She couldn't lie about those. Her emotions had always been right there for anyone to see. When she was happy, it shone in her eyes; nervous, she twiddled her fingers; aroused... her eyes darkened with desire. It was all there if he only looked.

But he'd been blinded by his anger and his—yeah, his fear. His fear that it wouldn't last.

"I do think you're brilliant, Vana. You taught me, and I was an unwilling pupil. I didn't want to know my family's history. I didn't want to know who Peter was as a human being. I was embarrassed by the stories and just wanted to wipe him from my life. But you wouldn't let me. You wouldn't allow me to deny him. You made me listen and learn, and you gave him to me.

"This house, his legacy, and the permanence behind it... I get it, Vana. You were right about football being a substitute for what I really wanted, a substitute that wouldn't last. I'd been so focused on keeping everything the same that I couldn't accept the differences, and then you came along, one big difference from anything I'd ever known, and you barged into my life with your magic and your hope and your determination.

"You wouldn't let me *not* see the world through your eyes, whether it was on a magic carpet or in your bottle or rummaging through memories in my attic. You've given me my family, Vana, and..." He reached for her hand. "And I'd like you to be part of it."

Vana couldn't say a word. Being a part of his family had so many possibilities that she couldn't get her hopes up. She was, after all, the woman who'd slept with him then made him forget it.

"Merlin explained it, Vana, what saying you loved me cost you. I know you can never say the words to me again, but—"

"No, Zane, that's not true."

"You *don't* love me?"

"No, not that. It's not true that I can't say the words. I do love you, Zane."

"But what about your magic and your immortality?"

"I don't have any magic left to lose."

"I don't understand."

"Look where we are." She swept her hands around the room. "We're not back in my third-floor bedroom. We're in my bottle and everything that happened has still happened. The Fates didn't send me back to that first night. This isn't a do-over. Remember when you said that you have one shot at life, that it doesn't come with do-overs? They gave me the option of traveling back to that night and reweaving our Life Threads so I could *not* say those words and keep my magic. But I didn't take them up on it, Zane. I elected to move forward with you. Without my magic."

He stared at her.

She took a step closer. "I'm not that person that they tried to make me be. I'm not cut out for The Service. Peter

313

knew it. That's why he never asked anything of me. Remember, he didn't have a big family. That's why he went around the globe picking up others who were as alone as he was. Those children? He so badly wanted me to be able to free them. That's why he sent me to my bottle that day—he didn't want any setbacks, and when the bear showed up and the stairs disappeared, well, he wasn't worried about what other people said. He was worried I'd get discouraged."

"But you won't be able to turn the children back without your magic."

"But DeeDee can and she's promised to do it."

"Then how about if they come live with us?"

"With... *us?*" Vana didn't know which to react to first. *"Children?"*

Zane tucked a strand of hair behind her ear. "They're going to need a family, and you and I both want one, right?"

"But how? Your condo isn't going to hold all of them."

"This house will."

"This house... What are you saying?"

"I'm saying that I'm turning down the contract offer and the network job."

"But—"

"Hear me out." He put his fingers on her lips, and Vana had to restrain herself from kissing them. "I've had a surprising number of opportunities open up to me since we were together, and one of them is to teach. Here. At the high school. Coach, too."

"But is that what you want, Zane?"

"What I want is you, Vana. I want you." He tilted her face up. "I love you. Your kindness and your generosity. The way you think of others and fight so ferociously for them. I love that about you. I'm not so fond of the time-travel thing, but I guess that's no longer an issue."

She shook her head. "I only did it to—"

"I understand why you did it. And I can't say I blame you. But that's behind us now. In the past where it should stay and never be revisited. I want a future with you. You said you can't take me to the future with your magic, but what about without it? Will you be my future, Vana? Will you marry me and let me love you? Will you love me back? Make a home with me? Raise the children—ours, the dishes, maybe even adopt a few? The children need us, Vana. And *I* need you." He gathered her hands in his, raised them to his lips, and kissed them. "I love you."

"Oh, Zane, of course I will. I love you, you know."

"I do. How could I not? It's not every day a man has someone give up all the magic in the world for him."

"But I didn't, Zane."

"But you said—"

"I don't mean genie magic. I don't *need* genie magic. I only need this. The magic of being in your arms. With that kind of magic, anything is possible."

Zane was lowering his head, her lips a whisper away, when a chartreuse beak poked between them.

"Uh, hello? You two lovebirds might want to hold off on the smoochie stuff for a few more minutes."

Merlin was in the house. Er, bottle.

"Stuffed and roasted, bird."

"Geez, you two really have no sense of humor." He eyed the two of them. "Of course, I guess that's understandable with the way you're wrapped around each other."

"Merlin, is there something you need?" asked Vana.

"Ah, such a leading question, Van." Merlin sighed, then whipped two things out from behind his back.

The first was a bottle of champagne. "Courtesy of Clotho. You're able to drink it now, you know, Van. Clotho said to tell you she's on Mount Damavand toasting the fact that you'll never interfere with her weaving again. And, this," he held out a wrapped gift box, "is from your sister. You might want to open it."

Vana took it from him and lifted the lid. "My gemstone!" The pink tourmaline had been set in a platinum setting.

"She thought you'd like to have this as a keepsake since you can't use your magic anymore. Oh, and whenever you're ready, it'll transport you out of the bottle. But no hurry. There's going to be a party going on out there. But no worries, you two. I know how to behave myself. So do the kids. Henry will keep the bottle all locked up, and Eirik will thump three times on the ceiling when the coast is clear. So, hang out, relax, what*ever*." Merlin waggled his eyebrows. "Try to have some fun this time, will ya?"

"Get lost, bird." Zane pointed to the bottle's opening.

"Yeah, I figured that's what you'd say." Merlin sighed. "Seriously, you guys are no fun at all." He disappeared in a puff of gold flames.

Zane took the ring from the box and slid it onto Vana's finger—the third one on her left hand. Where it belonged. "Merlin doesn't know what he's talking about, Vana. I think you're a lot of fun." He kissed her fingers. "Speaking of… what do you say about doing as he said?"

She led him over to the bed. "I say, your wish is my command."

Epilogue

C heck and mate." Peter slid his knight to queen seven, then sat back and intertwined his fingers on his chest while the High Master stared at the board in consternation. "That's 12,043 to 11,675. You're catching up, Adham."

The High Master sighed and whisked the chessboard onto the shelf behind him with a twitch of his finger. "I swear, Peter, if you hadn't been such a good friend to those be-wished individuals, not only wouldn't I have entertained your idea of Vana and Zane together, but I would have sent you to your kind's version of the Hereafter as soon as you'd gone into the Light."

"Then who'd give you a good game of chess? Every genie here is scared to cross you."

The High Master chuckled. "True. Who would have thought a mortal would keep me in check?"

"Twelve thousand and forty-three times."

The High Master raised his glass of mint tea. "So, my friend, those ideas I directed to the team owner, the superintendent, and the network guy worked out rather well, wouldn't you say? Are you pleased with the way things have worked out for your great-grandson?"

"Pleased?" said Peter. "I'm thrilled. Vana was like a

daughter to me. I couldn't be happier. But aren't you upset that she's lost her powers? Did you foresee that happening when you put Zane in her bottle?"

The High Master grinned slyly over the rim of his glass. "Lost them? If something is lost that implies it can be found. A very interesting premise when it comes to genies."

"I'm not following you, Adham."

"Just because you beat me seven times in a row does not mean you are the only master chess player here. "

Peter acknowledged the truth of Adham's statement with a toast of his own drink. "So what are you saying, exactly?"

"As Vana said to Zane, everyone has magic inside them. It's just a matter of tapping into it. And who but a genie to teach someone how to find the magic? I believe their daughter is the perfect candidate."

Peter spit out his tea. "Daughter? Why, no Harrison has had a daughter in two hundred years."

"Zane will be the first. And Vana will help her realize her full potential. Her full magical potential. By her second birthday, every one of those other be-wished individuals will be back to themselves."

"You mean, Henry and Fatima—"

"And all the rest. Including the gargoyles. They'll all be just fine."

Peter couldn't speak.

Especially when Adham added the final zinger. "Oh, and they're going to name her Petra."

The End

النهايـــه

Author's Note

Djinn are religious figures in Islam, and while I tried to incorporate that history and culture into my world-building, this story is based more on U.S. pop-culture references. No disrespect or insult to anyone's beliefs is intended.

Nor was there any insult or disrespect intended toward the Grimm brothers and their legacy, but sometimes Merlin doesn't know when to shut up. Honestly, the bird just gets so full of himself sometimes.

Thank you!

Thank you for reading *My Fair Genie*. If you enjoyed this story, please help others find it by posting a review on Goodreads, Amazon, Apple Books, Barnes & Noble… wherever you bought it. Feel free to share a link, tweet about it, Facebook it… All efforts are greatly appreciated.

I love to hear from my readers so check me out online and feel free to friend me!

www.JudiFennell.com
https://www.facebook.com/JudiFennell.Author/
https://twitter.com/JudiFennell

Sign up for my newsletter at:
http://JudiFennell.com/newsletter-signup/

Keep on reading for Jolie and Todd's story in the Once-Upon-A-Time Romance series, *Beauty and The Best.*

JUDI FENNELL

*A picture is worth
a thousand kisses*

Beauty
AND THE
BEST

A Once-Upon-A-Time Romance

Beauty and The Best, Copyright 2012 Judi Fennell

Cover by Kimberly Van Meter
Interior layout by www.formatting4U.com

Published by Mergenie Books

All rights reserved. No part of this book may be reproduced in any form or by any electronic or mechanical means, including information storage and retrieval systems—except in the case of brief quotations embodied in critical articles or reviews—without permission in writing from the author. Please contact the author at JudiFennell@JudiFennell.com. This book is a work of fiction. The characters, events, and places portrayed in this book are products of the author's imagination and are either fictitious or are used fictitiously. Any similarity to real persons, living or dead, is purely coincidental and not intended by the author.

For more information on the author and her works, please see www.JudiFennell.com

Chapter One

T here's a naked man in my kitchen.

The thought registered just as the terse, "Who the hell are you?" had Jolie Gardener spinning around faster than a figure skater on speed.

He had the nerve to ask this? He of the broad shoulders, six-pack abs, and other, nice, um, parts...

Really. A naked man. In her kitchen.

Well, *technically,* she was in a naked man's kitchen. Even more technically, she was in a naked Todd Best's kitchen—and there wasn't one hint of self-consciousness or embarrassment on his part.

Of course with that body, there shouldn't be. The guy *should* flaunt his nudity for the world to see. Which, at present, consisted of one single, solitary person: Jolie Gardener, aspiring writer and personal chef extraordinaire.

"Well?" His hands slammed to his hips.

"You're naked," she squeaked, which, really, was the only way to state that kind of obvious.

"I'm what?" Mr. Six-Pack Abs glanced down.

Jolie tried not to—so unsuccessfully it was pitiful.

"Shit," he muttered. "I am. I, uh, fell asleep last night..."

As butter sizzled in the new super-slick omelet pan on

323

the top-of-the-line range, Jolie's gaze alternated between some rock-hard abs and a scruffy eight a.m. shadow while her fingers danced along the speckled granite countertop in search of a napkin, placemat, oven mitt… something.

Mercifully, they scooped up a thick dishtowel that, in her world, would constitute a very plush, very luxurious hand towel from The Ritz or The Four Seasons, but which, here, apparently, was used to soak up water from designer flatware. She dangled it in the direction of Mr. *Au Naturel*. "Here."

He placed an empty bottle of Jim Beam on the island countertop with a *clink*, then took the towel with a grunt. "So, who are you, what are you doing in my kitchen, and would you mind turning around?"

She turned. "I'm the new girl the agency sent over."

"Hell. There better be some aspirin left," he muttered beside her, his bare (of course) feet making no sound on the limestone floor.

She peeked over at him.

His eyebrow soared skyward.

Right.

She turned back to the sizzling butter. Which had started to burn. Sigh.

He rummaged around in one of the drawers as she carried the pan to the sink. Trying to impress the new boss on her first day with his favorite omelet ranchero and she burned the butter. Not good, but then, it wasn't exactly her fault because nowhere in those papers she'd signed with her employment agency, Domestic Gods & Goddesses, was mention made of an optional dress code. And she didn't care how much they were paying her, nudity did tend to throw one off. As for the alcohol-before-breakfast debacle, she wasn't even going to address that. His rudeness said it all.

And here, *she'd* been worried about making a good impression on *him*.

A click of plastic bottle cap followed by a shake of the

bottle, the fridge opening, a gulp, then Naked Guy sighing punctuated the silence before she turned on the faucet. She cleaned out the pan, all the while the Naughty Girl side of her brain screaming, "Turn around!" with the other, Jolie side, going, "You *want* to keep this job?"

Self-preservation being the backbone of her existence since being dumped into the foster care system, she decided to listen to the Jolie side—no matter how much groaning Naughty Girl did.

Naughty Girl, however, couldn't resist a peek, and was rewarded with a swish of his longish golden hair, a flex of his well-defined arm, and an accompanying sizzle to her own nerve endings.

So not good. Jolie had known he was a hunk before she accepted this position. Had had quite the crush on him, too. How could she not? The guy had been plastered all over every magazine in the country for years, most especially here in his hometown.

Todd Best. *The* Best, as the media had dubbed him. And rightfully so. The man's landscape paintings were hanging in every high-end hotel, public library, and courtroom in the country. Even the White House, for Pete's sake. Not that she had an eye for art, but when a painting looked like the scene down the road and made her think she was standing there, feeling the leaves rustling by, smelling the fresh cut grass, hearing the birds singing in the trees and the ducks quacking on the pond, the whole set-up, that, to her, was talent.

And, of course, there'd been his fairytale marriage. But then, sadly, his wife had died suddenly and he'd moved out of their home, turned the reins of his company over to his brother, and put down his paint brushes.

Yes, Jolie had known *exactly* who she'd be working for. That'd been half the incentive.

"So, new girl, do you have a name? And what are you doing here today?"

Since he was talking, she assumed it was safe to turn around.

The old adage about making an "ASS out of U and ME" proved true.

Although he was the one with the A-S-S. And what a nice one it was. As was the muscled shoulder leaning against the stainless steel of the microwave above the stove, and the ninety-degree jut of his jaw line, the sculpted cheekbones, a perfectly proportioned brow, the fall of hair over his forehead...

She tore her gaze away from the visual smorgasbord and, traitors that they were, her eyes headed south.

Thank goodness he had the dish towel spread across his nether regions like a loincloth. But a hot guy in a loincloth was just as distracting as a naked hot guy. And she'd seen him in both. Or not in both. Whatever.

She ordered her eyes back on the pan. "Um yes, I do have a name, and as to what I'm doing here, I think that's obvious—burning the butter for your morning omelet." She raised the pan to illustrate and managed a quick push with her hip to get him to back away from the stove so she could start cooking again, praying all the while she wasn't hitting something vital.

Luckily, the guy had quick reflexes—or a good hunch—'cause he stepped out of the way before her hip came anywhere close to anything important, saving them the extreme embarrassment of *that*.

"How'd you get in?" Mr. Clothing-Optional asked.

Okay, what was the protocol here? How long did one actually have to converse with a buck-naked human being before someone said something about it? Or did a strategically placed dishtowel negate all observances of nudity?

"Look, um, *Mister*." What did one call their bare boss? Todd? Sir? *Big guy*? "How 'bout you go freshen up a bit and I'll make breakfast. We can have our chat when we're both, um, well, prepared for the day. 'Kay?"

"Fine. I'll get dressed. Then we'll talk."

"You do that."

As he sauntered—okay, maybe that was her overactive imagination, because could one *really* saunter with a Jim Beam-sized hangover?—from the fourteen-foot-ceiling kitchen with its state-of-the-art appliances that looked as if they'd come out of their packing boxes yesterday, so stainless steel shiny she could have used them as a mirror to fix her lipstick—if she'd worn lipstick—and she inhaled enough oxygen to jump-start primordial ooze.

Which posed a whole new set of problems for this job. How was she supposed to focus if she kept getting sidetracked by the physical?

But she would.

She could.

Heck, if she could outwit social workers and manage to keep her teenaged self out of the gutter, not to mention, actually *make* something of her life, she could certainly keep her own libido in check.

She had to. Her job, her livelihood, and all her dreams depended on it.

***

Each step up the goddamned grandiose stairway reverberated through Todd's skull, setting his teeth on edge and his stomach roiling. Why the hell hadn't the builder put carpet on these stairs?

Todd grabbed his head with one hand, keeping the other one hovering above his groin with the damned kitchen towel. It'd be funny if it weren't so ungodly pitiful.

He, a grown man, hiding his modesty behind a piece of eight-by-twelve cotton because he didn't have enough sense to pass out in his own bed.

He kicked open the bedroom door and grimaced. Bare, tan walls, minimal furniture, and the fucking king-sized bed mocked him.

He knew exactly why he'd chosen the couch.

And he wasn't about to dwell on it. He'd done enough dwelling last night. More than enough, apparently.

He barreled through to the bathroom, his refusal to dwell on the reason just one more part of the person he'd become in the past two years.

And the poor woman downstairs who'd had to witness the person he'd become last night… God, wasn't it just *perfect* she'd shown up this morning?

Todd grabbed the shower handle and turned the water full force to hot. He'd burn the alcohol out of his system if he had to. No one deserved that greeting her first day on the job. Even if it was his house.

Todd sucked in a breath as he stepped beneath the pelting liquid fire and realized he wasn't as tough as he pretended. He turned the spigot back to warm and leaned his forehead against the cool ivory tile, and listened to the phone ring in his bedroom. Let the machine get the fucking thing. He couldn't deal with the calls and the goddamned hounding.

Not today.

The water ran into his eyes and he wiped it away with the heels of his hands. Why *today*? Why'd she have to start *today*?

Why'd she have to start at all?

Why wouldn't they all just leave him alone?

***

"You see what you're up against, Jonathan?" The archangel, Raphael, waved his hand in front of the computer monitor in the executive office of Domestic Gods & Goddesses and the split-screen images of Todd and Jolie faded to a serene, heavenly blue screen saver. "Todd doesn't think he's ready to let go of his wife's memory and Jolie is still a work in progress. Getting these two together could be difficult."

328

Jonathan Griff took a seat on one of the burgundy chairs opposite the mahogany desk and sipped the lemonade Raphael had given him. Well, perhaps he gulped it. This was a big assignment. Todd was front-page news. Still. After two years out of the public eye, the man could have media coverage in an instant. He was high profile. He was hot.

What if Jonathan failed? Not only would Todd and Jolie, his Charges, suffer, but it'd be public. Then he'd never earn his wings.

Of course, personal aggrandizement was not what a Guardian should worry about. His Charges' happiness should be his sole focus.

He'd had some success in the past, but there always seemed to be *something* he never got quite right. Could he take that risk with such a prominent case?

"You can do this, Jonathan."

The archangel's words reverberated inside his mind—another talent Jonathan hadn't yet mastered. Why was Raphael offering him this assignment? The archangel had no malice in him so he couldn't want to see him fail. Perhaps he had an overabundance of Hope?

Jonathan, left eye twitching, touched the keypad and the close-up of Todd's face reappeared. The poor man was in so much pain and, while The Boss had a Plan for Todd, Jonathan couldn't bear to see someone hurting.

And then there was Jolie. No one should have to endure what she had as a child. She was trying so hard to be all right that she'd almost convinced herself she was.

But she wasn't. Not really. She played a good game, but she craved acceptance so much that she'd do anything to get it.

Well, almost anything.

Jonathan smiled, the twitch subsiding. He'd read her dossier. The girl had a fine moral character, as did Todd.

Character and a run of bad luck; that's what the two of

them shared. Not to mention the wellspring of love in their souls. That's why the request for their happiness had been selected for fulfillment.

Now it was up to him to help them along.

Jonathan set the lemonade on an antique walnut-inlay table beside him and hopped off the chair to stand before the archangel. If Raphael thought he was capable of this job, then he owed it to his Charges to be the best Guardian possible.

"Yes, sir. I believe I can help them."

~ * ~

Books by Judi Fennell

Royally Sunk

In Over Her Head
Reel's a merman without a tail, and Erica's terrified of the ocean. Only one thing could get her into the water: a gun. And only one thing could keep her there: the sexy merman who saves her life, only to risk his own.

Wild Blue Under
Valerie's a mer princess landlocked in the middle of the country. Rod is the prince who sets out to rescue her. But can they dodge a usurper's plot and make it back to the ocean before his tail—and his claim to the throne—disappear forever?

Catch of a Lifetime
Logan ran *away* from the circus; all he wants is for his life to be normal. The naked woman who shows up on his boat is anything *but* normal. Especially when Angel turns out to be a mermaid—with an angry sea monstress after her.

Making Waves ~ outtakes compilation
Read about The Incident that made Erica terrified of the ocean, the reason Valerie, the lost princess, was found, and how Logan's young son Michael found a mermaid The stories *before* the stories.

Bottled Magic

I Dream of Genies
Matt's luck has finally changed when genie Eden escapes her bottle and lands in his lap. Literally. And she vows never to go back in. Unfortunately for both of them, the guy who put her in there wants her back and he'll stop at nothing to get her.

Genie Knows Best

Samantha inherits her father's estate, complete with a genie who has one last master to serve before his indentured servitude is up. Sam's more than willing to set Kal free—until her greedy ex has decided that if he can't have Sam, no one can.

My Fair Genie

Zane's inherited the family mansion which he can't rid of quick enough to put the rumors of his family's crazy history to rest. Too bad the genie who's been the cause of those rumors has been set free to run amok once more. Only this time, it's his heart she's messing with.

Your Wish Is His Command ~ outtakes compilation

Find out how Kal came to be imprisoned in his lantern and why he needs to serve 1001 masters. It's the story before the story..

Once Upon A Time Romance

Beauty and The Best

Jolie is a personal chef by day and a romance writer by night. So when she gets a gig for the hot reclusive artist, Todd, she has the perfect hero for her book. Until Todd finds out and kicks her out of his kitchen, his home, *and* his heart.

If The Shoe Fits

Once upon a time, a long time ago, in a land far, far away, there lived a girl by the name of Cinderella. This is not her story. *This* is the story of Lucinda Isabella Casteleoni, who, like her namesake, has a wicked stepmother, two tacky stepsisters, and countless hours of hard work to (not) look forward to. But unlike that fairy tale princess, Bella's Prince Charming is nowhere to be found. Until a little old man with sparkling green eyes opens a shoe store down the street. Then the magic begins...

Through The Leaded Glass (prequel)

An accidental trip to medieval England has ad exec Kate scrambling for a way home... But can she bring the hot knight in shining armor she's fallen in love with back with her?

Fairest of Them All (coming soon)

BeefCake, Inc.

Beefcake & Cupcakes

Lara wants her cupcakes to be a success. Exotic dancer Gage wouldn't mind sampling them, but his work schedule to pay off his nephew's hospital bills doesn't leave him time to do so. Until a party where beefcake meets cupcakes and, *oh*, is it delicious!

Beefcake & Mistakes

When Bryan mistakes Jenna for a hooker and she realizes he's her adopted son's father, the mistakes and misunderstandings start to grow. But something else is growing between them, too. Sometimes, one wrong turn can be oh so right...

Beefcake & Retakes

Tanner his ex-wife to be out of his life forever, but when her grandmother has a stroke and he has to pretend to still be in love with Juliet, can he risk a retake on the one woman who never stopped loving him?

Beefcake & Snowflakes

Gina's had a crush on Darien since forever—until the day he humiliated her in school. Fifteen years later, he leaves her cold. Exotic dancer Darien has come back to town to set a few things to rights. One is the mess he made for Gina years ago… and *maybe* rekindle the flames they'd once had. But the only way to melt the snow around Gina's heart is to turn up the heat, both on the job… and off.

Manley Maids

What happens when three irresistibly sexy brothers lose a poker bet to their enterprising sister? They get hired out for her housecleaning venture. Now, the Manley Maids are at your service. Satisfaction guaranteed.

What a Woman Wants

Resort owner Sean plans to buy an historic estate, making a name for himself and making millions, so he moves in under the guise of cleaning the place to thwart the one condition of the inheritance. But heir Olivia and her menagerie get under his skin, and he finds that the poker bet that got him into this mess isn't the only game-changer.

What a Woman Needs

Movie star Bryan wants fame and fortune, not a repeat of his penny-pinching "normal" childhood. After the publicity surrounding of her husband's death, Beth needs is a normal life for herself and her children, and the movie star who lost a bet to clean her house—with paparazzi in tow—isn't it. But as flirtation turns into seduction, Bryan needs to convince Beth he's more man than a maid. Or actor. Because he's playing the lead in a reverse Cinderella story, and it might just be the role of a lifetime.

What a Woman Gets

Liam has no patience for women who spend a man's money without giving a thought to any actual work.

But to make good on his bet, Liam must not only tolerate socialite, Cassidy, he'll have to clean up after her when her father cuts her off. With no money and no home for Liam to clean, Cassidy has no choice but to accept a job offer—as Liam's new maid. But when sparks fly between them, will it be true love or just another messy affair?

What a Woman

MaryAlice Catherine is all set to clean her grandmother's friend's house, only to find the woman's cocky grandson whom she'd had a crush on growing up—and he'd known all along—is living there and she's mortified. Jared remembers it differently; Mac was always a bossy little thing, but he's not going to let her call the shots now. But with the two of them living in one house, there's no telling who's going to come out swinging.

What A Man Wants (coming soon!)

www.JudiFennell.com

335

About Judi Fennell

Judi Fennell has had her nose in a book and her head in some celestial realm all her life, including those early years when her mom would exhort her to "get outside!" instead of watching *Bewitched* or *I Dream of Jeannie* on television. So she did—right into Dad's hammock with her Nancy Drew books.

A PRISM Award and Golden Leaf Award winner, among others, Judi is the author of tongue-in-cheek romantic comedies about mermen off the Jersey shore, male strippers a la Magic Mike, and manly maids whose motto is... *Satisfaction Guaranteed.*

Check out her on social media to see the menagerie that shares her office, and check out her website at www.JudiFennell.com for excerpts, deleted scenes, reviews, and contests, as well as the chance to discover a whole new world!

Made in the USA
Middletown, DE
14 October 2023

40533641R00195